THE PAINTED MESSIAH

Also by Craig Smith:

Silent She Sleeps
(published in the United States as:
The Whisper of Leaves)

The Painted Messiah

Craig Smith

MYRMIDON

Myrmidon Books Ltd
Rotterdam House
116 Quayside
Newcastle upon Tyne
NE1 3DY
www.myrmidonbooks.com

Published by Myrmidon 2008

A catalogue record for this book is available from the British Library.

ISBN 978-1-905802-15-9

Set in11.5/13.5 pt Sabon by Falcon Oast Graphic Art Limited,
East Hoathly, East Sussex

Printed and bound in the UK by
CPI Mackays, Chatham ME5 8TD

3 5 7 9 10 8 6 4 2

For Shirley Underwood and Martha Ineichen.
I am blessed to have you both in my life.

Tyre

● Damascus

PROVINCE OF SYRIA

GALILEE

Capernaum
● Bethsaida

Tiberias
Sea of Galilee

● Nazareth

Caesarea
Maritima

ARABIA
(NABATAEA)

SAMARIA

● Samaria
River of Jordan

● Joppa
● Gerasa

JUDAEA
PERAEA

JERUSALEM

Bethlehem ●

● Machaerus

● Hebron

Dead Sea

Masada

TETRARCHY OF HEROD ANTIPAS

CENTRAL SWITZERLAND, PRESENT DAY

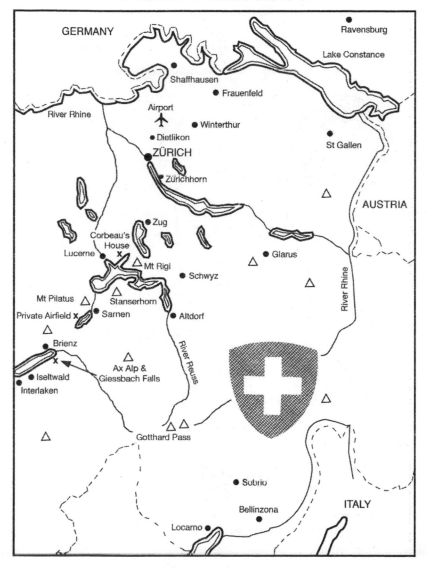

Prologue

Jerusalem
Passover AD 30

'Will those who have seen him in life know him by this portrait, Theophanes?'

'Most assuredly, sir,' the slave answered. Theophanes had no basis for believing this. Those who had known the Jewish messiah were themselves Jews. As everyone knew, Jews refused to gaze upon any human image.

'It doesn't look much like him now, though,' Pilate offered doubtfully. Theophanes studied the subject of his portrait critically. The man wore rags and a crown of thorns. His head was a bloody mass of contusions.

Theophanes had painted the Jew as he appeared, omitting only the humiliating effects of violence. With the eyes he had created the universal serenity of nobility sitting for a portrait. Theophanes was especially skilled at capturing this effect. In all other matters the slave was faithful to nature. The man was pleasingly robust – having plenty of muscle and a good layer of fat against the cold. His features were regular, the nose large and broad. The eyes were unclouded.

'Perhaps you have noticed, sir, all criminals have the same look at this point in their careers. This . . .'

Theophanes gestured toward his painting, '. . . is the face of the man you saw ride into Jerusalem.'

The prefect's chin kicked up slightly in response. His expression grew more comfortable. That man! The reference excited his confidence. That man had entered the city as the king of the Jews. 'The hair is wrong,' Pilate declared finally, for he would not rest until he had faulted the work of his slave. 'The beard is too short, Theophanes!'

This was not true but, as Theophanes had learned years ago under the lash of a whip, his master was incapable of understanding what he looked at. His sole concern with art – any art – was its power to impress fellow Romans and overwhelm the rest of humanity. He could not comprehend that what he saw he coloured with his own impressions. The hair and beard were correct. The slave had simply depicted what his subject would have looked like emerging from a Roman bath on a late afternoon, had he ever entered such a building. Rather than argue the point, Theophanes answered with the first lie that came to him. 'I have styled the hair and beard as your Jewish friend Nicodemus wears it, sir. I hope that was not indiscreet.'

Pilate liked this very much. Nicodemus, in his view, was the Jew all Jews should emulate. He cooperated with the Roman authority and paid handsomely for his favours. 'I see that now,' he answered thoughtfully. 'Very well, then. See that you attach it to one of the *imago* standards in place of Tiberius . . . and don't forget to hang the letters on the standard. That is the point, after all!'

'I-N-R-I. Jesus of Nazareth, King of the Jews.'

The prefect had already instructed his slave in this matter, but Theophanes was accustomed to hearing his orders twice. The Romans, as a race, imagined all other nations less attentive to detail.

'I want the standard with this man's image on the wall in my banquet hall in Caesarea when I return.'

'I am to leave Jerusalem ahead of you then?'

Theophanes felt a tremor of fear. Jerusalem was about to erupt in open revolt when they crucified this man. Inside the palace behind the shield of the prefect's guard one could expect a degree of security. In the streets of Jerusalem he would be exposing himself to the violence of roving crowds. They would be looking for easy targets once they had drunk enough courage to forget the fate of revolutionaries.

'Leave at sundown. It will be the start of the Jewish Sabbath, and no one will bother you if you are quick about it.' Pilate considered the matter briefly before he added with a slight, curdling smile, 'So long as they don't see what you carry.' Having given his orders, the prefect called to Cornelius, his most senior centurion, to lead the prisoner to his fate. Pilate then turned away from Theophanes.

One might as well say history itself turned away, for there were no records kept of the lives of slaves. As a rule, they counted themselves blessed above their own kind if their masters even knew their names. Other than chariot drivers the life of a slave inspired no comment, and even the greatest champions of the Circus Maximus in Rome left the arena for the last time without so much as a whisper following them to their graves.

Chapter One

Lake Lucerne, Switzerland
August 5, 2006.

Kate dropped into the lake without a sound. Still under the surface, she kicked away from the boat's stern, disappearing into a long dark alley that twisted between the other boats. Ethan followed nearly a minute later, returning to the surface in the shadows as quietly as he went in. He checked to see if the people beside their boat had noticed, but everyone on deck was looking at the long feathery streaks of a golden fire fading from the evening sky. Not a soul on any of the hundreds of boats surrounding them cared about what happened in the black waters below.

The lake beyond the boats was choppy. A cold summer breeze blew in from the Alps. The light of the pale, smoky moon was too faint to let him find Kate. He saw her only when the sky lit up in a blaze of white light, a silhouette against the shimmering surface of the water.

Kate had already stripped down to her wetsuit and was applying night camouflage to her face when he joined her. Scissor-kicking lazily to keep her head above water, she seemed like a beautiful lady before her mirror. Ethan studied her features while he stripped his own clothes away. Her face was striking, a pleasant mix of feminine delicacy and aristocratic boldness. Eyebrows, nose, and jaw were prominent and refined. It was a face cameras loved. The curve of her eyelids and sweet, round fullness of her lips missed cute by an eyelash. Her laughter had mischief and music. Her sweetness came with passion, her fury with anger. Descended from bastard English royalty on both sides, married and widowed to an English lord, she was tall and blonde, brilliant and connected: ambitious for risk and all things new. She could plot with the patience of an older woman scorned and then take what she wanted with the speed of an urchin.

They had met some years ago by pure chance, or so it had seemed to him at the time. He learned later that Kate was a woman who got exactly what she wanted and left nothing to chance. He had been with two other climbers in the Alps. They had hauled their equipment toward a fairly difficult rock, planning to spend the day ascending it. Kate was by herself with only a litre of water and a sweatshirt at her waist. She approached them while they were still preparing their lines and laying out the pitons. Without saying a word, though indulging herself with a look of casual interest in Ethan's lean muscular physique, she had started climbing. Ethan watched her for a moment before starting after her. It was his first climb without ropes, but he hardly recognized the danger. In fact, all he thought about was the woman ascending the rocks above him with the agility of a lioness. Even though he had considered himself in peak condition, he could not catch her.

'You climb without ropes much?' she had asked, when he had finally joined her at the summit.

He ran his hand through his short dark hair and smiled sheepishly. 'First time.'

He had a pronounced Tennessee accent in those days. Instead of putting her off, as it did with a lot of the Europeans, she seemed actually to enjoy it. 'Is it going to be your last?' She asked this with curiosity and a bit of a dare in her expression. Ethan could still remember grinning and shaking his head. It had been the most exhilarating climb of his life. 'I hope not.'

'Kate Kenyon,' she said and shook his hand.

The following morning they had headed toward the Tyrolean Alps, hitchhiking when they could, catching buses or trains otherwise. One afternoon as they clung to a tiny ridge of stone probably a thousand feet above a field of boulders, Kate had said to him, 'Think we could make a living doing this?' Ethan thought she meant as professional climbers, and laughed at her. She could make a living, but he was a long way from her level. In another few days he would be heading back to the States to start law school at George Washington, all this and Kate Kenyon nothing more than a pleasant memory. But she wasn't talking about rocks. A joke, she told him that night as they lay together in bed. But it was a joke that did not go away. Why did he have to go back? She could go with him, he said. And do what? Anything, anything at all. 'We could do that here,' she had answered. Two evenings before his flight, following what had promised to be their last climb, they were walking under a wall in Como, when she laughed and said to him, 'Come on!'

A moment later she disappeared into a darkened estate. Ethan knew what she meant to do. He knew, too, the smart thing was to walk away, but walking away wasn't really an option. He followed her over and had the thrill of his life stealing a lady's necklace and making love on a stranger's silk sheets. He had been following Kate over walls ever since. Nothing at all intimidated her. She came alive at the point where even the most courageous would hesitate. She loved risk as others loved adoration or money or notoriety. If it was possible, she would try it. If it wasn't, she would try to figure out a way to make it so. Physically, her conditioning and strength could still astonish him.

A golden palm tree etched itself against the black sky, the firework holding its form until the last glowing embers blinked away. As soon as it did, a staccato of heavy explosions boomed across the lake. From the boats huddled together at the centre of the lake a collective sigh drifted toward them. 'Ready, Boy?'

Finishing his face and his memories of those first weeks with Kate, Ethan dropped the tin and pulled on his skullcap. 'Ready, Girl.'

Like it was just another job.

They swam with only the top of their heads breaking the surface, moving quickly toward the dark peninsula closest to them. From time to time, Kate would roll quietly and look behind them, never breaking her forward momentum. The only time Ethan looked back he saw the light of a police patrol boat moving along one of the distant shorelines. Once past the peninsula they waded through a shallow marsh. Deep in the mud and weeds they found their inflatable, a Sea Eagle 9.2. It was exactly as they had left it the night before, well camouflaged and loaded with their equipment. They had stolen it six weeks before because it was light, easily handled and quick enough to get them to the other end of the lake and back.

While Kate cleared the brush away, Ethan inflated the keel and checked the pressure in the other chambers. Taking the grab lines, they lugged it toward the water, jumping in just as the craft cleared the marsh. Ethan dropped the ten horsepower motor into position and pressed the ignition. The Honda purred quietly to life, and he steered the craft away from the shoreline. Over the next three minutes they worked their way past three large estates. The great houses were darkened, apparently empty, easy targets but of no interest tonight. They pushed on and finally came to a small densely wooded hill. One lone mansion occupied the crest of it. To either side of the property, for nearly a quarter of a mile in either direction, there were no other houses, no lights, no roads. Just as the land began to rise up sharply, they glided into shore.

Kate jumped out first and pulled the raft over a stretch of gravel while Ethan heaved out their equipment. Wading back into the lake with their gear in a watertight bag, they swam another fifty yards or so, coming to a piece of grey rock that rose up almost vertically over the lake. Kate took the equipment and swam ashore. Ethan veered off toward the estate's private dock. This was secured by a high stone wall and closed off with a set of steel gates. It offered one large boathouse, built as a replica of the main house. In one of the two berths beneath it sat a luxurious Fountain 48

Express Cruiser. In the second was a Pantera 28, the fastest boat on the lake. Two Jet Skis were tied next to the Pantera. There were no lights on in the boathouse or around the dock. The perimeter was protected electronically. The slightest movement would trip both an alarm and security lights. Taking the bicycle chain lock latched around his waist, Ethan keyed it open and slipped under the surface. Close to the dock's entrance, he reached out blindly until he touched the moss-covered steel bars. Snapping the lock closed, he dropped the key and swept back from the gate.

He returned to the surface and swam back to Kate. She had already set out their gear in neat his and hers piles. Before he did anything else, he took a towel and began drying himself. Still in his wet suit, he slipped on a Cobra vest. Next he put on a pair of black pants and a matching jacket. Finally, he slipped on a pair of black sports socks and his climbing shoes. Both the pants and jacket had been specially modified by a seamstress in Milan Kate used for all her jobs. Every object and tool they would need had a reinforced slot to hold it tightly against the body. He inventoried each as he slipped it into place, reviewing the various points within Kate's plan: a silent whistle, a pair of thin leather gloves, handcuffs, a couple of lengths of rope, a small, flat steel crowbar, a Navy Colt .45 semiautomatic pistol with silencer attached, the first round already in the chamber, a combat knife, a small flashlight, a climbing pick, and a concussion hand grenade – in case things went to hell.

When these were in place, Ethan reached for a small backpack with a dart rifle attached. The pack fastened to his body snugly and offered a small ripcord neatly tucked away. One tug and a canopy would snap open. He could access the dart rifle simply by reaching behind his head. He finished with a full hood, night vision goggles, and a headset.

Kate began working over the tarp and rope with one of the towels. Together they dragged the tarp to the water, throwing the towels after it. As these sank into darkness, Kate whispered into her headset, 'Ready, Two?'

Ethan heard the second team's response, two voices answering in sequence, 'Ready, One.'

Kate turned to Ethan, 'Ready, Boy?'

Ethan gave a slight nod of his head, 'Ready, Girl.'

Kate walked up close to the rock and tipped her head back, planning her ascent one last time. Ethan did the same even though he had studied the rock a number of times from the lake. The stratification was typical of the area. It offered finger and toeholds all the way to the top. At about forty-five feet, a good third of the climb finished, the rock tilted, allowing for a rest, if he needed it. He was plotting his next move when he saw Kate start up the rock. She took the first ten feet in half as many seconds.

Ethan had made more than a dozen practice climbs under these conditions on a far more difficult rock. When Kate ran a job, she was nothing if not thorough, but they had used pitons and rope for night training. This was his first free climb in the dark, and it left him a bit uneasy as he began. Hazarding a glance in Kate's direction after he had started up the rock, he saw her passing the midway point. He listened a moment and caught the steady rhythms of her breath. His own methodical plodding embarrassed him suddenly, and Ethan pushed himself to emulate his partner. Never a smart thing to do. When he looked down, the distance was perfect for getting himself killed, too close for him to get to his ripcord in time, too far even to think about a lucky fall. He could see exactly the rock that was going to kill him, too. Angrily, Ethan stepped up his pace. He reminded himself just how easy this rock was. He moved quickly now for several steps, pushing off one fingerhold and reaching for the next without pausing to consider or to test or even to think. Exactly as Kate climbed.

Stopping at last if only to understand his progress, Ethan felt his nerves betray him. He began to reach for his next hold but then hesitated. Kate was waiting just under the top of the cliff and watching him now. Could she see he was getting into trouble? Hear it in his breathing? He made a long reach, and found himself unable to catch a decent toehold. He pulled back and probed more carefully. Nothing. He looked down at his rock and felt his hands beginning to sweat. All he could think about was a climb in the Bergell Valley some years earlier. The rock had frightened him before he began. About halfway up, fighting it every inch of the way, his fingers had suddenly released their hold as if they had a mind of their own. It happened sometimes when a climber was tense or frustrated or scared. If you were wearing a harness, you could kick away and hang quietly until you got your focus back. In a free climb you were dead.

For a moment, he could not bring himself to let go with

his left hand. It was the same thing that had happened on that day. First the muscles locked up. Then the fingers opened. Still clutching the rock, Ethan brushed his toe over the stone until he found a small crevice. It was not sufficient to hold him, only to take some of the weight out of his fingers. He looked now for another ledge, and realised his left hand had begun to cramp.

Taking his weight into his toes he finally broke free with his hand and tried to shake the blood back into it. As he did this, he stretched his left leg out, going for a fresh toehold, and almost fell when a cramp struck his hip. This was the point when you kicked out and laughed, trusting to your ground person and the rope. You lost, the rock won. Maybe you tried again tomorrow. Maybe you took up hiking.

He heard Kate now. 'Get left. You've got a decent shelf not more than ten feet away. Ethan tried looking for it. 'Trust me. It's there. Get to it now. Take your time, but do it, don't think about it.' It was not what she said, but the fact that she was there, that she understood he was in trouble.

Ethan focused on her voice with that faint, soft feminine British accent. He forgot his feet, his cramp, his fingers. Forgot death itself. 'Your left foot is on it, Boy. A little higher. Good.' He pulled himself higher, stepping into a thin shelf, and found another finger-hold, nothing more than a pocket within the stone. His hands felt soft, the cramp in his hip faded. He shook his hands but it was only habit. The blood was flowing, his strength returning. And then he found himself directly opposite Kate, both of them just under the edge of the cliff.

'I thought I was going to lose you,' she whispered.

'Cramps,' he said.

'They don't ask how, they just ask how far down. Are you good now?'

'I'm good.'

'Team Two, we are in place. Repeat. We are in place.'

The Palace Hotel, Lucerne

From the rooftop of the Palace Hotel Sir Julian Corbeau pulled his gaze from the explosion of colour in the sky over Lucerne and fixed his eyes upon the Contessa Claudia de Medici, a slender, middle aged woman standing close to the parapet. She had been in the country almost two decades without once venturing out to a social gathering of this sort. Corbeau wondered why she had finally relented. It wasn't a fondness for fireworks, he was sure of that. The bankers never failed to invite her, of course, but it was only a matter of form.

Her sole extravagance was her annual party for a hundred or so of Switzerland's social elite. Everyone Corbeau knew attended it. It was, they liked to say, the party of the year – littered with luminaries from around the world. When they had begun, Corbeau's troubles in America had created something of a scandal, and that may have been the reason she had overlooked him, but more recently, as America-bashing had become something more than just posturing, Julian Corbeau had enjoyed a burgeoning reputation in Europe. To be positively vain about it, Sir Julian was fashionable again. And still she had not extended an invitation.

He could not, of course, approach her directly like some blushing schoolboy anxious for her attention. He would not give her the satisfaction. He mingled with others. He talked about politics and society, as one does. He even talked briefly about a business venture with a French concern. Eventually, the contessa's name came up. The famous parties she threw. Hadn't he been to one of them? No, Corbeau answered. In fact, he said, he had been under the impression she was Jewish.

A bit of surprise at this. Not at all!

'My mistake,' Corbeau answered with a slight smile, noticing with satisfaction the sudden doubt in the other's face.

'Worth I don't know how many million,' the gentleman offered, as if that might make up for failings of the blood.

'Certainly not *the* de Medici family?'

'Married a poor cousin, I believe.' A careful, thoughtful sip of champagne. 'Got a title for her troubles, as I understand it. I believe she brought the money into the marriage, however.'

'Divorced, then?'

'I really don't know. She's very mysterious about her private life. I think he might have died, come to think of it.'

'Any idea how she came by her money?'

'I'm not sure, but I'll vouch for this, she has plenty of it.'

As the man who was speaking to him at the moment happened to be an officer in one of Switzerland's leading banks, Corbeau was quite sure of the contessa's bona fides. In fact, he had rarely seen such passion in a Swiss banker's eyes.

'And yet one never sees her,' Corbeau offered, as if baffled by her failure to embrace Swiss society.

'Rarely, I'd say. Shy of publicity mostly. When she accepted this evening, she wanted assurances there would be no cameras.'

'I wonder why.'

'If you can believe it, I think she is a genuinely humble person.'

'I was under the impression that humility had gone out of style.'

The banker laughed politely. 'An extraordinary woman, by all accounts. May I introduce you?'

She had lovely eyes, the contessa, so much so that one hardly noticed she refused to extend her hand. 'I've heard a great deal about you,' she said in French, though she was not French. The dusky skin and cool dark eyes intimated a far older race. She wore an exquisite ruby at her neck in a setting that looked to be a skilful imitation of jewellery from the Roman Empire, if not an original. Instead of a wedding band the Contessa de Medici wore an extraordinary antique cameo ring. It depicted two lovers holding hands. It might have been a Baroque fantasy of Arcadia, worth how many hundreds of thousands, one could only guess, but Corbeau was inclined to believe it was an original, worth closer to a million.

Corbeau's response to her courtesy was humorously self-effacing, a skill he had learned only with great difficulty. 'One should never listen to rumours. They are always so painfully accurate.'

'Rumours are all I can afford. You see, my work keeps me too busy to get out much.'

'You mustn't be a slave to your work. Life is to be lived!'

'I'm a slave to my passion, Sir Julian, which is scholarship.'

'The contessa is an author of some repute,' the banker remarked in a well-schooled French that sounded like a pale imitation compared to the contessa's.

'*The Forgotten Jerusalem*,' Corbeau answered, using the English title. 'I believe it is the finest book I've ever read on the Roman occupation in the first century.'

'Have you read a great deal of history, Sir Julian?'

'Not much of value, I'm afraid, but more than most people, I'm sure. Books happen to be *my* passion. Of course, I still manage to find time for the occasional evening with friends, so perhaps my passion is not as all-consuming as it ought to be.'

The banker, playing his part, explained that Corbeau possessed what was widely regarded as the finest private collection of occult literature in all of Europe.

With a faint smile to soften her obvious distaste for him, she asked, 'Are you a magician, then?'

It was a question Julian Corbeau generally despised. The contessa, however, seemed to understand what she was asking. Certainly she was a woman who knew the difference between parlour tricks and the work of a true magus.

'I don't believe in nonsense.'

'Perhaps I should have said *adept*.'

'That's another matter altogether. Unfortunately, I'm nothing more than an amateur. I enjoy reading about men and women with true occult powers, but that is my limit. I'm not sure what I would command of a spirit if I could in fact conjure one!'

'And I was under the impression that you are a man who knows exactly what he wants. You'll excuse me?'

'Extraordinary woman,' the banker observed as the contessa walked away.

Flushing angrily, Corbeau did not bother answering the fool. Extraordinary, she was, but there was something more to her than that. Corbeau knew hundreds of extraordinary people. It was his business to know extraordinary people! This one was different. This one had no fear of him.

Lake Lucerne

They put on their gloves as they waited for the second team to respond. For a moment there was no answer, and Kate repeated herself a third time. 'Team One in place. Do you read?'

An old man's voice answered. 'Almost there, Girl.' His voice came again after a beat. 'On target!'

Kate and Ethan began moving. A moment before they came off the rock and took hold of the retaining wall, floodlights washed over the entire property. A long wailing siren broke the silence. This was followed by several sharp blasts of a horn and a trill of electronic bleats. Over his headset Ethan heard a woman cursing in a rustic German dialect.

'Who put the gate in the middle of the road?'

The man soothed her, 'We made a wrong turn, sweetheart!'

They were talking loudly, their windows rolled down so their slurring voices might carry to the guardhouse. 'I did not make a wrong turn!' the woman answered angrily. 'Someone put a gate in the road!' It was a well rehearsed script, two drunken Austrian tourists on a summer evening with their fender pushed against the front gate of a millionaire's estate and making it clear that the accident was entirely the property owner's fault. Meanwhile Kate and Ethan scrambled off the face of the cliff and moved into the shadows to each side of the property.

They crouched in a shooter's tripod, one knee touching the earth, their dart rifles drawn and ready. For a moment nothing happened, and they were able to study the property for the first time up close. The house looked like a castle holding the high ground, but that was something of an illusion. Only the tower on the lake-side was actually medieval in its design. The house, though over a century old, was built for comfort. A large terrace opened off several glass doors at the ground level. Above this was a columned balcony offering yet another view to the lake. The property was nicely sheltered to either side by a small forest. It was secured by high stone walls, except at the back of the property where a vertical face of rock reached down to the lake and prohibited all but the most intrepid trespassers.

The lawn stretched out perhaps seventy yards from the house to the edge of the cliff. At the centre of it was a small concrete helicopter pad. Otherwise the area was open and green, giving a view to the lake and mountains beyond. Along each wall a gardener had indulged himself some years ago by planting numerous flowering shrubs and low, well-trimmed fruit trees. These presently kept the area closest to the wall in virtual darkness even when the security lights were shining and provided a natural screen against anyone looking out from within the house or monitoring the property with cameras.

Chances were no one was looking at the back of the property. Kate had created too much interest with her scripted drama at the front gate. In his headset Ethan could hear two car doors opening and closing. The siren stopped abruptly. The lights remained on. 'I suppose you're going to stand there in your fancy uniform and say this is my fault!' The old woman was talking to a single guard.

They knew the owner of the estate was in town, a VIP guest at the Palace Hotel's rooftop party during the city's annual fireworks. If all went well, the five men assigned to his personal security would be with him. Two guards remained at the estate. With one at the driveway, the second would be in contact with the police, hopefully informing them that at the moment there appeared to be no reason for assistance.

That left the two dogs for Kate and Ethan. They had come out of their kennels with the first alarm. Like the guards, they were focused on the situation at the front gate. When Kate blew her silent whistle, they came to a slight rise of land and looked anxiously for the source of the whistle. They were not inclined to leave the excitement at the front for less likely prospects here, but they were curious.

'Dogs are coming,' Kate whispered. Ethan could not hear the sound, but both dogs did. They began running at the same instant, bounding almost playfully at first, not quite sure where to go. When they had covered about half the distance between the house and Kate, they seemed to locate her. As soon as they did, they flattened down in full attack. Ethan blew his whistle, and the dog closest to him changed course without breaking stride. Dropping his gun sights into the dog's dark mass, Ethan squeezed the trigger. The Doberman flinched, tumbled, and then somehow got to its feet again its hind legs kicking wildly as it struggled to continue the attack.

Ethan dropped the dart rifle and pulled his knife as the animal lunged, but the drug had dulled its reactions. It fell short of him with a grunt and slid through the wet grass. The dog kicked once trying to get up, then groaned like a man in his bed and fell back for a long sleep. Ethan looked across at Kate. She was already pulling her dog by the skin of its neck into the thick foliage. Putting his knife back into its sheath, Ethan dragged his dog into the shadows, dropped his goggles into place, and started along the wall toward the house. Meanwhile the drama at the front gate continued. They wanted to see the owner. They weren't leaving until this was settled!

When he was nearly to the house, Ethan heard Kate. 'Ready, Boy?'

'Ready, Girl.' They cut across the lawn toward the terrace from either wall. A long loop of climbing rope hung over Kate's shoulder like a bandolier. They met under the house. Kate slowed her pace as she stepped first on Ethan's thigh, then his shoulder. Letting her momentum carry her up, she reached the second storey balcony guttering, kicked once and scrambled to safety. From there, she could throw her rope and grappling hook toward the tower roof. Meanwhile, it was Ethan's job to neutralize the second guard if Team Two could not take him down.

He drew his Colt and moved toward the corner of the house, leading with a quick peek. A uniformed guard walked out of the guardhouse and ambled lazily toward the trouble at the front gate. Ethan pulled back into the shadows. Team Two had drawn both men. The woman signalled this fact with her slurred speech. 'And you! What do *you* want? I said I wanted to speak to the owner of this dump! I don't need another uniform in my face!' Her husband tried again to calm her. They were just working a job like everyone else, he said. She shouldn't be cursing these poor fellows.

The second guard spoke in the same crisp High German as his partner. They were on private property. They were going to have to back up and leave unless they wanted to be arrested. Did they want to be arrested? Did they insist on going to jail for the night? There was no answer, nothing at all but the indistinct sound of two darts spitting out of two pistols simultaneously. Then Ethan heard the sound of two bodies hitting gravel. Kate and Ethan had twenty minutes, give or take – more than twice the time Kate had said they would use.

Looking up, he saw Kate walking up the side of the tower, her rope stretching down from the roof. He pulled the flat crowbar from the sheath on his thigh. At the French doors of the terrace he broke in with a single twist of his wrist. The lights were on inside the house. He returned his crowbar to its sheath. Moving from room to room with his back close to the wall, Ethan swept his handgun's sights into the empty spaces.

He heard in his headset Team Two's leader. 'Two sleeping at the gate! We're off!' The connection went dead.

Ethan finished sweeping the ground floor and began up the grand stairway. At the landing he heard a muffled explosion both on his headset and directly overhead. Kate was taking out the top of the tower with Czech Semtex. Ethan worked from room to room on the second floor. Quick and dirty, just to be sure. Kate had drilled him on this part. The house should be empty, but they had to assume the worst: an overnight guest, a guard they didn't know about, Corbeau changing his plans. She called it the catastrophe factor. In the main hall again Ethan walked down a narrow corridor.

This, according to the plans of the house they had stolen from the city planner's office some months ago, would take him to the library and tower. 'Coming in, Girl,' he said. He kicked through the locked door and found a beautiful room. Along two of its vast walls were built-in bookshelves. The third wall offered a bank of windows with a view to the lake, and a large, perfectly arranged writing table. The fourth wall had a set of pocket doors at the centre. These were presently closed. Each door offered three cast iron ornaments fashioned into the likeness of small black ravens. They appeared to function as door handles or some kind of medieval locking mechanism. From what he knew of their man, Ethan didn't trust them. He thought they might be booby-trapped, something Gothic, mechanical, and deadly.

'House is clear,' Ethan said, 'but stay away from the doors. I don't like the look of them.'

'We're on the clock, Boy,' Kate answered.

'Seven minutes,' he said.

'Five is better.'

The Palace Hotel, Lucerne

Jeffrey Bremmer, Corbeau's director of security, stepped out of the shadows and signalled his employer. Corbeau excused himself, and walked toward the man with a bit of curiosity. Bremmer usually handled his job without involving Corbeau. 'What is it?' he asked.

'A couple of drunks at the front gate set off the alarm.'

Corbeau looked out across the lake. He disliked any sort of disturbance that was not of his own making. Officially, he was still a US fugitive. The US could not act against him because he was under Swiss protection, but that didn't mean bounty hunters wouldn't try it. The US attorney, in a fit of pique when Corbeau had jumped bail after his indictment, had offered a one million dollar bounty to anyone capable of delivering him to a government willing to extradite him. That meant getting him out of Switzerland. In eleven years, two different groups had been foolish enough to try it.

'Austrians, apparently. A man and a woman . . .

sixty-something. They've been instructed to leave, but they're not cooperating.'

'Notify the police to be on standby, and give them one more warning.'

'I'll take care of it.'

As he watched Bremmer depart, cell phone to his ear, a strange dread took hold of Corbeau. It was not the first time the feeling had hit him. On three separate occasions over the past two weeks a wave of nausea had washed over him. His instincts told him his enemies were closer than he knew, but he could not locate the source. He had persuaded himself it was nothing, but *nothing* was suddenly becoming very insistent. Instinctively, he searched the rooftop looking for the contessa. She was gone. A camera spotted, no doubt.

He looked at the crowd. There were very few strange faces. Of those he didn't know he saw no one capable of successfully spiriting him out of the country. It was possible that was the plan, of course, but it was more likely something was going on at the house that was not quite what it seemed . . .

Well, the police were alerted. The road could be closed down in a matter of minutes. Everything should be—

Bremmer returned. He made no signal this time. Corbeau understood the look and immediately walked toward him. 'I'm getting no response at the guardhouse.'

'What about the police?'

'They are sealing off the road.'

'Good. Nothing more. I want to take care of this myself.'

Bremmer's smile suggested just how much he loved his work. 'I thought you might. The SUV should be at the front door by the time we get there. The second team is already moving. They should be at the house in three minutes.'

Lake Lucerne

Ethan went first to the bookshelves, checking the titles out of curiosity. Not surprisingly, given the man they were robbing, most of the library was devoted to the esoteric. He saw Pietro Mora's *Zekerboni*, a seventeenth century treatise on magic that he knew had been found in Casanova's possession and was instrumental in getting the famed lover convicted of sorcery in 1755.

He saw Aleister Crowley's *Confessions*, and fought the impulse to pick it from the shelves. He was sure it was a first edition. Crowley, at the height of his powers in the early twentieth century, was known as the wickedest man alive. He saw Madame Blavatsky's *Isis*, the complete works of John Dee, Dion Fortune's *Through the Gates of Death*, Éliphas Lévi's masterworks on magic, in the original French, *Le Dome et rituel de la haute magie* and *Histoire de la magie*. He saw Robert Fludd, W. E. Butler, Alice Bailey, Albertus Magnus, Pieto de Albano, Papus, Rudolph Steiner, and on and on. The library itself, book by book, if he could haul it out, was worth several million dollars on the open market, but tonight it was not part of the plan.

Tonight they wanted one painting – if it even existed. He moved to the second wall, which included biographies and secondary matter related to magic.

Hiding in plain view? He scanned the shelves, looking for anything that might conceal a small panel painting.

'Anything?' Kate asked.

'Not yet.'

'There's nothing in here!'

'Check the masonry. We're close, I can feel it.'

'What I can feel is we're running out of time.'

'We're okay.' He broke the lock on the desk with his crowbar and felt a twinge of guilt at the destruction of such a beautiful piece. Inside the only drawer he found a Mont Blanc and pale cream-coloured stationery embossed with Corbeau's coat of arms featuring a raven in flight. Beneath it were the words *Gare le Corbeau!* He looked at the two pictures on the wall separating the library from the tower. One of them was a faded print of a young girl, maybe nine or ten years old, sitting naked in an antique graveyard on what appeared to be her shroud. Her eyes were opened wide in apparent surprise at finding herself alive again. It was framed in a delicate grey. The framer had accented the grey with a thin, faded vermilion line. Pencilled in a tiny script was the phrase, *Nothing but the beautiful is true*, followed by initials and a date: O. W., March 29, 1899.

'We have the right man,' he said, and felt his pulse kick up. O. W. Oscar Wilde. He had been here a century ago. To see it again? Summoned? Gentleman that he was, Oscar had brought a gift – something to commemorate their first meeting? What Ethan wouldn't give to know that story!

'We're running out of time, Boy.'

Ethan turned from the print to the painting, a small

dark landscape of Golgotha after the execution. He walked toward it. It was a primitive black on grey study of the crucifixion scene after the bodies had been taken down and the crowd had gone home. Ethan reached out carefully to touch the thing. The frame stayed tight against the wall. Checking more closely he saw a tiny hinge behind the frame. When he pulled on it harder, the edge of the painting came off the wall like a small door opening. Inside he found a recessed, metal lever. Ethan pulled it, but nothing happened. Next, he tried turning it. The mechanism worked, but again nothing happened.

A booby-trap?

He looked at the raven heads on the pocket doors. No. The door handles provided the only trap Corbeau needed. This was the way in. The Knights Templar had used three empty crosses to indicate *the treasure*, or possibly the key to the treasure or even *the place of concealment*, depending on the context. It was not a symbolism widely recognized beyond Templar enthusiasts. The raven, on the other hand, was the essential ornament on Corbeau's coat of arms, under-scored by the words *Gare le Corbeau!* Beware the Raven!

He tried pulling the lever in its new position and dis-covered to his surprise the pocket doors began to slide back. Kate stood in the darkened room, her night vision goggles in place over her hood. She pulled these up and let them rest on her forehead as she stepped into the library. Ethan showed her the handle, the painting, and the print of the young girl. 'Look at the initials.'

'Oscar Wilde,' she said. 'Maybe *he* took it.'

'It's here, Girl. It's the Corbeau family heirloom.'

Ethan stepped into the gloomy tower. There were no light fixtures, no electrical outlets, only candelabras with half-burned candles set about the room. The room itself was a perfect circle. On the floor in a mosaic, Ethan recognized the Grand Seal of Solomon. The letters of the magical words were all written in a Greek script. Kate's climbing rope lay coiled upon it. It stretched up through the broken ceiling some twelve feet overhead.

Before the explosion there had been a ceiling painting. Most of it was gone, but Ethan could make out that it was the traditional occultist's Tree of Life with the ten emanations of God, each named in Greek letters. 'There's nothing here,' Kate whispered. For the first time she sounded anxious. Her burglar's heart had an internal clock.

Ethan studied the empty room. He saw the Masonic eye of God. Before it were two small marble pillars. A plain stone altar had been placed neatly between them. He walked around the room examining the stone benches built into the wall. 'Where would they keep the paraphernalia?' He studied the Seal of Solomon.

'We have to go.'

'It's here.'

'Doesn't matter. We're out of time.'

Ethan walked across the floor scrutinizing the intricate patterns and letters. He was looking for a telltale crack in the stone. He pulled his flashlight and began walking the circle of the seal. The stone had been laid over a century ago. There were tiny fissures and a bit of yellowing, but that was all. Kate spoke again, 'Time!'

Ethan looked toward the altar again. He focused on the eye. Was the eye staring at it? He spun around and looked at the wall, then walked toward it, shining his flashlight. Nothing. He went back to the library and touched the painting of the empty crosses. Which was it: *the treasure, the key to the treasure, or the place of concealment?*

Kate took his arm. 'Now,' she said.

Ethan pulled his knife and began cutting along the edge of the canvas. 'One minute. Then we go.'

She checked her watch. Nothing appeared behind the canvas. So the painting was *the* key. He tried to turn the handle but it did not move. He pushed it back into the wall, and the pocket doors began sliding together. He watched until the doors came together, then turned the handle as he had before. Pulling it out again, he watched the doors begin to open.

While they were still moving, he tried turning the handle. This time he got something. The lever snapped easily to a new position. The doors continued to open, but the wainscoting along the lower part of the wall slipped down behind the baseboard revealing three shelves. On the top, he saw a skull and crossbones sitting on a piece of white linen. The linen was wrapped around a small flat rectangular object.

'This is it,' he said.

Slipping the packet out from under the bones, Ethan hurriedly unfolded the cloth and came face-to-face with a portrait of Christ that was painted, if the legends could be trusted, inside Herod's palace in Jerusalem at the order of the prefect of Judaea, Pontius Pilate. According to the oldest reference to the relic, anyone who looked upon it would live forever and never grow old. The Templars had thought it inspired visions.

'Let's go, Boy,'

Ethan slipped the panel into a waterproof pouch and tucked it into the metal frame between Kate's back and backpack. 'Having any visions yet?' he asked.

'I'm seeing trouble.'

'Then we better go.'

A man appeared at the door to the library as Ethan said this. He was wearing a tuxedo and carrying a semi-automatic pistol in his right hand with the casualness of someone holding a drink. He was tall and trim, somewhere in his mid-thirties. He did not seem especially surprised to find two intruders wearing black silk hoods inside Julian Corbeau's library. In fact, he seemed to expect it. Kate reached for her pistol as Ethan drew his own gun, but they were both responding. The man was ready and appeared remarkably relaxed as he pointed his pistol at Kate and shot her.

Kate kicked back under the impact of the bullet as Ethan's Colt cleared its holster. The man turned his weapon calmly toward Ethan and fired again. This time he missed. Kate's weapon fired from the floor simultaneously, and the man in the tuxedo fell back against the door. A split-second later Ethan's Colt fired, striking the man's neck as he went down.

Ethan stooped down to check on Kate, whose smoking gun was still pointing toward the door. He found the bullet hole over her heart. 'I'm okay . . . I think,' she groaned.

Ethan probed the opening and discovered a hot

flattened piece of lead. 'Got to love the Cobra,' he whispered.

Kate came slowly up to her feet. Together they looked at the dead man sprawled against the door. 'Where did he come from?'

'I don't know, but if he has friends—'

They heard voices calling in German from the stairway. Two? Three? Ethan could not tell, and did not look forward to finding out.

'—we're in trouble,' she whispered.

'You get out with the painting.' He pointed toward the rope. 'I'll keep them busy.'

Ethan walked to the doorway of the library stripping his silencer off his Navy Colt. He grabbed the dead man's weapon in his left hand. A voice called up the stairs in German. 'Did you get them?'

Ethan looked back and saw Kate staring at him. 'Go!' he hissed. 'I'll meet you downstairs.'

It was a lie, probably the last thing he would ever say to her. It didn't matter though. The problem now was getting Kate out alive. All he had to do was live long enough to give her a chance. She could take care of the rest. He went down the tiny corridor fearlessly. He could not remember ever having such certainty or courage. Kate's life depended on him now and what he could do in the next few seconds. That was all that mattered. Two men in tuxedos on the stairway fired their guns simultaneously as Ethan rolled forward across the hall. He came up on one knee with both guns levelled on them and fired the weapons successively. One man went down under the barrage. The second pulled back. Another voice called from below. He heard footsteps ascending the stairs and came back to his feet – his retreat cut off. That was when Kate came out and began firing her Navy Colt without the silencer. One of the men screamed. The others fell back. Ethan fired two shots as he crossed the open area and came back into the tight corridor.

'Go,' he told her. 'I'll hold them until you're out!'

He turned out and fired three more shots to keep the men back while Kate ran to the tower. Pulling his grenade, he slipped the pin and dropped it in the tight confines of the narrow corridor. Kate was nearly out of the tower when Ethan took the rope and began climbing it with a rapid hand-over-hand. He heard the voices of two men as they came up the stairs. The grenade exploded before they got to it, but it slowed them down enough for Ethan to get to the roof. He pulled himself out with the help of his climbing pick.

Kate, covering him, dropped her own grenade into the tower and pulled the rope out. She reset the grappling hook and began down the side of the tower. Ethan watched the yard as she did, but no one came outside. He heard the grenade inside the tower explode just as he dropped off the roof and began rappelling down the tower. On the ground Ethan scrambled toward the wall. The lights in the house went off and a volley of automatic weapon fire poured from three points along the ground floor.

'AK-47s,' Kate whispered in the aftermath of the sustained burst.

As the next volley began, a man sprinted out of the house and moved quickly into the shadows of the wall opposite them.

'One in the yard,' Ethan said, moving carefully back until he found a tree and a rock that would give him something more than just concealment. 'I'm going to draw his fire!'

He fired blindly at the house once. As he did, the gunman in the yard responded with a long volley. Mulch and dirt blew into his face. Splinters of stone stung his neck and hands. As soon as the gunman open fired, Kate responded with three quick shots at his position. A scream of pain ended it, and then Kate was running for the cliff.

Ethan began squeezing off rounds toward the muzzle blasts inside the house. He continued firing until he was standing and moving across the brightly lit field. He fired until his ammunition was gone, then dropped both weapons and sprinted for the cliff. Kate went over, her modified parachute blowing out behind her.

Ethan got nearly two seconds of silence for his efforts, but then the automatic weapons began again. His legs felt heavy and uncooperative. The ground ripped crazily before him. He heard small cracking sounds as the bullets passed by his head. Logically, he knew he could cross the twenty-five yards in a matter of three or four seconds. Without cover, with automatic fire from two weapons bearing down, the final two seconds seemed like ten.

He fell once, rolling back to his feet, then, his legs betraying him, he staggered toward the edge of the cliff. He touched the ripcord a step before he went over – exactly as he and Kate had practised it. He felt the heat of one bullet pass him as he pulled the cord, and he knew with a sudden exhilaration he had made it.

That was when his back lit up in pain. Instead of

jumping as Kate had done, Ethan grunted at the impact and stumbled over the retaining wall. He heard the parachute open with a snap, and felt the drag of it pull him upright. It let him drift out toward the water without his assistance. His night vision goggles still resting on his head, he saw nothing before he plunged into the lake.

He waited for his body's buoyancy to take him to the surface, then fought free of the ropes and canopy. He tasted the lake water and nearly went under again before he wrestled free. He searched for the gunmen at the top of the cliff. All he saw was a mass of rock and the night sky. They would be heading for the boats.

A flash of light across the water caught his attention, and he whispered, 'Do you see me?'

There was no answer. He had lost his headset and goggles when he hit the water. He whistled, failing miserably, then found his flashlight and signalled once, hesitated, then twice more. Kate flashed her light once, and Ethan heard the outboard motor purr. He looked up toward the top of the cliff again. Still empty. Kate brought the raft to him and leaned over with her hand held out. He took her wrist and the grab line. Rearing up out of the water he fell across the raft.

Corbeau could hear them pulling away with a small outboard motor as he climbed aboard his cruiser. He signalled Bremmer toward one of the Jet skis and pressed the keypad by the pilot's wheel to open the gates of the dock. The cruiser's triple engines roared to life, but the gates did not move.

'Open the gates!' he shouted.

Bremmer pulled forward and tried the key pad. 'Jammed!' he called.

Corbeau swore angrily and killed the motor. 'Call the police!'

While Bremmer spoke on the phone, Corbeau cursed his folly and paced the deck. For days he had been waiting for another attempted kidnap, never imagining the real danger.

And now it was too late.

Chapter Two

New York City
October 3, 2006.

Because she had never gotten the field out of her blood, Jane Harrison came in from the west side of the park and took a piece of high ground for no better reason than to observe Thomas Malloy reading his newspaper. Malloy did his best not to notice. Jane had been his boss too many years for him not to play to her vanities.

He was seated under a canopy of golden leaves by one of the roads running through Central Park just off Fifth Avenue. Malloy had boulders at his back, a stream and woods covering his left flank. The weather was cool and cloudy and it was early, so there were not too many people in the park yet. At precisely the moment he had indicated they should meet, Jane walked down the hill, crossed a piece of pavement and sat beside him. Looking like an Upper West Side matron she arranged herself comfortably and began to work on a fairly impressive piece of needlework. It was a skill Malloy had not known she possessed. 'You've become a trusting soul since retirement, T. K.'

Jane Harrison was sixty-two years old, as trim and plain as the day Malloy had met her. She had not changed her hair in twenty-five years. Even the colour, a dull salt-and-pepper, remained a constant. Jane had been at Langley so long everyone imagined it was where she had started, but Malloy's father had told him years ago that Jane began her professional life playing the part of a disaffected expatriate wandering through Europe.

Following a series of raids and bloody assassinations of the Italian Communists, who were 'knee-capping' American tourists among their other victims, Jane transferred quietly into Langley, trading in her beads, long hair, and free love credo for the bureaucrat's uniform. She worked for a while as an analyst, then crossed the hall and rejoined operations at a supervisory level. Malloy had never confirmed the story, but legend had it that Ted Kennedy in his younger days had struck out with her at a party. Complaining bitterly about it, he had called her the Iron Maiden. True or not, the moniker attached itself, and that was still how most people referred to her. At least behind her back.

Malloy had met Jane shortly after Reagan began his second term. A young operative, Malloy's first tour of duty overseas had ended disastrously. He was expecting a life sentence inside Langley, probably as the Iron Maiden's Boy Friday. To his astonishment, Jane offered him a chance to redeem himself with the most coveted overseas assignments in the agency, a three-year tour of duty in Switzerland as a NOC, a NOC being any officer operating with No Official Cover. Years later Malloy realised what kind of courage it took for her to do that, but even as a young man he had been impressed by her confidence in him.

'I'm meeting the deputy director of operations for a notoriously paranoid government agency in Central Park, Jane. That means we've got guardian angels all around us. Why shouldn't I take advantage of the extra security and enjoy my newspaper?'

'Assume nothing, my friend. Didn't I teach you that?'

Malloy folded his paper and began scanning the classifieds. Jane's message to him was running again. So was his response.

The last time Malloy had seen Jane Harrison had been at his retirement party. Jane had told him when the time was right she would be able to offer him all the contract work he could handle, but for a while he was on his own. It was not the kind of promise supervisors offered at the typical thirty and thirty-five-year retirement parties. Malloy wasn't an old warhorse turned out to pasture and given promises so he could keep his dignity.

He had been an accomplished operative sidelined by the new director of operations. Rather than get old behind a desk he had taken his twenty-year-pension and walked. Jane made the promise. Like a good operative Malloy settled down with his cover and waited. He read the classifieds every morning, the *Times* when he was stateside, the *Herald Tribune* when he was abroad. Two days ago, Jane had finally run the lonely hearts advertisement they had agreed on. Malloy's answer ran the following morning setting up the rendezvous.

'What do you have for me?' he asked.

Jane concentrated on her needlepoint. 'You're not going to like it.'

'I'm going to go out on a limb here and guess that you've got something that involves breaking a number of federal laws without benefit of immunity.'

Jane ran a couple of stitches through her needlepoint while another jogger passed them. 'Nothing outrageous, I don't think. About as felonious as crossing against the light, but given the present political climate it's probably to our advantage to have a bit of credible deniability, just in case. An ex-operative with a chip on his shoulder, a grudge in his heart, and a history of pissing in the wind ought to be sufficient for the occasion.'

'I fit the profile.'

'I assume you know J. W. Richland?'

'The televangelist?' Malloy fought the urge to complain, but Jane caught his tone.

'A friend of the Administration, T. K.'

'Tell me you want me to cut his tongue out. I'll work for free.'

Jane was a good soldier, but even she smiled at this. 'Nobody has to know about this. We're sure not going to put it on paper, and I don't think Richland will either.'

'I'll know. Isn't that enough?'

'Don't tell me you've gone out and bought a conscience?'

'I've been thinking about getting one ever since I left the agency – as long as they don't cost too much.'

'They cost plenty, T. K., and give you nothing but grief.'

'Voice of experience?'

Jane looked out across the park, the shadow of a

smile playing at her lips. Italy – living her cover? It was hard to imagine Jane with a sex life, harder still to think of her belonging to the free love generation. 'I gave up the Girl Scouts years ago, T. K.'

'Could have fooled me.'

'Richland had a painting stolen from his estate. A few weeks ago he got a telephone call from an art dealer in Zürich who wants to sell the thing to him.'

'A ransom?'

'The preacher hands over twenty-five million, and he gets his painting back.'

'*Million?*'

'Who knew the Lord paid so well?'

Malloy thought about it for moment, and finally decided to ask the obvious question just to hear Jane's explanation. 'Why not go to the police?'

'Some question of provenance, I take it.'

'The Reverend J. W. Richland dealing in black market paintings? Wouldn't the *Times* love a piece of that?'

'Black market is such an ugly expression, T. K.'

'Almost as bad as smuggling.'

'Smuggling is the one thing you don't have to do. Charlie has asked Bob Whitefield to carry it in a diplomatic pouch. All you do is make the exchange and pass it to Whitefield at the Zürich Airport. Once he clears customs stateside, you take the thing back and make the delivery.'

'Why not just get Whitefield to take care of the whole thing?'

'If anything goes wrong, it won't be at customs, not with a diplomatic pouch. The risk falls to you.

Richland knows he's going to have to pay for this, by the way. As a favour to me I hope you charge him plenty.'

'Any indication that something might go wrong?'

'I got to be an old woman because I always expect something will go wrong.'

'Didn't I read that Richland is dying?'

'Old news, T. K. The doctors gave him six months to live eight or ten months ago. According to his new book, the preacher fired them all and went down on his knees.'

'Right. *Pray for a Miracle*. I tried it, but he's still on my TV.' Jane was silent, waiting. Not that he was considering a pass. Malloy had committed himself the moment he answered Jane's classified. If he walked away from this, he walked away for good. He wasn't ready to do that. 'So where do I find him?'

Jane tipped her head toward the south end of the park. 'He's at the Plaza. Ask for Mr Gideon.'

Slipping his city gun, a Sigma .380, out of its holster, Malloy tried to hand it to the muscle-bound plainclothes security officer guarding J. W. Richland's suite.

'That's okay,' the young man named Mike answered with an oddly soft voice, 'but I'll need this.' He reached tentatively for Malloy's cell phone. Malloy nodded permission and slipped his gun back into its tiny holster at the small of his back. The big man set the phone on a table delicately and brought a wand out of his hip holster. He passed it over Malloy's body, again with Malloy's permission. He was checking for transmitting devices.

'It's a funny world,' Malloy offered pleasantly, 'when a telephone is more dangerous than a gun.' Mike touched him lightly just to make sure Malloy was not wearing something as old fashioned as a miniature tape recorder, and agreed affably. It certainly was. Stepping away, he rapped his thick knuckles on the door, and Malloy heard the muffled voice of J. W. Richland.

The suite was a study in antique white: carpet, walls, furniture and curtains. At the window overlooking the park, a silver haired man turned cheerfully to receive Malloy. A young woman perched on a settee close by. Richland was average height, somewhere in his sweet-sixties. He wore a dark blue suit without the jacket, a white shirt, a scarlet tie and matching suspenders. The woman was a year or two beyond thirty. She had black hair pulled back tightly, not a lock of it out of place, lustrous dark eyes that missed nothing, and sensuously thick lips. Malloy was guessing she had bought the breasts.

She studied Malloy briefly with the air of one inspecting the hired help, then turned her attention back to Richland. It was enough to break the heart of a lesser man.

'Mr Malloy!' Richland shouted affectionately. He had his TV smile turned on, the Southwestern accent toned down. He met Malloy's gaze with intelligent blue eyes, and Malloy decided Richland didn't look like a man with a medical death sentence hanging over his head, no matter what his doctors said. Perhaps it was that thing the born-againers nurtured in abundance, overweening optimism. 'Thank you for coming on such short notice!'

Malloy was fairly sure no one in the last couple of decades had refused a meeting with J. W. Richland, short notice or not, but he answered in the spirit of the remark. 'My pleasure, Reverend.'

A curious thing happened as they shook hands. Richland met Malloy's gaze and let the moment stretch out a beat longer than necessary. He was not sure what the preacher expected to accomplish with this, but then it came to him. It was pure habit. This was supposed to be a great moment for Malloy, not a ceremony to be hurried through. Surely someday he would want to tell people about it. Shaking hands with J. W. Richland! Love him or hate him, it didn't matter. Richland was that big.

'You come highly recommended among people I respect,' Richland announced.

'Glad to hear it.'

Still holding Malloy's hand, he added, 'Are you as good as they say?'

There was a peculiar hint of challenge in this, but Malloy let it go. 'You know how it is these days,' he smiled and broke Richland's hold on him. 'A man is only as good as the PR firm he hires.'

Richland laughed with a bright explosion of mirth Malloy had a hard time disliking. 'Trust me, the real danger comes when you start believing your own press!'

'I'm a determined sceptic, Reverend, especially about my own press.'

'But you get the job done? That's what they tell me.'

This was serious. He wanted assurances. Malloy had not expected this and tucked it away to think about later. 'When I was twenty-four years old, a G. I. doctor in Beirut told meI don't die easily, sir. That's all I can promise you.'

Richland laughed grandly and clapped his hands. This was a gesture Malloy had seen him perform on TV. Usually when he did it he would say, 'Can I hear an Amen?'

'Don't die easily! My, that's good! He turned to the woman, who was still seated by the window. 'A man after my own heart, Nikki!' Then to explain himself, as if that were necessary, he said, 'Eleven months ago I had three doctors sit me down and tell me there was no way I was going to live another six months, Mr Malloy. You know what I did?'

'Yes, sir.'

Richland was not about to have his story interrupted, whether Malloy knew or not. 'I fired them! I took the medicine they were prescribing and poured it down the drain! Then I dropped to my knees and talked to the only One who has any say in the matter!'

Malloy smiled pleasantly, trying to decide how high to jack his fee.

'Nikki, come over here and meet another man who has cheated death!'

The woman stood and walked toward them. She had dressed for business in a dark blue pants suit and white blouse with a string of lustrous grey pearls, but she crossed one foot before the other – as if trained to walk for the pleasure of men. She reminded Malloy of a poisoned liqueur in a crystal decanter. He wondered if their affair had begun shortly before Richland's cancer or if like the angel of death she had shown up after the medical death sentence.

'Dr Nicole North,' Richland offered, 'Mr Thomas Killion Malloy.'

'Pleased,' she said without sincerity. Her voice had just a whisper of Texas in it, but Malloy, who possessed a discerning ear for language and accents, was quite certain it reached back three or four generations.

Richland waved his hand toward the couch and chair in the middle of the room. 'Have a seat!' he said. 'May I get you something? A croissant, coffee, juice? We've already had our breakfast, but I can call for something, if you'd like.'

Malloy had had a late night, and coffee sounded good, but he did not care to put off the meeting while they waited for refreshments. 'I'm fine,' he answered.

'Then let's get down to business, what do you say?'

'You need a painting brought into the States without attending to the usual formalities.'

Richland didn't care for the way he had put this, and for the first time since Malloy had walked into the room the preacher lost his smile. 'It's a bit more complicated than that.'

'Why don't you tell me about it?'

J. W. Richland glanced at Nicole North as if he wanted reassurance before he spoke. That wasn't especially interesting. He was dealing with an experienced intelligence officer, and he knew it. He could reasonably assume Malloy could read a lie almost as easily as he could tell one. What Malloy wanted to know, and what he could not find out by observing the preacher's body language, was whether or not he was serving the same stew to everyone.

'I acquired the painting a number of years ago, when there was not as much concern about . . .'

He looked at Nicole North for help. 'Cultural heritage.'

Richland nodded and repeated the phrase thoughtfully. 'A good thing in theory,' he said, 'but in practice if we went around returning everything we've dug up in the past one hundred years . . . well, you might as well close every museum in the Western world!'

'You think someone might have a legitimate claim to your painting?'

'Legitimacy isn't the issue, Mr Malloy. Any claim, any interference at all, and I won't see my property again.'

Malloy nodded as if he accepted this.

Dr North picked up Malloy's apparent scepticism. 'The painting was discovered at an archaeological site several years ago by my uncle – Jonas Starr.' She waited for a response at the mention of this name, but Malloy didn't react. He had never heard of the man. 'It's a twelfth century painting of Christ.'

'When I saw it,' Richland explained, 'I told Jonas that was exactly the way I had always pictured Christ. Do you know what he did? He handed it to me and said it was mine, just like that!'

'Where was the archaeological site?'

Nicole North considered the question without answering. Malloy couldn't decide whether she was dreaming something up or calculating how much truth she needed to give him. 'In southern Turkey,' she said finally. 'Not far from the city of Altinbasak.'

'And you think the Turkish government might try to reclaim it?'

'We're fairly confident they would if they found out about it. We also think they would have a lot of support if they took us into a court outside the United States.'

'Once it's back here,' Richland added, with a smile that confirmed his friendship with a sitting President, 'I don't expect we'll have any problems.'

'The thing is we're not sure we can trust the people we're dealing with,' North told him. 'It's quite possible that after we make the exchange someone might decide to tip off Swiss customs. The Swiss are well aware of Dr Richland's strong support for the President, and they would just love to create an incident to embarrass him.'

'The Swiss?' Malloy asked in surprise. The Swiss, he knew, had never aspired to create an international incident with anyone.

'They haven't forgotten the pressure America brought to bear on them over the matter of the bank accounts of the holocaust victims.'

As it happened, Malloy knew more about the bank accounts of the holocaust victims than he could admit. He was also, in select circles, an acknowledged expert on Swiss-American relations. Dr North's pretensions of authority on this issue indicated she didn't know that. 'When exactly did you lose your painting, Reverend?'

'Last winter,' Richland answered, levelling his gaze on Malloy. It was the kind of look an amateur gives for the Big Lie, which was strange because it was a simple, rather unimportant detail. More curious than anything, Malloy locked an accusing gaze on Nicole North. Unlike the preacher, she did not especially fear his powers of discernment. At that point Malloy decided they were handing out the same story to everyone. It probably wasn't in the President's interest to doubt an old friend, but he felt reasonably sure Jane and Charlie would not be taken in so easily.

'Last winter?' He managed to sound suspicious, as if paintings were rarely stolen in winter.

'February, wasn't it, Nicole?' Richland wiggled in his seat like a recalcitrant Sunday schooler.

'I think so. Yes.' Nicole North lied better than the preacher. She actually seemed embarrassed by Richland's discomfort.

'You went to the police, I take it?'

Richland looked confused and shook his head as he blushed. 'No. We . . .' His hesitation looked staged, but Malloy thought it was at least well-practised.

'Dr Richland has to be extremely careful with the information he provides the public,' Nicole North explained. 'We felt at the time if he filed a complaint, he would just be exposing himself and his ministry to possible criticism.'

They both seemed pleased with this answer and were therefore surprised when Malloy responded incredulously. 'You mean to say you didn't even file a claim with your insurance company?'

They seemed not to have thought about insurance, only the police, and Nicole North's eyes widened ever so slightly as Richland stepped into uncharted territory. 'No. The painting was a gift, you see. We didn't even know what value to put on it. Besides, the claim probably would have become public knowledge. You know how those things go.'

'We made considerable effort at recovering the painting, Mr Malloy,' Nicole North said finally. There was a bit of chastisement in this. They were hiring him after all, not the other way around. 'Both my security people and Dr Richland's made inquiries. Unfortunately nothing came of our efforts.'

'I really didn't think I'd ever get it back,' Richland explained. He looked like a stage actor who has stumbled back into the script. 'Then we got a call. A Mr Roland Wheeler of Zürich.' Richland gave Malloy a smile he no doubt reserved for annihilating enemies of the faith. 'He wanted to know if we would be interested in acquiring a twelfth century portrait of Christ.' Richland's expression suggested the transparency of such a ruse.

'Wheeler insists he is representing the owner,' North added. 'Naturally he refuses to acknowledge Dr Richland's claim of prior ownership. He's keeping it at a private bank in Zürich called Goetz and Ritter. From what we can tell, they don't run banks over there the way we do here.'

Malloy resisted a smile at this, and changed the subject. 'You're comfortable with the painting's authenticity?'

'I will be before I release the funds. I'm going over Sunday and will examine it Monday morning. If everything is in order and you agree to help, you'll join me Tuesday at the bank for the exchange. Once I've completed the transfer of funds, you'll take responsibility for getting the painting to New York.'

Richland squirmed uncomfortably. 'If something happened after you took possession, Mr Malloy, say for instance the police in Zürich stopped you, just how would you handle the matter?'

'If I take the job, I'll arrange matters so that nobody stops me, Reverend.'

'You didn't exactly answer my question.'

'Let me make something clear to you. How I work is my business. This much I can tell you: I'll either bring the painting to you or I'll be dead, and someone in my employ will deliver it.'

The Rev. J. W. Richland sat back and considered this for a moment. Malloy was a quiet, dark-haired man fast approaching fifty. He had never been the muscular commando-type. He had built his career on his insight into human nature, the art of persuasion, and by inspiring loyalty in those people he recruited to work for him. When he made a promise, he kept it. When he worked a job, he got it done – one way or the other. After a quarter of a century of handling whatever came at him, he didn't especially care to explain himself to amateurs.

'That's quite a statement,' Richland said finally.

'You're hiring me to do a job you don't think your own people can handle. It goes without saying you want someone who is ready for every contingency. When I tell you the police aren't going to stop me, believe it.'

'Well then,' Richland answered, 'I suppose the only thing left is to persuade you to take the job!' The preacher's expression suggested that he was a man accustomed to getting his own way but was not at all reluctant to engage in the hard give-and-take of negotiations. 'I propose an advance of ten thousand dollars to cover your expenses and another one hundred thousand dollars cash the moment you hand me the painting.' Richland seemed proud of his offer, as if he assumed Malloy would not have dreamed of asking for such a figure.

'I'm financing two security teams, one in Switzerland and one here. These people don't come cheaply, Reverend, and neither do I.'

Richland seemed surprised, but managed to ask politely, 'What exactly do you need?'

'One hundred thousand advance. Four hundred thousand cash when I hand you the painting.'

'That's ridiculous!' Richland tried to laugh, but he wasn't doing a very good job.

Malloy stood up and started for the door. 'I'm sorry I wasted your time. I thought you understood what you are asking me to do.'

'Now just a minute!'

At the door Malloy turned back and smiled cordially, ignoring Richland's protest. 'It was a pleasure to meet you both.'

'You're talking about a great deal of money!' Richland shouted.

'I'm sure you'll find someone in your price range,' Malloy answered with a condescending smile.

Nicole North spoke. 'You have a deal, Mr Malloy.'

Malloy looked at the preacher for confirmation, but J. W. Richland looked suddenly more like the woman's lapdog than a dealmaker.

Malloy and his fiancée lived in a converted warehouse that faced Ninth Avenue. Empty lots lay to either side and behind it. Two years ago a contact in Europe, using a series of dummy corporations to cover his tracks, had arranged to buy the building and asked Malloy to oversee its restoration and eventually to manage the property. The bottom three floors were still shells, but the platform elevator, original to the building, had finally passed inspection, and Malloy had converted the top floor into a small apartment with a large art studio for Gwen.

Gwen was a painter, one of the few who actually sold her works for a decent price on occasion. During the lean times, and there had been plenty of them over the past two decades, Gwen had covered expenses waiting tables. As it happened that was how Malloy had met her. A week later, a long dry spell broke for her, and Gwen sold a painting for close to forty thousand dollars. Her stock in the art world had been on the rise ever since.

Gwen was a short, slender, athletic woman with a boundless reserve of quiet determination and energy. She had an irreverent sense of humour and that rarest of all qualities, at least in modern times, common sense. She had dark intelligent eyes, short black hair, and pale creamy skin. As a Jewish kid growing up in Queens, Gwen said she had been a girl nobody noticed. That didn't seem possible to look at her now. She had been a radical most of her life. Disenfranchised from the power structure and suspicious of everyone who encouraged her toward moderation and responsibility and conformity, especially conformity, Gwen had spent, by her own account, the first decade of her adult life without so much as a passing nod toward discretion. In her thirties Gwen had understood the advantage of the single life, especially for an artist, and settled into a series of comfortable though distant relationships that would last a year or two and then dissolve amicably. Passion came at intervals. At forty Gwen still cherished a bit of the Revolution, but mostly she had come to terms with herself and her talent. She was one of the few people Malloy had ever met who had no regrets.

Whenever he was foolish enough to try to take inventory of the reasons he had fallen in love with her, the list, no matter how long, somehow failed to capture her essence. She had talent of course and wisdom and a wickedly quick wit. She had beauty, humour, fire, and an amazing gentleness. She was honest, charitable, and still curious about all things new. She had abiding friendships, a point he thought which argued for her integrity, and she could make friends easily, a virtual impossibility for most people at forty. Gwen could be silent for hours at a time, something Malloy loved about her because almost nobody except the occasional agoraphobic had that skill. She was moody when things went well, optimistic when others despaired.

There was an enduring bashfulness about Gwen's lovemaking, the hint always of a reverence for her passions, but on rare occasions she would summon the extravagant: a confession of historic interest or a fantastic proposition. Once just for the shock value Gwen had led Malloy by his hand into an alley and treated him like a decadent Victorian gentleman. Nothing quite defined Gwen but what he valued most was not a matter of character or beauty or style. It was the way Gwen saw her world.

She had the ability to find potential where others saw only wreckage. She had looked, for instance, at the hollow shell that was to become the centre of their life and knew at once she wanted it. She could see a face in the street, a beggar, a tramp, a cop, or a workman, and discover beauty where no one could imagine it. Malloy had seen Gwen turn the ravages of old age into a meditation on eternity, and for that alone he could have loved her.

He still nurtured the pleasant illusion that Gwen had found that same kind of untapped potential in him. At the time they met Malloy was a forty-something pensioner waiting for a call he was beginning to think might never come. Certainly, he imagined the better part of his life finished. Gwen taught him to believe it was still before him.

He entered the apartment as usual through Gwen's studio and was somewhat startled by the sight of a naked man sitting in a broken-down second empire loveseat. This was Rudy, one of Gwen's regulars. Rudy was a year or two past sixty. He possessed a surprisingly good build, and despite his best efforts had not quite erased the last traces of what had once been an extremely handsome face. He had long dirty grey hair and a three-day beard. Gwen and a second artist had taken positions in front of him some fifteen feet away. Gwen was seated and working with a stick of charcoal on a large sketchpad. She wore jeans and her favourite NYC sweatshirt. Malloy could tell by the way she barely glanced at him she was having a good session.

'It's not what you think, Tommy!' Rudy cackled. 'She just wants to look!'

'That's how it starts,' Malloy told him, as he stepped behind Gwen. She had three completely different poses of Rudy in various stages of completion tacked on a corkboard. They were all good, but the fourth, the one she presently sketched, had something special about it.

In this one Gwen included less anatomical detail in the groin. At the same time the sketch suggested a sexual potency missing in the other drawings. Rudy didn't have the classical features of horn and hoof, but Gwen had somehow captured the essence of an aging satyr. The power of it was in what she didn't show. Like most genuine accomplishments, it wasn't something that just happened because of a simple omission. Expression lay in the ambiguous shadows. A bit like his own work, he thought, but he could never quite explain it that way to Gwen.

The truth was he had never been completely honest about his work. She understood bits and pieces of it. She knew that he spent a good deal of his time tracking information, but not what he did with it or the people he watched most closely. It might have been awkward had she asked, but Gwen gave him space. Only once had she ever commented about his secretiveness. 'I'm never going to know if you're seeing someone, am I?'

It was supposed to be something of a joke, but like most humour there was a good deal of truth in it. Sometimes he wanted to tell her everything, a lifetime of caution tossed to the wind, but the old instincts stopped him. He compartmentalized his life. There was Gwen here. There was work there. His secrets had finally ruined his other relationships and even an early, misguided marriage, but Gwen was different. She accepted his silence about certain matters as part of his essential being.

After he had examined her sketch, Malloy walked around to see what Paul Sorrento had done with the same model. Paul had helped broker the sale of the painting Gwen had sold right after Malloy had met her. He routinely shared the cost of a model with Gwen, especially the males if it happened that Malloy was going to be out for the morning. The sketch Paul presently worked on focused entirely on Rudy's penis, a compact masterpiece of disembodied detail. His first sketch lay crumpled on the floor, a study of the same. Malloy looked at it, but could not see the flaw. Of course he wasn't Paul Sorrento. The artist gestured toward the sketch he presently finished. 'A hundred dollars for this one, T. K., if you want it.'

'I'm sure you'll find someone who can appreciate it.'

'I don't doubt that. I just thought you might want to broaden your horizons.'

Rudy laughed until he choked. 'Hey, Tommy,' he wheezed, 'if you don't tell anyone, you can have the real thing for fifty!'

Malloy smiled at the old man. 'You'd tell, Rudy.'

The best painting Gwen had ever done was an oil portrait of Rudy dressed in an out-dated tuxedo. Wearing a white tie and tattered black jacket, Rudy had seemed a study in contradictions as he posed for Gwen. When she had finished the painting, it was magnificent. In it Rudy was a man who had fallen and in doing so had lost his last fear. The old man's cold eye neither begged nor offered sympathy.

Gwen had sold it for seventy thousand dollars. Malloy thought she had let it go too cheaply. She said she might decide to do another, just for him. Edvard

Monk was famous for duplicating his best pieces. Why couldn't she? Malloy didn't know why she couldn't, but he knew she never would. The light would never be quite the same. Rudy would be a month or two older. He would scowl differently, tie his bowtie more carefully. Gwen knew it too. He thought it was the reason she had suddenly decided on a full figure painting. In this composition Gwen had achieved a visual mix of age, poverty, and Eros, something of the king of the tramps in his all-together. 'If you're not careful,' Malloy told the old man, 'you could become famous.'

'Fame get me my next drink, will it, Tommy?'

Paul Sorrento glanced up from his sketch. 'Fame can get a man all the drinks he can handle, Rudy.'

Paul Sorrento knew what he was talking about, but Rudy wasn't buying it. He broke his pose as he laughed. 'There's not that much booze in the whole world, Paul!'

'We're about finished,' Gwen said. This was a not-so-subtle hint for Malloy to leave them alone. He was disturbing the model's tranquillity. 'Another ten minutes, I think. Are you good for ten more minutes, Rudy?'

Rudy put himself back into position. 'You got the money, honey, I got the time!'

Malloy walked back into the apartment. Inside his office he snapped on his computer screen and began working up an e-mail for Captain Marcus Steiner of the Zürich city police. Even though they both had secure locations, Malloy employed certain preset code words. It didn't pay to be careless in Malloy's business, even among the good guys. He had learned that in Beirut. The bulk of the letter was straightforward. Malloy said he needed basic information on Goetz and Ritter of Zürich and a full dossier on an art dealer named Roland Wheeler. Marcus Steiner had been one of Malloy's key agents when Malloy worked in Zürich. He had also hired on for some dangerous work over the years, most of which involved protecting the interests of one of Zürich's local crime lords, who just happened to be the source of almost all of Malloy's intelligence-gathering outside the world of Swiss banking.

Once he finished the letter, Malloy called a former colleague. It was a workday for government employees, and Gil Fine answered his desk phone on the second ring. For a number of years Gil had been an analyst at Langley. At various points during Malloy's career they had worked with each other, though rarely on the same side of the ocean. As Gil Fine and Malloy had talked fairly extensively only a few weeks ago about a fugitive financier Malloy was tracking, they were caught up with their personal news and moved quickly to the point of Malloy's call.

'*The* J. W. Richland?' Gil asked. He seemed taken aback by the request.

Malloy laughed. 'Can I hear an Amen?'

'What's this about, T.K.?' Gil wasn't laughing.

'Richland needs a favour, Gil. I've been elected to perform it.'

'I can give you public record.' Even that much did not make Gil particularly happy.

'That works. I just want a little background on the guy. I also need something on Jonas Starr and Nicole

North. Apparently Starr is a relatively well-known archaeologist. North is—'

'Gorgeous.'

'That's the one.'

'Too bad you're getting married. She's single and worth several billion. That's with a "B" as in Boy, am I rich!'

'I thought I smelled money. She's not as single as she looks, by the way. I'd bet my pension she and Richland have something going.'

'You know Richland is terminally ill?'

'Read his book, Gil. The old boy is appealing the verdict.'

Gil laughed cheerfully. 'I did read it. It's not half-bad! Listen, I'll download what I have on them, but if you need more—'

'I'll have Jane Harrison ask your boss for it.'

'Are you working for the Iron Maiden again, T. K.?'

'Jane owes me a favour, Gil. If I need it, I'll call in my marker.'

'I'd be careful if I were you. Jane has a selective memory. The way I understand it, she only remembers the favours she does for others.'

It was Malloy's turn not to laugh. 'Jane has always done right by me.'

'That's because you always made her look good. Cross her and see how she treats you.'

Gwen slipped into Malloy's office and kissed the back of his neck as he was finishing up with Gil. 'A good morning?' he asked when he was off the phone.

'I think I decided what I want to paint. If I can get the light right, it could be nice.'

'The one I saw you working on at the end?'

She nodded, smiling. 'I didn't think you would like it. The others were more realistic.'

'The others caught the image. The last got hold of his soul.'

Gwen smiled at his observation, but didn't respond. She pretended to value his opinion about art, but they both knew he was a Philistine. 'How was *your* morning?'

'I talked to some people about a job.'

Malloy had led Gwen to believe he had worked with the State Department in Zürich, specializing in finance. Boring work for the most part, he had told her. Nodding toward the black nylon satchel he had set beside his desk, she remarked, 'You did more than talk.'

'A little travelling money.'

Gwen seemed surprised, but not particularly upset. 'Travelling where?'

'I need to take care of some business in Zürich. A couple of days there and then fly back.'

Gwen blinked in surprise. 'This is sudden.'

'A lot of money and not much work. I couldn't really turn it down.'

'What kind of work?'

'Same-old-same-old. Talk to the bankers. Try to figure out what they're not telling me.'

'Maybe I could come along. You know . . . see my man in action?'

'It would put you to sleep. How about another time, when we can do some sight-seeing?'

'Have you got a lot to do between now and when you take off?'

'Not a lot. Why?'

She tucked her hands between his legs. 'I was hoping to get some practice in this weekend.'

'Practice?'

'You know. For the honeymoon.'

Chapter Three

Caesarea Maritima
Spring AD 26.

Caesarea Maritima would have been impossible to anticipate, Pilate decided as his fleet sailed into the city's magnificent harbour for the first time. It was Roman in every detail, but nothing like Rome: Rome had grown over centuries; Caesarea had been built seventy years ago from a plan. At its centre Rome's streets were wide and straight. There were large plazas, harmonious entryways, and colossal statues at every turn. Beyond the centre the streets followed old footpaths. They were crooked, narrow and muddy. Whole blocks were filled up with tenement buildings, one street after the next, until even the sunlight could not penetrate through to the ground more than an hour or two a day. This left the pervasive stink of decay and mould. In Caesarea everything was clean and freshly scrubbed. Every road in the entire city was straight and broad enough to allow two chariots to pass – the Roman ideal. It was a city built on principles – not caprice and certainly not history. Nothing of importance had ever happened in Caesarea.

From the mouth of the harbour the temple of the

divine Caesar Augustus dominated the cityscape – honouring the city's namesake and making friend and foe alike conscious of its Western character, despite its location in the heart of the Orient, some sixty miles north of Jerusalem. There was an amphitheatre – which even Rome did not have. It was used expressly for gladiator events and this enabled the circus at the edge of Caesarea, unlike the Circus Maximus in Rome, to be used exclusively for races. A theatre was under construction and by all accounts it would be the crown jewel of a city devoted to classical ideals.

Pilate watched with interest as his flagship came in closer. The harbour had no natural features but had been created by two enormous walls reaching out to embrace part of the sea. Not only did they protect hundreds of ships, they also enabled a number of vessels to be loaded or unloaded simultaneously.

Sending his personal bodyguard forward to secure the dock before he stepped from the flagship, Pilate waited patiently for the last of his fleet to unload its cargo – two centuries of native Italian troops to reinforce the fourth cohort of the Fretensis Legion, then occupying the provinces of Syria and Judaea. Once these had secured the harbour alongside his bodyguard, Pilate sent his wife ahead of him to be received by the city magistrates. Finally, he was ready to disembark from his battle-ready trireme. The scarlet robe that he wore was too warm for comfort this late in April, but its gravitas lent him confidence as he strode down the gangway emulating the senators that he had seen leave their ships when he commanded the harbour at the imperial island of Capri.

Two years past his thirtieth birthday and a veteran of some fifteen years of military service, first as a cavalry-man in the wars against Germania and then as a tribune in the palace guard under the command of the empire's rising star, Aelius Sejanus, Pilate carried himself with confidence. He had curly black hair and a deceptively cheerful face. Physically, he had lost the first elasticity of his youth while gaining a good deal of weight, but he compensated for this with greater physical strength and an older athlete's skilful management of his resources.

A crowd had gathered to observe the new prefect's arrival, but Pilate noticed no one other than Valerius Gratus. Pilate would have recognized his predecessor by the equestrian's scarlet robe he wore, of course, but he knew the face as well. It was lean and cunning, the very image of the statues he had seen of the man in Rome some years ago. The two men knew each other's revered families, but they had never met. Gratus, a good ten years older, had endured the past decade in his post in Judaea.

While his wife rode with Gratus's wife in a horse-drawn carriage, Pilate sat alone with Gratus in the prefect's gilded litter, carried by eight powerfully built slaves. They headed south toward the prefect's palace, which Pilate had seen briefly from the mouth of the harbour – a gleaming white complex of buildings perched close to the city wall. Venturing the occasional glance from his curtained window, Pilate observed a mix of peoples and colours and costumes. When he asked about this, Gratus explained that more than half the people of the city were indigenous Greek-speaking

Syrians. The rest were Jews, Arabs, and Egyptians. After a moment, he added, 'The Jews create most of our problems.'

At Pilate's inquisitive look, Gratus continued hurriedly. Not that there were any serious problems in Caesarea. Not at all, really. Not like Jerusalem at any rate. He only meant to say that they offered a strong voice and were generally at variance with the desires of the city magistrates, the emperor's prefect, and the rest of the populace – the Syrian Greeks in particular. Warming to his subject, Gratus informed Pilate that in Caesarea the Jews were in fact hardly more than a vocal minority. They hated the city's luxuries but appreciated the opportunity to trade. In the city of Tiberias, the capital of Galilee, where there were no such commercial advantages, Herod Antipas had offered free land to any Jew willing to move to the city. Gratus gave a casual shrug of his thin shoulders. 'Only a few of the worst sort responded to the offer.'

'But Antipas is himself a Jew, if I understand it correctly,' Pilate answered.

Gratus's smile had a touch of exhaustion about it. He looked like a man ready to go home. Pilate understood the matter correctly, he said. The Jews, on the other hand, still had trouble with the concept. 'You see, the Hasmonians, from whom the Herods descend, were Samarian and Idumaean originally. They adopted Judaism only a century ago, so they are not real Jews, only converts to the faith for political convenience. Herod set the example and the present generation continues it. They honour the public ceremonies fastidiously. As for the rest, they are as Roman as you or I.'

THE PAINTED MESSIAH

'They are a strange people, I have heard,' Pilate
answered, 'the *real* Jews.'

'Incomprehensible, I'm afraid,' Gratus answered, his
mouth grimacing oddly.

'Sejanus believes all men, Prefect, are handled easily
enough if one understands the essentials of
management.'

'Sejanus was a boy when I left Rome. But tell me,
what does he say are the *essentials?*'

'Taken together men are like horses, driven by the
whip and restrained by the bit. One manages them
successfully when neither instrument is abused.'

Gratus' eyes momentarily registered the unintended
insult of this remark, but rather than show his
irritation, he pretended to be amused. 'With the Jews,
sir, one rides a horse whose ears inevitably lie flat
against its skull.'

Pilate thought better than to answer this. He had
never encountered a Jew in his life, real or otherwise.

'I look forward to learning a great deal from your
experience,' Pilate answered.

'Then I must disappoint you. I sail tomorrow at first
light.'

'A pity,' Pilate murmured with the satisfaction of one
anxious to get started with the business of governing
and in no mood for a tired old man's discourses on
history.

Pilate had lived so long on the island of Capri that he
had nearly forgotten the pleasures a city could offer.
Caesarea provided racing and gladiator contests,
jugglers, dancers and seemingly endless performances

of tragedy and comedy. Hardly a week passed when the new prefect did not entertain hundreds of individuals remarkable for their cosmopolitan character: Romans one night, Syrians, Egyptians, or Greeks the next, once even a delegation of Parthian ambassadors who came for the express purpose of paying homage to the beauty of the prefect's wife, meaning of course they honoured her distant cousin, the emperor Tiberius.

Pilate enjoyed the life, but it did not seduce him. His real passion was his work, and he turned to it the moment Gratus's ship cleared the harbour. An appointment lasted three years and it came with the understanding that a man returning to Rome after that amount of time, if he could last his full tenure, was expected to return as a wealthy individual. He had better, for his extended family expected it, and should he nurse any ambition beyond retirement to the countryside he would need money to win new appointments.

In Capri construction projects had continued steadily throughout his entire six years. His harbour was active, but Pilate's opportunities for financial gain had been limited both by the number of ships arriving and by the fact that the lion's share of building occurred on the Villa Jovis of Tiberius – the one man in the empire it did not pay to extort. Now he would have three provinces as his own, including two major cities and the greatest harbour along the eastern coast of the Mediterranean between Antioch and Alexandria.

The harbour itself was sufficient to make a man wealthy. Appropriate a fig here, a date there, he thought: over the course of a day a man could fill a shop with fruit! And tomorrow another. Then there was the copper, the iron ore, the timber, the precious building stones. Spices, fruits, grain, salt, beef, horses, sheep, pigs, goats – the list was endless. Men of business knew that everything moved swiftly with the Roman prefect's goodwill. The smart ones knew good-will came at a price.

The new prefect's first encounter with the Jews came early in his tenure and was unaccountably strange. The priests of the Temple of Jerusalem arrived by the over-land route some two weeks after Pilate had established himself in the prefect's palace. They came, he thought, two weeks too late. He therefore ordered them to wait in his courtyard just beyond the great hall until he had finished his business. Late in the afternoon, when he would normally retire to the palace baths for exercise, Pilate ordered his adjutant, the centurion Cornelius, to bring the priests into his presence.

Cornelius had long ago completed his required twenty-five years of service. A year or two shy of fifty he nevertheless maintained the extraordinary vitality of a man who has made a living with his physical abilities. Standing only an inch or two above average height Cornelius carried close to three hundred pounds, most of it muscle. He had never won a footrace, but then neither had he ever needed to run from the battlefield. Where he stood the battle always went well. His quick-ness with the short sword was legendary, his courage the sort that had made Rome the ruler of the world.

It was the custom of their generation for a Roman to shave each morning, but Cornelius's slave shaved his entire head for him. The effect was to reveal innumerable scars, lumps and dents. Cornelius had a broad, grim mouth and a long flat nose that had obviously been broken a few times. Like almost all senior centurions Cornelius enjoyed the prestige of a war hero simply by virtue of his rank. The backbone of the Roman infantry, such men were known to be the greatest fighters in the army. After a lifetime of war, many of these individuals were so skilled at combat that officers rarely made a critical decision without first consulting their most senior centurions. A centurion finishing twenty-five years could generally expect to retire to a farm in the countryside and live comfortably to the end of his days, but for men like Cornelius, still in good health, extended tours of duty were possible. These men would then generally work with commanders.

Pilate had a dozen tribunes in his service, children of wealthy senators and equestrians getting their first taste of military life. Such men were relatively useless and yet required a great deal of attention, being as they were the future of Rome. No commander could attend to business and give them much of his time, so it devolved upon the most senior centurions to see that they learned the workings of a Roman army.

Cornelius returned to the great hall a few minutes after Pilate had sent him to bring the priests in. With a rare and, to those who did not know him, frightening smile, the centurion announced, 'They refuse to enter the building, Prefect. They ask rather that you come to them outside.'

Pilate blinked in surprise. The prefect appointed the

high priest of the Temple of Jerusalem. The priests served him, as he served the emperor. He had rather have waited six months than give them the satisfaction of travelling first to Jerusalem, no matter how pressing his business with them. They had come to him after an unconscionable delay of a fortnight and now refused to see him unless he came outside his hall to meet them? 'Refuse?' he stammered. 'They *refuse*?'

'They fear they will contaminate themselves by entering a pagan hall.'

'That's ridiculous. Send them in!'

Cornelius gestured toward the *imago* standard, bearing the tiny bronze head of Tiberius, then swept his arm around the hall to indicate the other standards and pennants carried by the troops Pilate commanded. Many of these displayed the image of an animal. Besides these the hall quite naturally contained various stone images of gods and men – all contaminants to the Jewish sensibility. 'Their religion forbids them to look upon the images of men and beasts, Prefect.'

'Tell Annas—'

'The high priest is not here. He has sent his sons to greet Caesar's new prefect.'

Pilate stood, the back of his thighs aching, his chest heaving. 'The high priest is not here? Do I understand you correctly, Centurion?'

Cornelius seemed suddenly uncertain of himself. He reported only what the priests had told him, that is to say, what the servants of the priests had told him, and did not care to endure the wrath of an imperial officer – especially as it ought to have been directed elsewhere. 'That is the impression they have given, Prefect.

Perhaps I am mistaken, but I don't believe he is here.'

Having come to his feet and the end of his patience, Pilate marched out of the hall. By the time he arrived at the courtyard his fury was absolute. 'Bring the priests to me, if their religion allows them to stand in the sunlight!'

His guards responded to Cornelius's command, a quiet nod of the old centurion's head. The priests were brought through the gate of the palace like criminals herded by Roman infantry – a dozen-to-fifteen of them. Pilate did not bother to count. They were bearded and dirty. Their leader screamed incoherently at Pilate.

'You will speak Latin,' Pilate answered quietly. He had no training in Greek beyond a painful six years of reading Homer and the Greek tragedians and could not understand any but the most rudimentary phrases of the obscene *koine* Greek of the region.

Cornelius answered for the priest. 'They claim to know only Aramaic, Greek and Hebrew, Prefect.'

Pilate demanded to know what the man had said, and Cornelius spoke to him in Greek. When the leader answered him, Cornelius said to Pilate, 'He says we defile them by forcing them to walk under the Golden Eagle at the gate to the courtyard.'

'*Defile?*' Pilate longed for his short sword. If he had been wearing it at that moment, he would have rushed upon them at once.

'We need someone to translate this, Prefect. I know only enough Greek to buy wine and women.'

Pilate smiled without glancing at the centurion. 'I will remember that, Centurion, the next time I need either. Find us an interpreter then.'

Cornelius sent a tribune scurrying for one while Pilate stood on the steps of his palace facing the rabble of Jewish priests in perfect silence. They were, he thought, exactly as Gratus described, like horses with their ears flat against their skulls. At the moment they were talking among themselves furiously. They seemed to want to leave his presence, though Pilate's guard made that quite out of the question.

A young Syrian connected to the auxiliary cavalry arrived from within the hall and spoke to the priests. When they had finished talking in what seemed to be a heated exchange of Greek, the Syrian turned to Pilate. 'You pollute them, Prefect, by requiring them to stand before the standards of the Fretensis.'

Pilate turned and saw the familiar standards, pennants and banners arrayed over his door. As he still considered them and just what he wanted to do with these impertinent priests, the Syrian continued.

'In their religion they are not allowed to look upon human or animal images.'

Pilate gave Cornelius a pleasant smile he would have no trouble interpreting. 'Have we more than one inter-preter in the palace, Centurion?'

'We have many, Prefect.'

'Then you will inform this man that when he preaches to me again in his own words or speaks to these men anything but what I have said, I will have him cut open and hanged from the palace gates.'

Cornelius told the man in Latin, as if he needed to hear it again: 'Be advised, sir. Speak only the words of Caesar's prefect and the priests. Nothing more – on your life.'

The young man began to answer, then thought better of it and simply nodded.

'Tell them,' Pilate said, 'they may look upon the standards of the Roman Legions or they will die at the hands of those same men they insult. The choice is theirs.'

The translation followed promptly, and the Jews roared angrily. Some addressed Pilate, some spoke to one another. As it was not in Greek, but Aramaic, the translator began speaking to the Jews in Greek, asking them to speak a language he could translate.

'Execute him,' Pilate said.

Cornelius seemed not to understand for a moment, but as Pilate glared at the interpreter he understood and ordered his guards to take the Syrian by his arms. The poor man's urgency to get the Jews to talk in Greek was now forgotten. He screamed in Latin for Pilate to have mercy.

Pilate spoke quietly to Cornelius. 'Why is that man still speaking, Centurion?'

Cornelius gave no order this time, but drew his own sword and walked forward. He swept the point of his weapon directly down across the Syrian's stomach in a vertical slash. While the young man still stood with a look of surprise, his blood poured over the white marble steps. Cornelius ordered him suspended from the palace gate and the two soldiers holding the man began dragging him away – still screaming, for he had not yet expired from his wound. A third soldier went for rope.

The priests at last were silent.

A young tribune, pale and stricken by what he had

seen, was sent to bring a second interpreter out. Pilate showed the new interpreter his predecessor, now hanging over the road leading into the prefect's palace compound with his guts half-out of his body, and asked him if he thought he could do a better job.

The man said he hoped as much, and Cornelius explained his duties to him without a glimmer of emotion.

'Where is Annas?' Pilate asked the priests. The interpreter repeated the question in Greek.

The Jews consulted quietly with one another, determining their spokesman. He was elected quickly and spoke to Pilate with the respect one shows the emperor's prefect. 'The high priest regrets he is unable to make the long journey to Caesarea Maritima. His age does not permit it, but he hopes soon to meet you when you travel to Jerusalem.'

'I am not interested in regrets. It is the custom of the high priest to serve Caesar's prefect, not the other way around. You will kindly inform Annas that as his age limits him, he no longer holds his title.'

'As you wish, sir. May I kindly ask whom you desire to name in his place?'

Pilate studied the man's expression as the interpreter repeated his acquiescence in Latin. 'Who among you are his sons?'

They identified themselves. The man they had elected as their spokesman was not among that select group. That made him the one they were willing to sacrifice.

'And what is your name?'

'Caiaphas.'

'Are you a priest, Caiaphas?'

'We are all priests of the Temple, sir.'

'What is your relationship to Annas?'

'I have no familial relationship to him, sir.'

'Congratulations, my friend. You are the new high priest of the Temple of Jerusalem. Please me, and you shall become the second most powerful man in Judaea. Resist me, and you will envy the death of that unfortunate Syrian hanging at my gate.'

Hearing these words in Greek, Caiaphas neither blinked nor turned to examine the man whose only crime was to ask the priests to speak in a language he could understand.

Pilate liked that about his new high priest. He liked the man mightily, in fact. He then surveyed the other priests so he would not forget their faces, the sons of Annas in particular, then turned and walked back into his palace.

As an afterthought to his meeting with the Jewish priests, Pilate sent for one of the magistrates of long-standing to appear before him. Like the Jewish priests who left the courtyard, the magistrate passed under the corpse of the Syrian without daring to look at the open wound. 'In Caesarea,' Pilate said to the man, 'we hang all the imperial standards, including the *imago* which bears the bronze head of Tiberius. Is this not true?'

It was, of course, a matter of demonstrable fact, but the magistrate, who was also a Syrian, could not stop himself from answering lavishly. The standards adorned every public square and every public building. Was there a problem? Pilate asked how the Jews of Caesarea dealt with such an affront to their religion.

The magistrate grew more circumspect. 'They endure it, Prefect. As you know, their religion—'

'I should warn you,' Pilate interrupted, 'the last man who tried to explain the Jewish religion to me is hanging at the gates to my courtyard.'

'Of course, Prefect.'

'That is your answer? They endure it?'

'Caesarea is a Roman city, so the Jews adapt. They avert their eyes from the images.'

'Are you telling me there is not a single image of the emperor in Jerusalem?'

'Excuse me for saying it, but that would be an outrage, Prefect.'

'I am not so sure I will. The imperial standards adorn every city in the empire as a matter of law. *Every* city!'

'Not Jerusalem, Prefect.'

Pilate brought the matter up with his wife that evening over their meal. Did it not seem to her an insult to the Roman religion, this refusal to honour their emperor? In the east, after all, Tiberius was to be honoured as a god. Procula said she thought it exceedingly strange that a city should insult Tiberius in this fashion.

'In Caesarea,' he told her, 'where we have a great many Jews, they graciously allow us to hang the imperial standards as well as the golden eagle, the standards of the Fretensis Legion and all her cohorts and centuries. Perhaps you can explain to me the difference between Caesarea and Jerusalem.'

'I would not presume to explain politics to you, sir.'

Claudia Procula had the black hair and exceedingly large, luminous, brown eyes that distinguished all of the Claudii women, whom Rome inevitably celebrated as the most beautiful women in the empire. The matriarch of the clan, after all, was none other than Livia, the legendary wife of Caesar Augustus and mother of Tiberius. Unlike her great aunt, Procula did not seem especially attracted to power. By the age of twenty-one Livia had already divorced one husband, the father of Tiberius, in order to marry Augustus who, with her help, seized the imperial throne and held it for the next fifty years. As men liked to observe, when they were quite sure it was safe to say such a thing, Augustus had ruled the world, and Livia had ruled Augustus.

'I don't want you to explain politics to me. I only want your opinion. An objective consideration,' he answered. 'What do you think of it?'

'Sir, please. I don't know about such things.'

'Why does Jerusalem fail to honour – at the very least – an image of Tiberius? I will give the Jew his Temple, but don't you think he should grant honour to his earthly ruler?'

'It would seem so to me, sir.'

'To me as well.'

Following his dinner, Pilate sent a slave to find Cornelius. Cornelius was not to be found, however. The following morning as Pilate's barber shaved him and he dictated a letter to Sejanus, informing him of his decision 'to engage the sensibilities' of the Judaeans, Cornelius showed up.

'We are twelve hours behind schedule, Centurion, because I could not find you in your quarters last night.'

'If the prefect had only told me I would be needed—'

Pilate waved the matter away with a friendly smile, or as friendly as he got in the morning. 'Were you practising your Greek, Centurion?'

Cornelius nearly smiled in return. 'The Syrian women, Prefect, are beyond comparison, if I may speak freely.'

The centurion had told Pilate once that one woman was too many and two were not enough. So he took them by threes and was the happier for it. 'All of them, or have you a favourite trio?' Pilate's barber's razor hesitated as his eyes took in the huge centurion appreciatively.

'I have a favourite house, Prefect. The wine passes and the women are beyond—'

'—comparison. Yes. In the future you will please leave a forwarding address when you visit your wives, Centurion, so that the emperor does not grow impatient with his prefect. I want you to take three centuries to Jerusalem and raise the imago standard over the great door to Herod's palace. If I recall the plans correctly, it faces the Temple, so that everyone who goes to see the desert god may know the living god watches over them as well.'

'Yes, Prefect.'

'You will inform Caiaphas with a letter written under my seal that should any disturbances transpire inside the city as a result of this display, your orders are to crucify Annas and all of his sons. You will then proceed to the population at large, taking every hundredth soul regardless of responsibility, age or sex.'

'Yes, Prefect.'

'And tell Caiaphas that, in my religion, we honour

the images of all living things. Should he wish to discuss the matter with me, he had better bring his own interpreter. I find I am running short of them.'

'It will be done, Prefect.'

Over the North Atlantic
October 6-7, 2006.

Malloy downloaded everything Gil Fine had sent him, hoping to browse through the material during his flight to Zürich. Gleaned from various sources, some print and some electronic, it was the kind of material you would have gotten from a good library a couple of decades ago if you were ready to spend weeks tracking through the *Reader's Guide* and photocopying a few thousand pages. From the organisation of the material it was clear that Homeland Security had already done the basic work on Nicole North, Jonas Starr, and J. W. Richland. About half the articles on Richland involved the televangelist taking a resolute stand against sin. A great deal more was self-promotion, articles about Richland disguised as news. Finally, there was a small but persistent strain of real information, Richland's life as told by his enemies. The good stuff.

Despite a high profile and long tenure at the top, Richland's scandals had come and gone when he was still a very young man. There had been much made of it some years ago when Richland was a young preacher on the rise, but even then it was ancient history, nothing people could not forgive or at least overlook. Who hasn't been young?

The scandals were juicy, all the same. It seemed

Richland had begun his professional life working tent revivals at the age of sixteen. He preached hellfire and damnation, cured cancer, caused the lame to walk, the blind to see. By age nineteen, young J. W. Richland sold his tent and rented a church in downtown Ft. Worth. Things hopped for a while. People rolled in the aisles, talked in tongues, and sang the night away. Then, according to people who knew him in those days, a delegation of the younger husbands and middle-aged fathers appeared at Richland's office one evening after services and suggested the preacher consider a career in the military. The idea apparently made good sense, because the next day Richland enlisted. Ninety days after that he was in Vietnam.

According to Richland's own account of that time, the next several years were given over to worldliness. His enemies named names. There was marijuana and liquor without question. A number of sources talked about cocaine, amphetamines, and always a steady stream of sexual partners, with a notable penchant for the married ones. In the army Richland liked to brag about his tent revival days, the pretty girls and young wives who needed 'special counselling.' All of it a great joke.

After his tour of duty and an honourable discharge, he enrolled at one of the junior colleges in Fort Worth. Grades were shaky but passing. The lifestyle was more of the same. In Richland's account of his conversion, he had hit rock bottom and was half-drunk when he stumbled into an old-fashioned tent revival. It was the kind of event he had run so well when he was too young to know what gifts he possessed. Even knowing the game, and it was nothing but a game to him at that point, he wasn't immune to its power. While the preacher spoke that evening, J. W. Richland sat in the back row and wept.

That was the genesis of Richland's long journey back to faith. He met the woman he would eventually marry a year later in Bible class and soon after that transferred to a Christian college. At seminary he honed his oratory skills and fashioned a less radical dogma. When he returned to the ministry there were no outraged husbands, not even the hint of indiscretion. In fact Richland's return to the pulpit appeared to be a genuine conversion.

His ministry was even marked by a relative degree of sophistication, according to people who knew about such things. He was no longer healing the lame, curing cancer, and giving sight to the blind on a nightly basis. He built a broad base of support among the middle class and formed critical alliances with people who provided a sound financial underpinning to the ministry.

The most important early friendship turned out to be Nicole North's father. Nicholas North helped Richland exploit cable TV in the 1970s, letting him compete with the likes of Jimmy Swaggart, Jim Bakker, Pat Robertson, and Jerry Falwell.

Richland was not the biggest name in televangelism in the early days, but after Swaggart stumbled badly with a New Orleans prostitute and Jimmy Bakker went to prison, Richland took market share. While a number of preachers including Pat Robertson and Jerry Falwell began to politicize the evangelical movement,

J. W. Richland steadfastly refused to drift from his message. His strategy began to pay off by the early 1990s, the decade his face first made the cover of *Time*. Richland had become a household name. His refusal to deal in politics ended with the new millennium. Some thought because he had previously been reluctant to join the fray his support made the difference. He was a man, certainly, with a favour owed him.

Recent news articles on Richland dealt with his illness and dramatic refusal to be treated. According to some of the more reputable reviewers of his new book, Richland had returned to the message of his earliest ministry, proclaiming in effect that doctors weren't needed if one had faith. There was concern about the effects of such simplistic dogma, but on the whole the media treated Richland with surprising kindness, the result no doubt of the preacher's imminent demise.

When he turned to Jonas Starr, Nicole North's uncle, Malloy found a different kind of man. The founder of the NorthStarr Institute had spent his life promoting archaeological digs that, according to the institute's mission statement, 'verified Biblical history'. Interestingly enough, a long time member of the board of directors for the NorthStarr Institute was none other than J. W. Richland. Jonas Starr had been involved in Richland's comeback.

In fact it was Starr's influence with Nick North that got Richland's ministry on cable TV in the first place. Until his death Nicholas North had been an enthusiastic supporter of both men and the causes they represented. And Nicole North's father had the money to pursue any enthusiasm he fancied. Nick North came from old Texas money, meaning cattle and oil. By the mid-1980s, he had diversified into several industries and was rubbing shoulders with the likes of the Hunt brothers and Ross Perot. Jonas Starr, on the other hand, had been born poor. Possessing an amazing if undisciplined intellect and a faith in God that was so intense he even impressed his fellow Texans, Starr realised early in his life that he wanted to serve God. Having neither the voice nor looks for the pulpit, Starr discovered his true calling at the University of Texas: archaeology.

From the age of twenty onwards, Jonas Starr travelled the Middle East in search of proof that everything in the Bible was literally true. Nick North's sister, then a graduate student in archaeology at the University of Texas in Austin, was on one of Starr's earliest expeditions. Jonas Starr was clever enough to court her.

The marriage produced a great deal of success, with every significant discovery wildly publicized. Jonas Starr's greatest moment came in the mid-1980s, when he uncovered a six-thousand-year-old fishing boat in the mountains of eastern Turkey. Calling it Noah's Ark, Starr and his wife built a museum in Fort Worth to house their treasure.

Those members of the media sympathetic to the cause stressed the fact that Starr's boat was found where no body of water was known to exist, proof, it seemed, that a flood had carried it there. Radiocarbon dating supported the thesis as well, placing it almost exactly in the time of the biblical Noah. J. W. Richland, who apparently spent a great deal of television time reporting on the 'amazing discovery of Dr Jonas Starr', announced to his viewers that science had finally confirmed what the faithful had always known: the Bible was true not only in matters of the spirit but in matters of history and evolution as well!

Naturally the secular world struck back. Jonas Starr had found the hull of a boat in a region that had once been part of the sea. Moreover, the discovery of a boat in no way made it Noah's mythical craft. As one humanist put it, the only thing less trustworthy than the Bible's version of history was Jonas Starr's. Undaunted by his critics, Starr continued his life work, careful to stay close to the money of his brother-in-law and the publicity it could engender.

Following the death of his wife Jonas Starr's career seemed to stall. In the mid-1990s, at an exploratory dig not far form the ancient site of Antioch, Starr unearthed a Roman era drinking cup that he claimed was the legendary Holy Chalice, the cup Jesus had passed among his disciples on the night of his arrest. The media's initial response to the discovery was both credulous and excited. All that changed after one of Starr's own team accused him of buying the cup from Bedouin looters.

For a time Starr's friends stood by him, J. W. Richland in the forefront. Richland stressed the importance of the cumulative work of Jonas Starr. He said the people who attacked Jonas Starr were motivated by the fear that the Bible was ultimately right. Richland and others pilloried the graduate student who reported Starr's fraud, but the accusation did not go away. In fact other stories began leaking out. These suggested that in his desperate attempt to match the glorious finds of his youth Starr was always on the lookout for black-market treasures he would claim to have found himself.

After the Holy Chalice debacle, which even his friends later admitted harmed Starr's reputation, there were increasing accusations of fraud and a few notorious failures, the most prominent being a search in eastern Ethiopia for the lost treasure of Solomon. Heartily promoted before the expedition, the failure to find anything besides starving Ethiopians was advertised widely by a media that no longer took Jonas Starr seriously. In the late 1990s, after a series of disputes with the Israeli government, the Antiquities Authority of Israel refused to allow Starr permits to dig. There was even talk of keeping him out of the country altogether.

Whether by coincidence or as a result of the ban, the following year Jonas Starr resigned the directorship of his institute in favour of his niece, Nick North's daughter, Nicole. When Dr Nicole North, then twenty-seven, took control of the institute, people who bothered to comment suggested that the institute would inevitably fold. What they failed to appreciate was the unlimited funding North could make available to her institute.

Just how important that was became clear the following year when Nick North passed away. His will provided the institute with a seventy-five million dollar endowment. Moreover, as sole heir to her father's vast fortune, Nicole got the rest, a tidy seven hundred million in cash and liquid assets, as well as control of her father's business interests, worth roughly three billion dollars. Real estate and inventory valued at close to a billion dollars more put the inheritance at around five billion dollars: real money, as they say in Texas. That is assuming one could trust the accountants.

The last anyone had heard of Jonas Starr was the publication of his autobiography. He wrote only briefly about the Holy Chalice of Antioch, denying the charge of fraud, yet offering nothing beyond his good name as evidence of its legitimacy. Probably the only matters of interest came from Starr's recounting his earliest adventures. While these occasionally diminished the importance of his wife's participation, at least one sympathetic reviewer had referred to the couple as Mr and Mrs Indiana Jones.

Archaeological scholars who bothered to comment on the book asserted that there was nothing of value in the lifework of Jonas Starr. One academic journal called his autobiography a vanity publication. Another quoted a renowned French antiquarian who was even less kind. He called Jonas Starr 'a fraud, a liar, and a thief.'

At that point in his research Malloy was forced to shut down his computer. His plane would be landing in Zürich shortly.

Zürich, Switzerland
October 7, 2006.

Malloy held up a Swiss passport as he walked past the immigrations officer. He collected a single bag at the luggage carousel, passed through customs without incident, and ten minutes later boarded a train for Zürich's main station.

At the Gottard Hotel on the Bahnhofstrasse he spoke Swiss German and registered under one of the four names he had used regularly over the years, part of the agency-issued identities that stayed with an operative even after retirement, the assumption being old warhorses still had their uses. It was not usual procedure for an operative to try to pass as a native. Accents being what they are, it was probably the easiest method of drawing attention to one's cover, but Malloy felt comfortable with his Swiss German.

As opposed to High German, Swiss German is a language few foreigners bother to learn and almost none master. Having no written form, it can really only be acquired if one has an extraordinary talent for language or has grown up in Switzerland. Malloy boasted both talent and experience, having learned it in the streets of Zürich during the seven years his father worked at the American Consulate, then stationed in Zürich. Both a diplomat with the Consulate and intelligence officer for Langley, his father had spoken fluent High German, the literary language of the Swiss. His mother's second language was French, which she loved as some people love chocolate. Swiss German, sometimes called Farmer German, was his alone. Malloy's friendships had required it, and at seven one adjusts to necessity no matter its face.

It was this peculiar skill, the ability to speak as a native, that Malloy firmly believed had inspired Jane Harrison to offer him an assignment in Zürich at the beginning of his career. For the Swiss, the ability to

speak Swiss German is tantamount to uttering a pass-
word or offering a secret handshake. Getting access to
the private accounts of a Swiss bank had required all of
that.

Once in his room Malloy made a cursory examin-
ation for cameras and listening devices. Satisfied the
room was clean he settled down for a long nap. He
woke up just as the sun was setting. Still suffering from
a night without sleep, he ordered a pot of coffee sent up
and took a couple of hours to run through the remainder of the material Gil Fine had sent him. This mostly
dealt with Nicole North and North Industries and
turned out to be the least useful of the three folders.
Even though Dr North was neither a public figure like
J. W. Richland nor a publicity hound like her uncle
Jonas Starr, Homeland had culled material from several
hundred articles about her.

Of course as a major shareholder in most of the
media conglomerates producing the information,
Nicole North came off unscathed. In fact Malloy could
find almost nothing negative about the woman. She
was the belle of Dallas society, a major source of
charitable donations, a respected scholar, the dynamic
director of NorthStarr Biblical Institute, the driving
force for any number of church related issues, and of
course the chairperson of the board of a Fortune
500 company. If her managerial skills were a matter
of unrivalled excellence, the intimate looks into
her life were even more celebratory and shallow. Her
house was one of the treasures of Dallas. Her
munificence was sometimes for the public good,
sometimes just to help a stranger in need. All of it

carefully nurtured PR. And not a breath of scandal.

North's real passion appeared to be the NorthStarr Biblical Institute. Since taking nominal control of the institute, she had abandoned her uncle's passion for collecting and had begun retooling it so that many presently considered NorthStarr the premier evangelical think-tank in the country. It went without saying that a fairly substantial publishing concern had developed as a result of the Institute's new direction. The museum was still open, of course, but except for the occasional travelling exhibition nothing had changed since Jonas Starr had passed the directorship to his niece. There was still the hull of an old boat dominating the main floor and a brass cup carefully stored in a transparent high-tech security case. There were tools and scrolls and maps and video clips, all of it like a real museum. Just no crowds.

Malloy had hoped somewhere in the mass of files to get something about Nicole North's private life, especially her relationship with J. W. Richland, but that secret was too carefully guarded. While it was clear Dr North always managed to have an escort where an escort was appropriate, there was no speculation about her sexuality. She had been married briefly nearly a decade ago but the nuptials had been overshadowed by the groom's terminal cancer. He died a few months later. So far as Malloy could tell there had been no one since. From the context of various articles it was clear J. W. Richland was a family friend, but that was the extent of it. No one had linked the two romantically. Of course, they were not the kind of celebrities who inspired gossip.

Closing his computer down and having more questions now than when he began, Malloy headed out of the hotel for a walk along Zürich's famed Bahnhofstrasse. With all of the stores closed, the city's most expensive street was virtually empty. Malloy used his walk to reconnoitre the bank of Goetz and Ritter, which was close to the lake. That finished, he grabbed a streetcar, doubling back once to check for a tail, and finally entered the James Joyce Pub just after eleven o'clock.

The pub's interior came from a Dublin tavern called the Drury, said to be operating in James Joyce's lifetime, though it was not included in Leopold Bloom's journey through the city in the novel *Ulysses* on June 16, 1903. When the grand old Pub's time had come to an end and it was slated for the wrecking ball, the city of Zürich, to commemorate its most famous literary exile, purchased the interior and brought it to Switzerland. Drinks cost a small fortune, no doubt still paying off the freight charges, but the brass fixtures, mahogany bar, and decorative tiles were to die for. At least that was the opinion of Capt. Marcus Steiner, who insisted it was his favourite watering hole – as long as Malloy was picking up the tab.

The two men had met over four decades ago, when they were a couple of seven-year-olds. Then as now Marcus was small, inordinately thin, and brilliant. He had dark curly hair and intense brown eyes. His most striking talent was the ability to convey a perpetual look of innocence no matter what he had just done. It had worked then with an angry grocer who was look-ing for the kid who had stolen his apples, and it still worked inside Zürich's *Stadtpolizei*. Possessing the face of an honest Swiss, Marcus was nevertheless a born criminal. Being Swiss, he had resisted the siren call of his genius in favour of regular hours and a pension, but to compensate he had chosen a career in law enforcement – if only to be close to the thing he loved.

Compared to almost any other country in the world, the life of a Swiss policeman was boring in the extreme. In the city of Zürich one homicide a month was excessive. Thieves were known to steal wallets and then stricken by conscience return them by the mail with a letter of apology. Most humiliating of all was the fact that the occasional burglary and auto theft was usually foiled by the ever-vigilant Swiss citizen, leaving the Swiss police officer plenty of time for paperwork. Marcus had told Malloy things used to be even more boring for the police, but in recent decades Switzerland had begun importing a criminal element so that it could persuade itself Switzerland enjoyed the same problems as the rest of the civilized world. Marcus was an amateur pickpocket, a weekend burglar of some accomplishment, and on three separate occasions a contract assassin. On two of his three hits, all of which Malloy had authorized and paid for, he had been in charge of the investigation afterwards.

Malloy and his friend spent several minutes catching up, including talk about Malloy's upcoming wedding. When it came time for business, Marcus produced a bound dossier on Roland Wheeler. They were seated in one of the luxurious leather booths at the end of the pub. Besides the bartender and waitress there were five other people in the place, all of them smelling of Zürich money and respectability, all suitably removed from their conversation.

As Malloy began through the dossier on Wheeler, Marcus explained to him that Goetz and Ritter was exactly what it claimed to be: a small, exclusive, and extremely reliable private bank. For fifty thousand they let you through the front door. For a couple of million, you got personal attention, and for accounts in excess of ten million you dealt with Mr Goetz himself. The bank had remained in the same two families for five generations. Before that, Goetz and Ritter had sold mercenary soldiers to the various monarchies of Europe, making them a great deal of wealth in a country that hadn't very much at the time.

It went without saying that Goetz and Ritter did not run a perfectly legitimate bank in the American sense of the word. In the late 1990s, following the Swiss banking scandal concerning the lost accounts of the holocaust victims, the American government had negotiated new treaties with the Swiss, obliging Swiss banks to reveal information about questionable accounts, especially those of drug dealers, terrorists, and rich Americans attempting to hide their assets from the IRS. In theory America had finally breached the treasure house of the world's wealthiest criminals. In fact the multinational conglomerates cooperated grudgingly because they were vulnerable to reprisals, while the private banks such as that of Goetz and Ritter continued to operate as they had for the past couple of centuries.

The Swiss government had written the law. It was up to the banks to honour it. America had continued to pressure the Swiss authorities for more concessions, but so much of Swiss prosperity, twelve per-cent of its gross national product, depended upon finance that it was a losing battle. The Swiss had a weak central government for good reason. Besides, the Swiss had long ago decided it was foolish to mix money and morality. Voltaire had summarized the attitude perfectly even before the French Revolution and nothing but the interest rates had changed since his time: 'If you should happen to see a Swiss banker jump out of a window,' he said, 'follow him. You're sure to make money on the way down.'

'Wheeler is another story,' Marcus announced.

Malloy nodded and continued scanning Interpol reports on the art dealer. He was reading about one of a number of investigations involving stolen art. As with the other investigations it was apparent from the language that the art dealer enjoyed a degree of protection from the Swiss government that would not have been tolerated in other countries. It didn't take much effort to see why. Wheeler had moved to Zürich in the early 1990s, but he had extensive business contacts reaching back thirty years. During that time he had presented the city of Zürich with any number of financial gifts, the total running to something like fifteen million dollars, enough it would seem to make lasting friendships in the circles that mattered.

'He's careful,' Marcus explained when Malloy remarked on the city's reluctance to cooperate with Interpol's various art theft investigations.

'You mean by that he doesn't steal from the Swiss?'

Marcus smiled. He meant exactly that. 'What people

do beyond our borders doesn't really interest us, Thomas.'

From what Malloy could see of the reports, Interpol suspected Wheeler of somehow arranging certain acquisitions and then selling them to collectors, often Swiss, who were not particularly concerned about a painting's provenance so long as it improved the quality of their collection. As Swiss law protected patrons of the arts who had unwittingly purchased stolen property with a five-year statute of limitations, it was a convenient arrangement for all. From the point of view of the Zürich police, the principal investigatory agency, the missing element was Interpol's failure to link Wheeler to any criminal circles in Europe. How did he come by these paintings? Nobody knew. Was he a victim of others – duped into buying stolen goods? Interpol could not say and the Swiss were disinclined to pursue the matter. In fact, other than loose talk – a friend of a friend speculating on certain acquisitions, they maintained steadfastly that there was no hard evidence linking Wheeler to anything illegal. They could not in good conscience participate in the investigation by authorizing warrants or wiretaps against the man, his family or his business.

Marcus offered another sly smile. 'In over twenty-five years as a police officer, Thomas, I have discovered one thing always holds true. Evidence is extremely difficult to find if you refuse to see it.'

'Doesn't seem to deal in forgeries.'

'It's art. They all deal in forgeries whether they like it or not, but from what I can tell, that's not his game. He's a specialist. You want Monet, he'll find you a Monet. You want Leonardo da Vinci, maybe he has a couple in his attic he can let you have if the price is right.'

Turning the page, Malloy noticed Wheeler escorting a thirty-something Nordic blonde beauty. A typical trophy date, he thought, and was turning the page when he spotted the word *Tochter*. Tapping the photograph, 'He has a daughter?'

'Beautiful, isn't she?'

'Lives in Zürich?'

'She lives anywhere she wants, Thomas.'

'Katherine Kenyon.'

'Lady Kenyon, actually. Papa had the money, little Katie married the blood. On their honeymoon they climbed the north face of the Eiger. The husband and three other men are still up there.'

'I remember that. That was what? Ten . . . eleven years ago?'

'Something like that. You'd think an experience like that would keep her off the mountains. The only thing it did was convince her never to climb with ropes. Apparently, Lord Kenyon got dragged over by the other three. Lady Kenyon was able to cut the rope before she joined them. She came down alone – without ropes – and hasn't used them since.'

'Still climbs?'

'Swiss TV had a special on her about three years ago. At the time they were saying she was one of the top five climbers in Switzerland, which makes her one of the best in the world. You don't walk away from something like that.' Malloy closed the dossier and slipped it into the shopping sack Marcus had set between them. Marcus brought a holstered Sigma .380 off his belt.

'Loaded and very clean. I want it back when you leave, if it's possible.' By *possible* he meant unused.

Malloy wiped his friend's fingerprints from the holster and weapon, then slipped it next to his spine the way he wore his .380 in the States.

'I'm assuming your rates haven't changed.' He brought two bound stacks of thousand dollar bills from the pocket of his sports jacket and passed it to his friend under the lip of the table.

Marcus pocketed the money with satisfaction and listened to Malloy's instructions. When Malloy had finished, he smiled. 'Just like old times. Except we don't kill anybody.'

'Sounds like you've missed me.'

'Every cop in Zürich misses you, Thomas. Since you left, the crime rate has plummeted. They'll be talking layoffs pretty soon.'

Bob Whitefield was sitting in Malloy's darkened hotel room nursing a glass of Scotch when Malloy returned from his meeting with Marcus Steiner. Whitefield was a tall, heavyset man with a quick, watery smile and a soft, nervous voice. He had a couple of chins, a few remaining strands of black hair running across his scalp, and small, perpetually twitching brown eyes. The first time Malloy had met Whitefield was in Paris shortly after the new station chief had summoned him to a meeting. Malloy recalled every word spoken that afternoon. Whitefield was not a man for small talk. He had told Malloy that Charlie Winger wanted all western European field personnel reporting directly to Paris, meaning to Whitefield himself. When Malloy complained, pointing out that he had been reporting to Jane Harrison with some success for a number of years, Whitefield told him, 'You get with the programme, T. K., or you go home.'

Malloy had answered in conciliatory tones. He understood, he said. That was the way you worked in the agency. Agree, cook the books, file reports with discrete omissions, and do what was necessary. According to Jane Harrison, whom he had contacted at once, the arrangement was temporary. In her vocabulary that meant Charlie Winger was riding for a fall. It was one of the few times Jane had failed to come through for him, but in retrospect completely understandable. Charlie Winger had stormed the citadel like a man with friends above and below. What he wanted, he was going to get. Jane Harrison still had enough of a budget to run her own private war, but she was suddenly reporting to the director through Charlie. With hindsight, Malloy realised it was the beginning of the end of his career.

Malloy's second meeting with Bob Whitefield was every bit as memorable. Whitefield had told him his expertise was needed at Langley. 'I suppose congratulations are in order,' he had added without the slightest hint of irony.

This would be their third meeting. This time, at least, there would be no surprises.

'T. K., good to see you,' Whitefield announced pleasantly, as if Malloy had come for a visit. 'Care for a glass of your Scotch?'

Malloy settled comfortably in a reading chair and took the Scotch. 'I would have thought a station chief had better things to do than run errands for the big boys.'

Whitefield presented his patented watery smile. 'That depends on how big the boy is. I'd say helping out a friend of the President is worth it. I have to tell you, T. K., I was surprised to hear you agreed to slip back into the harness. I really was. I was under the impression you'd had enough of us.'

'I always thought it was the other way around.'

Whitefield seemed more relaxed suddenly. 'As I understand it, Charlie wanted you to have some different experiences so he could bring you up a few rungs on the food chain, and you got a little huffy about it.'

'I was inside every major bank in Switzerland, Bob. How are we doing now?'

Whitefield grimaced. 'We're getting up to speed, but it's been tough. With the new treaty in place, the Swiss promise all the cooperation in the world and deliver when they feel like it. When we need to know things, we go to the same people you used in the banks, but they won't work with us, or if they do they give us yesterday's news at tomorrow's prices.' Most of Malloy's contacts, the ones he listed in his reports, were cutouts, not people providing the real information. They looked good on paper, and they took a salary for the titbits they handed out, but they didn't know very much and provided even less. The people with real information were too critical to risk including in his reports. Beirut had taught him the folly of writing things down.

'It's a matter of trust,' Malloy answered. 'They'll

stick their necks out only if they know what kind of person they're dealing with.'

Whitefield's expression showed scepticism, but he didn't respond.

Wanting to change the subject, Malloy stood up, walked across the room, and looked out his window. 'I've been reading some of your reports from this summer,' he said.

'About Julian Corbeau?'

'Corbeau is one of my personal hobbies.'

'Corbeau is everyone's hobby, T. K, at least until we can prove something.'

Living now in Switzerland with a one million dollar bounty on his head, Corbeau had left America a decade ago under indictment. His interests in the Middle East were both extensive and complex, leading the sceptical to wonder if he might be one of the financial resources of the terrorists, but the Swiss refused to treat him as anything other than what he pretended to be, a legitimate businessman. According to a field report filed by one of Bob Whitefield's operatives, the Americans had finally stumbled across a tangible connection between Corbeau and a prominent neo-Nazi operative who went by the name Xeno.

Tantalizing as it had seemed, the connection involved only a single meeting with Corbeau's chief of security, Jeffrey Bremmer, in Hamburg. There were no telephone intercepts, no follow-up meetings. If the two were presently using cutouts, it was working. Nothing had put Corbeau's organization in direct contact with the man again. What did it mean? For Malloy, it was proof Julian Corbeau was dirty. Any kind of formal pursuit of

Corbeau based on the meeting, however, was impossible.

Corbeau's indictment was for tax evasion and illegal trading. These were not extraditable crimes in Switzerland. As far as the Swiss were concerned, the United States government was engaged in nothing more than harassment. It was their view that any surveillance of Corbeau was unwarranted and vowed they would promptly expel any individual thought to be attempting to monitor Corbeau's business activities. There was more naturally. The Swiss were rarely so blunt that they refused to cooperate, but those points where they did agree to help involved pursuing Xeno, should he ever cross into Switzerland.

'So what happened this summer?' He meant what had happened that didn't make the reports.

'We got lucky. We were watching some people in Hamburg and Jeffrey Bremmer showed up.'

'That much I got. Talking with the neo-Nazi underground. I'm wondering why.'

'Someone made a run at Corbeau this summer. Didn't make the papers, but he lost three men. A couple more of his bodyguards were wounded. My guess is he wants the people who did it, and he's brought in an assassination team. Whether Xeno is heading it or just running his surveillance, I don't know. This much I do know. Last summer Corbeau had five people around him at any given time. Now, we can't tell how many people are working for him. They're coming and going all the time. One estimate put the number at thirty-to-thirty-five guns.'

'So he's either going after someone, or he's seriously paranoid. We weren't involved last summer?'

'Freelancers, presumably, but we don't know. Corbeau wasn't even at his place when they arrived. Corbeau hears about it while he's at a VIP party in the city and sends his security team ahead to take care of the intruders. I'm not sure he was even there for the gunfight.'

'Maybe they didn't want Corbeau. Maybe they were looking to score some rare books.'

'You want a few thousand bucks in rare books or paintings, there are easier targets, believe me. You want a cool million with no questions asked, Corbeau is the product.'

'Not with thirty-five hired guns on hand.'

Whitefield smiled and shook his head. 'Not these days.' He shifted in his seat and took a sip of his drink. 'I understand our flight out is at fourteen-thirty Tuesday.'

'Glad to see the agency hasn't lost its touch.'

'We do our best. I'll meet you in the first class wagon on the twelve-o-three out of the Zürich main station, if that's okay with you. You can catch the train at a couple of different points along the way, but let's make the pass before we get inside the airport. I'll carry it through the flight. Once we pass customs stateside, you can take it from there. Anything comes up, this is your phone.'

Malloy checked the directory on the Tri-Band Whiteside handed him and found the numbers for Whitefield and Harrison already on the address book. He programmed in both his home number and Gwen's cell number as they talked. 'Any idea what you'll be carrying?'

Whitefield gave a satisfied smile. 'They tell me it's

safe to handle, compact, light, and extremely valuable to people who matter.'

'We live in a democracy, Bob. Remember? Everyone matters.'

Whitefield smiled and stood up, signalling the end of the meeting. 'Some of us more than others, T. K. Some of us more than others.'

Chapter Four

Caesarea
April AD 26.

The first of them appeared on the horizon just after dawn. They kept coming for the rest of the morning, a long ragged line of men walking at the side of the road from Jerusalem to Caesarea. They were not soldiers, apparently not even armed. Each man wore a filthy white robe, carried a blanket over his shoulder and a gourd on a rope, this last presumably filled with water. They possessed nothing else, nor was there any kind of supply train supporting them, as one would properly assume. They appeared to be headed for the city gates, but turned off and marched directly toward that point along the wall where the prefect's and his wife's apartments lay. As they arrived they continued moving their feet. Hundreds and then thousands joined them. All the while they chanted something in a language Procula did not recognize.

'What do they want, Lady?' a girl's voice asked.

Procula turned and saw one of her husband's lovers, a fourteen-year-old Egyptian slave, staring nervously toward the bearded men. 'You have nothing to fear, child,' Procula answered gently. 'They are unarmed.'

*　　*　　*

That evening at dinner Pilate entertained ambassadors of Herod Antipas. They had come to ask the prefect's presence in Peraea to honour the tetrarch's sixtieth birthday. The men had been in the city for several days and were only now admitted to the palace. Pilate did not care to visit Antipas until Antipas should see fit to visit him, but it was not as simple as that. Antipas's father was Herod the Great, who had been friends with Augustus, and it was said that Antipas himself had visited Tiberius for several days only a year ago. Antipas did not answer to the prefect of Judaea, of course, nor did Pilate inform the tetrarch of his actions. They were equals, after a fashion: one a soldier in the service of Caesar; the other a prince and ally.

As he indulged in wine Pilate became more cheerful, though he had still not consented to travel to Peraea. The ambassadors, not wanting to return to Antipas with a refusal, walked carefully around the issue of ten thousand Jews camped just beyond the city walls and talked of the pleasures to be found in the Orient. They spoke of how quiet the city of Tiberias remained, for example – not a single disturbance among its population. Their message was both subtle and clear: Antipas knew how to handle the Jewish population and could be a useful friend to an inexperienced Roman administrator.

Pilate did not care for their smugness and responded with a question to which he already knew the answer. The lack of any kind of substantial Jewish population had something to do with the city being erected over a Jewish cemetery, did it not?

The insult apparently scored nicely, for the answer

that came back from the senior ambassador had teeth. 'Many things affront the most zealous of the Jews – even something as seemingly insignificant as a small bronze head.'

Pilate gave a careless shrug of his heavy shoulders. 'It has been my experience that people adapt when they must. And not just the Jews! I myself awoke this morning to find my city under siege by two legions' worth of men who came with neither supplies nor weapons, determined to defeat me with prayers to their god.'

'Will you speak to them, Prefect?' one of the ambassadors asked. He seemed genuinely curious.

'I wouldn't presume to do so, but I am most anxious for their god to speak to me!'

One of the ambassadors laughed. 'What exactly do they expect him to say to you that will change your mind?'

It was Pilate's turn to laugh, 'One supposes an earthquake or bolts of lightning.'

'They won't last long,' one man remarked. 'How can they, fasting as they are?'

'I wouldn't be so sure,' another interjected. 'They are nothing if not fanatical, these Jews of Jerusalem.'

'Let them pray until their voices turn to sand,' Pilate snarled. 'The *imago* standard I erected last week will remain in Jerusalem for as long as Tiberius lives. It may not make the desert god happy, but by the gods-that-matter it makes *me* happy!' The ambassadors lifted their cups and toasted the courage of Pontius Pilate. Making his victory complete, Pilate announced to the delegates he and his wife would be honoured to attend Herod Antipas's birthday celebration.

The least discreet of them responded with spirit. 'You may march under your standards into Peraea, Prefect! We are not so sensitive as our neighbours to the south.'

The Jews were there the following morning and, because Procula's bedroom provided the best view, or so he said, Pilate came to her and ordered his breakfast brought to him. It was a first in their marriage. 'We should enjoy this incredible view together!' he told Procula cheerfully. 'I can't imagine why I haven't done it sooner.' From Procula's terrace she could look west to the sea, south along the desert, and east toward the mountains.

As they waited for their meal Pilate stood and directed his gaze at the early morning commerce inside the harbour – the only view he really enjoyed. Procula stood so that she could look out toward the sea and yet still watch the Jews. A fresh morning breeze swept in from the north keeping the heat of the morning in check, but the Jews caught none of it. They were in the sun already and murmuring their prayer like bees in summer.

'What is it they say?' Procula asked.

Pilate turned his gaze from the harbour and looked at Procula. 'What is it *who* says, my dear?'

Procula glanced toward the Jews. 'Those men. They chant something over and over again. I can hear the words, but I don't know what they mean.'

'Do not let them see you looking at them, Procula. It will only encourage them.'

'I'm sorry.'

'They will leave when they understand the utter futility of their prayer.'

'Of course. I know this. I was just curious.'

'They say, "God, turn his heart from stone." One is to suppose I am the man with the heart of stone.'

'All of this because of an *imago* standard in Jerusalem?'

'The priests of the Temple haven't the courage to die for their god on a Roman cross, so they rally an army of fools and send them through the desert to pray to their god in my presence, thinking it will inspire me to remove a little bronze head from the central portal to Herod's palace. The thing is not the size of your fist, my dear. They can't even see it. They complain only because they know it is there. That is what this is about – pure nonsense!'

Procula came out onto the terrace again at dusk. She told herself she wanted to see the sunset. Recalling her husband's advice, she did not allow herself to look at the suppliants. She was not sure how any of them could continue all day long, speaking the same phrase in a low murmur. What was it exactly? She tried to recall her husband's words. Something about his heart being made of stone.

Not long after they had moved to Capri Pilate had been talking pleasantly at dinner one evening, when he suddenly struck a slave who was serving them. With a fury she had never witnessed, her husband then rose from his couch and began kicking the boy. When he had finished, the slave lay on the marble floor bleeding and unconscious – close to death. After calling someone to drag the injured slave away, Pilate returned to his couch and began talking again in his normal tones. Later, when she was sure his temper had cooled, Procula asked her husband what the slave had done to warrant his beating. 'He looked at you longer than I thought appropriate.' Once the boy had recovered, Pilate ordered his castration and sold him on speculation to a merchant ship's captain.

There would be weeks when he seemed an utterly, absolutely normal human being, the man she thought she had married, but it never lasted. Power seduced him, it seemed, and he gave in to its seductions with a fury that left her trembling. It arrived for the first time in Caesarea late one afternoon after Procula had gone to direct the work in the kitchen. She heard about it in the excited chatter of her slaves and walked out to discover the disembowelled body of a bright young Syrian boy attached to the cavalry hanging from the palace gates. His crime? The slaves said the boy had not translated quickly enough for the master.

So it had returned after months of inordinate calm. It was no surprise really. Pilate had his feet under him now. That being the case, human life was cheap again.

'*God, turn his heart from stone!*' That was what the Jews whispered as the sun dipped into the sea. She did not care what Pilate said. He was not here to see it anyway. She turned and looked at them and did not pretend to do otherwise. They were shadows now, their voices like the chirping of nocturnal creatures. 'God, turn his heart from stone. God, turn his heart from stone.'

She heard their prayers even as she lay in her bed. She could not sleep, not for a long time, but it was not the noise they made. It was the prayer itself. Like these strange Jews, Claudia Procula had begun to repeat the phrase over and over – a prayer for the impossible whispered by the oppressed.

Pilate seemed irritable at dinner the next evening. He and Procula were alone for once, their engagements cancelled by Pilate without explanation. He wanted to know where the wine had come from. It did not seem up to standard. He was not sure the beef was cooked well enough. Had the fruit been imported from Egypt as he liked it, or was it from a Judaean field? When this last question could not be answered by his server, he demanded to see his steward. The steward came before the master nervously. Threats were issued. No beatings, however.

Silence followed until Pilate offered the smile he used on diplomats and merchants he wanted to cheat as he asked Procula quite suddenly, 'Was your day pleasant, my dear?'

'Very fine, sir.'

The smile seemed to curdle, the eyes to grow colder, but the voice remained as strong and cheerful as if he were speaking about good weather. 'Our visitors from Jerusalem . . . are they disturbing you?'

His courtesy had all the evidence of good training. In the first days of their marriage he had been less schooled and more genuine. 'God, turn his heart from stone,' Procula whispered to herself, first in Latin then in the Aramaic, or as close as she could approximate the sound. Then, for her husband to hear, 'I'm beginning to enjoy them. I think I will miss them when they are gone.'

Pilate laughed because he imagined she had made a joke.

'I thought this evening I could smell them,' he said, his smile simply disappearing. 'The wind had shifted, or the stink of them had simply saturated our apartments. I'm considering moving them further back from the city wall because of it.'

'But they have a right to petition the prefect?'

'They have the rights I allow them and no more!'

'Is it such a very important thing, this image of Tiberius?'

'It is a matter of principle. These people believe only their religion is important. I happen to believe my own is equally valid.'

'They do not protest the imperial standards in Caesarea, sir. They ask only for an exception to be made in Jerusalem, as it has been since the friendship between Augustus and Herod the Great.'

'Perhaps I should summon Cornelius and send him out to tell them their prayers are working. Pilate's wife defends Jews!'

From her terrace the following morning Procula smiled at the sight of the Jews still murmuring the same prayer. *God, turn his heart from stone. God, turn his heart from stone.* They still marched in place with the weary patience of holy men. She watched them openly now, sending for her breakfast so she could stay outside and enjoy the sight of them.

When Pilate's favourite asked about the strange men and what they were saying, Procula answered the slave honestly. 'They pray for your master because he is an important man.'

*　　*　　*

At dinner Pilate entertained friends of Philip, the estranged half-brother of Antipas. They had already heard Pilate would visit Antipas and were urging him in the gentlest possible terms to reconsider his decision. Antipas was passionately disliked by the Jews, they said. A show of friendship could have devastating consequences on Pilate's ability to govern.

'One need only look from one's window to see the kind of determination the Judaeans have when they are angry.'

Pilate, who might under ordinary circumstances have played these men against the ambassadors of Herod Antipas, listened sullenly up to this point. Once they touched upon the subject of ten thousand Jews standing before his bedroom window, however, he could no longer keep his silence. 'Do you imagine Caesar's prefect fears the prayers of madmen?'

The ambassadors seemed to understand their mistake and retreated to a more general discussion of Antipas's corruption. He had, after all, married his brother's wife. There was a time, of course, when Antipas had impressed Rome, but those days were past. He bore his father's name, they said, not his father's talents.

Pilate asked Philip's ambassadors if they would have him insult Herod Antipas, a man who, only a year ago, Tiberius received graciously into his palace?

'Before his sin,' one of them answered with an irritating confidence in his moral superiority.

'I must honour the friends of Tiberius so long as they are his friends. You would do well to petition Tiberius for sanctions against Philip's brother, if that is your desire. For my part, I pray only for peace and prosperity in our time.'

He left abruptly that they would know the subject was finished forever. He gave orders that the gentlemen might enjoy the evening in the prefect's palace. At sunrise they were to be shown the gate. He was not really angry with them. They were doing what ambassadors do. He had greater matters to worry about – namely ten thousand Jews at his throat! He could hear them at the banquet, in his bed, even in the great hall. It had been four days. They had not eaten in all that time, and he had not enjoyed a meal! Not a single moment of serenity! That night was the worst. They murmured incessantly, the sound coming as if from a single throat, and he could not sleep. At dawn he walked into Procula's bedroom as she stood on the terrace watching them – in spite of his instructions.

'By my calculations, they have gone eight days without food,' he said.

Procula blushed at being discovered in her disobedience, though she did not apologise for it. 'You startled me, sir.'

'How did you sleep?' he asked.

Procula stared out at the Jews as she answered him. 'I do not mind them, sir. Their prayer is like a song. I have grown very fond of it, actually.'

'Its meaning or its sound?'

She blushed but did not answer him.

'It does not matter,' he said. 'It cannot go on much longer.'

'Perhaps you should give them what they want.'

'Perhaps you should love your own life more.' At her

121

look of surprise, he continued, 'I do not take instructions from slaves or women, Procula. Those foolish enough to offer it, do so at their peril!'

'You asked me before any of this began if I thought it was a good idea.'

'You thought it was an excellent idea.'

'*You* thought it was an excellent idea! I simply agreed. I think now I made a mistake.'

'The mistake you make is resisting the will of your husband!'

Pilate awoke early the following morning to the sound of the prayer. He summoned his adjutant before he even left his bed. Cornelius came into his presence still fighting off the effects of the previous evening's drunkenness and still stinking of his Syrian whores. 'I want a cohort of infantry in full battle gear, assembled in the great stadium, Centurion, with a second cohort of cavalry in support. In addition to that, I want a century to escort our visitors into the stadium, where I will give them my decision. Make sure all but the century remain concealed until I give the signal for you to prepare for attack. At that point I will give them one last chance. Should they refuse to accept my decision, we will end it there – killing every last man.'

Cornelius answered that he would make the arrangements.

Pilate proceeded to his barber, where he dictated a number of letters. Then he enjoyed his breakfast of wine-soaked bread, eggs, and *mulsum*, a drink made of honey and wine. At midmorning his slaves dressed him for military combat, and he rode his horse into the great stadium. His escort included a half a dozen servants and a squad of officers. Joining Pilate at the gates to the stadium, Cornelius informed him that everything had been arranged. As Pilate rode into the arena the Jews accosted him with the same droning prayer to their god, and he congratulated himself on calling an end to it. When he had settled his horse in front of them he commanded Cornelius to silence them.

Cornelius lifted his arm. Slowly, inevitably the prayer ceased. 'You will tell the prefect what it is you desire of him!' he shouted in Latin.

The command was translated, and one of the protestors stepped forward. He spoke Latin with surprising ease. 'We desire that no image – either that of man or beast or pagan god – reside within the walls of the holy city of Jerusalem. It is the place of our Temple, the place where our God resides, and His commandments forbid us to look upon such images.'

'In all the empire one city alone resists the law requiring the public display of the *imago* standard,' Pilate answered. 'What you ask of me is to insult Caesar. This no intelligent man dares, but I will give you something. I am a reasonable man after all. Accept what I have placed within the city of Jerusalem, and I will not push for further concessions. Jerusalem has always been distinct from all other cities in the empire, because the Jews befriended Julius Caesar when he sorely needed friends. Augustus Caesar recognised this, and Tiberius carries the tradition forward. I change nothing. I only require that the universal law be applied universally! It is a matter of principle, which the prefects before me ought to have enforced but failed to do because of a lack of resolve.'

'You defile our city!' their spokesman answered.

Pilate, having quickly grown sick of that particular accusation, felt a stirring of rage and stared at the young man who flung his accusations about so recklessly. He was a thin, dark haired man of middle height with a beauty Pilate had rarely seen in an otherwise masculine figure. He had the eyes of a fanatic, the voice of a man people follow. 'As to the law,' the Jew continued, as if trained to rhetoric, 'your order is contrary to all agreements between our two nations. We therefore humbly ask you to remove the image!'

'What is your name, man, that I may know with whom I am dealing?

'I am called Judas,' he answered.

'A perfect name for a rebel. It was a Judas, as I recall, who nearly destroyed the Jews with war after the death of Herod. Centurion, give *our* Judas my answer to his prayer.'

Cornelius drew his sword and shouted his command: 'Soldiers of Rome! Prepare for battle!'

A moment later, horse and infantry appeared, weapons drawn and glistening in the midday sun. They came in squads and centuries, tightly grouped, just as they would enter a battlefield. They swept out from under the stadium seats and from under the flooring of the racetrack along the ramps the charioteers used to enter the track, flanking an enemy that found itself quite suddenly and completely at Pilate's mercy. Pilate gave an order to his centurion, who repeated it. The troops ceased their advance. 'Here is my answer to your prayer, Judas! What do you say to it?' The certainty of death swept through the crowd, and it was not without satisfaction that Pilate saw the effect. He let it take hold before he committed his troops to slaughter. 'Now, tell me, man. Are you prepared to die for the sake of one small bronze head inside the walls of Jerusalem?'

Pulling his hair ceremoniously away from his neck, Judas fell to his knees and ripped his tunic, exposing his neck for the Roman swords. 'To the last man!' he said and dropped his chin to his chest that the sword might cut him cleanly. Those closest to him, fell to their knees as well and pushed their long hair away from their necks, after his example. As others saw what these men did, they too knelt, until the entire stadium presented only Roman soldiers with weapons drawn and Jews kneeling submissively, every last man offering his neck.

Pilate's victory soured, but he commanded the centurion to have the men prepare to attack. 'Soldiers of Rome! Advance to battle!' Cornelius shouted.

'Your time is running out, Judas!' Pilate called.

Judas was the first to begin the chant: 'God, turn his heart from stone.' First hundreds, then thousands picked up the chant. 'God, turn his heart from stone.' Finally, they all recited it as they waited on their knees to die.

Pilate had only to keep silent and the racetrack would run with blood – for the sake of an image as common as the Roman Eagle! He nearly did. He should have, he knew, but something stopped him. The absurdity of the principle, perhaps. They were willing to give their lives for it, but he could not kill two legions' worth of men over something so insignificant. It simply was not worth that much carnage.

'Stand down, Centurion.'

Cornelius gave the order, and the troops obeyed crisply, stopping their march only steps from the first of the kneeling Jews. They would have marched forward with the same indifference. Did these Jews know that? Did they imagine their god had saved them? No, he thought. Pontius Pilate has spared your miserable lives, but he will not do it a second time! As soon as Judas understood that he had won, he stood. His people followed his lead and the prayer stopped. 'I will give you what you desire,' Pilate said to him. 'The *imago* standard will be removed before you return to your city. You have won a small battle, Judas, because your lives are not worth the trouble of taking – not on this occasion – but there will be a day when you offer your necks and I will take them and those of your women and children as well!'

As Pilate's words were translated into Aramaic, the exhausted men broke into a spontaneous prayer that was, finally, something other than the one they had uttered incessantly. Only Judas did not speak to his god. He kept his eyes on Pilate. Pilate recognised the challenge but refused to be drawn into it. He had given his order. As far as he was concerned the matter was finished.

To Cornelius he said, 'See to it that the *imago* standard is removed from Jerusalem with all haste, Centurion, and then show our visitors the road. If I must smell them for another morning, I will change my orders!'

With that said Pilate turned his horse and rode from the great stadium.

Lake Lucerne, Switzerland
October 7, 2006.

A couple of days after the break-in Julian Corbeau had begun watching the surveillance tapes in earnest. At first he was barely conscious of what he witnessed. Jeffrey Bremmer guided him through it. He watched in amazement as the two figures crossed his lawn – a virtual impossibility with his security cameras, except that his guards had been distracted for the two seconds it had taken. Room by room the male swept his house. The female climbed his tower with a rope. He did not see her again until she stepped into the library – there was no technology in the tower – but once she entered the library, the microphone recorded her whispers. She was English. Bremmer's consultants suggested that she was possibly an expatriate, as the accent had faded and had influences of Italian and German pronunciation. Her accomplice was American, quite possibly from Tennessee or Kentucky, but he had lived in a German speaking country for a number of years. The one called Girl was the leader, but Boy knew what they were looking for. The print Oscar Wilde had brought on his visit in 1899 registered with them both as proof the painting was in Corbeau's possession – which was exceedingly strange.

Violence has the extraordinary quality of seeming quite ordinary on surveillance film. A man in a tuxedo enters a room. Shots are fired. A second passes. The man is dead. Slow motion makes no more sense of it. Three shots fired in less than half-a-second. Two people down. One stands up again. The other rests in the corner of the screen, his chest and neck torn apart by two forty-five calibre bullets. Watching the tapes again the following week, every investigation stalled, Corbeau finally saw something. More accurately he saw what one rarely witnesses: Girl's physical perfection.

Corbeau's man entered the room and shot her. This was the point of interest. As she fell, Girl's weapon, including a lengthy silencer, cleared its holster. Before she hit the floor she fired the gun. Watching Boy, because the camera caught only his figure as Girl dropped behind Corbeau's desk, Corbeau and Jeffrey Bremmer had originally believed their man had missed with his second shot. In fact, the woman's bullet had struck Corbeau's bodyguard as he was attempting to shoot Boy. One could not tell for sure from the sound or the blood. The weapons of the thieves were silenced and all three shots seemed to occur simultaneously, but the smoke from Girl's gun preceded his bodyguard's second shot by a fraction of a second, meaning the bullet had struck him as he was pulling the trigger. Running the tape several times, it was clear Girl had reacted instinctively. She had not even been able to aim. Corbeau had inspected the wound himself. The bullet she fired had struck his man's heart. 'Could you have done that?' he asked Bremmer. Corbeau's chief of security was in fact the only man in the world Corbeau considered his friend. He liked to joke with the un-initiated that he and Mr Bremmer had been though fire together. It was, of course, hardly a matter to joke about inside the Order.

Bremmer smiled at Corbeau's question. He had been

hit wearing a vest that evening. The force of impact, he said, was overpowering. 'To be honest,' he said, 'I wouldn't have thought it possible – especially with such accuracy.'

'It was pure reflex, Mr Bremmer.'

'What are you saying? Special Forces? CIA? SAS?'

'One cannot train those kinds of reflexes. I think she's a professional athlete.'

Jeffrey Bremmer smiled. 'A British expatriate . . . and a world class athlete. We might be able to do something with that.'

'I want a list: any public mention of a female athlete roughly fitting Girl's description within the past five – make it seven years. We start with the media in Germany, Switzerland and Austria. If that doesn't give us a pool of names we can do something with, we'll include Italy and England. After that we'll go to all Europe if we have to, but we don't stop until we find her.'

Bremmer looked at his employer incredulously. 'That could take a great deal of time.'

'No. I want it done quickly. I don't care how many people it takes or how much money, Mr Bremmer. Hire a thousand, hire ten thousand! Our lives depend on this – or have you forgotten?'

'I have not forgotten.'

Three days later Bremmer appeared in Corbeau's office with a list of three hundred names, but there were ten he liked better than the rest. Corbeau examined the top ten names and tapped Lady Kenyon's name at the very top of the list. 'I want a full dossier on her in forty eight hours.'

By the week's end Corbeau had his thieves: Lady Katherine Kenyon and Ethan Brand, the owner of a bookshop in Zürich. He knew that Kenyon's father, Roland Wheeler, fenced the art they stole and he knew the bank Wheeler liked to use for exchanges. Tracking Wheeler's phone calls and flights out of the country, he knew the identity of the people preparing to purchase his painting, as well as the fact that they had employed Thomas Malloy and Bob Whitefield to transport Corbeau's painting to the States in a diplomatic pouch.

A knock at his library door interrupted Corbeau's reveries.

He called out in French, 'Enter, please!'

Xeno stepped into the room. When in the presence of Corbeau for the first time Xeno had touched his knee to the floor and kissed the grandmaster's ring. Now they ran things without the formalities that had once characterized the Order. Times change, as Corbeau liked to remark, and a man did well to change with them. Still, he missed the show of reverence that had once been a constant part of his rule. These days he had only his title to mark him out from others, and despite his outward show of accepting the ways of modern life, it left a bit of emptiness in his ancient soul.

'Your Eminence! The American couriers have just finished their meeting. Our names came up.'

Corbeau, who had long ago mastered his emotions, expressed nothing beyond mild interest at this news by simply lifting his chin and cocking a single eyebrow. Xeno reported the meeting in its entirety. Whitefield knew about the break-in at Corbeau's villa. That was to be expected. Since Bremmer's trip to Hamburg,

Whitefield had become more than a passing concern. He was in fact a danger. Corbeau's friendship with the Swiss was still intact, but the rumours of his connection to alleged neo-Nazis had begun to erode his once-unanimous support. 'Forget what they know and what they think they know. Tuesday it is finished for them, and make sure you arrange matters so that there is no danger for the painting.'

'I will take care of it myself.'

'You are known, Xeno. You cannot go near Whitefield. Besides, I want you to lead the team taking Lady Kenyon.'

At Xeno's apparent disappointment, Corbeau added. 'Give her to me without a mark on her and I will add a million dollars to your personal bank account.'

'You are too generous, Your Eminence.'

Corbeau smiled. 'You may want to survive Lady Kenyon before you speak of my generosity.'

Zürich, Switzerland
October 7, 2006.

Kate entered Ethan's bookshop a couple of minutes before closing. Sean Burri, at the register, called out to her as he finished taking care of an elderly man's purchases. Coming to the railing, Ethan watched Kate from the second floor as she ascended the open stairway.

The original design of the 16th century building had placed the living quarters over a butcher shop. The third storey had been used for sleeping. Renovating it when hc had bought the building seven years ago through a dummy corporation Kate's father had helped him to establish, Ethan had ripped out the centre of the second floor and entirely abolished the attic except for the enormous oak beams that had served as floor joists. He had then installed skylights and a wrought iron railing around the opening on the second floor. The effect was to integrate the first and second floors and to bring natural light down to the ground floor, making it one of the most beautiful shops in a city of beautiful shops. The downside of the design was privacy. To compensate, Ethan had constructed a tiny office on the second floor. That was where they headed as soon as Kate joined him.

Behind closed doors, she said to him, 'Drs North and Starr are flying in tomorrow morning. They want to talk to you about the painting tomorrow evening, then go to the bank Monday and have a look at it.'

'Talk to *me*? That's Roland's job. Remember? We steal it, he sells it.'

'They aren't buying Roland's story. They know it's stolen. That's not the problem. Dr Starr wants the provenance.'

'We told him. It's a Templar artefact. What else does he need to know?'

'The evidence you used to connect it to the Templars, I take it. Tell them everything up to Corbeau. That part they don't get, even for twenty-five million.'

'You think they're getting cold feet?'

'I expect they just want to know everything we know. My read on Dr Starr is once he's sure what we have is genuine, he'd kill to have it.'

'He's not alone, is he?'

Kate's face went brittle. 'Let's not go there again.'

'People are dead because we wanted that painting, Kate.'

'Bad people.'

'I don't care what they were. They were alive up to the point that you and I decided we should appropriate Corbeau's painting.'

'This one was yours, Ethan. Remember?'

'I'm just saying we have enough now.'

'Enough?'

'I'm finished with jobs.'

'I knew this was coming. I read you, Ethan. I know how you think.'

Ethan didn't answer. He could see the effect of his decision in Kate's eyes. They were finished once the deal closed Tuesday.

'You can't change what you are, Ethan. You're a thief and a good one. Why don't you just accept it?'

'What I am is in love with you. Everything else I can change.'

'If you love me, you had better love what I do, because it doesn't work any other way.'

'When is it over for you?'

'Who says it has to be over?'

'You're not going to be happy until you get yourself killed.'

'Is that what you think I'm trying to do?'

'I want a normal life, Kate.'

'Then find a normal woman.'

'Come on! I didn't mean—'

'I'm serious. If that's what you want, find someone clsc.'

'Would you try it straight? We can travel, climb, ski, skydive, take Polar expeditions ... I don't care! Whatever you want to do. Wherever you want to go. Just no guns and no more break-ins. I still see that man in the library.'

'The one who shot me without a word of warning?'

'Yeah ... that one.'

'And if I don't want to stop?'

There was challenge in her eyes, but he was ready, or as ready as one can get for something like that. 'Then maybe I need to think about things.'

'What does that mean?'

'We go straight ... or I leave.'

'You don't mean it.' Her smiled had lost its steadiness, but her eyes were still confident.

'If you don't think I mean it, you don't know me as well as you think you do.'

For a long, tense moment Kate stared at him. She was ready to say something that would not be easy to take back. Finally she settled herself. There was work left to do, and she still needed him, like it or not. That was how he read it, at any rate.

'I'll call you after the exchange and let you know what I decide. Meanwhile, don't forget. The Savoy Hotel, eight o'clock tomorrow evening, Dr North's suite.'

'Kate—' Ethan tried to take her hand.

Her hands shot up, palms out. She did not want to be touched. 'I'll think about it. Just don't push me.'

She left the door open on the way out.

Ethan watched her leave, knowing it might be the last time he ever saw her. The thought sickened him, but at least it was out. He had finally said what he needed to say. His share for the job, almost eight million dollars after expenses, was the leprechaun's pot-of-gold, the happily-ever-after of fairy tales, but it had come at a terrible cost. At thirty-one years of age Ethan should have known it would. Nothing is free, and no one knows this better than a thief. It had always been out there. They had practised using weapons. They went in armed on every job, knowing it might be the only way out. Because it hadn't happened before, Ethan had convinced himself it was never going to happen. Kate planned things too well.

Or so he had wanted to believe. He could live with what he had done – they were bad people, no question about that – but he didn't like it, and he was not going to risk having to do it again. It was only fair that he tell Kate the truth. There were no tomorrows in Kate's world, no long-term commitments. He knew that going in. You took her for what she was. You didn't change her. You didn't delude yourself by imagining she would ever settle down and live a normal life. She came from wealth. She had a title. She had everything anyone dreams of, a world of privilege that most women could not even imagine, but the only satisfaction Kate had ever found was in risking it all. She was good. That wasn't the question. It was possible she would never be caught, but that wasn't really the point. The point was Ethan had lost his taste for it when he had seen the man in the library shot to death. He had once imagined he would do anything for Kate. Anything! But there was a limit after all.

'I thought Kate was going to join us.'

Ethan looked up and saw Sean standing in the open doorway. He had not heard his friend come up the stairs. At least he had not registered the sound of his footsteps. For that matter he was not even sure how long he had been leaning against his desk trying to come to terms with his own decision. 'I think we just broke up.'

Sean smiled as if he thought Ethan was joking. 'You're kidding me?'

Ethan shook his head. He wasn't kidding.

'Another guy?'

That was exactly what it was, he realised with sudden clarity. Only the other guy had been dead for almost a decade. 'Nothing like that,' he muttered. 'Just . . .'

'You two are perfect together. If it's not another guy, what is it?'

'You want to buy this place?'

'*This* place? Sure, but I can't afford it. You know what kind of money I make.'

'Do you want it or not?'

'Sure, I want it.'

'I'll make you a partner for a thousand francs. You run the business, pay me rent on the building.'

'That's crazy. What about the inventory? You have a fortune tied up in books!'

'You figure it out and pay me back what you can afford, whenever you can afford it.'

'You're giving me your business – just like that? What's wrong with you anyway?'

'I think it's time to start a new life.'

Lake Brienz, Switzerland
October 8, 2006.

Early Sunday morning Malloy walked down to the train station and caught the first intercity out of town. Four hours and six transfers later, certain he had lost any possible surveillance team, if one even existed, Malloy arrived in the town of Brienz in time to catch the post bus on its run to Ax Alp. At the third stop up the mountain, he stepped off and started through the forest.

When Malloy had first arrived in Zürich, he had set up a freelance business as an editor and translator. With the occasional teaching assignment in the commercial schools it had provided a small but steady income, sufficient at any rate to justify his bohemian lifestyle. Advertising routinely in the Zürich newspaper he had culled some legitimate queries. To allay suspicions he generally took the work offered him. It was important to have a day job, a justification for his income and his movements. Editing was perfect. It let him work odd hours and allowed the occasional procrastination when his real work came under pressure. It also put him in touch with a wide circle of Zürich intellectuals and professionals.

One morning, about a year after he had settled into his routine and had begun establishing himself with people working in the Zürich banks, he received a call from a woman who inquired about the possibility of his editing her manuscript. An independent scholar with enough wealth to indulge herself, the Contessa Claudia de Medici had seemed legitimate, and her story was credible. She had already published her book in Italian and was preparing the English manuscript. Before she approached an American publisher with it, she said she wanted a native speaker with editorial experience to spend some time going through it. Malloy answered that he had no training in history or religion, but the moment he tried to suggest some people who might help her, she stopped him. Money was not an issue, and she didn't want just anyone working with her manuscript. She wanted him.

So the dance had started. Malloy had asked how she knew his work. A friend had recommended him. Did her friend have a name? Of course, but the contessa did not think it appropriate to mention it. At that point Malloy felt there was a good chance that Claudia de Medici was something other than what she pretended to be, but the woman intrigued him. He took her manuscript and dutifully began editing it at his usual rates.

Malloy had never really flirted with religion even as a young man. He knew virtually nothing about the origins of Christianity, nor had he much cared. All that began to change after he began working on the manuscript. Call it a sense of authority, expertise, passion. Whatever it was exactly, the contessa's writing left him spellbound. She talked about old Jerusalem as if she had walked its dusty streets. She spoke about what it was to be a Jew under the Roman occupation, then with equal authority what a Roman soldier must have experienced, stationed far from his home and culture, usually without wife and family.

There was no danger of a conversion to religion. Malloy was a committed sceptic in all things, miracles especially, but he could safely admit that the book had sparked a great deal of personal interest in the history of the Middle East and for that matter history in general. Finished with the job he mailed the manuscript back to her, as she had requested, along with his bill.

Somewhat to his surprise the Contessa de Medici made no payment. As a hungry businessman he was forced to send an overdue notice. This was answered with a note of apology, though still without payment. If he would care to drive to Interlaken, she would be glad to treat him to lunch at the Hotel Jungfrau by way of a formal apology for any inconvenience she had caused and, yes, pay her bill in full.

Malloy had not been able to find any photographs of the contessa and he was curious. Lunch sounded like a good idea, a chance to put a face to his mystery woman. Meeting her the first time, he was not sure what to think. She was decidedly older than he was, somewhere between thirty-five and forty, and yet it seemed to him he had never encountered a woman whose cool reserve and self-possession excited him so much.

Over lunch she mentioned entertaining anecdotes from the court of Tiberius as if it were gossip, not history, embellishing freely on the emperor's character. She even corrected what she called the misperceptions of Tacitus and Suetonius. She spoke with an authority that was both enchanting and convincing.

He waited for the inevitable questions about his personal life, the gentle probing about relationships. To his chagrin they never occurred. When their lunch was finished, the contessa passed an envelope across the table and thanked him for his excellent work. She excused herself, walked to the front of the hotel and had her man, Rene, drive her home. When he had composed himself, Malloy was vaguely affronted by the encounter. He even considered the possibility that she might be exactly what she pretended: a serious scholar, still rather young as those sorts go, who had forgotten to pay her bill in a timely fashion and wanted to make amends.

A few months later he received an invitation to a party at the contessa's villa on Lake Brienz.

Nearly a decade after that first party Malloy would consider the possibility that Claudia de Medici had arranged that first evening for his benefit. At the time he simply imagined himself lucky – an intelligence officer rubbing shoulders quite unexpectedly with people who had access to what he needed. The party was an extravagant affair which drew the country's elite, including bankers, industrialists, and politicians. It was an operative's dream. From that first party he established the contacts that eventually got critical information about the bank accounts of two Colombian drug lords and one ex-president of the Philippines. The following year he received another invitation, and every year after that another. At these parties the contessa would usually manage a greeting and perhaps an introduction to yet another luminary of Swiss finance, but she spent hardly any time at all talking to him. So it went for several years. She invited him to her party. He sent a thank you note afterwards. That was the extent of it.

Then one night the contessa telephoned him. It was past midnight, but she made no apology for the hour.

She said she needed help and could not wait until morning. He arrived at her villa at nearly three o'clock and met a young man who claimed to be a night watchman for one of the major Swiss depositories in Bern. He was wearing a private security uniform and possessed a photo ID, but it could have been forged. Malloy had no way of checking it on short notice.

That evening as he had made his usual rounds, the night watchman said, he had discovered the bank records of the holocaust victims set out before one of the furnaces with orders attached to the crates instructing bank personnel to incinerate the material. That would occur, he said, the following morning. To substantiate his story, the young man had stolen several of the documents and presented them to Malloy.

'Can you call someone, Thomas?' the contessa asked.

Given more time, Malloy could have worked up a respectable cover for himself, but there was no time. Over the past several months a multibillion dollar lawsuit had been pending against the major banks in Switzerland, claiming they had purposely concealed evidence relating to the holocaust accounts. The Swiss banking community had given repeated assurances that the records had been destroyed decades ago. They admitted that it was possible for certain individuals to have deposited money in the 1930s and subsequently for their heirs to have failed to make a proper claim to recover their assets. One needed a death certificate to close an account and the Nazi death camps hadn't been very good about that sort of thing. It was unfortunate, they said, but claims were at this point impossible to verify.

That they were lying was clear to everyone who knew the Swiss fondness for keeping records, but to prove it was another matter. Suddenly Malloy had it within his power to catch them in their collective lie. Tempting as that prospect was he had also known that he could be stepping into a trap, blowing his cover and getting nothing for his troubles besides expulsion from the country. In fact with anyone other than the contessa he might have hesitated. His training had certainly suggested she was a suspicious contact, but he had made no attempt to investigate her background because she had neither wanted nor offered information – or anything else. For all he knew, she could have been working for the Swiss banks instead of against them.

He trusted her, however. He could not say why. Instinct, he would tell himself later. When he was honest about the matter, he would admit he had been half-in-love with her since the afternoon of their lunch in Interlaken. It wasn't such a strange notion. Young men sometimes fall under the spell of truly self-assured older women, and the truth was she was not that much older. She had simply *seemed* beyond his reach at the time. Prompted by love or instinct, he still could not say which, Malloy took a dangerous leap of faith and called the American Consulate in Paris. A cover blown in Switzerland amounted to a one-way ticket home, but he would have risked his life that night. That was how much faith the contessa inspired.

By the following morning the American and Israeli consulates were actively involved. The night watchman was in good hands, and the contessa and Malloy quietly removed themselves from the inevitable media frenzy. No one ever knew they were behind it. Later, Malloy asked the contessa how she knew to call him. With her contacts in Bern, why not someone at the American Consulate? How did she know he could do anything for her?

'It was the right thing to do, Thomas. Let's leave it at that, shall we?'

And so they had.

Malloy had been inclined to lay the whole thing out to Jane Harrison in the aftermath, but that would have required changing his original story as well as betraying the contessa's trust. Moreover, the truth might have exposed him to the charge of acting as an unwitting agent for a foreign intelligence agency – he was still of the opinion she might be working for the Israelis. Stupidity was not a crime, but it was sufficient for re-assignment even if things happened to work out. Silence, on the other hand, left one's mistakes and questionable decisions buried and forgotten.

During the remainder of his time in Zürich Malloy had continued to attend the contessa's annual party, but they had never again met in private. With a free day on his hands and having not seen the woman for several years, Malloy thought it might be pleasant to drop in. It was more than a casual visit of course. He had been reading about twelfth century portraits of Christ for the past several days and could not quite comprehend J. W. Richland's passion for Byzantine icons. Assuming he could work the subject into a casual conversation, Malloy was hoping the contessa could give him some insight.

The contessa's villa sat on the side of Ax Alp

overlooking Lake Brienz. The building itself was a nineteenth century hotel that had fallen into disrepair by the time the contessa had bought it. After restoring it and taking up her year-round residence, she rarely left the property. Her sole extravagance was her annual party. If she visited friends or attended exclusive parties, Malloy hadn't heard about it, and the people at her parties were terrible gossips. She was a writer and a scholar. What she needed she sent for, everything from books to groceries. If she had wanted society she would not have bought such an isolated property. The solitude of the place was impressive, too. The building sat on a small plot of level ground close to a thundering cascade. It was surrounded on all sides by a dense forest that went on for miles. From the contessa's veranda, it was possible to see Interlaken at one end of the lake and the town of Brienz at the other. That was as close as she let herself get to civilization.

Her 'man', as she call him in English, Rene, stood at one of the doors to the house watching him as Malloy came down the mountain on a rather steep and sometimes treacherous trail next to the cascade. Another individual might have treated Malloy with a friendly wave of his hand, but Rene simply stared. Like the contessa, Rene's age was indeterminate. He could have been fifty or seventy. He kept his oddly battered head shaved and even though he was dark-skinned, there were no lines to offer any hint of his generation. He possessed hulking shoulders and a cinderblock torso.

Despite his age and size, Rene moved with the ease of an athlete still in his prime. Unlike his employer, Rene possessed no talent for language. His native tongue

Malloy had never been able to determine. The language he spoke with the contessa was a kind of pidgin Italian, though he freely mixed German, French, and English words into it, the accent inevitably misplaced. Rene's grammar, Malloy had decided long ago, was capricious.

One thing Malloy did not doubt was Rene's loyalty to the woman he served. In her presence, his eyes stayed on the contessa with the zeal and ferocity of a trained Rottweiler. When he had approached within fifteen feet, Malloy stopped and said to the man, 'Is the contessa at home, Rene?'

As this question was no doubt absurd, Rene did not bother answering him. He simply flexed his enormous fists and walked away. Malloy went to the veranda, intending to knock at the front door, but Claudia de Medici was already waiting.

'Thomas! This is a pleasant surprise! Have you moved back to Zürich?'

'I'm here on business for a couple of days. I found myself with a free afternoon, and I thought I'd drop by. I hope I'm not interrupting something.'

'Nothing that can't wait. Come in.' Malloy stepped into the elegantly furnished entryway. The contessa led him to the drawing room and began fixing them both a glass of Scotch.

'Are you working on a new book?'

'I have written my book. If I write another, it won't be for some time.' Her smile was almost bashful, her beauty as stunning as ever. In fact, it seemed to Malloy that she had not changed in the years since he had first met her. She was still a woman seemingly not quite forty, making her, he realised with a sudden sense of despair, over a decade younger than he was! 'And you,' she asked with a smile that suggested she had read his thoughts, 'are you still a freelance editor?' There was a bit of playfulness in this, something of an old joke between them, and Malloy smiled.

'Retired, I'm afraid.'

'Not entirely, I hope. You are far too young for something as dreadful as retirement.'

'I keep busy.'

'You are living in New York, I hear.'

'You must have good sources.'

'One of the advantages of having interesting friends.' Malloy resisted asking about her sources. The contessa was quite effective at gaining confidences, obstinate about keeping them. 'You are happy. I can see that much in your eyes.'

'I'm getting married this spring.'

'And you decide to step back into the life – in order to save yourself from your happiness?'

Malloy laughed at the jab. He had not thought about it like that, but he supposed one could see it that way. He certainly would not have been the first man to sabotage a perfect relationship. Still, he was reluctant to admit as much, even jokingly. Besides, he had never really left his profession – only fieldwork. 'If I wait any longer to get back into things, it will be too late,' he confessed.

'Perhaps it is not your destiny.'

'I believe we make our own destiny, Contessa.'

'It's my opinion that people are not thrust into hell because of their passions, Thomas. I think they jump in for the sake of them, but I'm not going to change your mind. I can see that. Why don't you tell me what brings you here? It has something to do with business, I think.'

The contessa worked as successful mind readers do. She read body language. She made grand assessments and waited for reactions. That she was sweet about it and seemed to enjoy him at some level made it less disconcerting, but the truth was her insights into his character had always left him wondering if she might really be clairvoyant.

'I thought you might be able to explain something for me.' The contessa tipped her head slightly, her expression curious. 'What do you know about twelfth century icons of Christ?'

'I know I enjoy them very much, though I would imagine I'm in the minority. What would you like to know?'

'A twelfth century Byzantine portrait of Christ – what would something like that be worth, say in mint condition?'

The contessa smiled as if dealing with a precocious child. 'That is difficult to say. Assuming it to be in excellent condition, you would have to know if it had been restored. Then there is the provenance. That would affect the price significantly. People interested in paintings of that sort value the history at least as much as, if not more than, the artistic merit. Many icons come with a portable altar. There might be a unique box or travelling case. Many of these are works of art themselves. Some are encrusted with precious jewels, which would add value beyond the particular artistic merit. A famous person might have owned it. A great deal of information about the royal family in

Constantinople is available from that era. The princess Anna Comnena, who met the first Crusaders, for instance, even wrote a book detailing her impressions of the army's leaders, including the relatively unknown Baldwin of Boulogne – the man the barons would ultimately elect as the first king of Christian Jerusalem. If it were her personal icon and you could prove it with documents, such a piece would be extremely attractive to some buyers – myself included, though I am not a collector – but without a great deal more information I couldn't begin to make a guess.'

'I have a general description of it. It's on a panel of wood, maybe a quarter of an inch thick, thirteen or fourteen inches tall and eight or nine inches wide.'

'Gold? Inlaid jewels?'

He shook his head. 'Here's the thing. The people involved are paying twenty-five million dollars for it.' The contessa's expression did not change, but Malloy was certain something happened – call it a twinkling in the eye or a moment of recognition. 'When I started trying to price comparable pieces, rare as they are, the pieces go for forty or fifty thousand up to half a million. Nothing is close to what my people are paying.'

'What is your involvement, Thomas?'

'I'm moving it for them.'

'Smuggling it?'

'Just moving it.'

'If the people are lying to you about the nature of the object you have to deal with or the price they are paying, my advice is to walk away. Better yet . . . *run*.'

Malloy smiled and shook his head. 'I can't do that. This is my chance to get back to what I do best.'

'Then I don't think I can help you, except to say you might be looking at something like what happened to you in Beirut.'

Malloy felt like a man who has just had the ground under his feet taken away from him. 'How do you know about Beirut?'

'People talk, Thomas. Rather, I should say, they whisper.'

'The people who know about Beirut don't.'

'A neophyte intelligence officer inherits half a dozen low-level agents who pass along outdated information. Some months later he is running a network of twenty-four agents and catches wind of an attack being planned against the US Marine base. He passes the information to his superiors and tries to discover specific details. The following day he is in a G. I. hospital with six bullet wounds. Eight of his people are dead, and the rest are evacuated. Two days after that, some two hundred and forty marines perish, and Reagan orders American troops out of Lebanon.'

Malloy tried to smile, but he didn't make much of it. 'They say we learn from our mistakes,' he said finally.

'Actually,' she answered, 'they say we *should* learn from them. The truth is that most people have a regrettable tendency to repeat them.'

'Do you know something I don't know, Contessa?'

'I know a great deal more than you do, Thomas, about a great many things. In this instance, I know that you never trusted your superiors again after Beirut and, because of it, you were so successful it caused problems that you could not even imagine. I know, too, that your skills aren't what they were. You have lost that scepticism you are so proud of, say what you will to the contrary, and you think you can handle this job without much trouble, because it looks like nothing can go wrong. You expect that once you do you will be back to your old tricks, not lying in your grave.'

Malloy felt a chill run down his spine when she mentioned his grave. 'Tell me what you know.'

'I know you are standing in a pit of vipers, but you don't see them because you are half asleep.'

Malloy wanted to argue or explain or at least to defend himself, but he resisted the impulse. A woman capable of bringing the Swiss banking system to its collective knees was not someone he cared to underestimate.

Chapter Five

The Palace of Herod Antipas, Peraea
Summer AD 26.

Although Herod the Great had been an extraordinary man, it was universally acknowledged his sons were not. They pretended otherwise, of course. They had learned pomposity at their father's knee. Philip ruled at a luxurious court in a tetrarchy to the north of Galilee. Antipas shuffled between Galilee and Perea with a great train of servants and officials of government in his procession. Each son dreamed of uniting his father's kingdom again, but in truth the time was long past when either of them might make a credible effort at it. Sejanus had made that clear to Pilate when offering him his present position. Judaea, Samaria and Idumaea belonged to the emperor because Herod's eldest son had been incompetent.

Rather than replace him with either Philip or Antipas, letting a once-prosperous kingdom perish in the process, Augustus had taken the contentious provinces as his own and restored the peace. According to Sejanus, Augustus's decision had proven the better course of action. Over the past three decades Antipas had repeatedly demonstrated the same capricious brutality as his elder brother, Archaelaus, while Philip's indolence extended to the point that he had lost his wife to his brother and did not rouse himself from his banquet couch to go and chase after her.

Pilate had been expecting to encounter a rather dull intelligence when he journeyed to Peraea to meet Antipas. Instead he discovered an urbane gentleman of sixty years, possessing a silky voice, a lively wit, and an engaging sense of humour. Antipas shared his father's less than substantial stature as well as his tendency to carry extra weight. Despite this he seemed an energetic man with lively black eyes that missed nothing inside the great banquet hall and probably nothing beyond his palace gate either, and though he did not trust the tetrarch, Pilate found, at least at the start of the evening, that he liked him very much.

Herodias, Antipas's new wife, appeared to be about half his age. She struck Pilate as a woman of obvious intellectual capacity with the imperious manner that came to women whose intelligence exceeded that of their husbands. Pilate's initial reaction to the woman was the curious thought that Antipas had not seduced her away from his brother for the sake of her beauty. He was wondering what magic potions Herodias had employed, when Antipas summoned her daughter into the hall to perform a dance. Salome was a tempting delicacy of some twelve or thirteen years, not yet ready for marriage but very close – and far prettier than her mother. Pilate enjoyed her performance but was curious enough about the family that he pulled his gaze from the dance to see how Antipas reacted to it. The tetrarch, he realised, was besotted with his stepdaughter.

Pilate's intelligence on the notorious marriage suggested that Antipas had fallen for Herodias shortly before his visit to Rome and persuaded her, through secret correspondences while he was yet abroad, to leave his brother and join him in Galilee on his return – as his wife. The role of Salome in all this had not been mentioned, but it seemed to him as he watched the newlyweds that Salome had been the critical factor, almost certainly, he thought, operating as her mother's agent. For what reason he could only guess.

It was not Pilate's business of course, but the possibilities inherent in the complex interaction of this newly forged family would interest Sejanus, and Pilate intended to make a full report once he was safely returned to Caesarea.

While Antipas almost certainly enjoyed the advantage of receiving a visit from Caesar's new prefect before bothering himself with a journey to Caesarea, he made every effort to let Pilate know he considered him his most honoured guest – at least until he had consumed so much wine that he no longer cared. Pilate and Procula reclined upon his right and left hand at the head table in a rare and somewhat unsettling mix of the two sexes at a banquet.

They were also the first to be introduced to the audience of some twenty courtiers and ladies. Antipas accorded them both lengthy speeches of praise. Procula's association with the Claudii seemed especially significant, though he was politic enough to praise her beauty above her family connections, and Pilate basked in the reflected glory of it.

The meal itself was decidedly Oriental and as ingeniously presented as anything in the court of Tiberius. During one of the latter courses Antipas became less interested in his food and more excited by the quality of the wine he served. He was the sort of alcoholic who loses none of his motor skills. Instead, as he drank, he became more animated and loquacious. On the subject of wine Antipas asked Pilate if it compared favourably to Italian vintages. It was indeed far superior to most of the wines Pilate had experienced, but he was too much of a patriot to admit it, and answered that in Rome one drank the wines of the world, which was to say, *Roman* wine.

Antipas, who probably should have understood he was making the prefect uncomfortable, pointed out that Pilate had avoided making any kind of judgment at all. Pilate turned his attention to Herodias, who drank with more care. He was quite certain she had never said anything she had not intended. 'As pleasant as the food and wine is I'm afraid I much prefer the gracious company of this evening.'

The compliment ought to have finished the matter, but Antipas clearly wanted to make his point, and his point was insult. 'It is useful to appreciate the differences in our cultures, Prefect, don't you think? It is not simply a matter of agriculture and climate, and how such affect the grape. The differences extend even to the way we choose to rule. I have heard the story, for instance, which I have every reason to believe is perfectly true, that you had, let us say, some difficulty with Jerusalem a few weeks ago. Is it so?'

'A prefect of Judaea has constant business with

Jerusalem, Tetrarch. I would hesitate referring to any that I have had so far as having difficulties.'

'My father dealt with nearly the same problem thirty years ago.'

'What problem is that?'

'The Jewish aversion to images. Don't imagine I am suggesting my father's method is superior to your own. I bring it up only to illustrate how the Oriental mind approaches a problem. My father, as you no doubt have heard, was a great friend and ally of Caesar Augustus. Like you, he took offence at Jerusalem's refusal to erect even the most modest of imperial emblems. After finishing the expansion and renovation of the second Temple of Solomon, he decided to place an eagle of pure gold on the outer gate of the Temple compound – the same image your armies place before every legion in the service of the empire.

'Naturally, as you no doubt did when you erected the *imago* standard over the great door of the palace, my father anticipated resistance from certain radical elements within the Jewish population. When they came to speak to him about it, however, he simply closed his door, and that was the end of the matter. Such was the nature of my father's character that none – none! – dared to provoke him with a demonstration.'

'As I recall,' Pilate countered, feeling as he did a regrettable flush of irritation creeping over his face, 'there was some trouble concerning that eagle, or am I mistaken?'

Antipas smiled as if he had anticipated his opponent. 'A great trouble! But not for Herod. You see when the priests learned that Herod lay on his deathbed, they chose to strike. The idea was sound enough. They understood Herod's successor to Judaea, my half-brother Archaelaus, must respond, but they gambled that the response would be measured, both because the protest had not occurred directly against him and because he might not yet feel secure in his power. Certain of the priests therefore arranged for two athletic young men to be lowered by ropes from the rooftop of the Temple while their companions occupied the attention of Herod's palace guard. It was quick work, the destruction of that eagle. By the time the troops arrived at the gate it was ruined.

'My father was in such a fury he came from his deathbed and met the criminals in his great hall. He wanted to know if these young men had no fear of him. They answered that their teachers had explained to them that God would grant them eternal life for the service of defending His Temple. Applying torture, Herod learned the names of these teachers and subsequently ordered the students tied to their teachers, that he might burn them simultaneously and so let them partake of the glories of Heaven together. He then ordered the first born of Judaea under a certain age to be caught and killed, for there was a rumour about that a maid had given birth to the Messiah, and he wanted to protect his line. When that was finished, when the streets were washed with blood I should say, he returned to his bed and died peacefully.'

'Do the Jews then believe in life after death – just as the Romans and Greeks do?' Procula asked. Perhaps, Pilate thought, she did not understand the insult Antipas had delivered. It didn't matter really. Antipas rankled at the irrelevance of her remark and lost some of his satisfaction.

Herodias smiled at the unconscious effect of the question and answered her. 'The Essenes believe in it as do the Zealots, who are not of any order but unite merely in the service of anarchy. The Pharisees remain ambiguous on the matter, Lady, as on all matters save the Law, while the Sadducees, whose families rule the Temple and own most of the businesses in the city, hold that this life is all that we have.'

'One might as well be an atheist,' Pilate answered, feeling some outrage at the notion of priests holding such a secular opinion. He knew atheists in Rome, but was himself an initiate of the ancient Eleusinian Mysteries, and therefore trusted that his eternal bliss after death was already arranged.

Antipas warmed to this new subject immediately. 'In my experience, Prefect, atheists make the best priests.'

'Are you then an atheist yourself?' Procula asked.

Herodias, perhaps observing the discomfort of her guests, or simply taking the opportunity of their discomfort, chided her husband gently with the answer she gave for him. 'My husband is an atheist only late at night when the gods sleep and he has drunk himself into oblivion. During the daytime and the early evening hours he honours every superstition known to humankind and even invents a few of his own. Otherwise, it seems to me, he would already have shown the courage of his convictions by arresting the prophet John for his open sedition.'

'The one they call the Baptist?' Procula asked.

'The very same. It is not as if he is difficult to find.

The man stands in the river Jordon every day at the same time and place.'

'I believe more Jews should follow his example,' Pilate quipped. 'I for one cannot understand their aversion to bathing.'

'Do you want to know why he hesitates?' Herodias pressed, quite ignoring Pilate's joke.

'Silence!' Antipas roared.

The chatter in the hall ceased. As Herodias well knew, Antipas had intended his command for only his wife, but she pretended he had silenced the crowd so they could hear her speech, and continued in a fashion that no Roman wife would have dared. 'It is because he fears the man will place a spell upon him if he does. Now I ask you, can an atheist fear the curse of a holy man? Have you ever heard such a thing?'

'I fear no such thing! John is simply more dangerous as a martyr than he is wandering around in the desert like a fool.'

'Your father had no such scruples.'

'The times are different.'

'As are the men.' Seeing her husband had no response to this, Herodias smiled pleasantly at Procula. 'Antipas believes your husband brought himself trouble with the Jews when he refused to kill ten thousand of them. Isn't it so, Antipas?'

'I believe an opportunity was missed to set an example, but each man rules differently and for different ends, as I have said.'

Pilate reached for his wine cup, reminding himself that he was a guest this evening and that this man, no matter how overbearing his insult, enjoyed some kind of friendship with Tiberius. 'I was prepared for disobedience,' he answered, quoting his own letter to Sejanus, which he wrote the morning after the affair. 'Receiving none, nothing at all beyond prayers to their god that I might change my mind, I chose to reward those individuals who petitioned mc in a perfectly legal manner rather than set an example of brutality. The difference between East and West, I suppose.'

'Do you mean to say, Prefect,' Herodias responded with a coyness Pilate found quite pleasant, all things considered, 'you did not fear the ghosts of ten thousand men?'

Pilate permitted himself a slight smile at his host's expense. He liked this woman far better than her husband! 'I confess, Lady, the thought did not cross my mind.'

The insult Herod Antipas delivered to him at the banquet stayed with Pilate much longer than it should have. Pilate tried to persuade himself that he was comfortable with his decision to show mercy. It angered him inordinately that Antipas, and certainly others, observed not his reasonableness but mistook it for an unwillingness to rule from a position of strength. He reminded himself what was obvious, that Antipas was insignificant, that Antipas was both brutal as an administrator and cowardly as a man. What mattered was the opinion of Tiberius, not the court gossip of a backwater tetrarchy run by a woman in all but name.

The emperor's opinion was waiting when he returned. Tiberius himself had sent the letter – not Sejanus. Pilate had not been sent to Judaea, he said, to create a war. He had been sent to maintain the peace and collect taxes. Agitating a hostile city made his work more difficult. On the other hand, having stirred resistance the emperor could not celebrate Pilate's choice to stand down without so much as a single arrest. The emperor regretted, he said, the unusual slowness of his response, but he had taken some effort to acquire an objective view before making his judgment.

The objective view was undoubtedly that of Antipas, Pilate decided after due consideration. Royalty must stick together despite whatever differences they held. In this instance it meant slapping down an equestrian. Well, it illustrated the importance of Antipas, if nothing else.

'Did you enjoy the company of Herodias?' Pilate asked his wife that evening as they dined alone in their quarters.

'I found her impertinent, sir. I would not speak to you in private as she spoke to her husband before us. I do not see how Antipas can stand it.'

'I should like it very much if the two of you became friends.'

Procula studied him from her reclining position at their dinning table.

'She may learn good manners from you,' he said with a smile. 'In turn, you may discover a great many things of interest.'

'I am not sure what you want, sir.'

'One imagines Antipas is a coward at heart – like his brother Philip. Herodias, on the other hand, is not. If she sees an advantage, I believe she will take it.'

'My friendship?' Procula asked.

'It will cost you only the trouble of visiting her should she respond to your desire to learn about her country and the local language. I will send Cornelius and a century of men to escort you, so you need not worry for your safety.'

'Am I simply to become this woman's friend or is there something more you desire?'

'What Antipas tells Caesar about us is what he believes, Procula. So long as Antipas sees our purpose as essentially opposed to his own I am diminished. If, on the other hand, he perceives a friendship between you and Herodias and Herodias herself campaigns actively with her husband to see us more favourably, our appointment here will be the beginning of an illustrious career, not the end of a modest one. What I want from you is nothing beyond a genuine affection for a woman who can be of service to our interests.'

'Then I will write to her at once.'

Tiberias on the Sea of Galilee
Fall AD 26.

Procula's second visit to the court of Herod Antipas occurred in the city of Tiberias in the province of Galilee and lasted nearly two months. It occurred after an exchange of letters in which Procula expressed an interest in learning something of the language and culture of the Jews.

Herodias appeared sceptical at the beginning, as if she read all too clearly Pilate's motives, but when she discovered in Procula a young woman more eager to learn from her than to spy, she gradually set aside her suspicions, or perhaps, Procula realised, accepted them and looked for her own advantage in the friendship.

It was Herodias's opinion that nothing should ever be said within the palace that one did not want others to share with Antipas. She therefore suggested carriage rides followed by walks. On such occasions, Antipas's soldiers and Cornelius's guard would withdraw to a discreet distance allowing free and frank exchanges between the women – the only ones they dared.

'Here,' Herodias gestured happily toward the countryside one afternoon, a week or so after Procula's arrival, 'we can speak as freely as trust in our friendship allows.'

'I hope that means as freely as possible,' Procula answered.

Herodias considered the younger woman thought-fully. By this point she knew a good deal about Procula's background, her life in Syria in the court of Germanicus, interrupted at his death, her return to Rome and subsequent marriage to Pilate at the age of fourteen.

'As we are speaking freely, perhaps you can tell me how the daughter of a senator and ward of a Prince came to marry an equestrian of no great distinction?'

'The emperor,' Procula answered as truthfully as she could, 'knew that I was in love. As the marriage was not against his own interests he allowed it.'

'In love! With Pilate?' Herodias laughed. She saw the plump, overbearing middle-aged bureaucrat and found Procula's statement improbable, but Herodias had not seen Pontius Pilate as she had – sitting on a black horse, a trim young tribune wearing the dashing black uniform of the palace guard.

'Pilate escorted the funeral procession of Germanicus from Brindisium to Rome – a journey of some thirty days.'

'And you became lovers along the way?'

'We never spoke.' Procula blushed suddenly, for those days were the most precious of her life, and she had never told anyone about them. 'Pilate managed to ride by my carriage each day, and we would look at each other. Once, he said to me, 'It is a long journey, is it not?' I was so excited I could not even answer him.'

'Are you still in love with him?'

'I still honour him, Lady.'

Herodias looked at the sky with a thoughtful expression. 'You are too pleasant to the man. If I may say so, I think he will notice you when he fears your anger or, better still, imagines you are willing to enjoy another man's interest. Beauty like yours is wasted if not employed to advantage. You could have any man in the empire with your family and beauty, and Pilate knows it. He only needs reminding now and then and he will behave himself!'

'You would have me become a shrew or a whore with such advice.'

'Tell me,' Herodias remarked, 'does he make an open show of his affairs or is he reasonably discreet about them?'

'Pilate is true to me.'

'You lie very badly, Procula.'

Some evenings after his dinner with businessmen in the

city, men he did not need to spoil with excessive attention, Antipas would summon Herodias and Procula to his cabinet, where he drank copiously and asked Procula about Rome. When he discovered a woman of some intellect and an appealingly straightforward manner, he pressed for her opinion of the political climate in Rome.

In particular he was interested in Sejanus, the prefect of the palace guard and virtual regent of Tiberius. Sejanus had taken control of the palace guard shortly after Tiberius ascended the throne. While others in Rome lost Tiberius's confidence through doubtful judgment or wavering loyalty, Sejanus, though still a very young man, had managed to turn Tiberius's trust into something very much like devotion.

'Sejanus is ambitious to a fault,' Procula explained, 'but politically talented.' The truth was Procula feared Sejanus more than any man in the empire. If he were to seize power from Tiberius, which was a very real possibility, she knew he would almost surely eliminate the last of the Claudii family, lest they mount a civil war against him.

'Everyone says it of him,' Antipas answered, 'and yet Tiberius continues to entrust him with new powers and titles!'

'Tiberius is tired of politics and perhaps tired of Rome as well.'

'One hardly knows which of the two one ought to flatter,' Antipas grumbled.

'Sejanus is too careful to boast,' Procula observed, 'but he anticipates the throne. That much is clear. By the same token Tiberius is too clever to name him as his successor.

That would leave him vulnerable to assassination. So long as he keeps the hope of legitimacy hanging before Sejanus he maintains the prefect's loyalty.'

'Do you think he could move against Tiberius, if he were . . . disappointed in Tiberius's choice of an heir?'

'Almost certainly.'

'Could Tiberius resist him?'

'That is the question everyone asks. Tiberius still has friends in the army, though by now they are the sons of the men he commanded. Sejanus, on the other hand, has no influence with the legions. Why should he have? He rarely leaves Rome.'

'There is no reason for it,' Herodias remarked. 'All the wars are finished!'

'A war would strengthen Sejanus,' Procula answered without thinking, and saw her mistake at once. Herodias's eyes flashed, for it had not occurred to her that Sejanus desperately needed the popular and military support that a great military victory and hero's welcome into Rome would afford him.

'It is a wonder Tiberius does not abdicate his throne and let Sejanus have the empire in name, as well as fact,' Antipas offered simply, for he had drunk a great deal that evening and was not thinking clearly.

'Gods die, Tetrarch. They do not retire. Tiberius lives only so long as he sits upon his throne, not one day longer.'

Procula found her evenings with Antipas and Herodias enjoyable because the tetrarch and his wife took her seriously. They valued not only what she knew but her judgment as well.

Other evenings were not so pleasant. Antipas would grumble about matters of history, specifically the ruin his brother had brought the Herodians. Inevitably he drank too much too fast and would demand his pleasure. What the tetrarch demanded those in his company must endure. That meant Salome would be summoned to dance.

One afternoon in the hills above Galilee Procula asked Herodias about it. 'Does it bother you when Salome must dance for the tetrarch?'

'Antipas married me because it was the only way he could be close to my daughter. I have simply worked it to my advantage.'

'Does Antipas sleep with her?'

'It is my daughter's business to make sure he believes he will have the chance sometime soon, mine to see that it does not happen, at least until I have all that I want. Rather the way Tiberius manages Sejanus, I suppose, only what Sejanus lusts for is the imperial throne, not a twelve-year-old girl.'

'And what is it you want?'

'What Rome will never give Antipas: the old kingdom of Herod. Do not look at me as if I am deluded. I know I must give Salome to one of her cousins and that the kingdom will be theirs in name to rule, but it will be mine all the same – or could be.'

'I do not think you are deluded. It is only that Tiberius will not risk any change in his policies.'

Herodias smiled prettily. 'Nor will he live forever – god though he is.'

Zürich
October 8, 2006.

According to everything Ethan had read about the man, and the online material about him was extensive, Jonas Starr was a lunatic, albeit a lunatic with money. The real fortune, however, belonged to Nicole North, Starr's niece by marriage and his successor at NorthStarr Institute.

During the negotiations for the sale of the painting neither Kate nor Ethan had spoken with the buyers. Kate's father, Roland Wheeler, had always handled the sale of their acquisitions. Roland took a third of the profit but for that he handled everything. He found the buyers. He created the cover story. Frequently, he even found the paintings he wanted them to acquire. This project had been different from the start. Ethan had found the painting on his own, using a combination of dumb luck, research and guesswork. There were no guarantees going in. To his knowledge no one had reported seeing Pilate's Portrait of Christ since 1900. Even the reference in 1900 was dubious, very possibly a dying man's last jest, but the more he had discovered about Julian Corbeau, the more Ethan became convinced Corbeau possessed the legendary painting. Before 1900, the only direct reference to it occurred in the second century writings of the theologian Irenaeus.

Kate and Ethan had approached Roland before the break-in to ask if he could find a buyer, assuming they could acquire the portrait. A few weeks later Roland told them he had a perfect fit. That was Roland's speciality. He had contacts in Europe, Asia, the Middle

East, South Africa and North America: collectors of art, artefacts, and manuscripts who were not very particular about legalities. He did the necessary research, and in this case was satisfied that the potential buyers would step up with a small fortune in order to possess in his terminology 'the mother of all icons.'

He was so confident in fact that, once Kate and Ethan had acquired it, he approached Starr directly at his home in Texas with a one-time offer of twenty-five million dollars. The oldest extant panel portrait of Jesus was a sixth century icon, the type of which was called Christ *Pantocrator*. This particular copy of the icon had resided in the monastery of St. Catherine on Mount Sinai in Egypt since its creation, a gift of the emperor Justinian at the inauguration of the monastery in AD 525.

With a painting almost five hundred years older and utterly unique, the enormous price tag was justified, even if its owners could never show it in public. Jonas Starr, knowing he could examine the piece before he made a final commitment, had pretended to accept Roland's narrative of the painting's history, perhaps fearing Roland would shop for a buyer elsewhere if he seemed too particular about its immediate past. Now, with the deal to be closed within twenty-four hours, he had questions.

In Roland's version, his associate had discovered the possible existence of the painting and approached the owner, who had imagined quite naively it was a piece from the Renaissance. Once they had used radio-carbon dating at the University of Zürich, he said, the owner had decided 'to trade it for something he cared about – cold, hard cash.' Whether Roland had promised Jonas Starr he could talk to Ethan at the time of the negotiations or whether, as Roland had told Kate, Starr had come forward with his request only recently, Ethan could not say. Roland handled Kate and Ethan as he did the rest of the world. He told them what they needed to know.

So Ethan appeared at the luxurious Savoy Hotel on the Bahnhofstrasse at eight o'clock Sunday evening. He was dressed casually in a leather jacket, jeans, and a flannel shirt. He had seen photographs of Nicole North, but there was still a moment of reckoning when she opened the door to her spacious suite. Dr North was an incredibly beautiful woman. Tall and slender with full breasts and a perfectly developed if somewhat lush physique, she had the sort of confidence that comes from growing up in the presence of great wealth.

It was not merely that others had taken care of her and would until the end of her days. It was also an understanding that between her wealth and beauty people found her fascinating no matter how she behaved. Despite that, by all accounts, she was a tireless worker, a friend to people in need, and a benefactor of worthy causes – the last person in the world Ethan would have expected to see mixed up in business like this. But here she was, playing the good niece to an old bandit.

What Ethan liked most about the woman was her voice. It had a touch of the South in it, and reminded him of his childhood in Tennessee, though the South of his youth was very different from Nicole North's genteel upbringing. She apparently expected Roland's associate to be a scholarly gentlemen and mistook Ethan for security, but then recovered nicely after the introductions. In fact, Dr North's eyes had a sudden and irresistible intensity when she understood that she was talking to the man who had discovered a painting that was believed lost for nineteen hundred years.

'May I mix you a drink? I have ... everything, I think.' She walked uncertainly toward her bar. 'We just got in a few hours ago. To tell you the truth, I'm not sure if it's morning or evening.'

'I'm fine, thank you.'

Jonas Starr entered as if on cue. He would like a drink, he said. According to his calculations it was one o'clock in the afternoon, Texas-time, but then Texas was a long way away! Starr was in his mid-seventies, with a full head of white hair and the kind of energy that is difficult to contain in small spaces. He was a thin man with a long nose and small bright eyes. His voice screeched with enthusiasm.

He was born to the working-class and obviously proud of it. Fifty years of wealth had not kicked it out of him either. In fact, those years had hardly made a dent. There was no mistaking Jonas Starr for a common man, however. He was an intellectual without the pretensions that so often accompany a person who lives for ideas.

The moment he stepped into the room and shook Ethan's hand Starr was on the attack. 'Roland tells me your painting was a part of the treasury of the Templars. I have to tell you, I almost passed on it for that very reason. I'm not a fan of the Templars, young man. In my book they were an overrated bunch of bankers with great public relations and not a shred of piety!'

Ethan smiled at the reference to banking. In the vast tradition associated with the Knights Templar it was easy to overlook their importance as the inventors of the modern banking system. In an age when land was the equivalent of money and generally the primary source of income, Crusaders had tremendous difficulties executing the simplest financial arrangements. Circumventing the laws against usury, the Templars developed a method whereby they would advance money to travellers in exchange for promissory notes secured with property in Europe. Prohibited from charging interest for these loans, the Templars provided their service out of Christian goodwill, asking only an administrative fee.

It was a game of semantics, fee instead of interest, but a clever one, and for nearly two hundred years, through the entire life of the Order, the Templars became the indispensable agents of commerce and travel. It was a system that made them not only wealthy but eventually – to their doom – the envy of kings.

'They were extraordinary bankers, Dr Starr, but by all accounts they were also the keepers of the Holy Grail.'

'King Baldwin the First carried the True Cross into every major battle after his defeat at Ramleh, just as every one of his successors did until it was lost to the army of Saladin in 1187. The Lance of Longinus inspired an exhausted and nearly defeated army to break out of Antioch and charge down on Jerusalem. Those relics were real, young man! Men and women of

every nationality and faith saw them and many eye-
witness accounts describe their effects on the Christian
and Moslem armies. Read the accounts yourself!'

'I have.'

'Well, then, you should have read that the notion that
they were the keepers of the Grail – whatever it was
supposed to be – is nothing more than a poetic fancy
that first appeared after the Crusaders lost Jerusalem.
Do you know why that is? It's because they needed the
PR! They wanted the financial support in Europe to
win Jerusalem back. The only Holy Grail the Templars
ever guarded was their bank vault! As soldiers they
were more foolhardy than brave, and if any of the
charges against them have even a grain of truth, they
did not deserve to wear the cross of Christ on their
tunics. The fascination with them is entirely out of pro-
portion to what they accomplished. I have my quarrels
with the Roman Catholic Church, but I'll tell you this
much: when the Pope shut down that outfit he did a
good thing!'

'I assume you've read about the head the Templars
allegedly worshipped?' Ethan asked.

'Baphomet,' Nicole North said with a touch of well-
schooled distaste.

'It was supposed to be the head of a devil,' Starr
chimed in agreeably. 'If it even existed!'

'Interesting, don't you think, that the Templars
would worship a head and not the Holy Grail – the relic
they were supposed to be guarding?'

'My argument exactly! There was nothing to guard.'

'I think the Grail and Baphomet are one and the
same.'

'That's ridiculous!'

'The curious thing about Baphomet is that, like the Grail, there was no consensus of opinion about what it was. Some said it was a rock. Some Templars told inquisitors it was a human skull. Others said it was a mummified head. Still others called it an image. The truth, I suspect, is that very few of the Knights Templar ever actually saw it more than once – and that during their initiation. If my guess is right, they would have encountered it then under the influence of hallucinogens. The point is Baphomet – the father of all wisdom – was an object worthy of their adoration. Those who belonged to command positions probably knew why. The grandmaster certainly did: it was not simply a painting of Christ, it was the True Image – painted in the lifetime of Jesus of Nazareth inside Herod's Palace at the command of Pontius Pilate.'

'Why not call it that?'

'My guess would be to keep the secret from the outside world.'

'You have any proof?'

'I had a document stating as much, but I had no proof until I was able to trace the painting to the Arsenal Library in Paris.'

'The Templar artefacts went to the Vatican, son!'

'Napoleon brought them to Paris after he tossed the Pope in prison.'

Starr eyed Brand curiously. It seemed he was not accustomed to being corrected.

'The other relics of the Crusades were made public. Why not the Holy Face?' Nicole North asked.

'The answer is in Scripture, Dr North. "Blessed are

the pure of heart, for they shall see in the face of God." '

Nicole North did not answer, but her mouth opened as she uttered an involuntary gasp. Her expression had suddenly lost all trace of scepticism.

'According to the Grail legends, whoever seeks the Holy Grail must have a pure heart. Without it, he will never find it. That was the requirement for every knight who joined the Order of the Poor Knights of Jesus Christ and the Temple of Solomon. They surrendered their personal wealth to the Order and renounced all worldly pleasures. Having met those requirements, the initiate would then be allowed to wear the cross of Christ and, if my theory is correct, see the face of God.'

'How did they get hold of the thing in the first place?' Starr asked.

'Baldwin had it by the time he was elected the first king of Christian Jerusalem.'

'You say that like it's a fact.'

'Baldwin came to Jerusalem by way of Edessa, Dr Starr.'

Jonas Starr's eyes lit up.

Ethan nodded. 'There are three distinct legends placing the Holy Face in the city of Edessa, all of them pre-dating its discovery inside the city wall.'

'Eusebius,' Starr answered, nodding. 'He calls it a painting made by no human hand and tells us Paul sent it to Edessa.'

'When you see the quality of workmanship, you'll understand why they believed it was created by no human hand.'

'The Holy Face of Edessa was taken to Constantinople in 900,' North interjected, 'two

hundred years before Baldwin. That same face disappeared in 1204, when the Crusaders sacked
Constantinople – a century after Baldwin's death.'

'You're talking about an image that appeared
on a piece of cloth – the legend that Jesus touched
his face to it and sent it to the king to heal him of
leprosy.'

'You don't think it's the same?'

'I think it's possible the cloth was a copy.'

'How did Baldwin find it?' North asked.

'Baldwin's Armenian friend, who directed him to
Edessa, must have known about the legend – maybe
told him the image in Constantinople was really only a
copy, that the king had the original somewhere in the
palace. I'm certain that after the death of King Thoros,
Baldwin would have had the power to search the palace
for it without asking anyone's permission.'

'And you think Baldwin gave it to the Knights
Templar?'

'The Templars organized in 1118, the year Baldwin
died, but everyone agrees the Templars were active
under the name of the Soldiers of Christ for at least a
decade before that. I think Baldwin organized them
expressly for the purpose of guarding his relic – which
makes him the model for the Fisher King of the Grail
legends.'

'The Fisher King is a myth,' Jonas Starr grumbled.

'Like most myths of heroes it was built from fact,'
Ethan responded. 'As you well know, the legendary
Fisher King was an old man who was incapable of
walking because of a wound he had received – according to some versions of the story – in the groin. That is

exactly what happened to Baldwin during the last year of his life, the same year the Order was officially founded. The Fisher King ruled in a far-away place that very few knights could even find. He was a recluse, he had a brother whose death came at the hands of his enemies, and he was exceedingly mysterious about what he possessed – refusing to name it. All of which fits perfectly with the information we have on Baldwin.'

'So how did you get your hands on the thing?' Starr queried, suddenly excited by the notion.

'Roland told you that.'

'Roland told me a story! I want the truth.'

'I've told you everything I can, sir. You understand, I think, this painting is not something you can display in your museum.'

Jonas Starr considered the matter quietly. Finally, he turned to his niece. 'Nicole, honey, how about you get me a fresh drink?'

As North walked across the room, Ethan's eyes inevitably studied her figure. It was all Starr needed. He pulled a compact pistol with a silencer attached from under his jacket and aimed it at Ethan's heart. 'For twenty-five million, son, I want the truth, the whole truth, and nothing but!'

'Do you want the painting or the truth, Dr Starr?'

'I'll take both, and if you're quick about it, I'll even let you walk out of here on two good legs!' He pointed the weapon at Ethan's knee.

Ethan looked up at Nicole North. She was watching him with the cold-blooded indifference of a pit bull. 'We need to know the name of the person you stole it from,' she said. 'The painting has no value to us without that information.'

'Why?'

'That's not your concern!' Starr screeched.

'Are you planning on eliminating your problem?'

'Answer the question, son, while you can still walk.'

'I stole the painting from a man named Julian Corbeau.'

'The American fugitive?' Nicole responded incredulously. 'The man is an avowed Satanist!'

'He is also someone who will go to any length to recover his property if he finds out you have it, and I'm under the impression he won't bother with the courts.'

'I don't understand his interest in a painting of Christ?' North pressed.

She did not fear Corbeau. What bothered her was that a sacred relic had been in the possession of a perfect devil.

'Sacred objects, Dr North, are believed to have special powers. For the faithful, that means healing, miracles, visions, inspiration. For people involved in the occult, like Julian Corbeau, religious objects can be used as a medium through which a master magician, or magus, contacts the spirit world – or at least pretends to. The holy object supposedly channels the energy and functions as a doorway between the material and spiritual worlds. The more holy the object, if you can quantify such a thing, the more potent the magic.'

'That's obscene,' North answered icily.

'I don't expect Corbeau is the first to use the painting in that way. I think the Templars involved it in ceremonies involving necromancy, perhaps even infanticide. Their corruption is too well documented to believe the charges against them were purely the fabrication of the King of France. From their humble beginnings as knights without property or fortunes, the Templars became the epitome of arrogance, their name synonymous with hypocrisy. They made an open display of defying their Order's constitution, and they were notoriously fascinated with the occult. Baphomet seems to be at the centre of it. Of course the priests who were searching for Baphomet on that infamous Friday the thirteenth in October of 1307 were looking for the face a devil – so they missed it – and the painting of Christ wearing a crown of thorns got packed away with all of the other objects of ritual and was eventually shipped to the Vatican.'

Jonas Starr holstered his revolver. 'Well, we'll put an end to this business with the occult, I promise you! Once we have it, only the people who love God are going to see this painting!'

'That's how the Templars started.'

'Well . . . we're not Templars!' Starr stood up and extended his hand by way of apology. 'No hard feelings about the rough stuff, I hope!'

'You still want the painting?'

'We have an appointment with Roland to look at it tomorrow morning at the bank,' Starr answered, dropping his hand when Ethan refused to take it. 'Assuming it's all Roland and you say it is, I guarantee you we want it!'

Ethan nodded and started for the door. 'Just one more thing, Dr Starr.' He looked at the old man without emotion. 'Don't think you can pull a gun on me twice.'

Jonas Starr's smile cooled, but his eyes stayed locked on Ethan. 'I'll keep that in mind, Mr Brand. I certainly will.'

Malloy called Gwen Sunday evening – her afternoon. She was painting, she told him, a self-portrait she didn't think he would care for. Too abstract. They talked about it, and it sounded interesting. When she asked about Zürich and if he had seen any old girlfriends, he was tempted to mention the contessa but resisted the impulse. He said he saw no one but silver-haired bankers.

On Monday Malloy spent the day dropping in on friends, catching up on private lives and gauging their willingness to resume contact. He tried Gwen late in the evening, but missed her. It was Monday afternoon in New York and there were a dozen good reasons why her cell phone was inactive. Still he could not help worrying about her.

He found Marcus Steiner after eleven o'clock that evening at the James Joyce Pub and sat down for a report on Nicole North's arrival in Switzerland. Marcus did not disappoint him.

'Dr North showed up yesterday in the company of a man named Dr Jonas Starr.' Malloy nodded thoughtfully. He had not expected Starr, but it didn't surprise him. Starr's expertise and experience would be useful. 'They checked into a suite at the Savoy, and had one visitor yesterday evening, a bookstore owner here in town named Ethan Brand.'

'What do you have on – Brand Books, right?'

Marcus nodded and took a sip of beer. 'The shop

has been around a few years. Brand has no record.'

'I know him. I used to stop in there sometimes. He's a sharp guy. A freak for medieval stuff. He told me one time he had a scholarship to Notre Dame. He was going to become a priest, but after he got there he found out about women.'

'He spent about twenty minutes with North and Starr, walked across town, downed four shots of Johnnie Walker Red, and went back to his apartment. You want me to keep watching him?'

'I guess not, but I'd sure like to know what he was doing with my people.'

'I can't help you, but your people went to the bank this morning. Roland Wheeler was already there. After about forty minutes Starr and North took a taxi to the university. This was around lunchtime.'

'What's at the university?'

'I was curious about that myself. We did a follow-up and found out they had an appointment to see the director of the radiocarbon laboratory.'

'They're dating the panel.'

'I dropped by later and flashed my badge. The director told me they had a chip of wood that was not the size of a nail clipping that they wanted him to test. The process doesn't take too long, and for a fee they will waive the standard four to six month waiting period.'

'Did you get an age?'

'Plus-or-minus forty years, he estimated the tree was chopped down in the middle of the first century.'

Malloy stared at his friend as if he hadn't understood.

'First century, Thomas.'

'They told me it was from the twelfth century.'

'They lied.'

'A first century portrait of Christ . . . I'm guessing there aren't too many of those around.' The price tag was beginning to make some sense now.

Marcus smiled. 'Hasan could find a buyer for us in Russia – ten, fifteen, twenty million? Who knows?' Hasan Barzani was the crime lord whose career they had both spent a great deal of time and effort developing. 'We stage a little incident, and presto, the thing just disappears!'

'I recall a lecture you gave me a few years ago about Swiss mercenaries. Once they sold their services, they never went over to the other side for a higher price.'

'It was a matter of national pride for five centuries, Thomas. We sold ourselves to the highest bidder, yes, but we gave good value. There is not a single example in the entire Chronicles of European history where a Swiss mercenary betrayed his employer. It's something in the DNA, I think.'

'So you would be the first?'

'Thomas! I would never do something like that. *You're* the one who cut the deal with these people. You can do anything you want. You're an American. You have no tradition! Me, I hired on to work for you. Tell me what you want, and I'll take care of it. You want the painting to disappear in Russia, it disappears! You want it to go to New York, I make sure it gets there.'

'Stealing a painting of Jesus is like dipping into the collection plate at church.'

Marcus shrugged indifferently. 'It happens.'

'It doesn't happen tomorrow.'

'You spent too much time in Switzerland as a young man. I think it rubbed off on you.' Marcus seemed vaguely disappointed, nothing more.

'Are we set for tomorrow?'

'I'll have two people across the river on one of the rooftops. If anything unexpected happens outside the bank, they're instructed to take care of it without consulting me.'

'Rubber bullets?'

Marcus nodded. 'Live ammunition for backup.'

'I'm going to need someone on the train with me . . . and a vest.'

Marcus seemed curious at this change in the plan, but he didn't say anything about it. 'I have just the guy, but he is pricy.'

'He worth it?'

'Let us hope you don't have to find out.'

Malloy passed another stack of bills under the table.

Marcus took the money without counting it. 'Someone will drop a vest off at the hotel before you go to the bank. Anything else?'

Malloy hesitated. He wasn't sure he wanted to bring this up, but it had been nagging him since his meeting with the contessa. 'You think I've lost my edge?'

Marcus gave a casual shrug of his thin shoulders. He kept his gaze locked on the room. 'People get older.'

'You're not answering my question.'

'I don't think it matters tomorrow. It's not like we're going to kill someone or steal the Mona Lisa. I mean, we're moving a piece of wood across town!'

'I got a tip. I don't know how good it is, but I

think there could be trouble – quite a bit of it, actually.'

'We can change the plan if you want.'

Malloy had considered it. It would be easy enough to disappear once he left the bank and then show up in New York, the painting carried by one of Marcus's people, but Whitefield's diplomatic pouch was a one hundred per-cent play against chance discovery by the customs authorities in both Zürich and New York. No other plan gave him that kind of protection.

'Let's stay with the plan, but we keep our heads up.'

Chapter Six

Jerusalem
Winter AD 26-27.

Jerusalem was nothing like Caesarea. Caesarea was a modern city born of imperial power. Jerusalem was inestimably old. Only the great Temple of Solomon, the tower of Antonia, and the palace of Herod were essentially modern. Beyond this small precinct of Judaeo-Roman architecture there was little of note for a foreigner to enjoy. Even the great structures Herod had refurbished in the Roman style lacked all manner of sculpture, so did not seem Roman at all. Arches and columns, acanthus leaves, ionic scrolls, Corinthian medallions, none of it was really Roman without the images of gods to finish the effect. Nor could the celebrated opulence of the East offer anything by way of recompense.

After a time, a sense of emptiness, one might almost say sterility, began to wear away at Pilate. He was expected to spend his winter in this dense, stinking, unwelcoming city, but he was ready to leave after only a few days. He was too good a soldier of course to complain or announce a sudden change of plans for the sake of his or his wife's comfort. So he endured.

There was one moment of amusement for him during that first long winter, a piece of accidental humour on the part of his wife. They had hardly settled in the great palace and were staring down upon the Temple across the great plaza when Procula announced in all innocence that she would love to go inside and have a look about. Could he arrange a tour for her? 'With three or four centuries of soldiers, I suppose,' Pilate answered, 'though I doubt we would ever get out alive.' At her look of confusion, he added, 'We are not welcome beyond the Court of the Gentiles, Procula. The Jews believe a well-bathed Roman might pollute the air and thus offend their God.'

It was not the last time they spoke of the culture of the Jews, of course. In Jerusalem one could not escape it. One saw them every day as they gathered before the Temple, conspiring possibly, worshipping perhaps, running their business inevitably. Soldiers stationed inside the city wore special armour lacking all human and animal insignia. Cohorts kept their standards covered and stored in the great armoury above the city on the mountain of Masada. Even the coins Pilate minted were peculiar in all the empire. There were no animals, no human bodies or faces, only pieces of grain for decoration. The Romans conformed so much it seemed Jerusalem ruled Rome and not the other way around.

'Do you like them, sir?'

'It is not my business to like them,' he answered his wife with stately indifference. 'It is my business to govern and to tax.' The truth was Pilate hated them. He felt as if his first encounter over the matter of the *imago* standard had left him looking impotent and foolish and, without really understanding the impulse, he anticipated the next protest as gladiators finally learn to anticipate the arena. It came sooner than he imagined. Without realizing it, Pilate set the thing in motion. It was, even in retrospect, an innocent mistake: unforeseeable to any reasonable person. Like many great catastrophes it began with a new friendship.

Nicodemus was known to all, Roman, Jew, Egyptian, and Syrian, as the wealthiest man in Judaea. He appeared one morning shortly after Pilate had settled into Herod's palace, and begged the favour of meeting the new prefect. Like others of his social status, Nicodemus had made his peace with the Romans when Herod's eldest son, Archaelaus, had very nearly destroyed Jerusalem through his incompetence. He was now an old man with a son, also named Nicodemus, a few years younger than Pilate. Father and son came together.

Nicodemus had sent servants to request an audience with a precious gift for the prefect's wife, a beautiful ruby pendant on a gold chain. As soon as Pilate saw it, he knew what kind of man he was dealing with and set aside his entire morning for the privilege of a meeting. Additionally, he arranged an honour guard within the great hall to greet Nicodemus and his son. Nicodemus took the assembled guard as his due but was wise enough to add to his gifts, offering with many apologies for its flaws an extraordinary cameo ring for Pilate's wife that featured a man and woman holding hands in silhouette. For Pilate he had 'four children of Solomon' waiting in the courtyard.

At Pilate's look of confusion Nicodemus explained that according to legend the ancient king of the Jews destroyed all of the horses in his kingdom, keeping only four mares, from which he intended to breed a race of horses like no other in the world – a desert animal, as tough as a camel, as quick as a gazelle and nearly as smart as the man who rode him! 'So quite naturally we call them the Children of Solomon. Would you care, Excellency, to see the four I have chosen for you?'

'They are truly magnificent!' Pilate exclaimed, as he admired the animals. Their heads were small and fine, the eyes bright and large, the tail high, the legs thin, the temperament fiery – four grey stallions, their thick manes braided with fine-spun gold laced with teardrops of pearls. 'But you must tell me what I can I do for you that is worth a gift of such magnitude?' he added after a moment of mesmerized admiration.

Nicodemus answered with a diplomat's skill: 'I ask nothing but your friendship, if such a thing is not asking too much.'

Nicodemus entertained Pilate and several other dignitaries at his farm on a number of occasions following that afternoon, sometimes letting the banquets carry on for days – Roman style. He did not cease with giving jewellery, always handed to the husband but with a polite mention of Claudia Procula's name. Along with his eldest son, Nicodemus took Pilate on long rides to show him the extent of his property. At times, he would even venture to advise Pilate as how best to govern Jerusalem, if he wished to avoid conflict.

Simple, really. Pilate, he said, needed to understand that he may have replaced the old priest of the Temple with Caiaphas, but Caiaphas had since married one of Annas's daughters, so he was now a son-in-law. 'As such, Caiaphas commands Jerusalem according to the will of his father-in-law.' The older man smiled at Pilate's consternation. 'Do not imagine,' he added, 'you can appoint another and have anything for your trouble but another marriage. The Roman prefect appoints the priest, but the priest invariably serves the Temple, which belongs to the Sadducees. Keep this thought in mind, as well. When you quarrel with the priests, you quarrel with all of Judaea. When you negotiate successfully with them, then you have negotiated with all of Judaea. Since it will cost you to defy their wishes, it should cost them when you acquiesce. They have the money. They have a great deal, in fact. It is the wise prefect who manages to get them to spend it to his advantage.'

On one of their rides, Nicodemus took Pilate to an arid tract of land and announced that he had acquired it quite recently for a good price. 'Virtually useless most of the year,' Nicodemus observed good-naturedly, 'it is adequate for pasturing goats in early spring. Of course most of them will be killed when the floods come through, but it is a beautiful piece of land otherwise, is it not?'

'Why would you buy such property, Nicodemus?' Pilate asked in astonishment, for it *was* beautiful, as deserts often were, but utterly useless.

Nicodemus' son answered for his father, 'It wants only water to change everything. A spur from the city's aqueduct could be run out here and this land would feed all of Jerusalem with its yield.'

'More than that. If we had water . . .' Nicodemus began wistfully.

Pilate considered the consequences in Rome of such a project. Tiberius was cruel by necessity; parsimonious by nature. Were he to discover that his prefect had diverted imperial tax money for a project such as this, Pilate would be lucky to escape with his life. He was therefore silent, seemingly a man incapable of understanding what was being asked of him.

'Paying for it,' Nicodemus added thoughtfully, as if comprehending his friend's hesitation, 'that is the real problem.'

'There's enough money in the Temple to build twenty aqueducts, Father,' Nicodemus the younger said.

'No question about that, my son,' Nicodemus answered with the same thoughtfulness, 'but getting them to release the funds is another matter entirely.'

'Perhaps I could speak to Caiaphas,' Pilate answered reluctantly. 'Land such as this – it seems a waste not to make it fertile.'

'Caiaphas will resist you unless you give him what he desires, Prefect.'

'And what is that, Nicodemus?'

Nicodemus smiled. 'What all priests desire, Excellency.'

Caiaphas hesitated when Pilate spoke to him, because, he said, he was not sure moncy was available. Pilate answered smoothly, having anticipated the objection. 'And there is one additional problem to consider.' The high priest waited expectantly.

'I would need to depend upon you to keep the peace in Jerusalem, as I would be forced to deploy all of my troops from the city for a year or more. In fact, I doubt I would be able to spend even a week in Jerusalem next year if we were to undertake the project. Of course I would make my soldiers available in case of emergency but otherwise, you would have to assume the entire burden of securing the city.'

Caiaphas was not so disingenuous that his eyes did not glisten at the prospect of ridding Jerusalem of the hated legions and taking credit for it in the process, but he repeated his ritualised hesitation. He must speak to the other priests about the matter. 'Have you an estimate of the necessary costs?'

Pilate presented the estimates. A few days later the gold was delivered into his treasury. That completed, Pilate ordered the majority of his troops out of Jerusalem to begin construction, and departed with the rest for Caesarea, a much wealthier man than when he had left it.

The first sign of trouble came later that spring when a protest erupted spontaneously in front of the empty palace of Herod over the matter of the aqueduct spur. Its shadow, the protestors announced, fell across a Jewish cemetery. Pilate could hardly believe it when he received Caiaphas's report of rioting. Attempting to settle feelings that had undoubtedly got out of hand, Pilate wrote to the priest to say that when the sun had changed its position following the spring equinox, the shadow would undoubtedly change as well. The next letter was more urgent. Rioters had broken into the palace, destroying a great deal of property. The aqueduct, they said, must come down or all of Jerusalem would burn.

Pilate ordered his most trusted cohort from the Fretensis Legion into the city disguised as part of the indigenous population. He likewise ordered his Syrian cavalry into the city in the costume of civilians. Finally, he summoned an honour guard under the command of Cornelius and proceeded to Jerusalem. His letter anticipated his arrival by less than forty-eight hours and promised a meeting with any of the population who wished to discuss the matter of the aqueduct with him. Arriving late in the evening, Pilate found most of the palace uninhabitable, or declared it such at any rate, and arranged to meet with those citizens who were concerned about the construction of the aqueduct in the great square before the Temple.

He sat virtually alone the following morning. His interpreter stood next to him along with two of his personal slaves to keep notes. These men were of course unarmed. Cornelius in full military uniform, supported by a dozen of the prefect's personal guard, stood back several paces from Pilate's rostrum. Pilate wore a toga bordered with a thin purple line, the mark of the equestrian class. His sword and dagger were concealed neatly in the folds. He looked into the crowd for faces of the Jews he had seen before, but he recognized no one. They blurred together into a mass of accusation and anger. Certainly, Judas was no longer a spokesman for the radical element within the city, but that was all he could determine. He thought that strange, since men like Judas did not fade quietly into oblivion, but must burn brightly for their hour of glory and then perish utterly. He had hoped this would prove to be the radical Jew's last protest.

He estimated as many as five thousand, the number well above Caiaphas's initial reports. As the priest had indicated, there was no leader, no apparent plan of action. People simply wanted an otherwise forgotten cemetery protected, though it defied all reason how a shadow across a grave could offend the dead. At Pilate's request Cornelius ordered the crowd to silence and the various spokespeople were asked to come forward as a group to explain to Caesar's prefect of Judaea the nature of the problem and their proposal for a solution.

Nearly a hundred men wanted to speak, though most of these merely volunteered for the privilege of shouting abuse at a Roman. Pilate did not begrudge them the pleasure. To his thinking it rather justified what was to follow. Still, as the shouting began to overwhelm Pilate's interpreter and the crowd pressed closer in its fury, Pilate began to grow wary. It was a late spring morning, already too hot to bear. The sun beat down directly on all of them as Pilate attempted to answer the charges in a reasonable and orderly fashion.

Having spoken his defence, a second verbal assault came, this from a young firebrand not much different from Judas – though neither as handsome nor as eloquent. As he spoke his supporters shouted their approval. In their excitement, they did not notice Pilate's men, dressed as Jews and desert travellers, filtering into their midst. There were two issues involved, the firebrand declared, two solutions necessary. First, the Romans must destroy the aqueduct and build it, if it must be built, over land that was not sanctified for burial using the imperial treasury, not Temple funds. Second, Rome must return the money stolen from the Temple to build the first aqueduct.

Following a great cheer for this speech, Pilate gave his answer. Slowly, but with force, he explained to them the commercial advantages of the aqueduct. Moreover, he added, it was absurd to imagine that he would throw away half-a-year's work because of a cemetery. 'For the love of the gods,' he exclaimed, 'do you hate water so much that you would turn fertile land to desert simply because its shadow falls on some beggar's grave?'

The crowd erupted noisily as Pilate's interpreter repeated his speech. A number of people rushed forward shouting incoherently, for the Jews were very fond of their dead, it seemed. When Cornelius had ordered them to silence, the firebrand told Pilate that beggars and kings slept in the same hallowed ground. 'Those who do not honour the dead,' he concluded, 'defile them!'

'Jerusalem needs water,' Pilate responded with calculated zeal. 'For the sake of the living, the dead are always silent. What do the dead care if a shadow falls across their cemetery? The living must drink. They must wash. They must eat the fruits of the land! For centuries you have been living in a desert. With Roman technology you find yourselves with all the water you need. We have turned a wilderness into a garden and yet I must travel from Caesarea to Jerusalem to explain to you the reason for your wealth!'

Another man stepped forward. The wealth, he said, was Roman wealth at the cost of Jewish lives. Pilate had emptied the treasury of the Temple, he added, for the sake of his bath!

'You speak of impurity,' Pilate said, letting the phrase linger. It was the signal to his troops. 'Impurity and pollution! And yet you people care nothing for bathing! You point at Roman administrators, men who wash themselves each day, and you have the audacity to suggest we are not worthy of entering your Temple because we are not clean! I tell you this, because the truth is obvious to all but yourselves. Your desert god has made you the slave of Romans for good reason: the very smell of you sickens him!'

They began screaming even before Pilate's interpreter finished repeating his words. They shook their fists and cursed him. They called on their god to avenge them.

Only when they recognized the screams behind them as those of the battlefield did they hesitate, and that was when Cornelius rushed to Pilate's rostrum. Pilate saw his centurion's sword slash through an outstretched arm. The blood of the wound hit Pilate's toga. Cornelius's men now formed a hard shell around the prefect, but the Jews no longer cared about Pilate. Soldiers, standing in their very midst, were sweeping their swords with calculated zeal. Those closest to Pilate took the first wave of the attack, falling like wheat before the scythe.

As a second contingent of his soldiers fought through the centre, hastening to his defence, the unarmed crowd began to scatter. Finding reinforcements coming in support of the first two centuries – these in full battle dress – they broke from the plaza and raced toward the road leading into the lower city, known as the City of David.

Those who could not move quickly enough, frozen by the mass of men before them, fell to the sword at once. The rest followed in a desperate, headlong rush from the plaza, only to come upon Pilate's Syrian cavalry. As the leaders recognized the trap, they stopped and tried to turn back. Those behind them, however, still ran forward. The result was both predictable and terrible.

The Syrians, having no love of the Jews, hit them with more ferocity than the cool veterans of the Fretensis Legion, urging their horses to trample those who fell to the pavement. The Jews who managed to retreat back to the Plaza were met again by Pilate's infantry and threw their arms up in surrender, but there was no surrender. Pilate greeted them with phalanxes of disciplined Roman infantry.

Twelve minutes after it had begun, no one remained standing who was not in the service of Rome. In all, four thousand Jewish men lay dead. Of the thousand or so surviving the massacre, Pilate gathered together all who were still whole and without significant wounds, and chose one hundred of them at random to be crucified along the road leading out from the Susim Gate – the so-called Gate of Kings.

The rest he released – that they might know his mercy.

Zürich
October 10, 2006.

The bank of Goetz and Ritter occupied an entire four-storey corner building one street east of the Bahnhofstrasse. It was built of stone blocks at the beginning of the twentieth century. Following the fashion of its day, the building advertised its opulence with typical Neo-Gothic excess. The architect had been especially fond of ivy leaves, grapes, angels and doves. There were micro-balconies serving no function and medallions to cover the occasional blank spots. Along the upper storeys, pilasters in each of the classical styles framed the windows, Doric at the second story, Ionic at the third, Corinthian at the fourth. The building was fairly typical for Zürich, but Malloy took a moment to study it again. At the front door the area opened onto a small circular drive. Parking was limited to a handful of customers, but allowed them access to three different exit routes from the city within a matter of seconds.

The problem was that once in traffic the choices were limited. If the police were seriously interested in intercepting someone leaving the financial district, they could do so at a number of neatly designed bottlenecks. This made bank robbery in downtown Zürich a low percentage play. The difficulties did not end there. Three sides of the bank were exposed, allowing the police open lines of fire from a number of rooftops. What the police could access others could as well. Walking out of the bank, Malloy would be vulnerable. That dimension he had eliminated as much as possible with two off-duty police snipers and a vest that he wore discreetly under a bulky sweater and jacket.

A safe, fast route out of the city was another matter.

Malloy walked to the fourth side of the building where the Limmat flowed quietly through the city. As it happened, a small harbour located next to Goetz and Ritter sheltered twenty or thirty private boats. Some fifty yards beyond the harbour, the river passed under a low ornate bridge pouring out of Lake Zürich.

At the front of the building again, Malloy found no armed guards, only a locked door. He rang the bell and when asked to identify himself responded in English, 'Mr Thomas.' He heard the buzz and click of the lock, then watched the heavy doors swing open. He walked into a small elegantly furnished reception area. A young woman greeted him pleasantly and called upstairs. Two minutes later a Ms Berlini appeared and escorted him to the elevator. She told him in English that both Mr Wheeler and Dr North had arrived some minutes before.

They were seated in the director's office when Malloy and Ms Berlini entered. Hans Goetz had strategically placed himself behind a large nineteenth century desk suited to the style of the building. Nicole North and Roland Wheeler were facing him. Both Wheeler and Goetz rose when Malloy entered, introducing themselves and shaking his hand with a military snap of the wrist in the European fashion. Goetz was a small neat man with white hair and a singularly florid complexion. His smile was friendly; his manners were impeccable. Like his desk, where every paperclip faced the same direction, Goetz was a man who took care of the details. Malloy had seen his type a hundred times over. They crowded the financial district's cafes, restaurants and bars. They were a cheerful and confident breed only so long as everything went exactly as they had arranged it. Their façade crumbled the moment anything went wrong. Such was the Swiss banker.

Roland Wheeler was in his sixties, the epitome of English self-assurance. He was tall and straight with silver hair and a dark tan that was both natural and appealing. According to the file Malloy had read, Wheeler kept a winter residence at Cannes, and a second in the south of Spain. It took Malloy only a moment to realize he possessed the urbane air of a man skilled at persuading wealthy clients to trust his judgment. For all his sophistication he was a salesman at heart. He took care of others. He gave advice. He made sacrifices over small matters that his clients might trust him all the more when it came time to purchase pieces of magnitude. Malloy thought Wheeler would be quick to understand the dynamics of a situation or the nuance of an expression, impossible to anger, unrelentingly attentive. And quite wealthy for the troubles he took.

Wheeler wore a charcoal suit, a gold tie clip, and a matching pair of gold cufflinks. Even by Zürich standards he dressed well. The most instructive piece of evidence about the art dealer was the way he included Ms Berlini in the meeting. Nicole North was a client. Hans Goetz was the director of the bank. Malloy was to be entrusted with a great fortune. They were all deserving of his attention and respect, but Ms Berlini was a functionary. Despite this, he treated her as a partner in the proceedings. Nor was it simple courtesy. She had, Malloy thought, earned Wheeler's respect. It was difficult to guess the extent of contact between them but easy to see that Wheeler had dealt with Goetz and Goetz's assistant on several occasions.

Dr North might have learned something from the man. Every gesture, every failure to make eye contact intimated an unconscious feeling of superiority. She was not only the person with the most money she looked as if she actually believed she was morally superior. Everything about her indicated that she half-expected someone to pull a gun. She clutched her package tightly, anxious to be finished with this unpleasant business. That wasn't going to happen until Goetz received a confirmation that the wire transfer of funds had been completed.

While they waited Malloy talked with the banker and art dealer about the weather. An exceedingly dry fall in Zürich, they informed him. Malloy observed that it was generally dry in the fall in Zürich. Was he familiar with the city? Malloy thrust his legs forward and leaned back comfortably. He had grown up in Zürich, he said. This elicited questions about his knowledge of German. Malloy answered in perfect Swiss German that his High German was barely adequate, but his Swiss German was pretty good. The accent and grammar of this sentence delighted both men, Goetz especially. It was extremely unusual, he said, for people to learn Swiss German.

Speaking now in High German, Wheeler agreed. He had lived in Zürich for over a dozen years. Even though he spoke High German fluently when he arrived, he still had trouble understanding the dialect. His daughter spoke High German, he said, but only under duress. She preferred Italian, which she spoke better than English, and hated Farmer German even more than she did *Brautwürst* and *Rüsti*. Having finished his speech, Wheeler seemed to catch himself suddenly and apologized to Nicole North. She must think them rude, he said, for excluding her. Malloy understood the exclusion was calculated, his show of good manners nothing more than a bit of emphasis to the insult, European style.

'Not at all,' North answered with a withering contempt she pretended to mask in a bright Texas smile.

Picking up the tension Goetz suggested that their business was almost finished. North gave the door a furtive look.

After nearly a minute-and-a-half of uncomfortable silence the phone rang. Hans Goetz answered it in Swiss German. Hanging up he told them the transfer had been completed.

Dr North handed Malloy the package like a woman giving her baby to a stranger for safe-keeping. 'You'll be careful with it?'

'As though my life depended on it.'

Wheeler laughed with just a touch of affectation. 'Come to that, I expect it does!'

Malloy set the package inside the book bag he had brought and waited for North to make her exit. North stood up quickly as if just then recalling her instructions. She flashed a petrified smiled. 'A pleasure.'

Her eyes shifted suddenly to the book bag. She

wanted to say something else, but instead walked out of the office hurriedly. Ms Berlini followed her. When she had gone, Wheeler and Goetz both seemed to want to comment about her abruptness but resisted the urge. To break the mood, Malloy asked about the weather forecast for the remainder of the week. The two men grew composed again. Decent today and tomorrow, Goetz told him, but a heavy fog moving in Thursday morning. Their talk of sun and fog and rain in the land of chocolate ended abruptly with the return of Ms Berlini. Dr North had departed from the bank without incident, she said. Malloy smiled affably at Wheeler and Goetz. 'It's been a pleasure, gentlemen.' In Swiss German he said to Ms Berlini, 'May I ask you to show me out?'

'But of course,' the young woman answered politely with a cool, though quite beautiful smile.

Inside the elevator Malloy spoke Swiss German commenting on the beauty of the bank. Ms Berlini answered that it was a comfortable place to work. 'And Mr Goetz?' Malloy pressed. 'A good boss?'

'One of the most respected bankers in Zürich,' she answered.

Malloy did not comment on the woman's evasiveness because he understood it. The banker reserved whatever residual sweetness that remained in his shrunken soul for his clients. Those who worked for him could count on tireless supervision, a work life in which no failing went unnoticed. Ms Berlini's polite response to Malloy's question was easily translated: Hans Goetz was a holy terror to work for.

In the lobby Malloy asked if he might use the

restroom. Ms Berlini directed him along a narrow corridor toward the back of the building. Once behind closed doors he telephoned Marcus. 'One minute,' he said.

In the hallway again he asked about the back door. Was it this way?

The young woman's face flushed slightly. She was not accustomed to obstructing the desires of her clients, but neither could she permit the slightest deviation in protocol. 'I'm afraid you can't use that exit unless it's an emergency.'

Malloy smiled. 'Let's assume it's an emergency. Is it this direction?'

'Yes, but—'

Malloy didn't wait for her to finish. At the back of the building he kicked the alarm bar on the door and walked out.

He headed toward the dock and arrived just as Marcus was pulling up in a stolen powerboat. He hopped into the vessel, chosen for its speed, and grabbed the M-16 Marcus had arranged for him. Jacking a shell into the chamber, he set the selector on full auto.

Marcus steered the boat back toward the centre of the river, the double engines roaring thunderously, just as two bank guards came out of the back of the building. Marcus's snipers opened fire, and both guards dived back inside the building. The boat passed under the low bridge that separated the river and the lake. As soon as they had passed it, Malloy drove the small crowd of pedestrians on the bridge to cover with a long burst of automatic fire. As he did so, he looked for someone who did not react like the others, but when he had finished no one was still standing. He set a second clip in the gun – live ammo this time – and turned toward the lake as the powerboat streaked across the water at close to fifty miles an hour.

'Are we clear?' Marcus asked without turning.

Malloy scanned the shoreline and lakeside harbour. There was still no activity except for the frantic excitement on the bridge, where the pedestrians were reaching for their cell phones. Already a quarter of a mile from the city centre, he and Marcus had the lake to themselves. 'We're clear!' he answered.

Marcus pulled his cell phone out and hit the speed dial. 'One minute,' he said. Only then did his shoulders lose their tension.

They used the private dock at Zürichhorn close to the casino. It was a couple of miles down the shore, impossible to reach quickly by car at midday. They cleared the boat with their weapons discreetly camouflaged and found Marcus's driver, an off-duty Zürich cop, waiting for them. Fifteen minutes later in heavy midtown traffic they crossed the very bridge they had motored under and made their way to the village of Dietlikon, halfway between the city of Zürich and its airport.

Malloy had a train to catch.

At the sound of the alarm, Hans Goetz reached for the telephone. His face turned crimson as he shouted questions. Meanwhile, Roland Wheeler sauntered to the window and looked down at the river. Dr North's courier was running toward the dock.

'It's Mr Thomas,' he told Goetz. 'He went out the back of your building.'

Hans Goetz looked at him uncertainly. Bankers always imagined the worst when they heard an alarm. Unauthorized use of an emergency door, on the other hand, hardly constituted a crisis, did it? Wheeler pointed toward the Limmat. 'He has a speedboat waiting for him.'

Goetz cradled the phone and walked to the window. It took him a moment to comprehend what he was seeing. His face cooled to purple. His breathing grew less agitated. At the sound of the automatic weapons both Goetz and Wheeler turned from the window and positioned themselves against the walls. As soon as it had ceased Goetz went to his phone again and dialled frantically.

'I know!' he shouted. 'I know that! But we are not being robbed!'

Ms Berlini burst into his office, her eyes wide with excitement and fear. Goetz, listening impatiently to the person on the telephone, finally shouted, 'Of course we need to call the police!' He slammed down the phone and looked at Wheeler and Berlini.

'I told him he couldn't go out that way!' Berlini said.

Goetz seemed to want to blame her, but caught himself. The problem was Mr Thomas. '*Amies!*' he shouted angrily. 'They're all cowboys!'

Wheeler laughed pleasantly. 'The American wants to earn his fee, Hans! So we have a bit of adventure.'

'The alarm will cost me—!'

'Pay it. What do you care? You made enough commission today you can afford it.'

'He could have *asked* to use the back door!'

'My impression of Mr Thomas is that he doesn't ask permission to do anything.'

Malloy saw three people at the Dietlikon train station, an old man holding a newspaper, the stationmaster, who remained inside the building, and an overweight middle-aged man wearing a dirty white trench coat. Marcus gestured toward the man in the trench coat as their Mercedes pulled into the lot. 'Max,' he said. Malloy, just finished with changing his clothes, glanced out the window. Max appeared to be one of a growing number of eastern European migrants flooding into the West. Nurtured on war and accustomed to taking what they wanted, they formed the new criminal class in western Europe and were capable of any violence. This one was in his late forties, dark and balding. He paced slowly, both hands plunged inside the pockets of his filthy trench coat. 'Max keeps a sawn-off shotgun loaded with deer slugs in the lining of his coat, Thomas, so be nice to him. He is very sensitive to criticism.'

Malloy smiled. Max looked about a sensitive as a fire hydrant.

'I'll meet you inside the airport. And don't forget my suitcase and computer.'

'They're in the trunk,' Marcus's driver said.

Malloy had changed out of his slacks and sweater into a pair of jeans and boots with a sweatshirt covering his vest. He wore a long leather coat and a baseball cap. He carried his package inside the morning's edition of *The Herald Tribune* and packed his borrowed Glock in a shoulder holster inside his coat. As usual he kept the Sigma .380 holstered and tucked into his belt at the small of his back. He bought a train ticket to the airport from the machine, checked his watch and sat down on a bench facing the tracks. With his back and right flank covered by the station walls and Max standing before him on the platform, one or the other of them covered all approaches.

A young girl with her schoolbooks came up to the platform shortly before the train arrived. Otherwise, the Dietlikon station was quiet. When the train pulled in, precisely on schedule, two teenagers stepped off. There were laughing and shoving each other like typical adolescents. Malloy watched their reflection in the glass to make sure they were exactly what they seemed to be. A thirty-something businessman was leaving the first class wagon just as Malloy started up the steps. Malloy waited for him to pass. When he was certain the man had walked on, he went into the train.

Other than Bob Whitefield there were two people inside the first class wagon, an old woman in her eighties and a young man in his twenties. Whitefield had situated himself at the front of the car and was reading a newspaper. The woman was seated at the centre of the wagon on the same side of the train as Whitefield, and the young man was at the very back also on the same side. Malloy already had his copy of the newspaper in his left hand. As he passed Whitefield, Malloy let his package slip out of the folds of the paper. Whitefield covered the thing at once with his own newspaper.

Moving down the aisle Malloy chose a seat one row behind the old woman on the opposite side of the aisle.

Max came into the wagon from the opposite end. Malloy did not look back in his direction, but he was certain Max had chosen the seat across the aisle from the young man. It was the only position that let him cover everyone inside the compartment.

As the train took off Malloy brought his Glock out and set it inside the folds of the newspaper. The plan was a simple one with high odds that nothing at all would interrupt a routine trip to the airport. Malloy and Max would follow Bob Whitefield until he passed through airport security. At that point Malloy would leave his weapons in a lockbox and pick up his luggage. With the rank of a captain in the Zürich City police force Marcus could move freely through the airport. He would keep watch over Whitefield until Malloy and Whitefield could board the plane. The only real danger lay between the Dietlikon station and the airport, but there were no stops.

During the five minute ride to the airport, no one came into the first class compartment, but as the train pulled into the tunnel a young man entered the wagon by the door closest to Bob Whitefield. He was tall and reasonably well built, somewhere in his mid-twenties. Dressed like an Eighties-style punker, a look that had not completely vanished among the German street people, he had shaved his entire head except for a Mohawk, which stood up in a series of long electric-blue spikes. He wore a black leather jacket with metal spikes at the shoulders and wrists. On his torn T-shirt was an obscene message Malloy could not read in its entirety. Worn-out army surplus pants and heavy black army combat boots completed the fashion statement. He walked past Bob Whitefield without looking at him, but when he saw Malloy he made a point of staring at him.

Malloy pretended not to notice the obvious aggression. He watched the young man's hands. They were empty at the moment, but there was a degree of energy about him that suggested he only wanted an excuse to reach for something, a knife most probably but possibly a handgun. In High German, Mohawk said, 'What are you looking at?'

'What is it, Marco?' Roland Wheeler asked his driver in Italian. They were three blocks from Goetz and Ritter.

'Police.'

Irritably, Wheeler looked around for signs prohibiting traffic. Marco did not usually make mistakes, but the banking district was practically impossible to drive in without breaking one law or another.

The police car slowed down in front of them and pulled onto the kerb. Marco pulled in behind them. The two policemen inside the patrol car sat quietly for a moment. Wheeler imagined that they were calling in for an update on the alarm at the bank. Once they realised who he was they would make a show of asking for identification and the car's registration, but that would be it. And if he was wrong, well, he could afford a traffic citation after this morning! He didn't care to be as silly about money as Goetz.

The policeman got out of their automobile slowly. They were typical Swiss officers, trim, muscular, exceedingly deliberate in their movements. They came to either side of Wheeler's Mercedes. The one on the driver's side of the car signalled for Marco to lower his window.

'Do it,' Wheeler said.

'*Guten Tag*,' the policeman said, using High German, instead of the ubiquitous *Grüetzi* of Swiss German. 'May I see your registration and driver's licence?' He spoke as if he knew they were foreigners, which was odd because Wheeler had a Zürich licence plate.

Marco stared at the man without responding, waiting for his employer to translate the instructions and tell him what to do. Wheeler spoke in Italian telling Marco to present his driver's license and the car's registration. Marco reached toward the console. As he did, the policeman swept his hand toward Marco's neck. Marco's enormous body jerked as blood splashed out across the dashboard and windshield. An odd strangling noise erupted from his throat. Before Wheeler could move, before he even realised he had no place to go and no weapon to reach for, the second policeman pointed a pistol at the window. He was aiming it at Wheeler's head.

'Open your door, please,' the first policeman said, still speaking High German.

Wheeler did not respond because he could not. He sat frozen in terror. The policeman on the passenger side of the automobile tipped his gun down until it was aiming at Wheeler's crotch. In English, he said, 'I will not ask you again. Open the door.'

Wheeler looked about stupidly, wondering what door he meant. Then he fumbled for the door handle. It was locked. He found the switch. He pulled the door handle and the gunman opened the door, gesturing for

Wheeler to slide across and make room. The policeman at the driver's door now jerked Marco's body out of the car and into the street. He settled behind the steering wheel and flipped the gear selector to drive.

They were moving again before Wheeler even understood what had happened.

'Dr North?' The uniformed policemen were both young and well-dressed. They pointed the machine guns slung across their shoulders politely away from her.

'Yes?'

'Would you be so kind as to come with us?'

Nicole was alone. She had only a small travelling bag with her and had already cleared security. 'What is this about?'

'Our supervisor asked us to bring you to his office.'

'I have a flight to catch.'

'That won't be a problem. This won't take long.'

The painting, she thought. They assumed she was smuggling it out of the country. Well, they could look all they wanted, but they were going to be disappointed. 'Why not?' she asked with a sudden smile.

Malloy did not answer the man. Having his moral victory Mohawk walked past him. At that moment a second young man appeared, like the first coming through the door closest to Bob Whitefield. This one had a yellow Mohawk. He was probably older by half-a-dozen years. Yellow Mohawk carried his leather jacket in his right hand. He staggered a bit as he turned back seemingly to close the door. His jacket gave an odd jerk. Malloy was processing this when he saw the barrel of a gun in the reflection of the glass across the aisle. It was moving from behind his headrest and nearly touching his skull.

Before he could react, the explosion of Max's shotgun sent Malloy's would-be-assassin to the floor. The man in the yellow Mohawk dropped his jacket and aimed his handgun at Max as Max jacked a second shell into his gun. Malloy tipped his Glock up slightly and fired once. The man jerked back against the door and slipped to the floor. Malloy stood up and brought his Glock around to cover the kid in the seat by Max, but he was down on the floor, his arms covering his head. The old lady stared silently at Malloy. Her expression was a strange mix of confusion and curiosity. She had not yet registered fear. Instinctively, he said to her in Swiss German, 'We make a movie. We're all actors!' Her face relaxed. For a fraction of a moment everything made perfect sense.

Malloy did not hear the next shot. He heard only the breaking of glass and Max hitting the floor. Expecting the gunman to come into the compartment, he settled his gun sights on the door behind Max, but the assassin stepped off the train as it was still rolling to a stop. He walked along the platform until he came to Malloy's wagon and lifted his weapon.

Malloy fired three shots and the man hit the concrete platform. His gun skittered away. The people around him broke for cover with a roar of panic. Max groaned loudly and struggled back to his feet. His face was grey and stricken. Malloy was watching him and did not see the man outside who shot him. He simply felt himself tossed back into the seats across the aisle. He heard the gun's explosion as he hit. Max's twelve-gauge deer slug answered. For a moment everything was quiet.

Malloy rolled to the floor. His breath was short and rapid. He touched the vest and found the hot metal slug buried in the padding. 'Platform is clear,' Max told him in English. 'If you are going, you better go now.'

Malloy took a deep, painful breath and crawled down the aisle. When he got to the front of the wagon he saw Whitefield stretched across his seat with a bullet hole in his forehead. Malloy took the package, pushed the dead assassin away from the door, and left the wagon. He found two sets of doors beyond. One faced the platform. The other accessed an empty track. Malloy tried the doors facing the tracks, but they were sealed shut. The platform in front of him was still empty except for two dead bodies. A train waited on the other side of the platform. Through the windows Malloy could see a number of people staring out in horror at the dead gunmen on the platform. Max came through the door. 'The cops are here in another thirty seconds. They are at the escalator.'

Malloy watched for some kind of movement on the train opposite them. When he saw nothing, he started through the door. Max brought his twelve-gauge forward as he did so. 'Get back!'

A movement at the bottom of the escalator turned into a gunman.

Instead of pulling back, Malloy dropped between the train and the concrete platform. He landed on a bed of crushed rock safely out of the line of fire. Max fired three rounds as Malloy scrambled under the train.

Coming to his feet on the other side, Malloy looked in both directions.

The tunnel was well lit at the station, but beyond the end of the train he could see only darkness. He took off at a sprint in the direction from which the train had come. Once out of the station and deep inside the tunnel he was forced to walk for several agonizing seconds. After only a few steps he heard someone running after him. Max? The assassins? The police? He didn't care to find out and began running again.

The light was pale at first, but it provided enough illumination that he could make out the shadows of the tracks as he came to the end of the tunnel. He broke into the daylight still running flat out. He watched the high concrete walls overhead. After fifty yards or so he climbed a steep bank and crossed a small strip of land. He jogged across a service road and entered a Credit Suisse parking lot.

There was a time not too many years ago when the Swiss left their keys in the ignition. Those days were gone. Swiss-owned automobiles now had alarms and J-bars like the rest of the world. The doors were all locked, and most of them were even relatively secure from a quick hotwire. The Dodge Shadow provided a nice exception to hot wiring deterrents though. When he saw one of them Malloy broke the glass with the butt of his gun and opened the door. Around the ignition lock was a plastic glow ring. By jamming a pointed object into the ignition and pulling down hard, he could shatter the ring and access the starter wires. All he needed was a pointed object. He looked around the car and saw nothing. Unfastening his belt, he jammed the tongue into the ignition and slammed the buckle with his fist. The glow ring broke, and he brought the wires out.

A moment later the engine sputtered to life.

Jeffrey Bremmer waited for the two private security men to bring Nicole North to him. It had cost him roughly ten thousand Swiss Francs for each. And of course no questions asked. The office cost him nothing. It belonged to a true Knight of the Temple.

The moment Nicole North arrived, he asked the two cantonal policemen to step outside and make sure he was not disturbed.

'You were travelling with Dr Starr,' he said to the woman in English.

The question put her off-balance for some reason. 'What of it?'

'Where is he?'

'What is this about? Who are you? I want to see some credentials.' It was the tough talk of someone who knows her rights, but North's eyes betrayed her. She was scared.

'I need to speak to Dr Starr.'

'I can't help you. If you want to talk to him, go find him. I have no idea where he is. Now may I go? I have a plane to catch.'

Bremmer walked behind the woman. The stink of her fear began to smother the sweet scent of her perfume. 'You may not go. You may not even live another fifteen seconds if you don't tell me what I need to know.'

North spun around to face him, but her courage, like the blood in her face, washed out of her. 'Who *are* you?'

Bremmer presented the opened blade of a razor. 'I am the man you answer and obey if you want to keep your face. Now where is Dr Starr?'

North grabbed the desk to keep from collapsing. Her eyes never left the exposed razor. Against her pleadings for her life Bremmer's only response was to tell her to give him the information he requested.

'He was going to follow the courier – Thomas Malloy. He wanted to make sure nothing went wrong.'

Bremmer made a phone call. He spoke in German so North would not understand. If Starr was inside the airport, Bremmer needed a team to find him at once.

The answer came back unexpectedly. 'We don't have anyone available. Everyone is looking for Malloy.'

Bremmer raged angrily, 'Malloy? What are you telling me? He got away?'

'We've put every extra man we have in the airport looking for him.'

'He was the only one who mattered!'

'I understand that.'

'I don't think you do!'

'Do you want me to call someone back to look for Starr?'

'No. Call me in ten minutes or as soon as you have Malloy.'

Off the phone, Bremmer looked at Nicole North and felt a moment of remorse. Sir Julian had given Dr North to him for the afternoon – anything he wanted after the interrogation – only this requirement: her death was to leave one unmistakable message – *Gare le Corbeau!* He had been looking forward to this afternoon for several days, and now suddenly nothing was settled. Malloy had gotten away with the portrait.

'What are you going to do to me?' North asked.

Kate called Ethan just as he was hanging the Shop Closed sign in the front door of his Zürich bookshop. Sean, the soon-to-be owner of the bookshop, was on the second floor of the old building opening and shelving the season's new mysteries.

'Check your bank account,' Kate told him.

Ethan paced nervously. 'I already have. It's great.' He glanced toward the second floor stacks. Sean was already pressing him about his decision to sell. What was he planning? What about Kate? Was it really over? Talking about roughly eight million dollars would pretty much confirm his suspicions that Ethan was involved in something more than an unexpected family inheritance.

'Happy?'

'That's a tough one,' Ethan answered. 'You know it's not supposed to buy happiness.'

Kate laughed pleasantly. 'But it certainly makes misery easier to handle.'

'Does it?'

'I've been thinking.' Her tone was serious. He was about to hear that it was over.

'About us?'

'About giving up the life, actually. I think you might be right. Quit while we're on top of our game.'

'You're serious?' Ethan felt dizzy with excitement. 'I thought you were going to tell me to forget it.'

'I thought I was, too, but then I decided working alone again . . . I'd probably get caught.'

'You're too good for that.'

'You're probably right. The truth? The truth is . . . I don't want to lose you.'

'I was sure you were going to call and tell me it was over. I mean, I just gave the shop to Sean.'

Kate laughed. 'Make him give it back!'

'No. I want to do something else. Maybe go to graduate school, try to become a professor.'

'Where?'

'Doesn't really matter. Just so I can be close to you.'

'Why don't you come down to the cabin this evening and we can talk about . . . you know . . . alternatives. I'm not going to sit at home and knit while you go to school.'

Ethan laughed, pacing excitedly. 'Sean and I are going out this afternoon. I'm signing the business over to him in the morning at the lawyer's office—'

Sean shouted from the second floor.

'That was Sean.'

'Say 'hi' to Sean for me.'

'I will. How about tomorrow afternoon? I can be there around one o'clock.'

'I'll see you then. Hey, one more thing. Do you want to get married next week?'

The door to his shop rattled. Ethan turned to see two men in suits. They were middle-aged. One of them was well over six feet tall. The second man was small and round, but even with a suit jacket on Ethan could see he was mostly muscle.

'I thought—' He had thought marriage was out, the last thing in the world Kate wanted. 'That sounds good, Kate! Let's do it!'

The taller of the two men held a detective's badge against the glass door.

'Listen, there's someone here. I have to go.'

'Is everything okay?'

The shorter man glanced toward the street. Ethan stepped toward the door and held his hand up, a gesture that announced he was coming as soon as he was off the phone. 'Everything's fine. You're serious? You mean like kids and happily-ever-after?'

'Why not? If we're going to do it, let's do it right.'

'Sounds great. I'll talk to you tomorrow.'

Ethan was still smiling when he opened the door for the two detectives. He spoke High German to signal to them he did not understand Swiss German. 'What can I do for you?' He figured it was a piece of paper he hadn't filled out correctly for the bureaucracy. That had to be it. There was nothing the Swiss enjoyed more than paperwork. The larger of the two men folded his badge away and shook Ethan's hand. A big soft hand, but the eyes, like those of his partner's, moved restlessly, cop-style, taking the room in at a glance. 'Zimmer,' he said.

The smaller man stepped forward and shook hands, 'Kemp.' His hand was small but the grip was brutal. For just a moment, his gaze settled on Ethan as if taking his measure.

'We'd like to talk to you about a few things,' Detective Zimmer explained.

'What kind of things?'

Sean ripped apart a cardboard box, and both men looked up in apparent surprise. 'Is someone here?' Zimmer asked.

'My business partner.'

'Ask him to come down,' Kemp said. There was nothing pleasant in the way he spoke. An abrupt language at times, German speakers habitually dropped in phrases of courtesy, such as *if you would be so kind, may I ask you, if it is no great trouble.* When he had first studied the language, Ethan had been amused by the artificial pleasantries. After close to a decade of living and working with the language, he understood Kemp's command pretended neither respect nor courtesy. It had all the charm of, 'Get his ass down here now!' Swiss police officers never talked like that.

Ethan studied both men with sudden dread. He thought Zimmer might soften the command, as the Swiss are prone to help others with their lack of manners, but Zimmer seemed as oblivious to the insult as his partner. 'Sean?' he called in English, his voice trembling. 'Could you come down here for a minute?'

Sean leaned over the railing and called out in English. 'Sure. What's up?'

'A couple of detectives,' Ethan answered.

Sean spoke to the men cheerfully in Swiss German. Neither man responded. He spoke again as he came around to the open stairway. Ethan could not quite understand this, but it had something to do with transferring the title to the business. Again neither man answered and it occurred to Ethan that the Swiss detectives did not understand Swiss German.

He wanted to shout some kind of warning but Sean was already down the steps.

Kemp pulled a gun. A silencer was screwed into it. 'Get over by the cash register,' he told Sean in High German.

Sean swore angrily and blurted something out in Swiss German. Ethan told him in English, 'Do what they say. It's a robbery. All they want is money.'

He didn't believe it. He was quite certain now that this had nothing to do with money – at least the money in the till.

'Have you got an office where we can talk?' Zimmer asked Ethan.

Ethan glanced once at his friend. 'Upstairs,' he answered.

'Let's go take a look at it.'

The big man pulled his own silenced pistol. Ethan started to protest that Sean wasn't involved, but the utter indifference in the man's eyes stopped him. He turned away and started for the stairs. He was now quite certain he would never walk down them again. Ethan was nearly to the top step when he heard the suppressed blast of a silenced weapon discharging. This was followed by the sound of Sean's body dropping to the floor and the curious tinkle of a discharged shell. Just that quickly and it was over for his friend.

Without really thinking about the consequences Ethan dropped his elbow back, sweeping his forearm across Zimmer's nose. The big man grabbed his face reflexively. When he did, Ethan kicked him in the chest. Zimmer went rolling backwards down the steps. Kemp got one shot off from behind the counter. Ethan heard the bullet pass with a crack. A second shot followed as he somersaulted between two bookcases.

Along each side of the balcony there were fifteen rows of open shelf bookcases placed tightly together with barely enough space for customers to slip in and look at the books. At either end of the room Ethan had set up another four cases. At the top of the stairs, a small aisle led back to his office, but once there he would be trapped. He looked across the room. Better, he thought, to stay here. The bookcases gave him cover. Not that it really mattered. They had guns. He had nothing but time.

And that was running out.

Sobrio, Switzerland

They used Helena Chernoff at the front door. Helena looked like a freshly scrubbed upper middle-class German housewife. She even had a bit of middle-aged perkiness in her step when she bothered. She wore a loose fitting shell that covered her armoured vest, black stretch pants and running shoes – just another weekend resident from the north invading the tiny mountain villages of southern Switzerland. She came hurrying up the winding stairs of the public walkway in front of Lady Kenyon's property and hesitated. There were two small cabins from which to choose. Helena glanced behind her nervously and started up the incline to Lady Kenyon's front door.

A six man team covered the back of Kenyon's property, three in the cabin next to Kenyon's, three more in the woods. Helena was alone in the front. Her backup was the man who was supposed to be following her. Xeno waited in the house across the street. Everyone carried two guns, one loaded with rubber bullets – for knock-down, if necessary – the second with tranquilizers. In addition, Helena had stun capacity in the sleeve of her jacket. If Helen couldn't get Lady Kenyon to open the door, Xeno would order the team at the back of the cabin to break in, but Helena was the first and best option. Lady in distress.

The first sign of a problem was Lady Kenyon's failure to open the front door for the innocent-looking Helena. Helena paced nervously, calling out in German as she knocked on the door, 'Hello! Is anyone home? Please! There is a man following me!'

Nothing. Kenyon was inside. They knew that much. The silence continued until Xeno whispered his orders. 'Back door, get ready!'

Helena called out with a touch of desperation. 'Can you help me?'

Lady Kenyon's cabin was typical of the area. It was built about two hundred years ago of thick timbers and roofed with grey fieldstones. It stood at the back edge of the village with a view to the valley and mountains beyond. Behind her property a steep rocky alpine meadow spread out for a couple hundred metres, then turned into a pine forest that was really only accessible by a single trail. If she got that far, the third team was waiting.

There had been some difficulty moving into position because of the openness behind the house, but the evening before Xeno had quietly installed his people in two houses. The first was below Kenyon's place, directly across a narrow road. From here Xeno directed the take-down. The other was next door to Kenyon's property.

'We have the back secure,' the back door team leader's voice announced over the headset.

'Hold your position.'

Xeno watched Helena's act at the front of the house with growing frustration. She moved with a skittering nervousness, calling again for help, and making a show of looking back toward the village as her backup came into view and walked menacingly toward her. He had been living on the streets on and off for the last couple of years, and looked it. He was not the sort of man a woman wanted following her.

Xeno gave it a count of five. When Kenyon did not open her door, he spoke into his headset. 'Take it down!'

Helena moved away from the front on the order and covered the side of the house. Xeno could see nothing, but he heard his two men enter the cabin. One of them shouted in High German, 'Police! You are under arrest!'

The second whispered to Xeno after a moment, 'She's gone!'

'She can't be gone! She's inside!' he answered.

'I'm telling you—'

Four gunshots sounded from within the cabin, and Xeno shouted to the others, 'Take cover!'

Zürich

Ethan heard footsteps on the stairs and saw Zimmer moving carefully. He did not appear to be sure of Ethan's position. Once he was off the stairs, he took cover among the bookcases. Maybe he imagined Ethan had a gun concealed up here somewhere. Kemp called to his partner in a language Ethan did not recognize,

Slavic, he thought. In response Zimmer dropped back toward the outside wall. At that point Ethan lost sight of him. Fearing the wall was no longer safe, he stepped to the railing. Kemp came out of the stacks below him and fired twice. The suppressed sound of his gun was barely audible. He shouted something and Ethan realised he was directing his partner forward. Having neither the railing nor the outside wall, Ethan scrambled for the other end of the room. Below him Kemp manoeuvred into a new position, firing four rounds without effect.

At the far end of the room Ethan slipped back toward the wall. He checked behind him and then ran forward but Zimmer had circled in the opposite direction and was waiting for him. From the length of the room, nearly eighty feet, his first shot would have been the end of it if Ethan had not somersaulted forward. He came up between two bookcases. Moving out to the railing, hoping to get across the room, he discovered Kemp had anticipated him.

Ethan rolled back to safety as Kemp fired three shots. Kemp called out again. No translation needed: We have him! Ethan had only a few feet of safety to either side. Once Zimmer came forward even that would disappear. The only hope, the only direction left, was up. The bookcases were eight feet high, their shelves made of half-inch thick poplar. He climbed them as easily as he would a ladder and got to the top shelf while Zimmer walked down the long aisle fearlessly. They knew now he didn't have a gun, and it was clear they had him trapped in a narrow aisle between two bookcases – both of his exits closed off.

Kemp shouted something from below, but if he saw what Ethan was trying to do, it didn't really matter. There were no other options. Zimmer came forward with his gun pointing at the floor, his eyes fixed on the space directly below Ethan. He started to look up as Ethan dropped across his shoulders. Zimmer collapsed under the force of Ethan's impact. As they fell, Ethan slammed Zimmer's head into the brick wall.

Kemp shouted again, but Zimmer was out cold – his head bleeding. Ethan rolled off him and found his pistol. Taking it and the spare clip inside his sports coat pocket, Ethan walked toward the railing quickly and quietly, tossing a book over the bookcases so it would land well away from his new position. It was all he needed.

As he stepped to the railing, Ethan could see Kemp following the sound of the book with his weapon, both arms locked in a shooter's V. With his second hand bracing his wrist, Ethan fired once and watched Kemp flinch as if hit. He rolled back to safety as Ethan fired twice more. From the shelves below, Kemp responded with a heavy barrage, driving Ethan to the outer wall. Ethan could hear Kemp change clips. He came forward quickly, hoping to catch the man exposed, but the room appeared to be empty. Ethan checked on Zimmer. The big man was sprawled out, just as Ethan had left him. He retreated to the end of the room, waiting, listening.

He came out quickly again. Kemp was still not to be seen. Hiding? Wounded? Dead? Ethan held the railing for as long as he dared, then retreated, moving along the outer wall on tiptoes. He went to the railing again, firing a single round to either side of the room below him, hoping to draw return fire, but Kemp remained concealed. Ethan held his position only briefly before he backed away.

He was about to persuade himself to try the stairs when he saw something that turned his guts to water.

Sobrio

Kate swung down from the thick rafters and checked her front window. The woman was gone, but the man she had claimed was chasing her was in Kate's front lawn scrambling for cover. She settled her gun sights on his broad chest and fired three rounds. Dropping her clip, she reloaded and headed for the back door. Stepping through the open door, Kate saw a fourth man at the side of her house and fired twice – both shots striking. Moving along the wall of her house away from the fallen man, Kate swung into the narrow alley between her cabin and a grain storage shed. Leading with her Navy Colt, she expected to see the woman but was disappointed. She turned and saw the man she had shot pointing his gun at her. She fired two shots instinctively, catching a shoulder and then his head.

They were wearing armour. The two men inside the house were dead, but the one in the front . . . probably not. And the woman? She was gone for the moment but might be circling the house to come in between Kate and the only direct trail into the forest. Her best chance was to get to the trees before they could flank her position. If she got that far, she could beat them no matter how many people they threw at her. Moving quickly across the open ground, Kate took the hill without looking back. Against a handgun she thought she could be out of range in a matter of seconds.

She did not see the woman, but she heard the gunshot behind her as she fell. On the ground, her hip on fire from the wound, Kate saw the woman coming toward her. Only then did Kate realize she had lost her Navy Colt. She sat up, scouring the ground for it. She felt dizzy. Brushing her hip, Kate felt the dart just before her eyes rolled back and the grey sky began to turn.

Her last thought terrified her as nothing had done since the death of her husband: Corbeau wanted her alive.

Zürich

Smoke came up through the airshaft at the centre of the room. Ethan could still breathe easily, but he tasted it already. Instinctively, he looked up. From the rafters to the skylight to the rooftop: the smoke would soon be thick enough that Kemp might not see him climbing out. He saw Zimmer staggering along the outer wall – across the room from him.

Zimmer was not looking for Ethan. He was getting out of a burning building. Ethan looked down. The ground floor of the bookstore had been swallowed up entirely in smoke. In a matter of minutes he would have no choice but to try to move – either down or up. He had installed the skylights himself and recalled the salesman telling him they weren't burglar proof, nothing was, but they were the safest on the market. At the time that had seemed like a good thing.

A silenced gunshot and a scream from below him interrupted Ethan's thoughts. He heard a body rolling down the open stairway. Stepping forward he could see nothing and realised Kemp had the same problem. He had mistaken his partner for Ethan.

Ethan took four steps back and ran for the railing, hurdling over it with his left leg leading, his right tucked and trailing. As he dropped into the white smoke, he brought his legs together. He kept his arms wide and loose, his feet ready for the explosion of impact. When he hit the plank floor Ethan used the last of his forward motion and rolled until he was behind the counter. He heard the spit of Kemp's gun chasing him.

He collided with Sean's body, saw the head wound, and scrambled as far as the front display window. He settled into a small space between the cashier's desk and the front door. His position gave him good cover and the broadest possible view of the open floor. For a long moment there was nothing to see but smoke. He had to get out, and was considering his chances of rolling through the display area and hitting the plate glass, when he saw Kemp scurrying for the back door. He was nothing more than a limping shadow but Ethan snapped-fired his weapon. The first shot had no effect. The second sent Kemp to the floor. Bounding over the desk and racing forward with the tip of the gun staying on Kemp's back, Ethan got within three steps, when Kemp suddenly rolled over.

Kemp fired quickly, going for Ethan's head. Ethan flinched and probably missed being hit because of it.

He did not give Kemp a second chance, but unloaded his pistol pointblank. He dropped his clip and reloaded. There was no time to check either man's pockets for identification. He didn't have to. He knew who had sent them and he knew there would be more. Ethan lunged across the open floor and found the back door. A moment later, he stumbled into the clean October air.

The cobblestone alley was so calm, so quiet, Ethan almost didn't notice the car parked directly in front of him. The engine was running. The driver blinked stupidly at him. For a second Ethan didn't understand either. Then he saw the driver reaching for something at his hip. Ethan did not wait or even think. He lifted his gun and fired Zimmer's pistol. He saw the man jerk, then slide down under the dashboard. Ethan walked forward until he was standing at the driver's side door and fired twice more.

He opened the car door and took the dead man's gun, the silencer already attached to it, and the extra clip he carried. He dug in his pocket for a wallet and found a private security badge and a photo-identity card giving the name Rolf Lutz. He took the wallet, badge, and ID. He pulled the corpse from the car and climbed in. Ethan settled himself for a moment and tried to think. If he went to the police or got picked up, Corbeau could get to him. His only chance was to find Kate. Together they could handle this.

He backed out of the narrow alley with the nonchalance of a man going home for lunch. He was all the way to Bellevue Plaza at the lake before he heard the first wail of sirens.

Lake Brienz, Switzerland

Still inside the city limits, Malloy hit the speed dial for Jane Harrison's cell number.

It was six-thirty in the morning, but Jane was wide awake. 'Yes?'

'Bob Whitefield is dead.'

Jane swore. A moment later she asked, 'What happened?'

'People were waiting for us at the airport. They hit as our train was pulling in.'

'Is the product safe?'

'The product is safe. I'll take care of the product. I just wanted you to know about Whitefield. The thing happened almost fifteen minutes ago. You need to get going on it.'

'Do you need transport or tactical support? I can bring a Special Ops team in from Stuttgart in two-to-three hours.'

'Not necessary, but tell our friends in New York there's going to be some delay – a day or two, I expect.'

'I'm here if you need me.'

Malloy disconnected and shut the phone off. The best anyone could do with that, even Jane, was to put him inside Zürich – which she already knew. He pulled his car back onto the road.

An hour later he parked his car in one of the large public lots close to the Interlaken East train station and caught a bus to Iseltwald on Lake Brienz. From there he had a choice of footpaths taking him along the lakeshore in the direction of Ax Alp. He took the high trail.

At the contessa's property, almost an hour later, Malloy saw Rene step out of the garden and wipe his hands with an unexpected delicacy. The old man offered no gesture of recognition and Malloy, after meeting his gaze fixedly, went directly to the front door of the villa. The contessa did not smile this time.

Fully conscious of the fact that he was echoing her statement to him the night she broke the Swiss bankers, Malloy said, 'I need your help.'

Given the differences between the two occasions, Malloy was not at all sure she would open her door for him, but she answered quietly and without hesitation. 'Come in.' When he had crossed her threshold, she asked if he wanted something to eat.

Malloy was quite hungry actually, but it hadn't occurred to him until she asked. For the past couple of hours he had been floating on an adrenaline high, his mind moving erratically as he tried to figure out what had gone wrong. That was gone now, and more than anything he just wanted to go to sleep. 'I could use a cup of coffee, if it's no trouble.'

The contessa smiled and began preparing two cups of espresso. She set out a glass and pitcher of water, a basket of bread, and an assortment of fruits. Malloy ate ravenously. As he did, he started to explain what had happened, but the contessa stopped him. First food, she said. Then talk. The silence they shared gave him confidence. He was not sure what had happened or even who had ordered the attack, but suddenly he knew he wasn't going back until he understood everything. It might take a day or two. It might take him several weeks. He didn't care. He couldn't afford to trust either Richland or Jane Harrison until he had more information.

'Now,' the contessa said, 'tell me why you have blood on your coat.' She reached out gently touching the dark stain in the leather.

Malloy told her the story simply and without embellishment. When he had finished, she asked, 'Did your friends set you up?'

'Not necessarily. If someone knew I was involved in this, he could have monitored my room from across the street with a directional microphone.'

'Who knew you were involved?'

'My friends. The buyers. Maybe the seller.'

'What's the motive, Thomas?'

He shook his head. 'I don't know. Money, I expect, but Bob Whitefield is a player. He could have been the target.'

Her eyes cut to the package Malloy had brought into the house. 'Do you want me to see it?'

'I was actually hoping I could talk you into keeping it for a few days – until I sort things out.'

'How about if we take a look at it and see exactly what you're asking me to do?'

The contessa stood up and went to one of her kitchen drawers. Pulling out a paring knife she cut the strings binding the package. Under the wrapping paper they discovered a length of linen cloth folded neatly around what felt like a small panel of wood. The contessa examined the weave with interest but said nothing. Finally, she unfolded it, revealing a small black panel of wood. A long crack ran through the centre from the base of the board to the top. At each corner and along the edges, the wood had been worn smooth, apparently from the repeated touch of human hands. Otherwise, there was very little damage. Even without Marcus Steiner's report on the radiocarbon dating, there was no question of its extraordinary age.

Turning the panel over, Malloy found himself staring at a painting of Christ wearing a crown of thorns. The condition of the piece was remarkable, the colours rich and expressive. 'The owners tested the wood yesterday,' he said. 'It's first century.'

'I didn't think it looked much like a twelfth century icon,' she offered with a scholar's wry sense of understatement. 'Bring it here. The light is better.' She gestured toward the worktable at the centre of the kitchen.

Malloy walked over to the table and found he was not quite able to take his eyes away from the figure staring out at him from the distance of two thousand years. The image depicted the head and top portion of the shoulders. Unlike the Renaissance portraits, this Christ was not a European. His skin was dark. The nose and lips clearly possessed Semitic features. Nor was he an especially young man, as tradition had it. He was closer to sixty than thirty, and he was not handsome. The face was gaunt, the skin leathery, but the eyes intimated both power and confidence. He wore the thorns like a royal crown. His blood glistened like adorning jewels.

'The perspective is slightly askew. Do you see how the highlights on the thorns and blood and in the eyes have a kind of randomness?'

Malloy had not noticed, but he saw what she meant.

There appeared to be no single exterior source for the light. 'Is that . . . good?'

'It is typical of Roman painting. The artists expressed a sense of perspective without understanding it.'

'You think it's authentic?'

'I do for two reasons. First, it's encaustic. All of the forgeries I know about in the 19th-century were tempera. Tempera is an egg-based medium that is easy to handle. Encaustic is made from bees wax and has to be applied hot with a spatula. A couple of thousand years ago, the best painters worked in encaustic for obvious reason. The colour holds and the shine was incomparable to anything then in existence. We have only really rediscovered encaustic in the last eighty years. It's possible, of course, that someone painted this recently on an extremely old piece of wood, but I don't think that is what you have here. See how the wood has been worn down by handling? In those same areas the paint has been compromised. This has been in existence for a great many years – long before twentieth century artists became reacquainted with encaustic techniques.'

'So it's not a medieval or Renaissance forgery?'

'I think it is exactly what it appears to be, a first century icon, probably Egyptian in origin. The best portrait painters were usually slaves who were either Egyptian or had trained in Egypt.'

'Worth twenty-five million?'

'Worth whatever the market can bear. It's one of a kind.'

From the doorway, Rene spoke. 'Get out!'

Malloy swung around in surprise. The contessa covered the painting and answered in a language

Malloy did not recognize. To Thomas, she said, 'You'll find some clothes upstairs that will fit you. The room at the top the stairs on the right. Take what you need. The clothes you have on will get you arrested.'

Malloy stared at Rene uncertainly. The contessa's man did not like him or his painting in the house. That much was clear. 'Are you sure it's okay?'

'I'll be up in a minute.' She saw Malloy looking at the painting. 'I'll take care of the painting for you. Don't worry.'

In the room at the top of the stairs, Malloy discovered four paintings that were similar in composition and style to the portrait of Christ he had carried out of Zürich. They appeared to be of great antiquity, apparently from the time of the Roman Empire, but they were not Romans. The clothing was colourful. The complexions were dark. The eyes were all black and shining. The subjects were common, every day people, probably upper-middleclass by the look of them.

After admiring them for a moment and wondering how the contessa had acquired them, he turned to the business at hand and found several overcoats that fit better than he had imagined they would. He chose the one that didn't look like it would draw much attention. It was not a tailored fit, but its roominess covered his shoulder holster comfortably. He wondered where they had come from. They certainly didn't belong to Rene.

He inspected the rest of his clothes. Except for a bullet hole in his sweatshirt he was presentable.

'That doesn't look too bad.' Malloy looked up in surprise at the contessa. He had not heard her climbing the stairs or walking on the creaky floors. 'Get rid of the sweatshirt. I think I have something across the hall you can wear instead.'

He smiled and stripped away his jacket, shoulder holster and sweatshirt. She looked at the vest with the bullet hole over the heart but said nothing about it. If she hadn't let him imagine himself lying in his own grave he would not have asked for it and would be at this moment one of several bodies at a crime scene.

'I just need to get back to Zürich. I should have a suitcase waiting for me there.'

'Let's get you there safely.' She started from the room.

'I like the paintings.'

The contessa stopped and turned back to look at them with the affection of a collector. 'They're supposed to be Egyptian mummy portraits from the second and third century, but I like to think of them as my children.'

'What are they really?'

'A window into the past.'

She stepped back into the room now and pointed out one of the paintings. Malloy had trouble following her hand because her fragrance stirred him. 'You see the similarity in style to your painting?'

'It's encaustic, isn't it?'

'Very good. The only one in the group that is actually.'

The tempera paintings hadn't the sheen of encaustic. 'So what are mummy portraits?' he asked.

'Sometime in the second century, Egyptians began having their portraits painted on panels of wood and occasionally on canvas. At the person's death, the relatives would then have the portrait slipped into the bandages of the mummy directly over the face instead of the traditional mask. The idea sounds strange, but the effect is wonderful. If the painting is skilfully done, it's as if you can see the actual person staring out from the bandages. Anyway, in the nineteenth century an archaeologist named Flinders Petrie began digging at an enormous necropolis in Fayum, Egypt, about forty miles from Cairo. Most of the paintings he recovered were in terrible condition, of course, but a few looked as if they had just been created. Naturally, once people saw them in Europe and America, there was an incredible demand for them. Economic realities being what they are, some enterprising Egyptians passed off quite a few forgeries for the real thing.

'Over the years our ability to date material has become quite sophisticated and a number of museums have been forced to remove what they had once thought was a second or third century masterpiece. It's virtually impossible these days to own the real thing. There are only about a thousand in existence. But, for a price, the forgeries are available, if you are enterprising about it. I don't really care when they were painted. I just love looking at the faces.'

She pointed at another painting, a woman staring out from eternity. 'This one went to the Petrie Museum in London but it became suspect when one of the curators realised there was no gypsum undercoat. The genuine paintings all had a base of gypsum. If you look closely, you can see why.'

'The wood grain shows through?'

She nodded like an approving schoolmarm. 'Otherwise

perfect. This one,' she pointed at a man's face, 'they found in the bandages of a woman's mummified corpse. It was at the Louvre for a number of years with the mummy before someone noticed the discrepancy and tested the age of the panel.'

Malloy pointed at the painting she had first indicated. It depicted a robust young man of some thirty years with dark eyes and a thick beard. He was beginning to go bald, but he was a handsome man all the same. 'The edges of the painting aren't rounded off like the others,' he remarked.

'In a mummy portrait they would trim the corners of the panel so that it would fit inside the bandages without making a bulge – but not on this one.'

'So it's a forgery?'

'It looks like a mummy portrait otherwise, though, doesn't it?'

'Is it genuine?'

'I haven't tested it.'

'But if it's encaustic—'

'Let me show you something I think you'll like. If you rub the encaustic with a cloth, the wax heats up so that the flesh seems almost to glow. Try it.'

Malloy took the sleeve of his sweatshirt and rubbed it, seeing the effect after a few seconds.

'Feel it,' she said.

He touched the paint and felt the warmth of it and smiled. 'That's amazing!'

'Almost like a living being, isn't it? Come on, let's find a shirt and get you on your way. Rene is not very happy at the moment and I think it might be a good idea not to push our luck with him.'

'Are you sure—'

'I owe you this for your help with the bankers, Thomas.'

'I made a telephone call. Not exactly high risk.'

'It was a lot more than that and you know it. You trusted me – and that made all the difference.'

As he was leaving, Malloy told the contessa, 'If something happens to me—'

She touched his lips with the tips of her fingers, a gesture that was too intimate for friends, but she did not pull back or seem flustered by her sudden show of affection. Instead, she held him with her gaze – as a lover might. 'Your eyes are open now, Thomas. You'll be fine.'

Zürich

Ethan found a cell phone in the glove compartment and tried to call Kate but got no answer. For several minutes, he focused on getting out of Zürich and planning his drive south. Sobrio was a mountain village perched over the Levantine Valley. The autobahn cut through it. Otherwise, it was a perfect wilderness dotted with tiny, ancient villages. It was two to two and a half hours from Zürich, depending on the traffic in the tunnels. The problem was that Ethan wasn't even sure if he should drive down there. He wasn't sure what he should do. He tried her number again, then Roland's cell phone. When neither answered, Ethan decided that Corbeau had moved against all three of them at the same moment. The more he thought about it, the more certain he became. There was no point in driving south. Kate was gone, escaped into the mountains . . . or dead.

That thought was unbearable and, almost reflexively, he tried her number again. The phone rang several times before her message service answered. She could have run, he thought with a thrill of hope, even knowing he was deluding himself. But it was possible! She could have dropped her phone getting away. He didn't have his phone, and he wasn't dead. Not yet, anyway.

He had to take the chance, had to drive to Sobrio. He found the autobahn at the edge of the city and started south. He checked his watch. He could be at Kate's cabin before sunset. And then? For the first time in their lives they had no backup plan. He tried Roland's cell phone, but Roland wasn't answering either. Ethan checked Lutz's cell phone directory. There were no names, only three cell phone numbers, all of them inside Switzerland. He tried the first two and got a phone out of service message. The next produced a pleasant chirp that was followed by someone speaking High German.

'And?' The speaker's tone, more than the word itself, suggested that he either didn't want to be interrupted or he expected a report without the usual pleasantries.

Ethan answered in High German with the same grimness. 'Brand is dead.'

'Problem?' The voice seemed to have a degree of curiosity. Phone contact was probably only necessary if something had gone wrong.

'He killed Zimmer and Kemp. I need to know what you want me to do.'

'You know what to do!'

'Did we get Kenyon?'

'They're flying her back now.'

Ethan muttered a satisfied, 'Good!' and disconnected. Pulling to the side of the road, he began to shake. Corbeau had Kate. Now what? He stared vacantly at the road signs, then at the cold grey sky. '*You know what to do*,' he whispered.

Corbeau owned an office building in the industrial town of Zug. He also had a vacation house outside St. Moritz. The first was not isolated enough for his purposes. The second was not large enough. If he was 'flying her back' from Kate's cabin, Corbeau would be taking her in a helicopter to his villa on Lake Lucerne.

Ethan was an hour away.

Zürich

Malloy caught a bus down Ax Alp to Brienz. From there he took a train back to Lucerne and another to the Enge station in the suburbs of Zürich. He kept his hat and coat on and managed to read his *Züricher Zeitung* with pretended interest. He called Marcus Steiner from a tram.

'Change of plans.'

'Tell me about it. I have been at it all day cleaning up the mess.'

'I need a safe house.'

'Let me see what I can do. Where are you?'

'I'll be at the lake across from the Congress House in a couple of minutes.'

'Max can be there in twenty. He's driving a black Mercedes.'

'Don't forget my computer and suitcase.'

Stepping off the tram at the Congress House, Malloy settled on a park bench amid some shrubbery and tried one more time to work out just what had gone wrong. Marcus, he knew, was not involved. Had his friend wanted the painting Malloy would be dead. Jane was a different matter. With Jane the mission was always more important than the personnel involved in it. That was understood from the opening gambit and it was something every field operative faced at some point. Sometimes it meant she didn't tell you everything. In this instance it was possible she was playing a game he did not understand. Possible, but not likely.

Charlie Winger made even less sense. Like Jane, if he wanted the painting, he probably would have worked things differently. Certainly his long-standing friendship with Bob Whitefield argued his innocence, even if he did not get along with Malloy. Whitefield was extraneous to the mission, an insurance policy against the long odds of Swiss Customs discovering the painting as it was being smuggled out of the country. Unless Whitefield was the reason for the attack.

A lot had changed since Malloy had worked inside Langley. Whitefield, for one thing, was more independent than when he first moved to Paris. But independent bureau chiefs, like freewheeling operatives, tended to be reassigned or forced into early retirement. As his superior, Charlie had no reason to want Bob Whitefield dead, not when a transfer was easy enough. Besides, this was about the painting. It had value. To people like North, Richland, and Starr it was priceless. The painting was at the centre of this. The people moving it were irrelevant.

Stateside a handful of people knew about J. W. Richland's favour. Of those no one at all knew when Malloy had intended to arrive at the Zürich airport. Whitefield had irritated Malloy as his supervisor, but nothing about the station chief of the Paris bureau had ever indicated Whitefield's lack of experience. He would have kept information concerning the rendezvous with Malloy to himself. That meant the only way someone else could have known about it was by an audio surveillance of Malloy's room when Malloy and Whitehead met and arranged the exchange. That was only possible if someone knew Malloy and Whitefield were involved. How had anyone anticipated Malloy would run the operation?

There were, as far as he could see, only two possibilities. Someone inside the agency had leaked the information to a third party or one of the buyers had said something. Agency personnel might sell information for the right price, but that kind of betrayal took time. Turning hard-core intelligence officers with the temptation of a quick buck just wasn't possible. In such a situation the approach was everything. A good approach took months, even years. There had to be a level of trust – like that which he had established with Claudia de Medici or Marcus Steiner. Given the nature of this job that wasn't really plausible. Mentioning Malloy's name to someone, on the other hand, was an amateur's mistake, what Malloy would expect from the ebullient J. W. Richland.

A black Mercedes appeared in the distance, its turn signal flashing, and Malloy walked to the sidewalk. 'Thanks for the help this morning,' he said in English as he slipped into the car.

Max shrugged his shoulders indifferently. 'That is what I was there for.'

'How did you avoid the cops, anyway?'

Max pulled out a detective's shield from his shirt pocket, 'Not too hard.'

Malloy laughed quietly.

'The story,' Max explained, 'is that terrorists assassinated a US diplomat. Swiss police responded with deadly force: five terrorists dead, one Zürich detective up for commendation. There is another Glock in the glove compartment, by the way. Why don't you take it, and I'll take yours. Marcus can substitute it this afternoon for the one I turned over to him as evidence. If we don't, my report isn't going to convince anyone.'

Malloy exchanged weapons, careful to clean his prints away on the gun he gave Max. 'What about the witnesses? They going to create any problems?'

'Both people who got a look at you thought you were one of the bad guys.'

'Have you talked with the Americans?'

'Somebody has. They turned up maybe thirty-to-forty minutes after the shooting.'

'Anybody looking for me?'

Max smiled, kicking up his shoulder. 'The friends of the dead guys, I expect.'

Approaching Bellevue Plaza, traffic came to a standstill. 'Fire,' he remarked miserably. 'Some bookstore got lit-up at lunchtime and traffic is backed up around the lake.'

Malloy studied the source of the black smoke for a minute. 'Brand Books?'

'You know it?'

'Best shop in town for English books.'

'Not anymore.'

A meeting with Starr and North Sunday evening and his shop burning to the ground two days later: that wasn't a coincidence. That was a chain of evidence. Brand was involved somehow. He just didn't know how.

'Did Marcus have any trouble finding me a safe house?'

'He said you didn't give him much time.'

'That doesn't sound good.'

Max's dark, stolid features broke into a crooked smile. 'It depends on your point of view, I suppose. In my opinion, a whorehouse has some real advantages.'

Chapter Seven

Zürich
October 10, 2006.

There are two districts in the old town of Zürich. Some would say two Zürichs. One offers an elegant mix of fashion and finance. At the centre is Zürich's Bahnhofstrasse, a promenade of cafes and sumptuous shops where window displays routinely offer fifty thousand dollar watches and necklaces so richly encrusted in jewels it would seem only royalty could wear them without blushing. The people who crowd this street are all business. They work here, and though they dress fashionably, they hardly seem to notice the golden temptations virtually within their reach. One finds of course the occasional tourist, dressed badly and wandering along the broad walkways with as little purpose as the pigeons, but mostly the crowd is young, urban, and upscale: the local elite, a pleasant mix of nationalities and languages and even colour.

Across the Limmat under the Gross Munster lies a bohemian Zürich. The buildings here are often three or four hundred years old. Gargoyles are standard fare. The alleys are paved with cobblestone and twist about in medieval whimsy. This is the part of town where one finds rare books, old paintings, antique glass and porcelain. Here, perfectly polished tables are frequently as old as the French Revolution and shopkeepers look more like Oxford dons than merchants in a hurry to move their property.

There is a degree of prosperity in this second Zürich that is astonishing, especially as the quarter makes an open display of strip clubs, blue movies, and an active population of prostitutes and addicts. It is an interesting place by day, hardly dangerous and not really so racy that you would notice the decadence if you kept your gaze straight ahead. But as the sun begins to set it becomes a different world.

Max dropped Malloy off in the heart of this district with instructions for where he was to go and what he should say. Malloy walked only a few blocks before he slipped into a small, ugly little tavern with no name. His jacket had the flavour of a working-class east European, so he should have fit in, but his suitcase and computer gave him away. The moment he stepped through the door everyone in the room stopped talking and stared at him.

'I hope you're in the right place,' a prostitute murmured in High German.

Malloy pushed through the crowd without answering and ordered a bottle of beer from a sullen bartender. Dropping twenty francs on the bar when his beer arrived, he said in Swiss German, 'Alexa working this afternoon?'

The bartender's eyes focused on Malloy briefly and then shifted toward the stairway at the back of the room. 'Alexa' was in.

The doors to three of the four rooms at the top of the stairs were closed. Hasan Barzani waited inside the fourth room. An AK-47 lay across the bed. Barzani was a tall man with a large square head and deep-set black eyes. He dressed like a workman in ill-fitting jeans, scarred boots, and a cheap leather jacket, even though he was worth over eighty million dollars. His method for earning his fortune was time-honoured and ugly: he sold the bodies of women, he stole the property of the middle-class and he murdered anyone foolish enough to stand in his way. Like every wealthy man Malloy had ever known, Barzani made no apologies for the way he had earned his money. Given the chance he would even indulge himself in justifications. He took care of people. He paid salaries to the families whose husbands and sons had once been free men and now sat quietly in prison. He had wealth, yes, but he had responsibilities as well!

All of which was true. What Barzani did not have was risk. Not for many years now. He was insulated from the crime he committed. He ran managers who ran networks. He owned corporations. He consulted lawyers. He even saw his own personal banker once a week. Barzani had started life the hard way, but he was not a criminal anymore. No, straight-faced he would tell you he was a businessman. And when people died, as people sometimes did, well, it was a tough business.

But he was nothing if not loyal and, for Malloy, Hasan Barzani came back to the streets. Malloy after all had not only financed him when he was nothing more than a petty crook with dubious connections to the major criminal organizations behind the Iron

Curtain, he had also taught the giant how to avoid what had become an embarrassingly long and intimate involvement with the police of Zürich. In return for this, in the beginning at least, Barzani really hadn't very much to give. Most of what he heard was outdated or simply incorrect. Malloy hadn't complained. He took what Barzani gave him and spent lavishly for it.

In time his patience had paid off. Barzani became an important man in Zürich with connections that reached all the way to Moscow. Weeks before the fall of the Berlin Wall, Barzani reported that things were changing, travel restrictions being lifted. The ubiquitous stream of East Germans trying to break out through the Austrian border had turned into an exodus. When he talked about Russia, he described the growing decadence, crumbling social institutions, and the kind of political awareness and concern that in any other country would have spelled revolution. Some of what he told Malloy Langley had flatly rejected as bad intelligence, either wishful thinking or an agent passing along what he thought his handler wanted to hear. For a time, even Malloy had begun to wonder, but once the wall broke, it became clear that Barzani was extremely well connected. In the early nineties while other field operatives were sending disturbing reports about what was becoming known as the Russian mafia, Malloy was providing names and job descriptions.

'Thomas!' Barzani shouted, as his face broke into a brutal smile. They hugged one another, both laughing spontaneously. 'What is this I hear from Marcus about you working again? I thought you were living the good life these days!'

'The President asked me to run an errand for him – as a personal favour.'

Barzani had the look of a man who has just learned that he is the heir to an enormous and quite unexpected inheritance. 'Well, we can't disappoint the President, can we?'

Lake Lucerne

Kate Kenyon came up slowly to a sitting position. She could see nothing, but felt cinders beneath her. For a moment, she could almost imagine she was outdoors but the air was too stale. What—? She had not even fashioned the question when she remembered the sting of the dart, the enveloping effect of the drug.

Julian Corbeau had her.

But where exactly? Carefully, Kate stretched her arms to either side. Finding nothing, she reached overhead. When that too gave her nothing, she tried to stand. Again reaching out, she concentrated on keeping her balance. It was difficult in perfect darkness, all the more so when she realised she could be anywhere – even at the edge of a cliff.

'You're awake.' The voice Kate heard belonged to a woman. Somewhere close to her, she thought, but for some reason she could not determine the direction. She was not even sure if the woman was standing or sitting.

'You *are* awake?'

A frightened woman, not the woman who had taken her out. Not Kate's jailer either. 'I'm awake. Who are you?'

'Nicole North.'

'How long have you been here?' Kate asked.

'I don't know. What time is it?'

Kate gave a dry laugh. 'I didn't bring my watch.' She knew from the tightness of her muscles and the general feeling of exhaustion that she had not been out for too many hours, but some time had passed. Three, four hours? It was maybe sunset, maybe nine or ten o'clock. Maybe midnight. In the dark it didn't really matter, did it? 'How did they get you?'

'They kidnapped me at the airport this morning. They got me inside a car, and I remember feeling something on the back of my neck, and that's the last thing I recall before waking up here.'

Here, Kate decided, was probably Corbeau's *donjon*. Before breaking into his villa in August, Kate had studied the building permits Corbeau's father and grandfather had applied for over the years. This part of the tower, according to the original blueprints, had a single entrance through the basement. The area was designated as a wine cellar. She had dismissed the area as a possible hiding place for the painting because of the quality of the air. It had not occurred to her that Corbeau might actually use his tower as a prison cell.

'What happened to your uncle?' Kate asked.

'Nothing. They couldn't find him. How do you know about my uncle?'

'I'm the person who sold you a painting this morning.'

For a long terrible moment Nicole North said nothing. Then sobbing quietly, she whispered, 'He's going to kill us, isn't he?'

'By the time it comes to that, we'll beg him to do it.'

Zürich

Malloy was sleeping when his phone rang.

'Yes?'

Jane Harrison spoke. 'They got Nicole North.'

'*Who* got her?'

'We don't know yet. What we know is this: Richland called his contact in the Administration; the director just told Charlie to take care of it.'

'Take care of what?'

'You're to turn the product over to Jonas Starr. Once he has it, Starr will arrange Dr North's release.'

'Let's pretend I believe that for a moment.'

'Dr Starr doesn't want any help on this, T. K.'

'If I turn the painting over to Jonas Starr—'

'Not *if*, when. That's an order, not a point for debate.' Malloy was silent, seething with anger. 'You'll get your payday. Starr has assured us that you will be paid in full. Look, he's got a team of mercenaries with him. They know what they're doing.'

'What's he doing with a team of mercenaries?'

'He brought them in.'

'More likely he was trying to track me and didn't get the job done.'

'Pass the product to him, T. K., and come home. You've done your part, and I guarantee you your money will be waiting for you.'

'You know the age of this product?'

'I know what they told me. Beyond that, I don't care, and neither should you.'

'Starr isn't going to trade it for his niece, Jane. It's not in his nature.'

'Call the man and do what he tells you, T. K.'

'And let North die?'

'Write this number down.'

'You call him. I don't want the man to have my number. Tell him I'll meet him at seven-thirty tomorrow at the *Rote Fabrik* in Zürich.'

'He wants the painting tonight.'

'I'm busy tonight.'

Lake Lucerne

Ethan Brand took a high point of land that was inaccessible to anyone who had not trained to climb rock. From this promontory he had a narrow view into Julian Corbeau's estate. He could see the front door of the guardhouse and some of the grounds. He and Kate had spent a number of hours hidden in the undergrowth at the top of this rock watching the routines of Corbeau's security detail.

The first thing he realised was that everything had changed. Formerly, Corbeau's security had been primarily focused on protecting his person from kidnap. He never left his compound without a five man detail, usually via his helicopter. The villa was secured by two guards in his absence. In addition to a ten-foot wall and a motion activated light and alarm system, there were two dogs. Against these obstacles, Kate had designed a plan to bait the guards and neutralise the dogs. From the start the problem had not been getting in safely. The problem had been getting out. For one thing the road around the lake was the sole link between the city of Lucerne and the village of Meggen.

The police could shut that down in a matter of minutes. The lake was no better. Assuming they could get to a boat, they faced a massive police response.

Kate's solution had been ingenious. They would wait until the summer fireworks. Then, amid hundreds of pleasure boats sitting at the centre of the lake, they would swim out to an inflatable, access the far end of the lake and return to the centre of the lake, sink the inflatable and climb back into their boat before the completion of the fireworks. With fifty boats on the lake, the police might have resorted to the tedious process of searching each vessel, but the summer fireworks had brought out closer to five hundred. Short of a threat to national security, the Swiss police would not inconvenience that many citizens – no matter how rich Corbeau was.

They had spent several months preparing for the incursion, not even sure the painting existed. They had risked their lives on the chance, and they had won. Or so they had thought. At some point Corbeau had learned their identities, and all the money in the world could not save Kate from him now. If she was even there, somewhere inside his villa, she was not coming out without a fight. And this time Ethan was not looking at a two-man security detail backed up by a couple of Doberman pinschers.

Watching Corbeau's villa for only a couple of hours convinced Ethan that he was looking at an armed camp. He had seen a dozen individuals walking from the main house to the guardhouse, but there were possibly twice that number. Certainly there were others in the field. There was always someone coming or going. There was no way to fight his way into the compound. But say he could get in with Lutz's badge and security pass. Say it was possible. He still needed to find Kate and get over the wall. Even then the fight would not be over. After using the police to close off the road, Corbeau would give chase, trapping them in the forest between the road and the lake.

The only sensible way to handle Kate's kidnapping was to call the police and tell them what had happened. And if he did the sensible thing? The police would need to take a statement. Once Ethan presented himself to the police, Kate would disappear, and Corbeau would make sure Ethan did as well. He could try to convince himself that the police would be neutral about the whole thing, but he had lived in Switzerland too long to believe it. Corruption as the rest of the world knew it was non-existent in the police force but, at the highest levels, people of wealth enjoyed unparalleled protection. It was unthinkable that they should be paraded before the media like common criminals. Entertaining as that was for the masses, it was bad business for a country that provided safe haven for billionaires.

The police were out, and a direct assault was out. Worse yet, he was looking at hours to formulate a plan, not days or weeks. He was working alone with only a couple of handguns, two silencers, and one extra clip of ammo. In his lonely vigil it was easy to imagine the ferocity of Corbeau's vengeance against Kate. The hard part was resisting a doomed assault on the front gate.

Zürich

Malloy stepped into the alley and followed the curving cobblestone lane up the hill to the nearest road. He found Max and Marcus Steiner waiting for him. 'How are the accommodations?' Marcus asked him.

'Can't complain.'

Marcus laughed quietly. 'Given the reputation of your host, I expect you mean you don't dare.'

'How did things end at the airport?'

'Everyone is on the same page. A career diplomat stationed in Paris spends a couple of days in Zürich before flying back to the States. A group of neo-Nazis target him as an American who works with the US government, and they kill him. These days they don't even need a reason. The important thing is not the story, Thomas, but how they knew you were going to be on that train.'

'Best guess is Roland Wheeler pulled a double-cross. The only thing better than twenty-five million is twenty-five million times two. Sell it, steal it, sell it again.'

'How did Wheeler find out?'

'I think the buyers gave him my name and he set up an audio surveillance on my room.'

'It's possible, I suppose. Wheeler started his professional life in Hamburg. Two of our hitters – the guys with Mohawks – were heroin addicts operating in downtown Hamburg.'

'Not exactly the kind of fellows who would be running in Roland's circle.'

'There was a Berlin accountant in on it too. Wheeler

has a number of clients in Berlin. Perhaps there is a connection through him.'

'What do you have on the Brand Books fire?'

'The investigation is ongoing, but they've got what looks like three people dead inside the building. So far the cause of death is unknown, but they should have autopsy reports by tomorrow morning. A man was found shot to death outside the building, just beyond the back door. It looks connected to what was going on inside. There are three entry wounds. They think probably nine millimetre.'

'We need to follow that up. If Brand was involved with Wheeler on this, it could be that Wheeler turned on him.'

'You really think Wheeler was behind the attack at the airport?'

'He's the thief in the crowd.'

'You might be right. He disappeared after the meeting this morning. The people at his gallery don't know where he is. He hasn't touched a credit card or used his cell phone all afternoon.'

'How long have you been watching his house?'

'Max called in two off duty Zürich patrolmen about three hours ago.'

Max spoke as he drove. 'I checked with them just before we picked you up. The place looks empty. They haven't seen a soul.'

'Are we going to have any trouble taking a look around?'

'He has a silent alarm,' Max answered. 'When the patrol car shows up, our people badge them and tell them we have it. Meanwhile, we go about our business.'

'The only problem,' Marcus added, 'is if we take something. The moment Mr Wheeler files a complaint our people are going to have to explain themselves. If it comes to a showdown between a couple of policemen and Roland Wheeler, Wheeler is going to win.'

'I just want information. We're not going to take anything.'

'I was hoping I could appropriate a Monet,' Marcus quipped. 'Do you think he has any he wouldn't miss?'

Roland Wheeler's property sat on the eastern shore of Lake Zürich in what had once been suburbs. The city had long ago converted the land surrounding his villa into a city park, giving Wheeler an uncluttered view along his shoreline. The house was not especially large by American standards, but it was undeniably grand in the old world manner. It was a two-storey structure of brick trimmed in limestone. It featured a large front portico and a terrace just off the second storey, a steep slate roof and the usual overabundance of Gothic paraphernalia. A small ornamental fence surrounded the property. Otherwise it was easily accessible. Max pulled his Mercedes up to the kerb close to the house and sauntered across the street to talk with the surveillance team.

'Still quiet,' he told them when he returned.

Marcus used a lock pick at one of the side doors. It was delicate work that he had long ago mastered. They were inside the house a few seconds later. A security panel greeted them, but they ignored the warning beeps. The furnishings were mostly antique. A great many were sixteenth and seventeenth century pieces. They had the warm, worn look of daily use. Malloy started in the bedroom, checking drawers and shelves for an address book. When he saw the familiar flashing of coloured lights splashing across the interior of the house, he walked to the window. The patrol car had responded within four minutes of the entry.

One of Max's off-duty detectives greeted them. He pointed toward the house, and Malloy, knowing he was only a silhouette, raised his hand in greeting. They did not get back into their patrol car immediately, but neither did they care to question the word of a fellow officer. The second off-duty cop ambled out into the street, and the four men settled into a comfortable conversation – probably about the weather.

'You need to see the office,' Marcus said, stepping into Wheeler's bedroom. Malloy followed him without comment. As they went, Marcus began muttering mournfully the names of the various painters Wheeler had hung so casually on the walls of his house. 'Cézanne . . . Gauguin . . . Picasso . . . Kandinsky . . . Klee . . . even my Monet. Do you think he would miss just one little Monet, Thomas?'

'You can always come back.'

'How do you say it in America?' He switched easily to English with a pronounced but pleasant Swiss accent: 'I want my instant gratification, and I want it now!' In Swiss German he added, 'What is tomorrow to a kid in a candy store?'

Wheeler's office gave the only evidence that the house had been searched. The file cabinets had been emptied, the paper burned in the office fireplace. The computer monitor remained, but there was no sign of the computer itself.

As they were finishing their search of the office, Max entered the room. 'Got something,' he announced in his gruff manner. Both Malloy and Marcus looked at him expectantly. 'You'll probably want to see this for yourself,' he said.

They found Roland Wheeler's corpse sitting inside a basement cabinet, his thighs pressed into his chest, his heels pushing against his buttocks, his chin settled neatly between his kneecaps. The art dealer still had on the grey suit and scarlet tie he'd worn at the bank. His flesh was cool. Rigor mortis had set in. A bullet had been fired at close range into the back of his skull.

Marcus considered the corpse briefly before asking Malloy, 'You still think he's the one who ordered the hit at the airport?'

Lake Lucerne
October 10, 2006.

Kate heard the squeak of a steel door opening and saw a faint grey light wash across the cindered floor. Despite her dread she glanced around her prison cell. The ceiling was roughly twenty-five feet above her. As she had guessed this was Corbeau's tower, the lower two-thirds of it to be exact. There were half a dozen chains with handcuffs hanging from the walls and a number of torch holders. Beyond the dark shadows overhead, if she could possibly climb that high across the smoothly jointed stones, a thick stone floor waited. She had been hoping to discover some way out, but there was no exit except through the steel door.

Three uniformed guards stepped into the room as

Kate came to this conclusion. Each man carried a burning torch and a short-barrelled shotgun. As the torches flickered, the shadows of the men danced across the walls behind them. The scene inspired the disheartening observation that in Corbeau's world medieval brutality enjoyed all the advantages of modern technology. She was in a Gothic nightmare, held inside an impregnable medieval *donjon* by jailers who dressed in corporate security uniforms. A bit of electricity might have made things seem almost normal.

When each man had placed his torch in a stand, Julian Corbeau entered the room with an oddly unsettling majesty. He was in his mid-fifties, trim, small and unnaturally erect. Ethan's research indicated the man had not spent a single day in military training, but it was hard to believe. He presented himself as the consummate general. She knew collectors from every nation, people with whom her father had dealt over the years, men and women who operated outside the boundaries of law with the arrogance that comes of owning politicians, but she had never seen a man with as much self-assurance as this one. It was as if he imagined himself invested with the powers of a deity.

Giving North no portion of his attention, Corbeau looked at Kate as if shopping for delicacies. He did not care if she feared him. This was not a show of power. He wanted only to enjoy himself. When it seemed he had, Corbeau glanced in the direction of the guards who had placed themselves along the wall. One of the men stepped forward and presented his weapon as if offering it for inspection. Corbeau took the shotgun and pointed it at Nicole North. It was the first time he had even considered North's presence.

'There is nothing I would enjoy more than killing you, Dr North,' he announced in English. 'Fortunately for you, you have some value if your uncle decides to trade my painting for your life. That said I don't particularly care about the condition of your body as long as you are alive, so you would do well to answer my questions quickly and honestly.

'You, Lady Kenyon,' he said shifting to Italian but in no other way directing his attention away from North, 'are a different matter. I extend to you the rights and courtesy due a prisoner of war. For the time being I have no intention of causing you even a moment of pain. Not a bruise if I can help it. If you don't cooperate with my interrogation, I tell you freely, nothing at all will happen to you.'

He shifted his gaze to Kate, and without smiling still managed to express his amusement. 'You don't look as if you believe me.'

'I don't.' Kate told him in English.

Corbeau nodded and the guard who had presented him with his weapon walked up to Kate, touching her shoulder gently. In German he said to her, 'Against the wall, please.' Kate gave way under the pressure of his fingertips and felt the cold masonry against her shoulders. The guard spoke again in German. 'Your hand, please?' Kate presented her hand. She could imagine that he meant to separate it from her body. That was a thief's punishment, but as there was nothing she could do to prevent it, she simply steeled herself for the inevitable – whatever it was.

Gently, with all the courtesy of an escort helping a

woman from a car, he lifted her wrist until it was above her head. The cuff snapped over her flesh with surprising ease. Startled, Kate looked up and saw the handcuffs. With her free hand she swung angrily at the guard catching his nose with a swift, sweet crack. The young man covered his face with his hands and began to bleed. A single cry of pain had escaped his lips as she broke his nose, but that was the only sound he offered.

'Shoot her,' Corbeau said in German. He spoke with the indifference of a man who has given such an order numerous times. Both guards levelled their weapons and fired once at Nicole North. North screamed as she was thrown back against the wall and then fell to the cindered floor. After a moment of stunned silence, North gasped in pain and gave a violent, inarticulate scream.

'Rubber bullets,' Corbeau said in Italian, his eyes holding Kate's gaze with a lover's intensity. 'I expect right now she thinks she's dying. As I understand it, the pain is nothing compared to having one's flesh burned away. Perhaps you'll refuse to cooperate again and give her a chance to find out. Now, if you would be so kind, give this gentleman your hand, and for the sake of your friend here do not make me ask anything twice. I assure you, I will unchain you both after we have talked, but I've seen the video surveillance tapes of you in action, and to be honest I won't feel entirely comfortable until you're secure.'

North stayed on the floor, her groans still loud.

Corbeau told his guard in German to ask Kate for her hand.

The guard stepped up to her quietly, his nose dripping blood. 'Please?' Kate let the guard snap the cuff around her wrist. Next he cuffed each ankle.

It did not help Kate's fears to watch her gentle guard lift North up roughly by her arm and slam her against the wall. He actually threw his head back and forth, letting his blood splatter across North's face. As she cringed and shrieked, he cuffed her wrists and ankles brutally. That accomplished, he ripped her clothes away. Certain now of what came next, North broke down. Her prayers for pity meant nothing to Corbeau. He was not even looking at her. His eyes remained fixed on Kate. His promises to the contrary, Kate was sure Corbeau meant for them both to be raped before he proceeded to the more delicate arts of the Inquisition.

'Leave us,' Corbeau said in German. As the three guards left, he passed the weapon back to the guard.

When they were alone, Corbeau walked over to examine North's wounds. She whimpered quietly as he touched her flesh. 'What do you want?' she asked.

In Italian Corbeau said to North, 'If you ask me politely, I will have fresh clothing sent to you at once.'

'What are you saying?' North shouted in sudden anger. 'Speak English! I don't understand you!'

Without taking his eyes from North, Corbeau continued in Italian, 'If you tell her what I just said, I will give her clothes soaked in acid.'

'What does he want?' North demanded of Kate. 'Tell me what he's saying!'

In English he answered, 'Pray to your God, Dr North. I understand He can be a great comfort in times like this.'

North screamed as if he had pierced her with a knife, and yet Corbeau had done nothing to cause it except to mention God.

Corbeau left her and walked to Kate. North's screaming subsided with each step he took away from her, but her breathing was laboured and shallow and fast. When he was standing in front of Kate, Corbeau said in Italian, 'Who broke into my house with you this summer?'

Kate answered in English. 'A man I know in Rome.'

Corbeau walked to one of the torches on the wall. Taking it with an affectionate gaze at the bright, flickering fire, he stepped toward Dr North. Her screams turned into a mad panic.

'Ethan Brand!' Kate shouted.

It did no good. Corbeau swept the torch over North's feet. He seemed indifferent to the changed pitch of her screams or her wild contortions. Her voice was like nothing Kate had ever heard, and something inside her broke. She had imagined she could resist, that no matter what he did he would not have the satisfaction of seeing her beg, but Corbeau understood Kate's singular weakness: she was human.

'Leave her alone!'

Corbeau carried the torch with him as he returned to Kate. His eyes swept over her shoulders to her breasts, across her hips and thighs – a look Kate had no trouble understanding.

Corbeau's smile was almost friendly. 'And if I do?'

'What do you want?'

'I want the truth! Don't imagine you are betraying your lover. He is already dead.'

Kate's eyes burned. Her throat closed off. For a terrible moment it seemed that she could not stand.

'If it is any comfort, he killed two of the three people I sent to interrogate and execute him. A very physical man, your lover. I only wish he had been one of mine.'

Kate blinked tears from her eyes. Until that moment, she had never truly hated anyone. It was an emotion that left the extremities cold, the centre very hot. She did not care that it would cost her life. Had she been free in that moment she would have killed Julian Corbeau. What was hard was accepting that she could do nothing. Ethan was gone, and she could not even cry without giving this sadist pleasure.

'Who were the people at the front gate?'

Kate glanced at Nicole North. Much as she might have wanted, she could not refuse Corbeau. She actually wanted pain. It would have given focus to her rage, but she could not watch North's suffering. 'They were Austrians. I don't know their names. My father knows them. I only met them once.'

'You don't know their first names?'

'We didn't use names.'

Kate's eyes cut to North, who was watching her with fearful intensity. She had apparently worked out that her pain was connected to Kate's answers.

'I shouldn't worry too much about them, if I were you. They're both dead. Helga killed herself this afternoon. Poor soul wasn't very bright about it. She drank some kind of drain cleaner. From what I understand, she suffered a great deal. Hugo was found about an hour ago in his favourite tavern in Vienna. Someone had castrated him in the WC and left him to bleed away. Messy business, I take it.'

'You miserable bastard.'

'I have a very long reach, Lady Kenyon, in case you hadn't noticed.'

'You won't get away with this.'

'Your father said almost the same thing to me this afternoon before I put a bullet in his head.'

Kate lunged toward the man in fury. When her chains held, she nearly ripped her arms from her shoulders. It was her turn to scream.

Corbeau walked over to Nicole North, who began to tremble uncontrollably as he approached her. 'Stand up, Dr North.' North did not respond, seemed incapable of it. 'Stand up or I shall burn you again. Would you like that?' North stood but only for a few seconds. Her legs could not hold her and she used her chains to support her. 'How did you find out about my painting?' Corbeau asked, swinging the torch carelessly close to North's hair. North cried quietly, her terror so complete she had already lost the will to resist and certainly the power of discourse.

'She didn't!' Kate shouted. 'Ethan found it!'

Corbeau turned away from North, but remained close enough to set her hair on fire if he did not like Kate's answer. 'A letter in the Bill Landi collection at the University of Denver, as I understand it?' he said.

'If you know why do you ask? Why are you threatening her?'

'Tell me about the letter.'

'Landi was in Paris in 1900 to study painting. He met Oscar Wilde one evening in a tavern. For the price of a drink, Wilde told him a story about a portrait of Christ Pontius Pilate ordered painted on the morning of the crucifixion. The man who possessed it, he said, was immortal, the risen ghost of Jacques de Molay. Landi thought Wilde was making it up – I mean obviously he was making some of it up – but he wrote to his brother about it, because he was excited that he had met Oscar Wilde.'

'How did Mr Brand come across the letter?'

'You should have asked him that before you killed him.'

'I'm asking you.'

'Someone wrote to his website with a question about Pilate's Portrait of Christ. Ethan had never heard of it, but he was curious and started looking around. Eventually, he got something on it and wrote back with a source, which is what the person wanted. Out of curiosity he asked where this person had come across the reference and the writer sent him a copy of Landi's letter.'

'You're not telling me something,' Corbeau answered.

'I'm telling you what I know. Landi was a fairly successful artist and architect in Denver. When he died, his papers were donated to the university archives.'

'Who wrote to Mr Brand?'

'I don't know. He has ... *had* ... a website.' She struggled to keep her voice from breaking. 'He got letters all the time from people who wanted information. Most of it they could have picked up in any primer on the Middle Ages, but sometimes he ran into something interesting. At first, I didn't know anything about it. He didn't get me involved until he had already found you.'

'He *found* me – just like that? Someone mentioned the existence of an obscure painting on the internet . . . and he found me?'

'What he knew was this. The owner of the portrait lived in Paris in 1883 and somewhere in Switzerland in 1899. He had the name of an Englishman Wilde visited in Switzerland in 1899. I don't know the relationship between this Englishman and your grandfather, but Ethan found something.'

'You're lying to protect someone.'

Kate said in Italian, 'I'm doing the best I can to protect someone right now by telling the truth!' In English, she added, 'Maybe Ethan didn't tell me about some of it, but I saw a photocopy of Bill Landi's letter. That much I know is genuine.'

'Whoever wrote to him about the letter understood his abilities as a thief.'

'That's not possible.'

'If I found you someone else could have as well.'

'You think one of your own people was behind it?'

'I give my people what they cannot achieve on their own – even *with* the painting. It is why they are devoted to me. It was someone outside the Order – an enemy.'

'It was dumb luck.'

'There is no such thing as luck. But let me ask you something. You stole my painting . . . for the money? You had no other agenda?'

'We stole it to see if we could.'

Corbeau seemed to accept this, even to appreciate the

motive. 'Then I think you would agree with me. You failed quite spectacularly.'

'May I ask you a question?' Corbeau's expression suggested a willingness at least to entertain her query. 'What happens to us once you get your painting back?'

Corbeau smiled darkly. 'Dr North will probably seek medical attention for her burns.'

In Italian she asked, 'What are you going to do to me?'

'That is the more interesting question.' Corbeau smiled with a sweetness that frightened her. He seemed almost willing to tell her but then shook his head. 'I think we shall wait for the answer to that. Besides, you would not believe me if I told you.'

Zürich

Max drove Malloy to the old town shortly before midnight. Marcus Steiner turned the scene over to another homicide detective, claiming he had too much to do assisting at the Airport crime scene, and then went back to his office to check for updated reports on the fire at Brand Books.

Malloy tried to call Gwen and finally got through. 'I've been in the city,' she told him when he asked where she had been. 'Why?'

'Nothing. Just . . . worried.'

'Has something happened?'

'No . . . just . . . the usual. I might have to stay on a few days more though. I don't want you to worry. I'll call when I have things worked out.'

'How many days?'

'I'm not sure yet.'

They spoke a few minutes more and then disconnected. Setting the phone down, he stretched out on the bed, hoping to get an hour or two of sleep. His phone rang almost at once. It was Marcus.

'We had a Marco Brunetti with his throat cut this morning in the financial district. He was wearing a gun in a shoulder holster and carrying a licence for it. A couple of our detectives got to work on it. Guess who employed Marco.'

'Roland Wheeler.'

'I am going though the phone records on Wheeler. The next to last call he makes is to Brunetti's cell phone, straight after his meeting with you. The last call he makes is to Kate Kenyon's cell phone.'

'The daughter.'

'I pulled up the files on Lady Kenyon and found out that the Ticino Cantonal Police think she was kidnapped from her weekend cabin in the mountain village of Sobrio early this afternoon. Here is the interesting thing, Thomas. I asked for Kenyon's cell phone records, and the last call she made was to Ethan Brand.'

'Whose bookstore burned down this afternoon . . .'

'I still don't have anything on the three bodies inside the bookstore, but the man in the alley was not an innocent bystander. He was wearing an empty holster. We don't know if he was killed with his own gun or if whoever shot him took the gun afterwards. They ran his prints with Interpol and just got the name – Rolf Lutz. He's a smalltime hood working out of Berlin. Five years in prison for extortion. After that several more arrests but no convictions, everything from assault to possession.'

'Oh, and one more thing. The reason I called, actually. He had a clip on his belt but no cell phone. Maybe some fireman picks it up or maybe his killer takes off with it. I don't know, but this afternoon and this evening we got about ten different people calling Wheeler. Only one of those numbers shows up on the list of calls to Kate Kenyon's cell phone. Whoever was calling made several attempts in a period of about ten minutes, and then stopped trying. It's not Brand's cell phone, but I am thinking that it could be Brand.'

'You think Brand got out?'

'Somebody killed Lutz.'

'So your theory is he kills Lutz and takes his phone and starts calling Kenyon and Wheeler?'

'If they're in this together that's the natural thing to do.'

'Have you dialled the number?'

'I thought I'd let you try it.' Marcus read the number to him. 'This one is on me, by the way.'

'Not with the risks you're taking!'

'I forgot to tell you, the people who shot Roland Wheeler walked off with his Monet.'

After a moment to absorb what his friend was telling him, Malloy simply shook his head and laughed. 'What's the world coming to?'

Chapter Eight

Lake Lucerne
October 11, 2006.

At eleven-thirty a panelled van left the front gate of
Julian Corbeau's estate. The lights stayed on for several
minutes but no one walked from the guardhouse to the
villa. The activity Ethan had seen earlier had settled
down. The appearance of the van was the first vehicle
coming or going in over half an hour.

When he and Kate had planned the burglary of
Corbeau's villa, they had spent long hours watching the
routines. Corbeau's director of security ran people on
twelve-hour shifts, sometimes three days a week and
sometimes four. Shift changes occurred at midnight
and noon. The guards used their own vehicles. The van
was something new, but the schedule looked to be the
same.

Before they had settled on the evening of the summer
fireworks over Lake Lucerne, Kate had said she thought
the best time to hit was shortly before the end of shift. The
guards would be comfortable, bored and all too ready to
accept the obvious, two drunks at the front gate. Her idea
was sound, but Ethan was looking at a different kind of
incursion. He needed that moment of disorientation that

CRAIG SMITH

comes with an unfamiliar environment. The van, he was sure, would bring fresh guards in and remove those people who had been watching Corbeau's property for the past twelve hours. At that moment and not a moment before, Ethan intended to drive down to the front gate and talk his way through – or die.

While he waited, trying not to think it might be the last minutes of his life, Lutz's telephone vibrated in his pocket. Pulling it out, he checked the number out of curiosity. It came from a cell phone issued in the Bern region – not one of the numbers in his address book. A supervisor? Maybe even Corbeau's head of security? He memorised the number just in case it could prove useful and pushed the button. 'Lutz.'

'Ethan,' an American voice announced with un-expected casualness, 'this is Thomas Malloy. I used to come into your bookshop when I was living in Zürich.'

Ethan's initial reaction was stunned confusion. By the time he spoke, using German and announcing that the caller had the wrong number, it was too late. If Malloy had had any doubt, Ethan had convinced him of his identity. Coming to terms with this, he actually remembered Malloy. It had been a few years, but the face came back: an older man, dark hair, dark eyes, trim, handsome, quiet, intelligent. A freelance editor and translator, he thought, or something like that. What was *he* doing in the middle of this?

'Roland Wheeler is dead, Ethan. Kate is missing. The police think it might have been a kidnapping. Right now it looks like you and I are the lucky ones, but I don't think we're going to be lucky for long if we don't start telling each other what we know.'

274

'I don't know what you are talking about, sir.' Ethan continued to speak in German, but Malloy persisted in English.

'I need a name, Ethan. Tell me who is trying to kill us and I might be able to save Kate.'

In English, Ethan answered, 'Don't call me again, Mr Malloy.'

The minute he was off the phone, Ethan was sure Corbeau had put Malloy up to calling him – a friendly voice, a helpful offer, a bit of innocent confusion about who was after him! Bremmer must have figured out that Ethan had Lutz's phone. Tracking the calls probably. Maybe tracking him with the call . . .

He turned the phone off.

He looked at the gate some seventy yards distant and very nearly decided to walk away. He wasn't going to get through with Lutz's badge. They knew the truth, probably had the bodies identified. Corbeau had sources in the Zürich police department. He had sources everywhere! Even Thomas Malloy – a nobody-expatriate! And if he drove off? What then? How much life did he have, knowing he had left Kate to die?

When the van returned, Ethan prayed. He had not prayed since he had lost his faith in his third year at Notre Dame but he prayed anyway. He prayed as the dying pray. He finished it, as he had when he believed, by making the sign of the Cross, and felt unaccountably at peace with his decision to go in. Inside the car he checked his ammunition and visualised the property one more time. When the van departed again, presumably taking Corbeau's first team of guards back into Lucerne, he drove to the front gate.

Two men inside the gates pointed AK-47s at him. A third guard approached him from the shadows of the wall. He, too, had a Kalashnikov pointed at Ethan's head. Ethan rolled his window down and held up Lutz's security badge as he had seen the others do all evening. He kept his expression indifferent and muttered his name with an exhaustion he did not feel. 'Lutz.'

'Where is your ID?'

As it had a photo Ethan couldn't use it. 'I lost it in the fire,' he answered.

'Lutz!' The guard called to the men behind the steel bars. 'Badge, but no ID!'

One of them used a cell phone. In German the man with the phone said to the rover standing next to Ethan's vehicle, 'Ask him where he has been!'

Ethan snarled angrily. 'I was in a fire. I lost two people. What was I supposed to do? Drive straight here and bring the police with me?'

The guard relayed this to his supervisor, and suddenly, magically, the gates to Julian Corbeau's property opened. The guard who had made the phone call pointed toward the kennels. 'Park over there and report to Mr Bremmer at once. He wants to know what you got from Brand.'

Ethan acknowledged his instructions with a tired nod of his head. One of the dogs came to attention as he parked the car. The other, the one Kate had shot, seemed indifferent. Wiping the car of his prints he left the vehicle and walked toward the side of the house where he knew he would find the only outside entrance to the basement. As he went Ethan took care to study the wall. He thought he might be able to grab the top with a running start, but Kate needed a step. A shed had been set up close to the wall. It could work, he thought, but it was exposed. Farther back along the wall the house would offer better cover for them. He noticed a wheelbarrow behind the half-closed doors of the shed. It was the old-fashioned kind of wheelbarrow, deep and heavy and wide. Perfect. Ethan walked to the shed and opened the doors, careful not to leave his fingerprints.

The guard at the door to the basement came to attention. 'What are you doing?' Like those at the front gate he spoke High German without the usual Swiss accent. Corbeau imported his talent.

Ethan pulled out the wheelbarrow before he answered the guard. 'They told me I stink.'

The guard laughed.

Ethan gave him the rough edge of a smile. 'So I'm going to clean out the kennel and let them smell that!'

'Forget those guys! But I've got to tell you, I can smell you from here! What happened, anyway?'

Ethan turned the wheelbarrow over carelessly and kicked it close to the wall. He appeared reluctant to give up his idea. 'You ever been inside a burning building?' he asked.

The guard lost interest in the wheelbarrow. 'That one was yours?'

Nodding, Ethan walked toward the man. One of his guns was tucked into the waistband of his jeans, only partially covered by his flannel shirt. It didn't matter if the guard saw it. Lutz was an assassin after all. 'Can I get some fresh clothes and a shower downstairs?'

'Sure. They have clean guard uniforms in the laundry room, if you don't mind looking like security.'

Ethan glanced purposefully at the guard's uniform. 'I don't mind. That's how I started out.'

The guard was a young man and no doubt aspired to greater things. Ethan's remark gave them something in common. 'You hear about the airport? Malloy and some Zürich detective killed five of our people. Can you believe it?'

Ethan stopped and offered the guard a look hc hoped passed for concern, but he was thinking . . . *Malloy*? 'Glad I wasn't there,' he muttered finally.

'Well you lost two, yourself!'

'Going into something like that,' Ethan answered reflectively, 'you think you can control the situation, but the truth is you never know.'

The guard nodded. 'If I get bored sitting out here tonight, I'm going to think about those guys that didn't make it. You know what I mean? I could be in a body bag right now.'

'You and me both,' Ethan answered, and started on.

'Where are you from anyway?'

Turning to answer, Ethan kept his hand close to his belt. 'I'm English!'

The guard smiled. 'I thought you had an accent!'

The basement door closing behind him, Ethan hurried down the stairs. Entering a commons area, he found several lockers, most of which were padlocked shut. In the next room he saw a stack of fresh uniforms neatly folded and starched. He grabbed a shirt, a pair of pants, and a towel. In the kitchen he found a butcher knife and slipped it under the towel.

At the end of a long narrow hall leading to the tower, he found two uniformed guards playing cards. They were wearing side-arms and obviously keeping watch on the tower. Three short-barrelled shotguns leaned against the wall close to them. 'What are you doing here?' one of them asked. He too spoke High German.

Ethan approached the man as he answered in German. 'I need a shower.'

'You just walked past the showers!' the other guard grumbled. He spoke in the tone one takes with imbeciles.

Playing the country oaf, Ethan offered a sheepish smile, 'You're kidding me! I didn't see any showers!'

The man pointed back down the hall. It was a gesture that opened his defences, and Ethan brought the knife out, sweeping it across his neck. Finishing, he spun behind the second man, who had dropped his cards and was reaching for his weapon. He drove the blade fiercely through the man's back, covering his mouth with the towel to muffle his scream.

The first man was still holding his neck. The second trembled in shock. They rolled from their chairs simultaneously.

Ethan cleaned the knife handle of his prints and went to the tower. Throwing the bar up and away, he opened the steel door and called into the darkness. 'Girl?'

'Boy?' The voice didn't even sound like Kate. He heard the scrape of cinders but saw her only when she stepped into the light of the doorway. Her sweater was smudged, her jeans were stained and her blonde hair desperately needed attention, but Kate had never looked more beautiful.

'Are you okay?'

'I'm fine.' Kate glanced back to the darkness. 'She's not.'

'What are you talking about?'

'Nicole North is here.'

Ethan walked into the tower and found North lying naked on the cinders, her face to the wall. 'Dr North, we're going to break you out of here, but we have to be quick about it. I have some clothes out here—'

'He burned my feet. I can't even walk!' she moaned, barely turning from the wall.

Ethan looked back at Kate and said to her in German, 'We have to jump the wall. It's the only way out. There's no way she can get over it.'

Kate answered in German. 'We can't leave her here!'

'We have to!'

'Nicole,' Kate said, 'we can't take you with us, but I want you to promise me you'll hang on. No matter what he does or tells you, trust me, I'm coming back to get you.'

'If you want to help, call the Plaza in New York,' North answered. 'Ask for Mr Gideon.' She looked at Ethan. 'Make sure they know where I am and that Corbeau's ready to trade for the painting. If you do that for me . . . I'll give anything you want!'

'I'll make sure your people know,' Ethan told her. 'Just hang on.'

North looked at Kate. 'You're breaking out?' Kate nodded. 'Aren't you . . . scared?'

Kate smiled at her. 'Of course I'm scared. Scared is good. As long as you're scared you know you're still alive.'

*   *   *

Taking the handguns from the dead guards and fishing out two spare clips from their belts, Kate chambered a round in each gun and asked, 'What's the plan, Boy?'

Ethan pulled both handguns out of his jeans, thumbing the safeties off. 'There's one guard outside the basement door. I put a bullet in his head and we jump the wall. After that we run like hell.'

'That's it?'

'If we use the silencer, they might not even notice you're gone for a few minutes.'

She managed a grim smile. 'Hope I can remember it all.'

Kate could spend months looking at a job, talking about the possibilities. 'I didn't have much time to put something together,' he said.

She kicked one shoulder up. 'Better than sitting in the dark and waiting to die, I guess.'

'I thought so.'

In the commons one of Corbeau's bodyguards was waiting for Ethan. 'There you are! Bremmer wants—'

Ethan could not decide whether the man noticed Kate or that Ethan was carrying two guns. It didn't really matter what prompted it. The moment he realised something wasn't right, he reached under his sports jacket. Ethan had no choice but to lift one of his pistols and fire.

Corbeau's bodyguard lost his handgun when he fell. Instead of reaching for it, he touched a device attached to his belt and said, 'Kenyon—!'

Ethan's second shot stopped him. Kate came up next to him. Together they looked toward the basement ceiling expectantly. Maybe the transmission had not made any sense or he hadn't depressed the button. Maybe they still had a chance.

When the siren screamed a few seconds later, Kate and Ethan looked at each other. They were caught. Ethan's shoulders slumped. He was ready to give up but Kate shook her head, her eyes on fire. 'No surrender, Boy. Promise me! No surrender, no matter what!'

Ethan nodded, glancing doubtfully toward the basement door. 'If you can get that far,' he said, 'there's a wheelbarrow set up at the wall to give you a step.'

Kate nodded toward the door at the top of the stairs. 'Open and drop,' she whispered.

Ethan took a deep breath and ran up the steps. He dived into the base of the door with the heels of both hands and the door broke open. The guard he had talked to stood about ten feet out from the door, his Kalashnikov set on full auto. As the bullets ripped over Ethan's head, Kate fired two shots from a position well below the threshold. The guard kicked back. Ethan crawled over the threshold and settled both handguns on the front of the house.

Kate came up the stairs, hurdled over him, and sprinted to the wall. Kicking off the wheelbarrow, she caught the tiles at the top with both hands. She had one leg over when three guards came around the corner of the house. Ethan dropped one of them as he was raising his weapon toward Kate. He wounded a second. The wounded guard, along with the third man, pulled back to cover.

Firing his weapons until they emptied, Ethan came to his feet. Perched at the top of the wall and using it for cover, Kate began firing steadily toward the front of the house. As Ethan caught hold and swung his leg over the wall, an AK-47 rattled in the distance. The bullets seemed to climb up after him. He felt masonry stinging his face, then heard Kate's weapon discharge. The automatic fire ceased, and Ethan shouted, 'Go! Go! Go!'

Together they dropped into the forest.

Whatever ambient light they might have enjoyed was lost inside the woods. They stood in absolute darkness. They were not dressed for the cold, but such was their predicament they hardly noticed.

'Which way?' Ethan asked as he placed his spare clip into one of his guns, stripped the second gun of its silencer and left the weapon in the leaves. There were essentially two directions away from Corbeau's property. They could come out of the forest somewhere along the road or at the lake. Trying to avoid either they would eventually find themselves exposed on both sides.

'Lake.' Kate's voice had regained its certainty.

'Take my hand!' Ethan told her. They had only a few precious minutes to get as much distance as possible from Corbeau's property before his people came out in force, but inside a dark wood time counted differently. Without a flashlight or night vision goggles, they were reduced to feeling their way. Every step forward brought them into some obstacle, tree branches mostly, but rocks and hollows as well. Pushing for speed only made it worse. They had spent a great many nights in the mountains. They had made a good living working in the dark but they had always carried equipment to help them manage. Suddenly, they were blind, seemingly hemmed in on all sides and forced to move with painstaking care. It was no way to run for your life.

When he unexpectedly discovered nothing in front of him, Ethan took advantage. The first several steps took them over a reasonably level terrain – seemingly the break they needed. The next sent them tumbling through the air. He actually touched ground about twenty feet below his last step, and then dropped again. Hitting a bank of soft clay, he slid another fifty yards or so. By the time he had come to a stop, Ethan understood he had come out of it in one piece. His only concern was Kate. 'You okay, Girl?' he whispered.

'You walked us off a cliff, Boy.' She was close to him. Her tone suggested she wasn't hurt.

'I was hoping you didn't notice that.'

Kate came close, her body touching his, her forehead brushing across his jaw. A moment later her lips touched his. 'We're going to get out of this, Boy.'

'Promise?'

'I promise.'

'Still want to get married?'

'More than anything. When he said you were dead—'

'I know. I had the same feeling when I found out he had you.'

Above them Ethan could hear Corbeau's people setting up a perimeter along the road. Inside Corbeau's dock, the engines of the Pantera and Fountain rumbled. The WaverRunners screamed.

Kate and Ethan were nearly at the lake, but it was too late to matter. Corbeau had them surrounded.

*   *   *

They got their first glimpse of the water once the Fountain got to open water and shone its spotlight across the landscape. They settled behind a fallen tree just off the shoreline. On this particular finger of the lake the opposite shore was about five hundred yards away by water, nearly three miles distant by road. In the Fountain's spotlight, Ethan could see that the sleek Pantera carried a driver and two gunmen. Both boats settled some fifty to eighty yards out from shore while the Jet Skis began a sweep along the shoreline. It took only a few seconds of watching them for Ethan to realise that Corbeau expected them try to break out at the road. The boats were simply holding the perimeter.

Kate gestured toward the two Jet Skis. 'You ready to hitch a ride?'

'They'll blow us out of the water if we do.'

'Give me the extra silencer.' Ethan handed it to her.

The Jet Skis sported no running lights and only a single headlight, so they were hard to find, but when the Fountain's light splashed over them, Ethan had only to lose his gun sights in the shadow of the rider and squeeze softly on Kate's '. . . three!'

Their guns spit quietly and the Jet Skis skittered out from under the recoil of the falling riders. Kate fired six more rounds before catching the spotlight on the Fountain. A split-second later, gunmen on both boats opened fire on the shoreline. The assault was terrifying for its intensity, but a Kalashnikov on full auto is good for only a few seconds. The moment the gunfire ceased, Kate popped up and shot the headlights of the Jet Skis. When the second assault from the boats had finished,

Kate took the Pantera's spotlight out with three shots and turned the lake to darkness. The gunmen responded with another wild volley, but they had neither sound nor muzzle flash to help them.

Kate reloaded, and they left their cover while the gunfire continued sporadically. They crossed an open stretch of shore and dived into the marsh some twenty yards from the Jet Skis. Ethan heard Kate slip into the frigid water and followed her. He shivered and resisted the urge to shout at the cold. The Jet Skis were still idling as they climbed on the saddles. Ethan changed his gun to his left hand and recalled the hours of shooting on the range with both hands – Kate's idea – because she always wanted a backup. When Kate's engine began to whine, Ethan rolled the throttle back on his machine and felt it rise up out of the water like a living beast. He could not see Kate, but he followed the sound. She was headed, he realised with some surprise, straight at the Pantera.

The gunmen on the speedboat opened fire first. They were shooting at sound. Kate and Ethan aimed at the muzzle blasts. Both men went down, but Kate kept going at the boat, firing until her weapon emptied. Ethan caught the driver with a shot just over the bow with what turned out to be his last bullet. Dropping his gun in the lake, he leaned forward and turned the throttle the last inch.

The Fountain's engines roared in response, but it was a forty-eight-footer and came around slowly. For several seconds, Ethan kept his focus on the lights of the tiny village on the opposite shore. Three hundred yards, two hundred yards, one hundred . . .

He risked one backward glance and saw the Fountain gaining speed, but the race was already finished. He drove the Jet Ski up a grassy bank next to Kate. They sprinted together for the shadow of an old barn. The guns on the Fountain were easily within range but, on a moving boat aiming at moving targets a hundred yards distant, they had trouble. It was all the luck Kate and Ethan needed. From the old barn, there were a number of buildings that provided a fairly decent line of retreat, and soon they were running along a narrow alley safely within the village.

At the two-lane highway, even without weapons, Ethan realised the chase had turned to their advantage. They were in the foothills of Mount Rigi. It was a vast area spotted with tiny villages, isolated farms, open meadows and dense forests. For the space of several minutes they ran for higher ground. It got them the distance they needed and kept their wet clothes from bringing on hypothermia. When they came to a reasonably flat road, they ran flat-out for nearly half a mile. They saw a security light at a barn a couple of minutes later and headed for it. They let the dog bark at the end of its chain while Kate hotwired an old truck. They were rolling when Kate snapped the heater on and finally spoke. 'Nice plan, Boy.'

Zürich

'Tell me you didn't just raid Julian Corbeau's compound,' Jane Harrison said.

Malloy stood up and started pacing in the tight confines of the room. 'Corbeau? When was this?'

'Just after midnight your time.'

He checked his watch. It was four in the morning – still evening for Jane. 'I don't know anything about it.'

'Corbeau is telling the police the CIA just attempted to kidnap him. The Swiss ambassador wants assurances we aren't involved.'

'Any chance this is connected to the painting?'

'You tell me.'

'I have no idea, but if I had to make a guess—'

'Get the product to Starr, T. K., and get out of the country before we get dragged any further into this . . . mess!'

Jonas Starr's Mercedes pulled into a small parking area at the *Rote Fabric*, a defunct ceramics factory the city used for cultural events. The area was quiet at seven-thirty on a Wednesday morning. Both Starr and his driver waited in the car while Starr's two bodyguards got out and headed directly toward Malloy.

They were big men. By their manner he was guessing they were ex-military. They were both carrying MAC-10 machine pistols. 'Hands in the air,' one of them commanded.

When they had disarmed Malloy, Jonas Starr stepped out of his Mercedes. Starr was a tall, thin man with a weathered face. He wore a cashmere coat that could almost let him pass for a Zürich businessman. Only his voice betrayed him. His voice was pure Texas.

'Where is my painting, Mr Malloy?'

'The painting is safe, Dr Starr.'

Jonas Starr smiled. Under different circumstances it might have passed for charming. At the moment it suggested nothing so much as impatience. 'Unfortunately, my niece isn't.'

'If you would care to tell me who kidnapped her, I might be able to help.'

'As I understand it, your people have instructed you to hand the painting over to me. Now why don't you do that and we can leave here friends?'

'I didn't make my deal with you, Dr Starr. I made arrangements with Dr North and the Reverend Richland. Those are the only people I'm taking orders from.'

Starr glanced at the two men to either side of Malloy, his smile transforming into a snarl. 'I don't think you're in any position to bargain.'

'That's because you don't understand my position.'

Malloy gestured toward the roofline of the building closest to them as five gunmen appeared.

Starr, seeing his position so utterly compromised, shouted indignantly. 'What is this?'

'My guns, gentlemen?'

Starr acquiesced and the guard with Malloy's weapons handed them back. Holstering his Sigma and Glock, Malloy told him, 'You're free to call and complain about this, but the minute you do, your painting disappears into Russia. Once it's there neither one of us is ever going to see it again.'

'Name your price, Malloy. How much is it going to take to get you to walk away from this?'

Malloy smiled. 'How about Richland tells me what he wants me to do.'

'Are you serious?' When Malloy didn't answer him, Starr reached for his cell phone. A few seconds later he said, 'Jim, I'm standing here with your good friend Thomas Malloy. He tells me he wants you to tell him to release the painting to me.' Starr passed the phone to Malloy.

'Reverend?'

'I understand you ran into some problems, Mr Malloy.' J. W. Richland's voice sounded as if he had just been pulled from a deep sleep, but he was trying to be cheerful.

'The important thing is I've got your painting. I can bring it to you if you want, or I can exchange it for Dr North's life. You tell me what to do.'

'I thought I made it clear to the people you work for, Mr Malloy—'

'I work for *you*, sir.'

'You're to give the painting to Dr Starr! He'll make arrangements for Nicole's release.'

'I can't do that.'

'You want to tell me why not?'

'Dr Starr isn't capable of handling it. He proved that this morning.'

'It's not your choice to make!'

'You're right. It's your choice. Do I bring the painting to New York, or do I use it to try to save Dr North's life?'

'You do what you're told to do, mister!'

'You're not following me, Reverend. Now listen closely. If you go to your friends or if you tell me one more time to give it to Dr Starr, your painting disappears. Now what do you want me to do, bring it to New York or use it to save Dr North's life?'

With a sigh of resignation the preacher answered. 'Bring me the painting, Mr Malloy.'

'And Dr North?'

'We'll do what we can!'

'The painting can save her, Reverend.'

'You don't know that!'

'No, I don't. But I'm willing to bet my life on it.'

'I can't risk it.'

'Risk what – *my* life?'

'You act like I enjoy this!'

'It's Julian Corbeau who has her, isn't it?'

'I can't let a man like that have it . . .'

'Reverend, I can get her out. He'll make the trade. Don't let her die for the sake of a painting.'

'Bring the painting to New York, Mr Malloy.'

Malloy tossed the phone to Jonas Starr and walked away.

'Where are you going?' Starr asked him.

'When you write my cheques, Dr Starr, I'll be glad to answer your questions. Otherwise, you can go to hell.'

Lake Brienz

Malloy slipped into a waiting van and was driven to one of the city's underground parking lots. There he found Hasan Barzani's Porsche. Five minutes later he was driving it through heavy traffic toward the town of Brienz. From Brienz he circled the lake and headed up Ax Alp. He parked the Porsche in the woods and started down the mountain toward the contessa's villa. The trail was steep and crooked, sometimes following the contours of the rock, sometimes the course of the cascade. At the contessa's property,

Malloy found Rene raking the yard. 'Is she here?' he asked.

Rene turned back to the leaves without bothering to respond.

'You want your painting?' the contessa asked, when she saw him at her front door.

Malloy smiled. 'If you haven't sold it.'

Opening her door, she let him into the house. 'I don't think I would have had any trouble if I had wanted to.' She led him into her parlour and gestured toward the table. She had rewrapped it.

'How many people do you think would buy it if they knew it belonged to Julian Corbeau?'

The contessa's smile faded. 'There are a great many fools in the world, Thomas. I wouldn't have to look far.'

Malloy slipped the package into a small backpack, which he tossed over his shoulders. 'I've been trying to figure out why someone would pay twenty-five million dollars for a painting that could never see the light of day.'

'For that kind of collector, secrecy is part of the thrill.'

'Not the people I'm dealing with.'

'I'm not sure you understand what you're dealing with.'

'Actually, I think I do. I've got a two-thousand-year-old painting of Christ. The former owner is ready to commit any crime to recover it and the future owner is prepared to make any sacrifice to keep it. What's not to understand?'

'Tell me about the people who purchased it.'

'Have you ever heard of the Reverend J. W. Richland?'

Her face showed recognition. 'A dying man.'

'What does that mean?'

'He has cancer. He thinks the painting has the power to give him back his health.'

'He can't seriously think—'

'Dying men are dreamers, Thomas. He does not *think*. He *believes*.'

'Believes what? What is this thing going to do for him? He's trading the life of a woman who loves him for a piece of wood!'

Malloy never raised his voice. In the presence of the contessa he rarely ventured a certainty. His outrage surprised him. It was not the meeting with Jonas Starr that bothered him. Starr he had anticipated. It was Richland's remark about risk. The painting had meant more to him than the woman he loved. A great deal more.

'What are you talking about?' the contessa asked with a show of curiosity.

He told her about Nicole North's kidnap, his meeting with Starr, his conversation with Richland.

'You can't understand them, can you?' she asked.

Malloy shook his head. 'Corbeau will make the trade. North doesn't need to die.'

'I believe you're right, but the question is what are you going to do?'

'What I hired on to do, get the painting to New York.'

'And Dr North?' Malloy stared at the fireplace without answering. 'You intend to leave her to Corbeau?'

'I didn't make the decision!'

'You are making it right now, Thomas.'

'You know how many people I could lose trying to rescue her?'

'I am wondering what you lose if you don't at least try.'

Malloy met the woman's gaze. 'She's not innocent.'

'Not too many of us are.'

From inside his tool shed Rene saw a man taking up a position high over the villa on the far side of the cascade. He moved with the precision of a soldier. Two more men came down the mountain as Rene left the shed with his tools stacked in his wheelbarrow. These men climbed across the rocks over the path Malloy had descended a few minutes earlier. Finally, as he ambled into the garden, Rene noticed a man walking along the trail well below the contessa's villa. Like the first man, he was on the opposite side of the cascade.

With the patience of a tired old handyman, Rene crossed the bridge and pushed slowly into the forest. A moment later he began running.

Malloy left the contessa's villa and headed back up the mountain toward Hasan Barzani's Porsche. Five minutes above the property the path cut away from the cascade, following a trail perched over a deep rocky chasm. The trail itself remained comparably wide and comfortable at this point, but both his training and instincts kicked in. Directly overhead was a wall of rock. To his right he was looking at a three-to-four-hundred-foot drop to a bed of stones. He was vulnerable to attack here and enjoyed no possibility of retreat. When he had come this way before, he had not been carrying the painting and he had the advantage of holding the higher ground. Now he was moving forward without knowing what lay ahead. Even as he understood his mistake, the first man appeared on the rock ahead of him. 'Stop right there, Malloy!' he shouted.

Malloy threw himself back against the rock, but the cover was only partial, and a voice behind him called down, 'All we want is the painting. Put it on the trail and back away from it, and we'll let you live.'

Malloy could see the man had an easy shot down at him. He looked at the treetops of several saplings. They came up out of the rocks beneath his trail and rose up some five to ten feet overhead. He didn't consider the matter. Had he done so, he might have hesitated. He took a step and dived toward the most promising one in the bunch. Catching it as he left the trail and swinging out over the chasm, Malloy pulled his Glock from his shoulder holster and fired one shot at each man. It was a spectacularly athletic moment of gunplay – and it very nearly worked. He saw the dust of the rocks next to each man's head, and then his only chance had passed. Dropping the gun, he grabbed the sapling with his free hand and held on as he plunged toward the rocks, praying the tree would hold.

When the treetop hung below its roots, its tender trunk bent in a great arch, he looked at his situation realistically. The results were mixed. He was some ten feet beneath the trail and able to grab hold of some rocks. From here the two men had no shot at him, but neither could he escape. The way up offered a slow, precarious climb across heavy boulders back to the trail and the two gunmen. Below him he was looking at a sheer drop off. If they came for him he still had his Sigma. Given the natural cover the rocks provided, he could maybe keep them at bay for a few minutes at least.

It looked to be a stalemate for the moment, but the moment did not last. From across the cascade the first shot echoed through the canyon. A third gunman had positioned himself directly across from him and had an easy shot at him from dense cover. Malloy had no defence and finally admitted it. 'Okay!' he shouted, 'I'll give you the painting!'

A second shot sounded. Like the first, the bullet was not even close to Malloy's position and, for a moment, he was not sure what was going on. Then he saw Rene come out of the trees carrying a MAC-10. The contessa's handyman looked at Malloy with what might have been amusement in another man, and tossed the machine pistol to the rocks below. He then turned and disappeared into the woods again.

When he had finally climbed off the rocks and made it back to the trail, Malloy found the two gunmen dead. He checked the body of one of them and found a cell phone. Spotting Jonas Starr's number among the contacts he pressed the send button and heard Starr answer. 'Did you get it?'

Malloy tossed the phone into the canyon without answering and grabbed the dead man's MAC-10 machine pistol and two spare clips.

There was no answer at the contessa's front door. He

circled the house, searching for some sign of a break-in. Finally, he forced the back door. He searched the downstairs for some sign of life, calling out as he went from room to room. Upstairs, where she had sent him to change clothes, Malloy saw that one of the mummy portrait forgeries was missing. The encaustic. Nothing else had been touched. He tried to remember the face in the painting, but it didn't come to him. It was . . . just a man's face. Only the sensation of touching its waxy surface remained . . . and the scent of the contessa as she stood close to him.

When the front door opened, Malloy settled the selector of the MAC-10 on full auto and peeked out from the room. Rene stood at the bottom of the stairs. 'Out!' he shouted in German. 'You have done enough already!'

Malloy came down the stairs. 'Where is the contessa, Rene?'

'Gone.'

'Gone? What are you saying? Is she okay?'

'Get out, Malloy. Just go.'

'Rene! Tell me! Is she safe?'

'She is never safe.'

'I can help.'

Rene's ugly round face seemed almost to smile. 'I have seen your *help*!'

Malloy did not understand, but neither was it his business. The contessa was gone. She was apparently safe, to a degree at least, and Rene had proven himself more than capable of protecting her. That was all he knew and all he had a right to know. He looked back toward the room where she kept the forgeries.

'One of the paintings upstairs is missing.'

Rene nodded without showing any surprise.

'Did she take it?'

'What does it matter? You have driven her out of her home – bringing those gunmen here! Can she at least have a single painting?'

Malloy wanted to say something more, but Rene went to the kitchen. Conversation finished.

Chapter Nine

Interlaken, Switzerland
October 11, 2006.

With some difficulty Malloy found the GPS chip Jonas Starr's security people had planted on him that morning when they patted him down before his meeting with Starr. They had placed it under the belt loop of the holster of his Sigma. Even knowing what he was looking for, he almost missed it. He tossed it in the lake, tucked the MAC-10 under his jacket and took off jogging in the direction of Interlaken.

Forty minutes later, nearly at the end of the lake, he stopped at Iseltwald. While he waited ten minutes for a bus, he called Marcus Steiner.

'I want you to get the product to New York for me. Can you do that?'

'I can't get away, Thomas, but my brother can probably catch a flight out tomorrow morning.'

Matthias Steiner owned his own company and travelled extensively. A sudden decision to make a flight to the States probably wouldn't raise any flags.

'Great. I'll have to get you the money later. Am I good for it?'

'It's on me, Thomas.'

'Monet?'

'My wife loves it.'

'I'll be in Interlaken in an hour. We can make the exchange there.'

'It will take me three to get to you. What can I say? The paperwork you generated is killing me.'

'At least there's no more talk of layoffs.'

'There is that.'

'I'll be at the bar in the Jungfrau.'

Malloy's next call was to Hasan Barzani. He had run into some trouble, he said and had been forced to leave Barzani's car at the side of the road on Ax Alp. The car wasn't important, Barzani answered. He wanted to know what kind of trouble Malloy was in.

'The fellow we did business with this morning. He tagged me with a GPS chip and set an ambush.'

'Doesn't sound like it was a very good one.'

Malloy laughed. 'It was plenty good enough, but I got some unexpected help.'

'Are you okay?'

'For now.'

'Anything I can do?'

Malloy hesitated. Quite a bit, he was thinking, but decided to take it slowly. 'Maybe. Let me get back to you.'

'Just say the word, Thomas.'

'You don't know what it means to me to hear you say that right now.'

'We can't let down the President!'

Twenty minutes later, his phone vibrated. He didn't know the number but answered it.

'This is Kate Kenyon. Ethan said you called last night and offered to save me.'

'I did, but he told me not to call him back.'

'The situation has changed, Mr Malloy. We could use your help, if you're still offering it.'

'What can I do for you?'

'Julian Corbeau has Nicole North. I want to get her out.'

'What's your interest in Dr North?'

'Last night I watched Corbeau burn the flesh from her feet.'

'My God.'

'This morning we called the people North told us to contact. They're acting as if they don't know what we're talking about. I'm assuming that means they're going to keep their painting and let Corbeau kill Nicole.'

'And you don't care for that?'

'I told her I'd get her out.'

'What do you have in mind, exactly?'

'Why don't we get together and talk about it?'

'I'll be in Interlaken tonight. If you want to talk, it has to be there.'

'That's fine.'

'I'll meet you in the park across from the Jungfrau Hotel at dusk. And come alone, if you don't mind.'

Malloy passed the painting to Marcus over drinks and sandwiches, then walked out of the hotel and across the street. The sun had already set behind the mountains, the dusk arriving with a light fog. He kept his hands plunged into his coat pockets. His right hand held his tiny Sigma. His left went through the pocket lining and held the MAC-10 automatic pistol under his coat.

In summertime the park would have been filled with backpackers and tourists, but in mid-October it was empty. The night was cold. He took a seat on the one of the benches well back from the road and wondered if he was about to make the biggest mistake of his life.

When Kate Kenyon came toward him, she kept her hands in her pockets.

'You know who I am?' she asked.

'Lady Kenyon.'

She smiled. 'That would make you Thomas Malloy.'

'Where's Ethan?'

'At the moment he has an AK-47 pointed at the back of your head.'

Malloy let his coat slip back, exposing the MAC-10. 'Safety is off, in case you're giving signals.'

'Have you talked with Corbeau?'

'I don't really have anything to say to the man.'

Kenyon brought a cell phone out of her coat pocket slowly. 'I have a number that will probably work. I want you to call him and set up an exchange for tomorrow morning. Tell him to have his helicopter at his house before six o'clock and you'll call him with instructions for the exchange between six and six-fifteen. Tell him you'll give him fifteen minutes to get to a place of your choosing – or the deal is off.'

Malloy thought about this. 'What are we giving him when he gets there?'

Kate smiled. 'His painting.'

'I don't have it.'

'Does he know that?'

'No.'

'Then make the call, Mr Malloy. You look like you can play a pretty good game of poker.'

'You want to explain how we're going to handle the exchange without the painting?'

'Let's see if he takes the bait first.'

The voice that answered spoke High German with the tone of a man taking a call from a subordinate. 'Yes?'

'Mr Corbeau, please,' Malloy said in English. 'I have a painting of his I think he'd like to have back.'

'Who is this?' the man answered in English.

'Thomas Malloy.'

'Give me your number. Someone will call you back within the hour.'

'Get Corbeau on the phone now or I burn the painting.'

'This will take a minute!'

'Then take it.'

After nearly a minute another man spoke in English. 'Sir Julian is unavailable. If you have anything to say, he has authorised me to act on his behalf. However, we will not agree to extortion, nor will we engage in any illegality.'

'You ought to see the fire I've built,' Malloy answered.

'We're trying to cooperate!'

'As far as I'm concerned if Corbeau doesn't want to talk, he doesn't want his painting.'

Another voice spoke now. 'What is it you want, Mr Malloy?' Corbeau.

'First I want information.'

'About?'

'Dr North.'

'I can give you Dr North in reasonably good health, assuming you can give me something in return.'

Malloy looked at Kate Kenyon. He didn't like acting on faith but he had no choice. 'Tomorrow morning between six and six-fifteen have your helicopter and Dr North ready to move. I'll give you fifteen minutes to get to me after I call you. When you show up, you get your painting and I get Dr North. You want to play games or renegotiate . . . I burn the painting and start shooting.'

'You burn the painting and Dr North dies.'

'It either happens tomorrow morning or we're finished talking.'

'Fifteen minutes isn't a great deal of time.'

'It's all the time you need. I want no more than four people on the helicopter, including the pilot and Dr North. You show up where I tell you and everyone goes home happy.'

'How do I know I can trust you?' Corbeau asked.

'You're the man holding the high ground. You don't like what you see below, fly off and do what you have to do.'

'And how do you know you can trust me?'

'I'm gambling that you want your painting more than you want to kill me.'

'I need to think about this, Mr Malloy.'

'Think all you want, but come six o'clock tomorrow morning you're going to have to make a decision.'

'We need to get out of town now,' Kate told him. She wiped the prints and set the phone on the park bench. 'Come on.'

They started walking across the park toward one of the side streets. A dark nondescript van turned out to be their destination. 'You can have the back.'

Malloy kept his finger on the trigger of the MAC-10 as they approached the vehicle. He saw only one man inside.

'Is that Ethan?'

'I lied about the gun. I thought you'd trust me if you thought I was afraid of you.'

'You aren't afraid?'

'I have it on good authority Julian Corbeau wants to kill you almost as much as he wants to kill us. That makes us . . . like new best friends.'

Ethan Brand sat at the steering wheel. 'Sorry about the way I acted last night,' he said when Malloy had climbed in. 'You kind of caught me in the middle of something.'

'You were breaking Kate out?'

Ethan started the van and pulled away from the kerb. 'Getting ready to.'

Kate turned in her seat. 'You told Ethan last night that my father had been killed. According to the news this morning, the police didn't find him until last night. I'm curious how you knew so quickly.'

'I was the one who found him.'

She blinked, not entirely successful at holding her tears in check. She was a woman who had not had time to come to terms with her grief. 'Corbeau told me he was the one who put a bullet in his head.'

'Someone did.' After a long, painful silence, Malloy said, 'Maybe you two better tell me what you're arranging for tomorrow morning. I'm not real comfortable working in the dark.'

'I need you to make a call tomorrow morning. Beyond that, your involvement is optional, though we could use a hand.'

'What kind of involvement?'

'Let me tell you something about Julian Corbeau. If you negotiate an exchange – even if you had the painting – he'll come after you later. So the only chance for any of us is to disappear permanently or finish this tomorrow.'

'You're going to kill him?'

'Actually, we thought we'd kidnap him.'

Malloy sat back in surprise. 'It can't be done.'

'Of course it can. All we have to do is get him over the border. After that the US can extradite him. The man is worth a million dollars if we can do it.'

'You can't get him off his property, let alone out of Switzerland. You have any idea the number of people he has around him right now?'

Ethan was driving, listening, but at this he answered drolly with a fairly pronounced southern accent. 'The only thing we know for sure is he had quite a few more yesterday.'

'You did that . . . alone? He was claiming the CIA tried to kidnap him.'

'I walked in alone. Coming out, I had Kate.'

'So how many people does he have left?'

'We think over a dozen,' Kate answered. 'Maybe as many as twenty, but they won't all be at his villa. He's keeping his guards in town and shuttling them out to his place in shifts. The hired guns are in and out, or at least they were yesterday.'

'How many of us are going in?'

'Three of us, if you want to help.'

'I can get us whatever guns and manpower we need. All I have to do is make a phone call.'

'Assuming you're up for it, we have everyone we need. Any more people and we'd just risk showing our hand.'

'Three against twenty?'

'The numbers aren't that important,' Kate answered. 'What matters is we catch him looking the other way.'

'The exchange?'

'Do you have any idea what we stole from him?' Kate asked.

'A two thousand-year-old portrait of Christ.'

'There's more to it than that,' Ethan answered.

'Looks like we've got some time on our hands. Why don't you tell me about it?'

'Well, to start with, it's not a portrait, it's *the* portrait . . .'

Lake Lucerne

Corbeau finished his phone conversation and asked Jeffrey Bremmer to send for Helena Chernoff and Xeno. Bremmer returned with them, and the three stood before the grandmaster. Two of Corbeau's bodyguards stood in the room as well, their backs to the wall. After describing the call from Malloy, he asked Helena, 'What is he thinking?'

'He expects you to fly somewhere and make the exchange.'

Corbeau glanced at Bremmer, who nodded in agreement.

There were five mountains easily reached by helicopter inside fifteen minutes – perhaps a couple more farther out. Each provided alpine meadows, heavy boulders, extensive cover and no one around for miles. Each was large enough that it would not be possible to anticipate a particular point of exchange, and a proper surveillance of all five mountains would require a great many more people than Corbeau had presently engaged. As he ran through the possibilities, it seemed the logical option was to play it straight, as long as Malloy did.

'What do we lose if we give him North?'

Bremmer shook his head. 'Nothing but time.'

'What if it's a trap?'

'If the police are involved, we'll know in advance,' Bremmer said.

'The danger,' Corbeau explained, 'is that he takes our hostage and we get nothing.'

'As things stand we don't have very much with the hostage,' Bremmer said, with a shrug of his shoulders. 'We've approached Richland in New York and so far we have no response. It's as if he doesn't care.'

'Malloy is handling it for him,' Corbeau answered after a moment of reflection. 'I expect he has instructed Richland not to respond.'

'Malloy won't risk losing a hostage over a painting,' Helena Chernoff answered. 'He's a professional. As far as he's concerned the trade can happen, so it *should* happen. The risk is if we try anything. He'll have something ready, just incase.'

'Back up?'

'He has resources inside the country. He'll have

people with him, but there is no point in risking the hostage's life if you go along with a trade.'

Corbeau turned to Bremmer. 'I'm going to trust him. It's the best chance we have right now. Call my pilot and have him here and ready to fly before six tomorrow morning.'

Interlaken

'The Knights Templar?' Malloy asked sceptically. He had got the rough history of Pilate's Portrait of Christ: from Jerusalem to Edessa, its three centuries buried in the wall of that city, its accidental discovery by workers repairing the fortifications, and finally its acquisition, in 1098, by the crusader knight Baldwin of Boulogne.

'Baldwin founded the Templars to guard the image. When they were brought down two hundred years later, the priests who found the painting didn't recognize it as Baphomet, the head the Templars allegedly worshipped, so they sent it along with everything else to the Vatican archives. Five hundred years later Napoleon took possession of the Vatican and moved the Templar artefacts to the Arsenal library.

'According to what Oscar Wilde told a young painter in Paris about a month before he died, there were people in Paris who recognized the painting for what it was and began using it in ceremonies involving necromancy – raising the spirits of the dead. At some point, Corbeau's grandfather joined the circle. He revived the Order of the Knights Templar and proclaimed himself possessed of the risen spirit of Jacques de Molay – the last grandmaster of the Temple.'

'How was Wilde involved?'

'Corbeau was apparently recruiting members from the most prominent families in Europe . . . and men of talent. Wilde fit into the second category. His popularity and skill as a writer, along with his love of decadence, would have made him a very appealing candidate.'

'But wouldn't he have sworn an oath of secrecy?'

'According to his biographer, Wilde loved secrèts. He just wasn't very good at keeping them. Besides, when he told Bill Landi about the painting and how it had inspired his Dorian Gray, he was a dying man. He had nothing to lose, and I'd like to think maybe he finally recognized Corbeau for what he was.'

'A charlatan?'

'A monster. The original Templars were deep into the occult. According to the official charges against the order, they were accused of sacrificing infants. I don't think that's quite what was going on, but it's close. You see, there are two ways for a spirit to take possession of someone. For a temporary possession, which is the most common, the ghost simply occupies the body of a living person and speaks through him. The more permanent possession occurs when the magician tricks his victim into believing he or she is dead. At that point the spirit leaves the body so another spirit can steal into the presumed corpse. When the magician revives the body, the ghost comes back to life in the flesh of the victim – and stays there. Meanwhile, the departed spirit wanders between death and life.'

'You don't really believe in that nonsense?'

'You can take away the soul of a child in any number

of ways, Mr Malloy – you don't need magic to kill the very young. I think Corbeau's Knights Templar have simply ritualised the process. They take a child and raise him to believe he carries in his heart the spirit of a fallen Templar. In Corbeau's case he would have been taught secret rites of magic from his earliest childhood, seduced by shadows and strange sounds, taught the memory of being burned at the stake, given a taste for power and a longing to avenge his supposed enemies. Plus, he holds in his hand – or he did – the only true likeness of the face of Christ. Why shouldn't he believe he's Jacques de Molay?'

'You're saying he was raised to be insane?'

'Psychopaths make the best generals.'

'Let's say I buy the Templar connection and some of what you're telling me about Corbeau. At least he believes it, even if I don't. I still have problems with this painting being a portrait of Christ. You say the man who was to become the first king of Christian Jerusalem shows up in Edessa and finds it?'

'We have independent confirmation that such a painting existed in Edessa. It's not just a theory.'

'But that doesn't mean the painting is authentic. It could be just a first century icon. Nothing connects a painting of Christ back to Pontius Pilate – except the legend.'

'There are two sources that state a painting of Christ 'made by no human hand' – whatever that means – came out of Jerusalem and into the possession of a King Abgar of Edessa in the first century. Another reference, by Irenaeus, mentions a painting of Jesus made by Pilate when Christ walked among men.'

'But this material is . . . what? A few centuries after the fact?'

'Irenaeus writes about a century-and-a-half after the Crucifixion.'

'Well, what's a couple hundred years between friends?'

'Point made. A long time.'

'Very long compared to a human life.'

'Wilde referred to it as *Pontius Pilate's Portrait of Christ*. I don't know where he got the idea, but the logical assumption is he got it from Corbeau's grandfather.'

'. . . who got it second hand from the Knights Templar. Let me ask you something.'

'Okay.'

'Why would Pilate want to make a painting of Jesus?'

'In some Eastern traditions both Pilate and his wife are saints – because they defended Jesus against the Jews.'

'Pilate had a wife?'

'Book of Matthew: Pilate's wife had a dream that Pilate was about to execute an innocent man, and she sent a message to her husband, begging him not to do it.'

'Any idea why Pilate would care to have a painting made of a man he was about to execute?'

'I can't help you there. All I know is the reference to the painting pre-dates any other legend of the True Image. That doesn't mean it exists, but it does mean a lot of people thought it did. The last step, believing Pilate is responsible for having it made, that's your leap of faith – if you care to make it.'

As he said this Ethan pulled off the highway and drove toward a small private airport. The hanger was closed, the lights were out.

'We're here,' Kate said. 'If you can get some sleep, now is probably a good time. Come four o'clock tomorrow morning things are going to hop.'

'Sounds good,' Malloy answered.

'There's a cot in the hanger.' She handed him a key. 'Make yourself at home.'

'Where are you two going to be?'

'We've got a tent set up about a mile back in the woods.'

Chapter Ten

Caesarea
Summer AD 29.

Wearing the toga of a common citizen, Senator Publius Vitellius sailed into Caesarea on a merchant ship. Pilate first knew he was in the city when he saw the wax impression of the senator's signet ring. The moment he recognized it, he cleared his morning schedule.

In his youth Vitellius had been the friend of Prince Germanicus, later his most trusted general. Following the death of the Prince – which many believed Tiberius himself had ordered – the empire had been on the verge of civil war. Instead of exciting the crowd and rallying the legions around his own banner Vitellius had sought a peaceful resolution – one which spared Tiberius the humiliation of accusations and yet brought to justice the very man many believed Tiberius had sent to assassinate the Prince.

In the aftermath of these events Vitellius became a close ally of Tiberius and was accorded the supreme honour of owning the villa closest to Tiberius's Villa Jovis on the Isle of Capri. Despite this, the two men were never intimate. Tiberius was too cunning to expose himself to a man whose best friend he had murdered. In Rome men might do business with one another, but they never forgot a debt of blood.

Pilate had first met Vitellius when Pilate commanded the Guard escorting the remains of Germanicus from Brindisium to Rome. Over the course of a month of travel the two men had spoken only twice, but that was sufficient for Vitellius to appreciate Pilate's potential. When they were in Rome, Vitellius used his influence to promote Pilate's career.

Despite the patronage Vitellius had offered him Pilate did not anticipate meeting with the senator. In fact he would have preferred never to have seen the man again.

'You have done quite well for yourself, Prefect,' Vitellius observed pleasantly when they met *in camera* in Pilate's cabinet close by the great hall. Vitellius had aged considerably since the two men had last met. His hair had gone to grey, his complexion had lost its colour but the essential man remained unchanged. He was persuasive, shrewd and dangerous.

Pilate could not anticipate the purpose for Vitellius's arrival in Judaea, so he answered with the extreme modesty of a corrupt civil servant. 'I aspire only to serve Rome, Senator.'

'That is good, Prefect, because Rome has need of such loyalty.'

Such statements inevitably required the sacrifice of one's own life and Pilate felt a chill take hold of him. 'I will do what I can, but I hardly need remind you that I command only half a legion of Romans. The Syrian cavalry, like any of our mercenary forces, is loyal only in the sunshine.'

'You will not need an army, only a bit of discretion.'

'The Senator knows he can trust me.'

'Tell me, Pilate, have you heard of the Jew they call Yeshua? He's a Nazarene, I believe.'

Pilate felt the tension leave him. 'I've heard of him, but have had no dealings with the man. He makes trouble in the hill country of Galilee, not in Judaea. Antipas endures him no doubt because he fears all holy men. What about him?'

'He has become a danger to the peace.'

'Not the peace of my provinces.'

Vitellius pressed the issue. 'There are many who believe the man is preparing to declare himself the Jewish Messiah.'

Pilate offered a condescending smile. 'So what if he does? He's is an indigent. He has no base beyond Galilee, no money, no weapons, not even the makings of an army! As I understand it only the poor and the desperate and a great many women follow him about. If he declares himself the Jewish king, I'll respond if Antipas cannot or will not handle it. Until then—'

'A man named Judas Kerioth has become one of his followers, Prefect.'

'I'm not familiar with the name.'

'Really? I was under the impression you had dealt with the man. "The most dangerous man in Judaea," I believe you called him in one of your early reports.'

'*That* Judas. Of course I'm familiar with him, and I stand by my opinion. A very great danger. But if I may I ask . . . are your sources quite certain the Nazarene has not pledged himself to Judas?'

'Friends in Galilee tell us the Nazarene is something more than he seems.'

'Be that as it may, Judas did not strike me as a follower of any man.'

'Perhaps he has found someone who inspires him.'

'If it's really so—'

'We have reports Yeshua has raised the dead, a young girl, in point of fact, the daughter of a leader of the synagogue in Capernaum.'

Pilate smiled, shaking his head. 'In the East, Senator, these kinds of stories attach to magicians and self-styled holy men. One ought not to make too much of it.'

'This is more than a rumour. The wife of Antipas – a very sensible woman, if I am any judge of character – talked to the girl's father. He was reluctant to admit the truth but did so under torture. On another occasion, it is reported Yeshua met and fed five thousand men with a few loaves of bread and a handful of fish. It may be perfect nonsense, but if the man is as innocent as he seems, what is he doing meeting five thousand men in the desert?'

'I see the problem! I will look into the matter at once.'

'There is no need for that. A course of action has already been determined. We need only for you to press Antipas to arrest this Yeshua as quickly as possible and deliver him to you in Jerusalem. Once he is there I want you to execute the man as an example to the next would-be Messiah.'

That did not seem such a very great thing. 'I will contact Antipas at once.'

'Just so we understand one another. I want you to make sure Yeshua's followers are left alone.'

'That is a mistake, Senator.'

Vitellius blinked in surprise.

'—to leave Judas free, I mean. It would be a far better idea to execute Judas alongside his master. I have dealt with this man! Believe me, you do not want him free to make trouble, especially in Jerusalem!'

'Your command has given you a great deal of confidence.'

'Thank you, Senator.'

Vitellius's face darkened. 'I did not mean to compliment you. You have your orders. See you obey them.'

When Vitellius had left him, Pilate considered his predicament miserably. Tiberius imagined the affair was as simple as a public execution to set an example, but he had not seen ten thousand men present their necks for Roman swords because Judas had set the example! He had no idea what passion these Jews possessed and what an utter lack of concern for their lives they felt when their blood was up.

Summoning Cornelius, Pilate explained his orders. 'Permission to speak plainly, Prefect?'

'Of course.'

'I think Herodias has discovered the fuel for a great fire.'

'I am not sure I follow you.'

'A war in Judaea can only benefit Sejanus and the house of Herod. I believe Herodias has found someone capable of starting it.'

'This Yeshua?'

'You, sir. Outnumbered as we are, there will be no resisting the kind of uprising Judas can lead against our garrisons after we have crucified the Jewish Messiah.

Afterwards, your death will be the excuse Sejanus needs to march on Jerusalem. Once he avenges your death and breaks Jerusalem as he has always wanted, Tiberius will not be able to resist him. Sejanus will have the army and the population behind him and will force Tiberius to adopt him.'

'But the order comes from Tiberius!'

'Are you quite sure of that, Prefect?'

Pilate sighed. 'No, but if I attempt to go to Tiberius to ask if he has issued it, Sejanus will know.'

'Then you will do as you are told . . . and prepare for the worst?'

'I think I must.'

Caesarea
Fall and Winter AD 29-30.

Despite Pilate's request for Antipas to arrest Yeshua, the holy man continued to work openly in Galilee. Inquiring after the delay, Pilate learned that Yeshua made a habit of working in a crowd for a few hours and then moving quickly away, always a step ahead of Antipas's agents. 'It is like chasing the wind,' the tetrarch's envoy reported *in camera* some months after Pilate had asked the tetrarch for his help.

Alone with the prefect later, Cornelius begged the opportunity to offer his opinion. Pilate was feeling the pressure in the unexpected delay and looked to the man eagerly. By all means, offer an opinion!

'If one desires to catch the wind, Prefect, one cannot chase after it foolishly in the manner of Antipas. One must construct a sail and await its pleasure.'

'Anticipate him, you mean? It is impossible! Patrols find thieves who have established campsites for themselves in the wilderness, but this man stays here one night, there another. He has no fixed camp, no home. There is no anticipating such a man! I know only this. He avoids Tiberias, Caesarea, and Jerusalem.'

'I cannot speak about this Yeshua, but Judas is not a fool. If he knows Antipas is after his master, he knows time is running out. If he stays in the desert long enough, he is finished, but in Jerusalem, at the Passover, he will find an army wanting only its king.'

Jerusalem
Passover AD 30.

When Nicodemus heard that Pilate and his court were in Jerusalem, he invited the prefect to visit him at his farm for a couple of days. Arriving under an unusually heavy escort at midday, Pilate spent a long afternoon in his friend's luxurious private baths, followed by a celebratory banquet that evening.

The following morning Nicodemus and his son took Pilate into the desert to show him the wonders the aqueduct had accomplished. The transformation was impressive, and Pilate congratulated his friend. 'You are a visionary, Nicodemus!' he exclaimed.

'On the contrary, my friend, you are the one who has brought additional prosperity to all of Judaea.'

'I fear Judaea prefers death to prosperity.'

'I am not sure what you mean.'

'There is much talk these days of a Jewish king, the long-awaited Messiah of prophesy. Are the people really so naïve, Nicodemus, that they believe they can throw off the Roman authority simply by trusting a man who pretends to work miracles?'

'There are men who excite the crowds, but they are for the most part disenfranchised. They find their strength in the villages, where the people dress themselves in rags and spend the day working for a piece of bread that you and I would not find fit to toss to our dogs. In the cities, these people have no audience.'

'I met a man some years ago who seemed capable of inspiring the people of the city.'

'These sorts of men are rare and far more dangerous to the peace.'

'I am wondering if you know him – Judas Kerioth.'

Nicodemus's eyes brightened at the name. 'He is the son of a wealthy merchant in the city. As I recall, he fell in with certain radical elements and has been disinherited for it.'

Nicodemus's son spoke. 'Judas is a disciple of the rabbi I told you I had met, father.'

'The one who despises money?' Nicodemus exclaimed with a laugh. 'Tell Pilate what he said to you.'

'I was travelling on business and heard the man speaking. The more I listened the more I liked what he said. He wasn't one these men who wants to get rid of Rome. He talked instead about the Kingdom of God. I went to him afterwards. I thought I could help him, but when I asked him what I could do for his sake, he told me I should sell all that I owned and give it to the poor, and then join him in the desert.'

'Can you imagine it?' the older Nicodemus responded.

Pilate did not answer, but looked at the son again, who said in all seriousness, 'I was almost tempted to do it.'

'Why?' Pilate asked him. He was curious more than anything.

The young man offered a mysteriously happy smile. 'I suppose because it had never occurred to me that I could.'

'He wants to destroy Rome,' Nicodemus answered, 'Men like that are all the same!'

'My father and I are not in agreement about the rabbi.'

'That is because my son was still a baby when Judas of Galilee seized the Temple. He does not remember what it was like then.'

'I have heard the stories, Father.'

'Stories are one thing. Blood is another! There was a time when I was quite certain Jerusalem would become the next Carthage – her people killed, the city razed, the earth sown with salt.'

'He talked about God, not revolution!'

'Could you find this man, if you wanted?' Pilate asked. Nicodemus and his son both turned and looked at him curiously. 'If he is the great healer I've heard about,' Pilate explained, 'I could use his services.'

'He is difficult to find,' the young man answered somewhat evasively.

'Perhaps if he comes to Jerusalem, you could inform me?'

Young Nicodemus tipped his head as if it were no great matter to him. 'If we can help, you know we will.'

In private Pilate confessed the truth to the elder Nicodemus, who listened thoughtfully to the matter before announcing his opinion. 'Your centurion is right, I think. Sejanus wants a war. He knows you will do your part because you must, and he hopes Judas will respond appropriately because he can. He still has a great many friends in Jerusalem.'

'I cannot ignore direct orders.'

'What if I were to take care of Judas? The others who follow this Yeshua are simple men. Without their rabbi and certainly without Judas, they couldn't possibly inspire a general uprising against the Roman garrisons.'

'My orders are specific, Nicodemus. The followers are to be left alone. If Judas turns up murdered, Sejanus will know where to place the blame. If I murder Judas, I might as well slice my own wrists as well.'

Nicodemus considered the matter quietly before telling Pilate, 'Follow your orders, then. Follow them . . . explicitly.'

Pilate's face betrayed his excitement. Until that moment he had faced death, either by the hand of the Jews or his own after losing his garrisons. 'You have an idea?'

'Let us call it a chance: for the two of us and for our families – and for Jerusalem.'

The people began leaving the city as soon as the sun had set upon the Sabbath. By dawn, well over fifty thousand of them lined the road leading to the Susim Gate, the Gate of Kings. At midday their Messiah rode into their midst, his path strewn with palm leaves as he rode toward the city on the back of a donkey.

'The wind arrives,' Cornelius remarked drolly from the battlements.

Pilate nodded solemnly, unable to pull his gaze from the spectacle. 'I hope we have not caught more than our sail can manage.'

'If we have, then we will die like Romans, Prefect.'

'All things considered, Centurion, I had rather live like one.'

Nicodemus' slaves watched for Judas Kerioth at his parents' house. He appeared after dark on the second evening of their watch and entered by a side gate. An hour later he came back into the street. The slaves were waiting for him. They handed Judas a scroll held together by a piece of wax with an impression of the signet ring of Nicodemus. Recognizing it, Judas opened the letter eagerly and read by the light of the slaves' torches:

The Kingdom of God is at hand, my friend.
—Nicodemus

Judas looked at the slaves questioningly. Their leader told him, 'My master wishes to speak with you this evening, if it is possible.'

Judas followed the slaves to a house within the city and came before Nicodemus the Elder. 'Your master is wanted by the Romans, Judas,' Nicodemus told him by way of greeting. 'He hasn't much time left.'

'Antipas has chased him for the better part of the last year without effect.'

'Antipas is an old fox whose teeth have rotted away from eating carrion. Pilate is not. Pilate will find him . . . sooner or later.'

'It may be we find Pilate first.'

'You have the army for it. It seems a shame your king hesitates to use it.'

Judas's eyes flashed at the insult, but he did not speak.

'The Jews have never been more ready to fight, nor more certain that the time has come. They want only inspiration and a commander to lead them!'

'Rome has always been kind to you, Nicodemus,' Judas remarked. His tone was casual, but his point was made. He did not trust Nicodemus.

'I pay well for the kindness, but I am tired of it. Their greed is insatiable. I had rather buy the services of an army to defeat him than pay Pilate another penny for his goodwill.'

Judas smiled. 'Are there armies about that are for sale?'

'Herod Antipas is easily bribed.'

'We want nothing from that man!'

'And nothing is what he is selling. The moment you turn on the Roman garrison the Governor of Syria will order three of his legions to march south on Jerusalem. These he will support with three auxiliary units of Syrian cavalry – thirty thousand men under arms. He will ask in addition that Antipas bring an army into the field before he proceeds to Jerusalem. If Antipas delays, the Romans will wait. That is when you will strike.'

'Have you spoken to Antipas?'

'My gold will say all that is necessary, but I will not waste it on dreamers and fanatics. I need to see a man who can lead Judaea against the Romans before I will spend money on revolutions.'

'That man is among us now!'

Nicodemus shook his head. 'I have seen men like your master more times than I care to count. They possess every advantage the Lord can give a man and then hesitate at the critical moment. Nations rise and fall because of their indecision. Who can say what stops them from seizing the moment? Certainly not courage. Perhaps they think that in time their opportunities increase. I do not know. I *do* know this. The nation of Israel cannot be born again without spilling the blood of both Romans *and* Jews. Let Pilate have your master. Let him hang him as he intends from a Roman cross. Let him do it before all the Jews on the day of our Passover.'

'You cannot be serious!'

'You saw the people receive him in Jerusalem. You saw the hope in their faces. Tell me! Will the people not ache with the loss of such a leader?'

'They will burn with fury,' Judas muttered, 'as they always do when they see the Romans humiliate us.'

Nicodemus nodded solemnly, his dark eyes catching the younger man's and holding them. 'Some men are born to lead, Judas, and some to inspire. Since you were very young people have known it was in your nature to lead. Why do you hesitate when you see what the death of your master will inspire? Do you not remember Moses? He placed a serpent upon a cross and set it before his army. So it will be when you hold up the death of your master before our people. Your time has come to fulfil your destiny, Judas. The Kingdom of God is at hand. Give Pilate Yeshua and Pilate will give you Jerusalem.'

'I cannot give Yeshua to Pilate and then lead his army into battle!'

'Why not? What happens under cover of darkness will stay in darkness. No one will ever know. Besides, it is not his army you will lead. When you are King of Israel they will have forgotten even the name of Yeshua. Men will speak of Judas Kerioth as the Messiah of prophesy. And they will be right!'

As Judas considered the prospect that he would become the true Messiah, his eyes glistened with excitement. 'Can you buy Antipas off?'

'It will be easy enough. He is already in Jerusalem.'

A cloud of doubt now came over the younger man. 'Rome will not stand for it. They will send more than a handful of legions against us if we defeat the legions stationed in Syria.'

'Learn from the mistakes of the past and you will keep what you have won. Once you have annihilated Pilate's forces and defeated the Syrian legions, you can wait to be crushed or you can march on Egypt. The Egyptians will see your courage and rise up against the Romans themselves. When that happens, you can make an alliance with them and finish the work they have started. Afterwards, you would do well to entice the Parthians to join your cause. They are bitter enemies of Rome and will seize the opportunity you offer them. A united army under your command can sweep across Africa, breaking the legions before Tiberius has awakened from his midday nap.'

'You make it sound easy.'

'It is never easy to sacrifice those we love, no matter how necessary. I make it sound possible. Because it is.

Rome rules us because we let her. She will fall when we refuse to kneel down to her authority. The moment waits only the man with the courage to seize the opportunity and the vision that makes men follow him. Do I look at him or shall we wait for another generation before we throw them off?'

After a moment of silence, Judas answered, 'Tell me what I must do.'

'It is not safe to stay in Jerusalem, Lady.'

Procula stared uncertainly at the centurion Cornelius. The hour was late. She had already retired to her bedroom and was reading by candlelight about the Passover of the Jews. Cornelius's enormous frame filled her doorway. 'What are you talking about?'

'Pilate arrests the Jewish Messiah this night. By morning, the whole city will know it. When that happens, there is a good chance they will storm the palace. I cannot protect you if that happens, so I have arranged your escape this evening. You will please dress for travel and follow me.'

'Pilate sends you?'

'He would have come himself, but this evening is critical to our chances.'

'Answer my question. Did Pilate send you?'

'No.'

'Nor should he have done so. I am a Roman, like yourself and Pilate and all the rest who sit in this wretched palace. I will not flee the fate others must endure.'

The enormous round face of the centurion flushed with exasperation. 'You do not want to be here tomorrow, Lady. You have not seen how soldiers act against women after a battle.'

'What has Pilate done, that he brings this upon us?'

'Your husband answers an imperial command, nothing more.'

'Regarding the Jewish Messiah?'

'I have said more than I should.'

The foreboding of what was about to transpire no doubt triggered Procula's dream, though she believed, as was the custom of the day, the dream was divinely sent.

It was a simple and awful vision: a man crucified, as many had already been. But this was different. Those who watched did not keep their distance, as they ought to have done, but stood at the base of the cross and caught his blood as they could, smearing it upon their foreheads first and then upon the heads of the others who could not get close enough.

Coming awake suddenly, Procula whispered to the night, 'He is the Paschal Lamb!'

Climbing from her bed, she told the slave girl sleeping on the floor in the corner of the room that she needed to speak with the officer of the guard at once. The girl scurried quickly from the room and returned a few moments later with an officer and an escort of guards.

'I must speak with Pilate,' Procula told the tribune as she pulled a cloak hurriedly over her night clothes.

'The prefect is busy, Lady.'

'It is the middle of the night!'

'It is soon daylight, Lady, but he is already engaged in business.'

'Take me to him then.'

'That is not possible. The prefect sits in the great hall. He will not be called out nor is it allowed for a woman to enter.'

'Take me to Cornelius then.'

'Lady, I am not authorized—!'

'I am not asking a favour, Tribune. I am giving you an order!'

'The centurion attends your husband.'

'Then take me as far as it is legal for me to go, and tell the centurion I am waiting to speak to him. Cornelius himself can decide if he wants to come outside.' The young officer considered his options briefly, then gave a curt nod and invited Procula to follow him.

Herod's palace was a monstrous place, busy at every point with vast, meaningless frescoes of vegetation and imaginary landscapes devoid of human and animal life. One great room after another opened off a series of vast hallways having no function other than to create a sense of awe. They walked for nearly ten minutes before they came to the great hall.

Procula waited several minutes before Cornelius appeared. 'What is it, Lady?'

'Pilate must not execute the Jewish Messiah!'

'He has no choice.'

'The man is innocent!'

'That means nothing to a Roman prefect. Politically, he represents—'

'You don't understand! I have had a dream. I have

seen what will happen! This man is the sacrifice of the Passover!'

Cornelius shook his head. 'Dreams do not always—'

'His blood will mark out those who are to be spared when the Angel of Death comes! As in Egypt, before Moses led his people to freedom, it will pass over only those who have the mark of his blood. The rest of us will perish! Not the first born, but all of us – our whole world! If Pilate kills this man, Rome falls!'

'I will tell him of your dream, but it will change nothing, Lady.'

Cornelius departed, and the tribune who had escorted Procula told her, 'The prefect has no choice in the matter. The Jews themselves demand it.'

'Demand what?'

'Demand that the pretender be put to death. Your husband resists them. He says he can find no fault with the man, but they threaten him with the wrath of Caesar if he refuses.'

'The Jews are invoking the name of Caesar?'

'Your husband has already sent Yeshua to Herod Antipas, hoping he would make a judgment, but Antipas refuses to oblige him.'

A second officer listening to this added, 'I hear the prefect still refuses to execute the man. He says he will take him before the Jews themselves and let them decide. The priests are furious about it, too, but your husband will not be swayed. He will spare the man if he can.'

Procula did not answer the young officers, but she did not believe Pilate defended a Jew. In her experience men did not change their nature without reason. If

Pilate was quarrelling with the priests over the matter of a single Jew, he had a good reason – and it was not for the sake of kindness or out of a sense of justice. Pilate did not possess those virtues. He was up to some evil. Though what it was she could not even begin to guess.

Theophanes sat down at first light and began to paint. Pilate wanted the King of the Jews, not a criminal, and that is what the painter created. His subject was probably thirty-five or thirty-six years old. Maybe a year or two younger. His face was dark from the constant exposure to the desert. He was balding, and there was a touch of grey at the temples. Theophanes caught the image exactly as he would have been before his arrest: a man who enjoyed food and drink and a bit of laughter to keep the spirit alive – not one of these ugly, thin, sad ascetic sorts who hate the good earth upon which God has put them!

The slave painted quickly, not because Pilate was in a hurry, but because the medium demanded it. As soon as he applied the hot encaustic to the warmed gypsum-treated board it began to cool. As that happened it became progressively more difficult to manage. Had he chosen tempera, Theophanes would have had an easier time of it. Tempera was more forgiving, but encaustic was far superior when it was handled correctly. The satiny finish was as close to life as paint could get, and it kept its lustre and colour indefinitely. Theophanes left tempera to lesser men. He worked only in wax.

As he finished the portrait, Pilate approached in order that he might make his habitual complaints. 'Will those who have seen him in life know him by this portrait, Theophanes?'

Pilate presented four men to the crowd in the great plaza before the Temple, announcing that he had condemned each man to death, but that in honour of the Jewish Passover, the Jews could free one of the criminals.

The crowd was small and surly, the better portion of them rounded up from the streets and the majority not even Jewish, but there were enough bodies that had turned out to call it a crowd. Those who recalled the massacre on this very spot, and almost everyone did that morning, hardly looked at the criminals. Their eyes watched the Syrian cavalry lined up in battle formation at either side of the Plaza. Three centuries of Roman infantry in full battle dress completed the square containing them. Cornelius stood behind the criminals and raised his sword. Each man caught a few wild cheers, save one: the man named Yeshua, who inspired not a single voice. 'Is this not the King of Jews?' Pilate shouted at them. 'No one stands with his king? Not one of you?'

They were quiet. They hardly breathed. Pilate could hear the clap of horse hooves on the cobblestone at the edge of the plaza. 'Is this man to die – this man you adored as your Messiah only a few days ago?'

The priests began the shout, and the others picked it up quickly – *Crucify him!* As each man shouted, another joined him until all of them cried in unison: *Crucify him! Crucify him! Crucify him!*

Pilate signalled to Cornelius to silence the crowd. The

prefect walked to a bowl one of his officers now carried forward. 'The man is blameless,' he announced grandly. 'If the Jews want him to die, he will die, but I wash my hands of the matter.'

The thunder broke with the fury of armies colliding and stirred an animal fear deep inside Pilate's chest. Walking out to one of the terraces, he looked up at the still blue sky and wondered what had made the sound.

The answer came half an hour later when the storm hit. It came with wind and rain. The earth shook so that tiles fell from the ceiling of the great hall. Fearing for his life Pilate ran out of the building and into the shrieking wind. There he saw trees collapsing, debris and leaves blowing wildly through the air like arrows on a battlefield. He could not see the great Temple of the Jews, the rain was so heavy, and for a moment he thought the desert god had been awakened from his long sleep.

Procula found him on the porch only partially protected from the rain. The wind still howled. The storm had emptied the Plaza and had driven the Roman guard to cover, so they stood alone before the palace, only their slaves to attend them. 'You have murdered an innocent,' Procula shouted, 'and this is what comes of it!' She swept her hand out toward the storm and darkness.

'I did not kill him, Procula. The Jews have done it!'

'Is that what you are telling Rome?'

'I had no choice. The Jews forced me to do it! I had to keep the peace, didn't I?'

'The *Jews* forced you? Who rules the Jews, Pilate?

What death did the man die but a Roman one?'

'I tried to save him, but they would not have it!'

'Tell your lies to someone who does not know you so well!'

'Take care, woman, or—'

'Or what? Will the Jews demand you kill me as well?'

The son of Nicodemus visited Pilate in the company of another wealthy man. They were asking for the body of the rabbi. Roman policy was to leave criminals on the cross until the stench of human decomposition had passed and the birds had finished feeding. Pilate might have refused easily enough by citing the law, but he was moved by the presence of Nicodemus the younger, whose favour he wanted to keep, and by the politics of the moment. He had challenged the Jewish nation and he had won by skilfully passing his own guilt in the matter to their collective head. It did not pay to keep his victory before them.

Better, he thought, to let this thing finish quickly and quietly. They would not move against him until sundown tomorrow, because of their Sabbath. By then they might have organized again, might have found someone capable of stirring their passion for blood, even if Judas had been discredited. Pilate did not need to give them a point of focus for their rage. He told Cornelius to give orders that the three men be finished off and taken down before sunset. 'Throw the two thieves into the sewers for the rats to strip, but see that the body these men seek is given to them.'

Before he left, Nicodemus asked for a word in

private. Pilate granted him his request out of reverence for his father.

'I appreciate what you have done today,' the young man said. 'I know it would have been easier politically for you, if you had not resisted the Temple authorities.'

'Sometimes it is not enough simply to want to do the right thing,' Pilate answered.

'But it is! It is all that matters. That is what the rabbi taught us! Our victories and failures do not make us what we are: our intentions do. What we hold in our heart is the only action that matters!'

There was no kind way to answer such naiveté, so Pilate remained silent, as if contemplating a great wisdom.

After the sun had set and the Jewish Sabbath had begun, Nicodemus the Elder showed up. As Procula had refused to join him, Pilate was eating alone and left his meal to meet his friend *in camera*.

'The priests have called Judas to them and paid him for giving them Yeshua.'

'Did he take the money?'

'He threw it at them and ran into the streets.'

Pilate smiled.

'They have already spread the rumour that Judas sold his master for a few pieces of silver. He is ruined and knows it.'

'And the others?'

'Make a show of your troops for a few days and you will hear nothing more from those men.'

'There will be no revolt?'

'Who is to lead it? And against whom? The Jews have

killed their Messiah, not Rome. I heard you say it yourself.'

Lake Lucerne
October 12, 2006.

At three-thirty Kate knocked on the hanger where Malloy had spent the night and greeted him with a thermos of hot black campfire-brewed coffee. She pointed toward the woods behind the tiny airfield and told him, 'We've got bacon, sausage, and eggs and more coffee when you're ready.' She tossed him a pair of night vision goggles. 'Just follow your nose.'

He joined them fifteen minutes later. Ethan prepared three eggs for him and piled on the meat. 'A Tennessee breakfast!'

'He *thinks* it's Tennessee. I keep telling him it's English.'

Malloy looked at the pork doubtfully. For the sake of Gwen he had begun to follow Jewish dietary customs, if not their faith. 'I don't know,' he said, pushing the meat from his plate back into the pan, 'I'm a little tight this morning. I think the eggs will be enough.'

'When was the last time you jumped?' Ethan asked.

'Jumped?'

'With a parachute.'

Malloy looked at them in the flickering light of the fire. 'Where are we jumping?'

'We're going to pay a visit on Sir Julian,' Kate answered. 'You didn't think we would be driving up to the front gate, did you?'

'The last jump I made was about a quarter of a century ago.'

'You trained on the round parachutes?'

Malloy nodded and took a sip of coffee. 'The last of the old school.' He could still remember the impact. As a kid it hadn't been pleasant. The idea of it now left his knees sore.

'You ever use a rectangular canopy?'

'I never jumped again after jump school. If a job required a maniac, I usually out-sourced it.'

'The good news is,' Kate said, 'you're going to love the new canopy. You've got nothing to worry about. You remember the old paratrooper boots? They're out. People jump in tennis shoes these days. Even beginners land standing up . . . and smiling. Handling is easier, too. A morning like this with no wind, if you land in a treetop it's because you want to.'

'Usually when people talk about the good news, there's some bad news too.'

'There's a little bit of problem with your drop zone,' Ethan told him.

'*A little bit?*'

'You've got about twenty to thirty yards between the cliff and the rotary blades of Corbeau's helicopter. Sounds like plenty of room—'

'Not really.'

'It's enough, but you have to be careful. You come in too low and you smack into the side of a cliff. You come in a little high and the rotary blades suck you in. Other than that,' he smiled, 'no problem.'

'Eat your eggs,' Kate laughed, 'and don't worry

about the jump. Odds are we'll all get shot before we touch down.'

They cleared camp quickly. That finished, Kate pulled three parachutes from the van. 'We didn't pack these ourselves,' she said, 'so we repack them now – with gloves.'

What struck Malloy was the compactness of the modern parachute. It strapped onto the back with a container that was smaller than the average backpack. Almost nothing was the same, except that the canopy itself was still as difficult to pack as ever. The problem was getting the air out. It took patience and method, and Malloy had neither at four-thirty in the morning. Ethan came over and helped him. 'I don't see the ripcord,' Malloy told him.

'There isn't one. At the bottom of the pack you pull the drogue chute out. That catches the wind and pulls the bridle. The bridal pops the pin,' he said, pointing to his already packed container, 'and then the D-bag comes out.' The D-bag held the canopy.

'You do this often?' Malloy asked.

'Kate does quite a bit with a group. I join them sometimes on the weekends.'

The pilot arrived at five and began preparing the Cessna C-182 that was parked in the hanger where Malloy had slept. While he did this, Kate ran through the inventory of weapons she and Ethan had collected the previous day with the help of a well-connected friend in Zürich. It was an impressive armoury even by Malloy's standards. There were three Viper vests with side and crotch panels, combat headgear, and four AKS-74s – the airborne troop model with folding metallic butts

– and six Steyr tactical machine pistols. Of these, Kate holstered four of them on her person, one at each thigh and two at the belt, handles out for a cross-draw. She stowed two extra clips of 9 mm ammunition. They had half-a-dozen MK3A2 concussion grenades, three each for Kate and Ethan, three headsets for communications and three sets of handcuffs, one for the pilot, one for Corbeau and one just in case. They all had several lengths of rope. In addition to her four machine pistols, Kate carried a holstered Navy Colt .45 at the small of her back and one of the Kalashnikovs strapped across her chest. Ethan carried two Kalashnikovs across his chest with two Steyrs holstered to his thighs. He had climbing rope tucked into his jump harness and an ice pick at his belt that he wore like a handgun. Kate and Ethan each carried a combat knife in the right boot. Everyone wore gloves and a tight fitting hood.

Handing Malloy his armour and one of the AKS-74s, Kate said to him, 'I'm Girl, he's Boy, you're Man. No names, no faces showing, no prints and hopefully no blood. It's okay to leave weapons and clips behind. Everything's been reported stolen. 'What about yours?'

'Clean,' Malloy answered, wiping his guns for prints as he spoke.

'Your job will be to secure the helicopter, preferably with the pilot still alive. After you do that, hold your position. Use your MAC-10 if you need a burst. Otherwise set the Kalashnikov on single shot and keep our retreat clear. If we don't fly out, we don't get out.' Malloy examined his weapon, but he was comfortable with it. Unlike the American M-16, the Kalashnikov's first selector was full auto, the second single shot. The weapons were otherwise relatively comparable, with the Russian model being somewhat lighter and less inclined to jam but more difficult to handle in a prone position because of the length of the clip.

'Corbeau keeps the helicopter pad at the centre of his backyard. His pilot always flies in from the lakeside and faces the house. You'll come in behind his position a few seconds before us. It will still be dark, but the security lights ought to be on for the helicopter, meaning we don't trip the alarm when we drop in. The last fifty feet or so all three of us will be visible, assuming anyone is looking up, but there's supposed to be a light fog this morning, so we might catch a break. If our timing is right Dr North should be somewhere between the house and the helicopter when we drop. Ethan and you can take out the escorts – headshots if possible. If anyone is wearing armour it will be the people going with the hostage.

'You make sure North gets to the helicopter. If she has trouble walking, you might have to help her. Ethan can provide some cover for you if you need it, but you're going to have to assume at least some of the fire is going to be coming from a position only you can respond to. Once she is inside the helicopter, the light armour should keep her safe from small arms fire. We figure three, maybe four minutes inside the house. It's going to feel like ten, so get down close to the ground and get comfortable. We have one chance at this guy. If we lose him today, he'll hunt us down, and he won't ever stop.'

Inside the tiny Cessna Malloy met the pilot, an amateur flier from Bern and a good friend of Ethan's.

He was preternaturally cheerful considering the hour.

They were in the air less than a minute later, sweeping up alongside the dark shadow that was Mount Pilatus and then circling back under the peak of Stanserhorn. As the plane pushed for altitude, everyone grew quiet. At eleven thousand feet the pilot turned toward Rigi and called out to Kate. Kate took a moment to get oriented with the lake and then checked with Malloy and Ethan. Everyone was ready to jump.

'Make the call,' she said. 'Tell him to meet you at Lake Pilatus on Mount Pilatus. You'll have a bonfire burning, so he can find you.' As Malloy hit the speed dial, Kate signalled to the pilot to turn the engine off. They were floating in the darkness, earth and sky indistinguishable.

Corbeau answered his phone at once. 'Yes?' he said, speaking English.

'I'll meet you at Lake Pilatus on Mount Pilatus. I've got a bonfire started so you can find me. If I don't see your helicopter by . . . six-twenty, don't bother coming.'

'We need to talk, Mr Malloy,' Corbeau answered.

'No we don't.' Malloy disconnected and shut the phone off. Then he looked at his new partners. 'We're on the clock, people.'

Corbeau finished his call and looked at Bremmer, who shook his head. 'He wasn't on long enough, but they got the number and they're tracking it. They should have a location in a few minutes.'

Corbeau nodded and let his gaze sweep across his library bookshelves. He was seated at his desk. Xeno,

Jeffrey Bremmer, and Helena Chernoff stood directly before him. Two uniformed guards stood at attention across the room.

'Something is wrong,' Corbeau announced quietly. His manner was thoughtful, as if still putting together his impressions. 'Malloy's voice was not quite right.'

'He's nervous,' Xeno answered. Xeno was leading the team taking North on the helicopter and was already wearing armour.

Corbeau shook his head. 'That wasn't it. It was more like . . . a man who is bluffing. I don't think he has the painting.' Having said this, Corbeau looked at Chernoff for confirmation.

'It's possible,' she answered. 'If he sent the painting to New York, he might still try to save North.'

Corbeau looked at Bremmer. 'What does a man do if he doesn't have the money to pay a ransom?'

Bremmer smiled. 'He fills a bag with paper and brings a gun to the exchange.'

'He's setting a trap for us.' Corbeau was suddenly sure of himself. 'He doesn't have the painting.' To Xeno he said, 'I want you to leave North here, and take Helena in her place. When you fly in, if Malloy is exposed, shoot him and get out of there. If he's concealed, wait on him, but don't set down. He'll have people with him, but they're not going to move against you until the hostage is safe. Work it right and you can be out of range before they understand what you've done.'

'What about the others?' Chernoff asked.

'I don't care about the others. I want Malloy.'

'And if he has the painting?' Xeno asked.

Corbeau shook his head. 'He doesn't.'

'Tell the pilot you're to go to Lake Pilatus,' Bremmer added. 'He'll know where it is.'

'Do you know the terrain?' Xeno asked.

'It's somewhere on Pilatus, so I expect—'

'It's on the north slope,' Corbeau said, 'and it's not really a lake. It's a marsh, reputed to be the last resting place of Pontius Pilate, thus the name. The place is isolated with lots of trees and rocks and steep hills surrounding an open meadow. That means Malloy is going to own the high ground if you set down, so make sure you don't.'

Bremmer looked at his watch. 'You have twelve minutes. Let's not keep the man waiting.'

Once Chernoff and Xeno had left, Bremmer asked, 'Do we need Dr North?'

'I suppose not.'

'I was promised an afternoon with her.'

'Take the whole day,' he said. 'As it turns out, she's of no value to us. But when you finish, leave the body where it can be found quickly. If nothing else those who claim the corpse will take us to Richland and Starr.'

Bremmer's cell phone rang. 'That will be the cell phone location,' he said as he reached for the phone. But then he stopped, his eyes locking on the mist just beyond the library windows, as if he could not believe his eyes.

'Oh, my God,' he whispered.

The cold rush of air against his face disoriented Malloy momentarily, but Kate's voice came over the headset. 'Just float and let us catch up with you.'

At the far end of the lake a few lights shining through the fog marked the city of Lucerne. To the east a pale light washed over the horizon. Otherwise the landscape was perfectly black – mountains, lake, and sky. Ethan came floating in beside Malloy, 'We're heading down there,' he said over the headset and pointed at a speck of light.

A freefall from ten thousand feet lasts a little over half-a-minute with normal speeds reaching one hundred twenty miles per hour. Despite the wild sensation that came with any jump, there was an odd feeling of being in control. To an extent that was true. It was possible to roll, perform somersaults, dive for speed, or slow down. All that really mattered was getting stabilized before deployment, and that was the only thing Malloy attempted to do from the moment he dropped out of the plane. When Kate slipped up on his right, her voice sounded in Malloy's headset, 'Deploy chutes on five, gentlemen.' Ethan and Kate arced away as she counted it out.

Instinctively Malloy reached for his ripcord and felt a moment of panic. No ripcord . . . and no reserve. Then he remembered and reached around and pulled the drogue chute out. The small pilot chute caught the air and began pulling the bridal out of the container. He heard his canopy unfurling and then felt the familiar impact of the material catching the air. He looked up, but could not see the slider descending down the ropes. Without the slider, the parachute would have deployed instantly, decelerating his speed too quickly for the equipment to handle. With it the lines stayed untangled, and deceleration was more gradual. At full deployment

Malloy took the toggles and tried to get a feel for his equipment. The wind whistled instead of screamed now, but beneath him the world seemed eerily quiet.

'You need to accelerate,' Kate said. 'Pull down on one of the toggles until you make a three-sixty. Not too tight! Nice and easy. That's it. Now just float and steer towards the light.'

As they closed in, Malloy could actually see the cliff rising up over the lake, the helicopter, the high walls surrounding the estate, the villa and the tower – all shrouded in a light mist. They were still above the light, still invisible from the ground, but once they dropped into the light the euphoric silence of the world below would end with a clatter of automatic weapons.

Kate pulled hard on the left toggle. The effect was twofold. First, it sent her into a three hundred and sixty degree turn far tighter than the one Malloy had executed several thousand feet above. Second, as she straightened out of the hook turn, her momentum shot her forward at close to thirty miles an hour. Called a turf-surf among aficionados, the manoeuvre was usually performed a bit closer to the ground and allowed the parachutist to skim a couple of feet above the grass for about thirty metres or so. The risk of the move was unintended impact with the ground, but Kate's danger was different. She was headed right for the second-storey windows of Corbeau's library. A foot too high or low and she collided with a stone wall. On target, she broke glass.

The lights were on. Corbeau sat behind his desk. Bremmer stood in front of him. Two uniformed guards stood at attention by the door.

As she came toward the window, Kate lifted her legs at a ninety degree angle to her body.

The rotor blades on the Bell 407 were whirling as Malloy drifted in closer than he would have liked. The pilot was fiddling with his control panel, not thinking about his blind spot. In fact, he probably didn't have a fear in the world. Just after Malloy hit the ground, while the canopy still fluttered, he cut free and ran toward the pilot's door. He jerked a lean, athletic man about his own age from the cockpit, tossed him to the ground, handcuffed his wrists and tied his ankles.

Ethan came in toward the roof a bit higher than he intended. He pulled down hard on both toggles. This tightened the canopy and caused a sudden drop. He hit the slate roof with the force of a six-foot fall.

He stripped his parachute away and freed one of the AKS-74s. As Kate swept into Corbeau's library, Ethan walked calmly to the edge of the roof. At the sound of Kate's Steyrs he took out the two guards at the front gate and then turned to catch the first security guard exiting the guardhouse on the run. Ethan hit him with two taps. The next guard was at the door before he realised it was an ambush. Ethan's first shot struck his neck, the second his forehead. He tossed a grenade through the window of the guardhouse and then ran along the ridge of the roof toward the other end of the house. Directly above the basement entrance at the side of the house, Ethan saw two men below him. Another was already out in the open and struggling to get his Kalashnikov ready to fire. All three men wore armour, but North wasn't with them. Malloy took the lead man with a single shot to the head. Ethan dropped a grenade on the other two and then finished them with headshots.

He turned back and saw two men run out to the second storey terrace, spinning and firing on full auto at Ethan. Malloy took one. Ethan dropped the other.

At impact with the windows, Kate used a cross-handed draw to produce two Steyr tactical machine pistols. The two guards had their weapons raised when she took them with her left hand. Bremmer, who was stilling reaching for his sidearm, Kate took down with her right.

When she had emptied both weapons Kate dropped them and pulled a fresh Steyr from one of the holsters on her thigh. She finished the guards and Jeffrey Bremmer with kill shots as she walked toward Corbeau, who had risen from his seat but had made no attempt to reach for a weapon.

'On the floor!' Kate told him. When he hesitated, she pulled her Navy Colt with her left hand and fired once into his leg. Corbeau went down hard, screaming incoherently. Kate kicked him in the face, breaking his nose.

Tossing the Navy Colt aside, she forced Corbeau's hands behind his back and locked his wrist's together with cuffs. She set the Steyr on the floor next to him and then tied his feet with a length of rope. 'Your package is in the library, Boy,' she announced.

'Grounds are quiet, Girl,' Ethan answered.

'Man?' Kate asked.

'No sign of North,' Malloy answered.

'We'll find her.'

Taking up the Steyr, Kate walked toward the narrow hallway leading out of the library. 'I am clearing the second floor, gentlemen.'

Leading with a concussion grenade Kate walked toward the main hall, ready for resistance, but the hallway before the stairs was empty. Kate went room by room through the second storey, tapping closets, wardrobes, and doors with small bursts of gunfire before opening them.

When she had assured herself no one was at her back, she reloaded and headed for the stairway. 'Second floor is secure, gentlemen,' she whispered.

'I'm coming in,' Malloy announced.

'Hold your position!' Kate said.

'Position is secure.'

Chernoff and Xeno were at the bottom of the stairs when they heard the sound of automatic weapons in Corbeau's library. Xeno started back, but Chernoff took his arm. It was too late to help Corbeau, and they both knew it. They heard more shots, from the roof this time, and then the sound of a grenade exploding close to the guardhouse.

Three men came running toward the stairs, but Xeno stopped them. 'Wait for them here,' he said, signalling them to either side of the stairway.

He signalled Chernoff toward the back of the house. At the windows overlooking the backyard she saw the pilot in the grass. Next to him was a man wearing headgear and a hood. The helicopter was empty, the blades still twirling. She heard shots and another grenade exploding on the opposite side of the house. She crossed the main room heading to the front window. 'One in the back!' she called.

At the front of the house the gate was still closed, but both guards were down. 'Both guards down at the gate!'

Slipping out the side of the building not far from to the basement entrance, Chernoff found three more down. She looked up at the roof as she pressed close to the side of the house. One man holding the pilot. Two or three on the roof. Another pair on the second storey . . .

Against three times that number! It didn't make sense. There had to be a second wave coming through the tunnel from the lake or hitting the front gate – or both.

Which meant it was time to go.

She hit the wall on the run, snagging the tiles at the top and swinging one leg over. Pulling her Glock free, she studied the woods beneath her but saw nothing besides the predawn shadows and wisps of fog.

From Chernoff's position atop the wall she could see the helicopter and the pilot through the leaves but not the other man. Had he seen her? Was he coming?

She waited, watching the backyard with her gun ready. When he broke from behind the heavy cover of the tree branches close to the wall he was running toward the house. Chernoff fired three shots at the man, two in the chest for takedown and one in the head when he hit the ground. Then she took aim on the pilot and put one bullet in his skull. In case they were hoping to use him to fly out.

She heard a single gunshot fired from close to the front gate but couldn't see who had fired it. It didn't matter. She slipped both legs over the wall and dropped into the brush. Like Brand and Kenyon, Helena Chernoff headed in the direction of the lake.

'Man is down!' Ethan shouted. Even as he said it, a bullet hit him in the back. The impact sent him sliding headfirst toward the edge of the roof. His first coherent thought was that the slug had not penetrated his armour, but he was going to die from a headfirst plunge from the roof. He snagged his ice pick from his belt and swung its point through the slate. The immediate effect was to throw his body to one side. Getting both hands on the pick, Ethan's legs arced round and ended up hanging over the roof's guttering.

Pulling himself back and standing up again, Ethan saw his Kalashnikov had fallen into the shrubbery. He brought his second weapon off his chest, snapped the folding metallic butt into place, and climbed the steep grade back to the top. The man who had shot him was already through the front gate and starting toward the house. The rover. Ethan hit him once with a headshot and then strapped his weapon back to his chest.

Extending a length of his rope, he looped one end around the chimney and ran for the edge of the roof. At the end of his rope, his body swung back toward the house, and broke through the library window. He landed only a few feet from the devil himself.

Kate rolled a concussion grenade down the main stairwell, then pulled the second Steyr. Wielding both guns she was almost down the stairs without incident when two men slipped into position from different hallways – one in front of her, the other at her back.

Seeing the muzzle flash of the Kalashnikov in front of her, Kate leaped over the bannister, emptying both weapons as she dropped. She hit one man hard but the second pulled back too quickly.

Tossing the empty machine pistols aside as she rolled, she freed her Kalashnikov and came to sitting position with her back to the wall.

'I think I could use some help,' she whispered.

Kenyon's shots had pounded against Xeno's vest, forcing him back to cover. For a moment he waited, his chest heaving, his breath fast and shallow. He could hear Kenyon calling for help and signalled the man next to him that there was still someone on the second floor. 'Wait for him,' he whispered as he sent the man to the other hallway.

Ethan had already tossed Corbeau over his shoulder and was coming to the top of the stairs when he heard Kate ask for help. Dropping Corbeau to the floor, Ethan descended the stairs with his AKS-74 on full auto. 'I'm on the stairs,' he said. 'Man, are you hit?'

There was no answer.

Xeno leaned against the wall, holding his weapon close to his chest, the muzzle up, his finger pressing the trigger.

He heard Brand's voice above him. 'I'm on the stairs.

Man, are you hit?' And then he was coming down the steps. Like Kenyon he jumped the last two metres and hit the floor hard.

The moment he did Xeno swung out, his gun level and set on full auto.

Ethan saw Kate on the floor, her shoulders leaning against the wall. She had one gun but two hallways to cover. Jumping over the bannister he dropped the last six feet. As he did a uniformed guard moved into view in the living room with a handgun. His first shot hit Ethan, but he dropped when Ethan opened fire. A second man came in low, sliding across the floor on his shoulder with a Kalashnikov on full auto and using the corpse of the man who had just fallen as cover. Ethan swept the point of his weapon down across him but the clip emptied out. He heard Kate's firing directly under him, but was not conscious of the Kalashnikov at his back until a spray of bullets slammed him face first into the wall. He dropped across Kate, tossing his emptied weapon aside and pulling one of his Steyrs. The man in the living room came up, having reloaded and opened fire again, but Ethan hit him with a long blast from the Steyr.

As he spun to cover the other hall way, Kate slumped lifelessly to the floor.

'Girl is down!' he called, touching the torn armour over her heart. 'Talk to me, Man! Repeat. Girl is down!'

The moment the shots started Xeno felt a strange stinging sensation close to his hip and another in his arm. As he rolled back to cover, half-a-dozen rounds slammed into his chest and side.

He checked his wounds, one in the arm, one close to the hip below the line of his vest – and one, he realised, in the centre of his chest, the bullet having penetrated his vest.

That one scared him, but at least he was still standing.

Malloy sat up like a man pulled out of a deep sleep. 'I'm coming,' he muttered and tried to stand without much success. He could not remember where he was and it occurred to him he might be drunk, at least until he looked around and saw his helmet, headset, and the AKS-74.

The helmet, he realised, had taken a round – which explained the wooziness and headache. As he collected the gun, like a boy gathering his shovel from the sand-box, he realised the voice he had heard calling him back to consciousness could not have come from the headset. He had lost that when he was hit.

It must have been the memory of Gwen telling him to wake up. He smiled at the thought of so many mornings coming slowly awake while she coaxed him out of bed and he tried to talk her back in . . .

He heard a shot fired without understanding its source. Even the distinctive crack as it passed his face and the thunk as the bullet struck the earth several feet behind him made no immediate impression. The next bullet struck him squarely in the chest. That had the effect of awakening him to the fact that he was exposed and someone was still trying to kill him.

He rolled hard to the left and kept rolling when he heard more shots. When he came up, he pulled his MAC-10, located the man at the edge of house by the muzzle flash of his gun, and levelled his weapon. He felt the hard punch of a bullet strike the heavy padding at his shoulder. The gunman was going for the head. He answered with a burst that hit brick and danced toward flesh. The man spun round once like a dervish, his arms reaching out as he dropped to the gravel.

Malloy came to his feet slowly, his head throbbing now. Loading a fresh clip, he began a broken-field run toward the house. At the terrace Malloy did not bother opening the door, but crashed through the glass. He saw Ethan squatting protectively over Kate's prone figure, and understood at once something was wrong.

As the two men recognized one another they both relaxed. Just then a gunman stepped into the open with his Kalashnikov on full auto. Malloy dived across the floor and came up in a seated position firing a full burst as several rounds pounded into his vest. The man went down, and Malloy tossed his emptied MAC-10 aside. The wind knocked out of him, his chest and stomach heaving, Malloy crawled across the room and joined Ethan.

Xeno staggered back along the wall looking for others, but no one was left. At the front of the house he could see three men down just inside the opened gate. If there was someone still on the roof it would be suicide to try to get to the cars.

He thought about going over the wall, but with his wounds he realised he couldn't make it.

He heard glass breaking, weapons firing, the cry of a man hit, and then one of the weapons clattering across the floor.

His only chance was to get to the tunnel and then make his way down to the boats. From there he could get across the lake.

He closed the basement door quietly and limped slowly down the wooden steps. He stopped midway and reached under his vest to touch the blood. He checked its colour – dark. That meant the bullet hadn't punctured a lung. He reached under his armour again and felt a piece of the bullet wedged into the bone. Unless it was just a fragment, that was good. It might hurt like he was dying but it wasn't going to kill him. Just a broken sternum, an arm and a hip. Xeno took a long, painful breath and finished descending the steps. Fighting nausea and dizziness he leaned back against the handrail, trying to clear his head. There was still time, but it was running out. He had to move. He had to get out. He just needed to get past the nausea and he was going to be all right.

He took a deep breath and looked across the basement toward the door to the tunnel. He took a step and the floor seemed to tip out from under him as the room twirled. He was conscious and sucking air when he hit the concrete, but then everything went black and cold.

'She's dead,' Ethan whispered. His voice was tinged with awe. The possibility of Kate's death seemed never to have occurred to him.

Malloy touched Kate's vest. Like Ethan's and his

own, it had been ripped apart by several bursts of the Kalashnikov's 5.67 millimetre ammo.

At least there was no blood. Or maybe he just hadn't found the wound yet. He pulled her hood back, exposing her neck and jaw. He stripped his glove off and laid his fingers across her neck, praying he was wrong, but the carotid artery was silent.

He looked at Ethan, whose eyes behind his hood were wet and dilated, and then made sure Kate's mouth and throat were clear. Pinching off her nostrils Malloy brought his mouth to Kate's cold lips and breathed. He pulled back and then breathed into her lungs again. He heard Ethan praying and whispered his own.

On his third breath Kate stirred. A moment later her eyes fluttered opened. She coughed and then grabbed for air with a sudden, desperate gasp.

'We need to get her to a hospital!' Ethan cried.

'No hospitals,' Malloy answered.

'What . . . what happened?'

'You stopped breathing,' Malloy answered. He said nothing about her heart.

Kate lay back, staring at the ceiling. 'We have to go,' she said after a moment. She took a deep ragged breath. 'Get Nicole and let's get out of here.'

Ethan hesitated.

'Go!' Kate told him. 'The police will be here any minute!'

At the mention of the police Ethan seemed to shake himself out of his trance and stood to leave the room. Before he went he saw Malloy had no weapon. He put a fresh clip in one of his Steyrs and handed it to Malloy.

He pulled the other from its holster and headed for the basement.

The lights were on, but it was quiet. Unlike the upper floors of the house, the basement's air was clean.

So why was there fresh blood on the steps? He studied the drops and smudges on the steps and handrail. On the floor just beyond the staircase he saw a large, glistening stain that had not yet dried.

He crouched down, looking out farther across the open floor, but the trail ended at the bottom of the stairs.

He came down another step, searching the recesses and shadows of the room. A bloody trail that began and ended on a staircase . . .

He looked to either side and took another step. That was when he put it together. *Under the stairs!*

The Kalashnikov began firing as Ethan leaped over the last six steps and rolled out across the floor. Coming up in a squatting position, he saw the strange popping of splinters as the bullets broke up through the steps. He squeezed down softly on the trigger of his Steyr, his burst ripping into the wooden staircase in a ragged figure eight.

The AK-47 finished first but only by a fraction of a second. Ethan heard the gun drop to the concrete floor and tossed his own aside, reaching for the combat knife in his boot.

At the same time the man staggered out from under the stairs. He was holding a pistol, bringing it up slowly toward Ethan. He was hurt and bracing himself on the staircase, but Ethan had no cover. And no choice but to attack.

The bullet hit his armour like a fist driving into his midsection just as Ethan collided with the man. He kept his knife low and brought it up under the webbing of the vest. He felt the muscles give way reluctantly to the power of the steel. He heard a gasp of pain. He felt the body heave and then the blood pouring over his gloved fist.

He heard the gun hit the floor and saw the man's eyes darkened. A strangled rattle cracked from deep within the man's throat as he slid across Ethan's chest, hips and legs.

'Boy! What's going on?' Kate on the headset.

For a moment Ethan could not find his voice. He simply stared down at the man and the bloodied knife sticking out of him.

'Boy! Talk to me!'

He answered. He was fine.

'Trouble?'

Ethan picked up the gun. 'Not anymore.' He checked the clip in the pistol and took the weapon with him as he headed toward the tower.

As he swept the rooms, quick and dirty, just in case, Ethan heard Kate telling Malloy to get Corbeau.

He pulled the crossbar up and opened the steel door leading into the tower. Nicole North stood in the dark wearing a coat but no clothing beneath. She was shaking, her hair was wild, her eyes wide with apprehension. She had no way of knowing if she was about to executed, traded, or rescued.

'It's okay,' Ethan said, remembering his hood and

what he must look like. 'We're here to take you home.'

When they heard shots in the basement, Malloy started to move, but Kate held his arm. She still had her head-set on and said, 'Boy?' The shots ended, but then they heard a pistol shot. 'Boy!' Kate shouted. Her eyes dilated with fear. 'What's going on? Boy! Talk to me!'

She listened. 'Trouble?' she asked and then seemed to lose her tension. To Malloy she said, 'We need to get Corbeau.'

She was still breathing with difficulty, but she was sitting. 'Are you hit?' he asked her.

'I'm fine,' she muttered, but she didn't look fine. She was moving slowly and her focus seemed to come and go. Like someone back from the dead and still sorting out priorities.

Her eyes cut around the room nervously. 'There was a woman . . .'

Malloy shook his head. 'Haven't seen her.'

Kate tried to reach for one the emptied weapons.

Malloy handed her the Steyr Ethan had given him and pulled his Sigma .380.

On the second floor, like the first, the gun smoke still hung in the air and with it the unmistakable stink of the firing range.

He found the bodies of three men in Corbeau's library, but Corbeau was missing. He went back to the hallway and began searching the rooms.

'Corbeau's gone,' he shouted.

From below he heard, '. . . the tower!'

Malloy entered the library again. He heard someone running up the stairs, a voice shouting. Were the cops at the gate? He thought about going back, getting out while they still had a chance, but they couldn't leave Corbeau behind. Better to give up to the cops than that.

He stepped toward the pocket doors, reaching for one of the raven heads as Ethan came into the room shouting, 'NO!'

Malloy stopped, his hand inches from one of the raven heads. 'What's the matter?' he asked.

'Step away,' Ethan told him and grabbed a book. He walked forward and tossed it against the cast iron raven's head. A bright tiny steel needle shot out of the beak half an inch, a poisoned teardrop of clear liquid forming on the tip.

'*Gare le Corbeau!*' Ethan told him, his eyes fixed on the raven.

Malloy translated the phrase in reflex: '*Beware the Raven.*'

'It's on his coat of arms,' Ethan said as he walked over to a painting not far from the doors and pulled it from the wall. Recessed in the wall was a handle which he pulled and turned. The pocket doors opened, and Julian Corbeau stood inside the darkened chamber of the upper tower, his hands still cuffed behind his back, his ankles still tied together. 'How did you get in here?' Ethan asked, but Corbeau was silent, his eyes cold and impassive.

Ethan tossed him over his shoulder like a sack of grain and headed out of the library.

Kate was standing up when they got down the stairs, Nicole North beside her. North was barefoot and apparently naked under the coat. As Malloy got closer he saw the burns on her legs and feet – the ruined flesh.

When she saw Corbeau, North's eyes grew round with terror, but she said nothing. She had Kate beside her and that seemed to give her some measure of courage.

Malloy, covering their retreat, was the last to the helicopter. As he came he saw the pilot face down in the grass.

'The pilot took a round,' Ethan said as Malloy scrambled into the cockpit. 'You know how to fly one of these?'

Malloy shook his head.

'I downloaded the manual from the internet yesterday. Didn't look too hard, but just to be on the safe side you'd better get in the back and strap-in.'

Malloy retreated to the cabin and sat down opposite Julian Corbeau. In the distance he heard police sirens coming along the road from both directions. The sky was still open and silent.

Kate was seated next to Corbeau. Nicole North had taken her place at the other end of the cabin, as far as possible from Corbeau. 'Ethan said he just read the manual yesterday on how to fly one of these things,' Malloy said to Kate. 'Tell me he has a sick sense of humour.'

'I told you to keep the pilot alive.'

The helicopter lifted a few feet over the concrete pad, tipped oddly down and then careened wildly toward the cliff. As they shot over the retaining wall, they suddenly had all the altitude they needed, but Ethan's acceleration somehow sent the Bell plunging into the darkness. He was able to pull it up and skim across the surface of the water for several seconds before he finally got a feel for the craft and started to climb. Once a crash was no longer imminent, Malloy checked his watch. The whole thing from the jump to the near-crash had lasted less than twelve minutes.

'We're headed back to the airport,' Kate told him. 'The Cessna will take Ethan and me with our friend here to Milan. You take the van and make sure Nicole gets to New York.'

'Everyone have passports?' Malloy asked.

'We got ours yesterday,' Kate answered. 'Sir Julian isn't going to need one.'

Malloy looked at Nicole North. She shook her head. Malloy could call Jane and get something arranged for her at the US Consulate in Bern. He didn't have his either but he would call Hasan and get someone to meet him at the airport with it, his luggage and his computer.

'Before you spend the reward money,' Malloy told Kate, 'I'm going to ask Sir Julian a few questions. If I don't like the answers – we'll dump the body over the lake.'

Corbeau smiled. He wasn't buying it.

Malloy drew his Sigma and pointed it at Corbeau's head.

'How did you know I was going to take the twelve-o-three train from Zürich to the airport?'

Corbeau's eyes answered Malloy without fear. Finally he offered a sliver of a smile. 'I've been interrogated by experts, sir. Don't think you can brandish a gun and get what you want.'

Kate pulled her knife and held it against his ear. 'The

US attorney will pay me as long as you're alive. I don't think he cares how many body parts are missing.'

The blood drained from Corbeau's face. 'What do you want to know?' he asked.

'How did you find us?' Kate asked.

'I found you . . . on a hunch. Once I had you my people put together your team easily enough. With intercepts and phone taps, it wasn't too difficult to find out the identity of the buyers. At that point—'

Corbeau's eyes flitted toward some point behind Malloy's shoulder. They grew round in terror and then there was a gunshot.

The bullet struck between Corbeau's eyes. His head kicked back, and then his body slumped forward. Malloy shifted his Sigma quickly, only to realize that Nicole North had gotten hold of a handgun. She was still holding the weapon and staring wildly at Corbeau's corpse, as if she half-expected him to come at her. Kate sprang across the seats and took the gun from her, but it was over.

Nicole North had taken her revenge, and there was nothing more to do about it.

Chapter Eleven

New York City
Friday, October 13, 2006.

Malloy got Nicole North safely to Bern and arranged to meet her, Richland, and Starr late the following evening in New York at an apartment on the Upper Eastside. The Plaza, he said, was no longer safe.

The apartment belonged to a freewheeling venture capitalist whose private bank accounts in Switzerland Malloy had happened to discover over a decade ago. Rather than reporting his findings to the Treasury people, Malloy had, in the parlance of the agency, turned the man. He travelled widely. He had contacts in Africa and the Middle East and Indonesia. Sometimes he knew things, and what he knew he would pass on conscientiously. Malloy had handled the extortion delicately. His agent considered himself a patriot and a friend. Asking the use of his apartment was a bit unusual, but he made the arrangements on short notice without grumbling. It's what patriots do.

The apartment offered any number of refinements including a working fireplace trimmed in Florentine marble. A fire was already burning brightly when Nicole North arrived with her entourage. Jonas Starr was sullen, a man expecting accusations. J. W. Richland wore his TV smile and Mike, the bodyguard, looked well-advised to be prepared for a double-cross. There were others downstairs. Starr and Richland and North had not come this far to lose the painting in the streets of New York, but it would have been unseemly to crowd the room with guards. Besides, Malloy had left specific instructions with Dr North. Richland, Starr and she were all needed for the exchange to take place. In addition, he let them bring one person of their choice. They could come either armed or unarmed – he didn't care – but no telephones and no recording devices.

Richland's bodyguard, the soft spoken Mike, carried the money. Malloy made a show of checking each of them for transmitting devices and noted that both Jonas Starr and Mike carried handguns. There was a degree of exasperation over the show Malloy made of searching them, but at least Dr North and the Reverend Richland recalled treating him to the same indignity and submitted themselves to the inconvenience with a proper sense of irony.

Once out of the foyer, they entered the living room and saw the painting. Malloy had set it on the table, propped up so that they could all see it in the reflected light of the fire as soon as they entered the room. Both Starr and North had examined the painting in Zürich under florescent lighting. By firelight the colours shivered, the eyes came alive, and the highlights in the blood danced. It was easy to imagine the thing invested with divine power. It was beautiful and frightening and tempted even a confirmed sceptic to bend his knee in its presence, a thing of such majesty and beauty that it seemed not to have been painted by human hand.

Richland could not help himself. He walked across the room and knelt before it, bursting into an impromptu prayer that soon became incoherent. Talking in tongues. It was his, and his excitement was something more than a love of antiquity or even the whisper of legends. The contessa had been right. He really believed the face of Jesus – this Jesus painted on wood – would heal him of his cancer. His prayer ended, the preacher turned tearfully to North. 'It's like nothing I've ever seen, Nikki!'

'Are you satisfied?' Malloy asked him.

Richland pulled his gaze from North and stood up again. 'Very satisfied, Mr Malloy. You've done . . . exactly what you told us you would do!'

'I want you to call Jane Harrison. Tell her everything is fine. If there is something you don't like about the way I handled this, tell her.'

Jonas Starr answered from across the room. 'That wasn't part of our deal.'

When Malloy didn't respond Richland stepped into the silence. 'That's okay, Jonas. We had a few tense moments there. I think we can do this much for Mr Malloy.'

'You went over my head. Some people might be tempted to think I didn't do everything in my power to get this painting back to you, as per our agreement. If you don't call them, that's always going to be there.'

'I completely understand.'

Malloy hit the preset code on his phone and handed it to Richland. Richland was gracious and friendly. Not just a good job, he said. Under the circumstances, an extraordinary job! No complaints! Sure. Sure, there were troubles, but that had nothing to do with Mr Malloy! No, he had handled himself as a consummate professional. Above and beyond!

Richland's voice, manner, and natural eloquence were undeniable. When he finished, he caught Nicole North's gaze and nodded. North then signalled Mike the bodyguard to hand over the money. 'The painting is yours,' Malloy told them, taking his fee. 'And my responsibilities for it are finished. As per our agreement.'

At that point Kate and Ethan entered the room. Jonas Starr screeched angrily, 'What is this?'

Ethan walked toward the portrait, still in Richland's hand. 'This? This is mine.'

Richland smiled nervously. 'I'm afraid not, young man.' He gestured for the bodyguard's help. Mike reached under his sports jacket, but Kate presented her weapon with such speed Mike was looking at her gun before he had even touched his own weapon.

'Nicole,' she said, 'tell this man he doesn't have to die this evening.'

'It's okay,' North said to Mike. The young man let his hand drop to his side again.

'You can pull a gun on us, young lady,' Jonas Starr grumbled, 'but I'm here to tell you, you will not leave this building with that painting! I've got twenty people outside waiting for us!'

Ethan walked toward Nicole North, stopping within arm's distance of the woman. 'Tell him. Tell him what you promised me the night I found you in the tower.'

North seemed uncertain. 'I don't . . . I don't know what you're talking about.'

'You said you'd give me anything I wanted if I would just call the Plaza and asked for Mr Gideon.'

'I didn't mean this!'

'You said it, and you meant it. *Anything*. Well, this is what I want.'

'I don't remember! I was under duress! I would have said anything!' She looked anxiously toward Richland and her uncle.

Kate holstered her pistol. 'I remember. I also remember that Mr Gideon didn't take our call. The person who answered his phone said he was busy. We told him what it was about and he told us the matter was being taken care of.'

Nicole North looked at Richland.

'If someone called, I didn't hear about it!' he answered.

'Tell her what you told me,' Malloy said.

'I don't know what you're talking about!' Richland tried to smile, but it took some effort.

'What did you tell him?'

Flustered, Richland stabbed a finger at Malloy. 'He refused to give Jonas the painting so we could negotiate your release!'

'That's not quite the entire story, Reverend. Put your hand on Jesus there and tell her the truth.'

'How dare you!'

'What did you tell him?' North demanded.

When Richland could not bring himself to answer the question, Malloy said to her, 'I gave him a simple choice. I said I could use the painting to get you released or I could bring it to New York. I told him if he didn't like those choices he would never see the painting.'

'What did he say?' North spoke to Malloy, but her eyes stayed on Richland.

'He told me to bring the painting to New York.'

'*My* painting,' Ethan added.

Jonas Starr stormed angrily toward them. 'You are not taking this painting!'

'Give him the painting,' North said.

Richland hesitated. Jonas Starr shouted, 'No!'

'Give it to him!' North answered.

Richland seemed incapable of responding.

Starr reached for his weapon, but Ethan drew his so quickly, the old man had no chance. 'Do you really want to do that?' he asked.

When Starr hesitated, Ethan moved in and took his weapon.

'What do you want? Name your price,' Richland shouted. 'Anything but the painting!'

'The painting is my price.'

'Give it to him, Jim!' North cried. '*I* paid for it, and if it's what he wants, it's what he gets!'

Ethan holstered his gun and unloaded Starr's weapon, pocketing the clip and tossing the gun aside. Next, he relieved Mike of his weapon. Finally, he took the relic from Richland. For a moment it looked as if Richland could not bring himself to let go, but when he finally did, Ethan asked, 'Is it mine?'

'It's yours,' North answered. She studied Richland's face as she said this. It was as if she was really seeing him now for the first time.

Ethan looked at the painting for a long, sad moment, then stepped to the fireplace and tossed it into the flames.

Richland screamed and lunged forward. He actually got his hands around the wood as the wax boiled and ran across his hands and arms.

In agony the preacher dropped the thing and curled up on the floor screaming. Nicole North, who knew something about the pain of fire, came to him and held him as he wept.

She was still holding him when Malloy, Kate and Ethan walked out.

Chapter Twelve

New York
December 2, 2006.

Malloy stood outside the Rockefeller Centre watching Paul Sorrento and Gwen skating. They were hamming it up for his benefit, but were actually pretty good. The Christmas lights were on. People were milling about at the edges of the rink and for a moment he simply forgot the crowd.

'I understand you have been looking for me.'

The voice behind him belonged to the Contessa Claudia de Medici and Malloy turned expectantly. 'My God . . .'

Affecting the look of a prosperous middle-aged New Yorker, the contessa wore a black cashmere coat, a scarf, beret, and gloves. Watching Malloy's reaction, a confusion of surprise and pleasure, her eyes had a familiar spark of mischief.

The Contessa de Medici's disappearance had been overshadowed in the media by the deadly attack on Corbeau's villa, but Malloy had followed the investigation closely. He had even returned to Switzerland to track down financial leads he knew the Swiss police were unable to pursue. He got nothing for his trouble. She was gone. Her money lay untouched in her accounts. A week ago the Swiss police had finally given up, declaring the contessa and her handyman 'victims of foul play.'

'Don't look so surprised, Thomas. You of all people should know I'm not without resources.'

'I'm just happy you're okay.' Saying this, Malloy's eyes cut from the contessa to search the crowd.

'I'm by myself at the moment,' she said, 'but Rene is still with me, if you are wondering. Having difficulty learning English, of course, but then he was never very good with his German either.'

Malloy smiled fondly. 'The man makes himself understood.'

'That he does.'

'What happened to you?' he asked. 'When I came back to the house after . . .' He glanced around. Too many people were able to hear them, and he wasn't sure quite how to finish his question.

The contessa gestured for him to follow her, and they made their way out of the crowd. When they were alone, she said, 'When I heard the gunshots, I thought Corbeau's men had come. There was an old tunnel leading out from under the house, and I used it to make my escape. Once Rene found me and I understood what had happened, I realised I couldn't go back.'

'With your contacts in the country—'

'I didn't care to tell the police what you and I were up to, and if Rene was going to stay out of prison, I could hardly refuse to make a statement. My only legitimate option was to disappear.'

Malloy shook his head. 'I should never have dragged you into this.'

'If you hadn't come to see me, I think you'd be dead.'

'That would have been my problem, not yours.'

She raised one shoulder carelessly, as if her losses didn't amount to very much. 'I knew the risks when I decided to go after Corbeau.'

'I don't understand. *You* went after Corbeau?'

She offered a wry grin. 'There are a couple of things I neglected to mention the last time we talked.' The contessa took a moment, letting her gaze sweep across the crowd. Seeing nothing to disturb her, she said, 'About a year ago Ethan Brand received an e-mail at his website asking if he knew anything about a painting of Jesus made in King Herod's Palace on the morning of the Crucifixion.'

'*You* wrote the e-mail?' Why, he wondered, hadn't he suspected her of setting the thing in motion? She had motive, opportunity, and the means to do it – the essential elements of determining guilt – and he had missed it. Had he imagined she had brought down the Swiss bankers over the holocaust accounts only to retire from the public stage?

'I had Rene send it. Credible deniability, I think you call it in the editing business – or whatever it is you do. At any rate, as I was an expert who also frequented his bookstore, Ethan asked me about the legend one afternoon. Naturally, I told him what I could.'

'You knew Ethan would try to steal it?'

'I expected he and Lady Kenyon would do a good deal more than try.'

'They *are* good.'

'Corbeau needed to be stopped, Thomas. I was not the only person who thought it, but I knew how to do it.'

'What about the letter Ethan read – the kid who talked to Oscar Wilde? Was that a plant?'

She shook her head. 'I had traced the Templars' painting from Edessa to nineteenth century Paris some years ago, but from that point on I had no further luck. I was fairly sure Oscar Wilde had encountered it or at least had talked to someone who had seen it—'

'Because of *The Picture of Dorian Gray?*'

The contessa smiled fondly, as if mentioning an old friend. 'Wilde told a different story every time someone asked him how he had got the idea to write about a magical painting. I knew he had spent most of one winter in Paris in the early 1880s. During that time he met everyone connected with the secret and occult societies that were in fashion then. I had been looking at various individuals in Paris, but if something was going on, the players were keeping it a secret. Finally I started in on Wilde's acquaintances and came across Bill Landi.

'He only turns up in Wilde's biography because when his parents found out he had spoken to the infamous Oscar Wilde, they cabled for him to return home on the next ship. It makes a good story, of course, but as I read about it, I realised the two had spent most of an evening together in a tavern and that it was the last evening Wilde spent out of his bed. I thought Wilde just might have been in the mood to tell a secret, and so I chased down Landi. He turned out to be a fairly prominent painter some years later, and his papers went to Denver after his death. It was there I found the most incredible tale Wilde ever told in a letter Landi sent to his brother the morning after his encounter with Wilde. With that and some Swiss property tax records I was able to track the painting to Corbeau's grandfather – also named Julian. He was chased out of Paris for some unsavoury activities and living on Lake Lucerne. Suddenly a lot of the rumours about Julian Corbeau began to make sense, and I decided to bring the man down.'

'Was Ethan in on it from the start?'

'He had no idea I knew what he intended to do. I was just a rather naive resource he thought he could use without showing his hand.'

Malloy smiled. 'I bet you were surprised when I showed up at your door.'

'More worried, than surprised, Thomas. To tell you the truth I had imagined it was over, that Corbeau would chase after shadows for a while and never find his painting. I had no idea it was still in the country.'

'You didn't think I should get involved?'

'You obviously were and it was clear you weren't about to walk away from an agreement, so I thought it best to remind you of your mortality.'

'If the point was to eliminate Corbeau,' Malloy said, 'why not just come to me – or one of your other friends? Kidnapping him might not have looked feasible, but an assassination could have been arranged without too much trouble.'

'The point, Thomas, was to steal the painting. It was at the centre of Templar ritual and magic – the reason for the Order's existence.'

'We burned the painting, contessa.'

Her eyes showed curiosity, nothing more.

He shook his head. 'The idea of Richland holding up the face of Jesus on TV and selling copies to the faithful was worse than anything we could imagine.'

'I expect all three of them had decided to keep it out of the public eye. Reserved for the elect of the faith, so to speak.'

'Just like the Templars . . .'

The contessa's smile turned cold. *'Blessed are the pure in heart.'*

Malloy shook his head in disgust.

'Do you find it curious,' she asked, 'that a painting of the Saviour turned believers into monsters but left you, Ethan, Lady Kenyon, Roland Wheeler, and even Hans Goetz unaffected?'

'The believers wanted a miracle. For us the only magic in that piece of wood was the cash it could generate. What I want to know is how *you* resisted it? If I understand you correctly, you'd spent years searching for the Holy Face. When you found it, instead of acquiring it by some means, you arranged to pry it from the hands of one criminal and turn it over to another. That must have been hard to do for a woman of faith.'

'How do you know I wasn't tempted?'

'By the way you handled it when we looked at it in your kitchen. I could see you were curious, but you weren't like the others. You weren't afraid that now you had it in your hands someone was going to take it away.'

She nodded, pleased it seemed he had understood her response. 'There was a reason the Edesseans buried that painting in their city wall, Thomas. You have only to look at the fruit it bore in a matter of days – the death and betrayal it inspired – to know it was an abomination.'

'You don't really think it was evil?'

'Not at all. The evil existed in the hearts of those who adored it. The painting simply provided the stimulus for them to act.'

'Was it the face of Jesus, do you think?'

'You mean did you commit a monstrous crime?'

He smiled sheepishly. 'I guess that's what I mean.'

'Corbeau got what he deserved, Thomas. As far as I am concerned the devil he prayed to can go to hell with him.'

'Just a painting then – some face?'

'Who knows? Maybe it was a pretender, a charlatan who passed himself off as the risen Christ. There were certainly enough of them around.'

Malloy looked away. 'What do you do now, Contessa?' he asked.

The brittleness that had overtaken her features softened as she considered her prospects. She looked at the passing figures, the bright Christmas lights, the laughing children. 'Now that I am presumed dead in Europe and living as a penniless middle-aged immigrant in the land of opportunity?'

Malloy laughed. 'You make it sound almost romantic.'

'Things are not really as desperate as they seem. I may have left a fortune behind, but I can retrieve most of it before they declare me legally dead. And I had a little something to take with me.'

'The painting you took when you left?'

The contessa smiled. 'Rene tells me you wanted to know why I chose that particular one and left the others.'

Malloy looked away again, watching the crowd. He

was still not sure if he trusted everything the contessa told him. 'I'd almost convinced myself you had gotten your hands on the True Image and we were all chasing after the face of a first century impostor.'

'I took that particular painting and left the others for the simple reason that it was not a forgery. Combined with an antique ring and necklace I had in my possession, I got resettled without too much discomfort.'

'You sold your painting?' He was surprised.

'Don't be silly, Thomas. I used it and the jewellery as collateral on a personal loan I took from a friend in Geneva.' She nodded in the direction of the ice rink. Gwen had stopped skating and was looking for Malloy. 'I had better go. Your friends just noticed you're not watching their show.'

'Will I see you again?'

Their eyes met and the inevitable feeling of desire swept over him. 'That is the question, isn't it?' she asked. The playfulness was gone. Their long history as friends and allies lay between them like a tangible thing.

'That's the question,' he answered.

The contessa leaned forward to kiss his cheek, her eyes suddenly quite sad. 'For now,' she said, 'this had better be goodbye. As for the future . . . let's leave that in the hands of God, shall we?'

Pulling back to arm's length, she held Malloy with her dark, luminous eyes all too briefly before she turned away.

A moment later the Contessa de Medici had melted into the crowd and was gone.

Epilogue

Caesarea, Samaria and Rome
AD 30-41.

There was no mention of Pilate's first administrative embarrassment resulting from his failure to raise the image of Tiberius in Jerusalem, but nobody missed the point when they saw the portrait of the man named Yeshua in Pilate's banqueting hall. 'In Jerusalem,' Pilate announced to anyone noticing the portrait hanging from the imago standard, and everyone did who wanted to please Caesar's prefect, 'the Romans might not be allowed to display the image of the emperor, but in Caesarea the Romans show an unsurpassed open-mindedness by giving a place of honour among the Roman standards to the *imago* standard of the King of the Jews.' The pleasure of the joke lasted many weeks before Pilate told Cornelius to have the standard repaired and to discard the image of the dead Jew.

The following year Tiberius's sister-in-law, Antonia, received a courier from Caesarea with a message that she passed on to the emperor. In it a number of the activities on the part of the emperor's 'most trusted servant' were spelled out, including Sejanus's covert attempt to start a war with the Jews. Tiberius rallied from his lethargy and managed without great difficulty to eliminate Sejanus and his allies, including Senator Vitellius. Afterwards he exiled Antipas and Herodias to Gaul. He then settled back into his semi-retirement in Capri and lived for another half dozen years.

During that time Pilate remained as the prefect of Judaea, Samaria, and Idumaea. The event that finally prompted Pilate's resignation was the appearance of yet another Messiah: a Samarian holy man named Simon Magus. Simon had an army that worshipped his image in its many manifestations. Among them was a portrait of Simon wearing a crown of thorns, for he preached that he was the culmination of the greatest prophets, including the most recent and notorious, a man named Yeshua, whom some, he said, mistakenly believed was the Messiah.

His followers prayed to Simon's images morning and evening in the belief that doing so would guarantee they would neither age nor taste death. Since they imagined themselves immortal, they were ferocious if un-disciplined fighters, but they had not their general with them when it mattered. With a force of some three thousand and outnumbered nearly two to one, Pilate met and exterminated the radical sect in a single engagement. He crucified all who did not perish on the field of battle and gave orders to hunt down Simon Magus as well. Simon fled into Syria, however, where his cult of worshippers persisted for many centuries, for he was a persuasive man and a magician of extra-ordinary skill, having learned the arts of necromancy in Egypt, where the priests still worshipped Hermes the thrice-born.

By chance, Pilate's victory in Samaria was marred by a deep wound in his groin. Though painful it did not at first appear to be life-threatening. The ensuing infection however nearly took his life. In fact, the prefect's doctors gave Procula no hope when he fell into a coma some five days after the battle. They suggested she make a sacrifice at the temple of Asclepius, the god of medicine, for it was the only chance he had.

When that failed to bring relief, Procula called on Cornelius, then living in semi-retirement in Caesarea and practising his medical skills, such as they were, among the poor. He had become a Jew since leaving Pilate's administration. But for a bit of foreskin he had sacrificed, he was still the same – still the great hulking figure and still the great passion to protect Pilate's wife. Arriving with only a bit of ointment that he put together from his own garden, the old centurion applied it to the festering wound and broke the fever within minutes. Pilate awakened from his long sleep an hour later – refreshed and cheerful.

Some weeks later, though fully recovered, Pilate resigned his post in Judaea, pleading disabilities. Tiberius's health was failing, and the son of the glorious Germanicus was set to become the new emperor. Rome was about to enjoy a renaissance that Pilate did not care to miss.

Caligula was twenty one years old when he came to the throne. He was handsome and popular and found his treasury brimming with the fortune that Tiberius had refused to spend. Sejanus was gone, the Senate had lost the last of its potency, and the world answered to the whims of the man who sat on the imperial throne.

For years a virtual prisoner on the Isle of Capri, Caligula came to Rome like a hungry tiger. He wanted pleasure and parties – parties like the world had never seen – and he wanted to be worshipped as a god. Because he had a tremendous imagination the costs were staggering and nearly bankrupted the once over-flowing treasury. Warned of the dangers of spending more than he possessed, Caligula refused to cut back. Instead, he turned his mind to replenishing the imperial fortune.

Summoning great numbers of nobility to his palace for banquets it would have been treasonous to refuse to attend, Caligula would choose one among his guests – always the wealthiest and usually the most corrupt. He would then entice his victim into signing a will that left everything to Caligula. The enticement might be the promise of not executing all of the man's children as he watched, taking only a few of them instead, or raping the wife and eldest daughter, while sparing the younger children.

Those who resisted beyond these reasonable entice-ments were tortured until they signed anyway. Once the will had been examined by various witnesses, Caligula would then devise an entertaining end for his victim as his guests watched. One was drowned in a cauldron of soup. One was turned into a human torch while Caligula pretended to study his will. Some played games of chance that let them live so long as their luck held. One played Adonis, another Attis, a third Heracles wearing the poisoned cloak his wife had given him. One was grilled on a spit while he was still alive, then served 'very rare' as an entrée to Caligula's terrified guests.

By the time the senators and equestrians of the city understood just what kind of madman ruled them, they discovered an even more horrifying fact. The plebeians of the city hated them with such passion they actually celebrated Caligula's crimes and wanted only the privilege of watching his imaginative executions in the Circus Maximus.

Having an audience fully appreciative of his genius, Caligula found new inspiration.

When Pilate's invitation to the palace arrived one morning, he waited until Procula left the house, then quietly retired to his bath and opened his veins.

Denied what was reputed to be a great inheritance, Caligula refused the family of the Pontii permission to bury Pilate, insisting instead that Procula – the sole heir of her husband's fortune – come alone to the palace afterwards with her husband's ashes. The emperor wanted to grieve in private with his cousin.

Following a depressingly simple funeral, Procula returned to the city. While she was still in the plaza before the great house Pilate had bought for them on their return from Judaea, Procula freed her slaves, bid farewell to the Pontii, and took the urn bearing her husband's ashes.

At the front gate she was turning the key when Cornelius stepped out of the late afternoon shadows. 'Centurion!' she said in bewilderment. She had not seen Cornelius in over two years and had assumed he was still in Caesarea. 'What are you doing here?'

'The palace guard is waiting inside your house, Lady. They do not intend to let you take your own life, if that is your intention.'

Procula felt a moment of panic but then steeled herself with the courage expected of a Roman matron. 'Honour me with your sword,' she said, 'and I will give them no say in the matter!'

'I will do better than that. I will get you out of Rome.'

'If they are inside my house, they are in the streets as well!' She looked out across the plaza and saw several groups of men engaged in conversation. Some she had seen earlier in the day but only now recognized this was not a coincidence. 'Please, Centurion! Give me your sword!'

Cornelius took her hand and placed it gently on his forearm. Considering her exalted station, she ought to have been insulted or outraged, but in fact she found comfort in his touch. 'I will not let you die, Lady, but you must trust me.'

Caligula's spies began to converge on them as soon as Cornelius and Procula turned back from the house and entered the plaza. They came slowly at first, carefully encircling their prey like hungry wolves wary of a trap. Two slipped in behind them, two others approached from either side. Three came at them directly. Their circle tightened at the centre of the plaza.

Cornelius seemed not to understand the danger at his back. He watched the men before him with the steady gaze of a man who has faced many battles, but Procula knew the men behind him would make the first move.

Why, she wondered, had he chosen an open plaza for his last fight?

The ambush that hit Caligula's men came silently, half-a-dozen arrows whistling down from various rooftops. The assault left three men writhing on the paving stones. Before their companions could even understand what had happened Cornelius struck one of the men behind him, the move so quick Procula did not even see him pull his sword.

The three still standing did not wait for a second volley from Cornelius's archers but turned and ran for their lives.

With the Praetorians searching wagons and carriages at every gate of the city, it took twelve hours to spirit Procula out of Rome. In the end, Cornelius's companions – People of the Way, as he called them – used a rope and basket and dropped her over the city wall. At the coast his friends arranged for a cargo ship to take them as far north as Genoa. From there they travelled north into the Alps. The journey was arduous and slow, but along the way they always found friends. One night Procula might sleep in a barn, the next in a mansion.

In Helvetia Procula took Pilate's ashes to a remote mountain and spread them across an alpine marsh. That evening she returned to the village quite late, but Cornelius begged permission to speak with her *in camera*. A matter of some importance, he said.

After she had let the old man enter her modest rooms, Cornelius pulled a small panel painting from beneath his coat. 'Do you remember this man?' he asked.

Procula took the painting from him and studied the image. She could still hear the raucous laughter Pilate's joke excited among his Roman visitors – the king of the Jews with his own *imago* standard!

'I remember.'

'When Pilate ordered me to destroy this, I took it into my chambers instead. Morning and night I found comfort in the calmness of his eye and the purity of his spirit. When I touched the image, I felt something within me begin to kindle that has not yet burned away.'

Procula let her fingers touch the waxy surface and could imagine that same kindling in her own breast. She studied the features of the Jewish Messiah more closely. He certainly didn't look like a god – or even a king, for that matter. He wore no crown of any sort, no insignia at all. He seemed . . . more the sort of fellow to run the harvest or build a temple. In the company of his friends he would speak plainly and when he made a bargain, he would keep it.

'Tell me,' she said. 'Was he really such a man as this?'

'Take this and keep it with you. I think in time you will know the answer better than anyone, what sort he was.'

Procula was startled by the centurion's proposition and tried to hand the image back. 'I am not worthy of such a gift! If you must give it to someone, seek out a person who is truly good.'

'I led him to his death without a flicker of conscience. His friends hid in fear on the only occasion when he ever really needed them. The man he called his Rock denied knowing him, and his most zealous follower sold him to the priests of the Temple for a few pieces of silver. Tell me, Lady, where am I to find anyone who is *truly* good?'

Procula shifted her gaze until she was looking at the great round ugly face of the centurion. This was not a gift of kindness. Cornelius, she realized, was asking her to take a burden from him. This was the only image ever painted of this man, a man some now were calling the son of God. To keep his image safe was to keep it secret from everyone. That was burden that only grew heavier as time passed, unless it was given away or shared.

'I will not take it from you, my friend,' she said, 'but this I will do for the sake of your kindness to me. I will help you keep it safe. So long as we travel on the same road, let it be *our* responsibility. Who knows? Perhaps the good that was in this man will remind us that there is always some good things that need to be done – no matter what the cost. But I ask one thing in return, and it is not a small matter.

'Ask it and it is yours.'

'I want you to take me to the people who walked with this man. I want to know what they heard and what they saw when he walked among us.'

Procula was in Corinth hoping eventually to travel on to Jerusalem when she learned of Caligula's assassination.

Her first thought was a practical one. It was now safe for her to go back to Rome. In fact, she was quite confident that Claudius, the new emperor, would see that Pilate's property and fortune were restored to her.

That meant no more labouring for others and counting coins out at the marketplace for a bit of food. A second marriage would even be possible, if she wanted it. She was still young enough and would certainly be rich enough to attract the most prominent men in the city.

The thought of her fortune stopped her. How many people had Pilate robbed for the sake of his gold? How many Jews had he murdered to build an aqueduct for the pleasure of a rich man's bribe?

She had turned her face away from Pilate's crimes all her married life. She had told herself it was not her choice to do these things but having lost everything, Procula knew the truth. With Pilate's earnings came Pilate's sins, and so long as she possessed his fortune or had hope of possessing it or gave in to the occasional regret at losing it, she was bound to every crime he had committed.

In Jerusalem she would be without resources, but she would be among those who had heard the words of Jesus . . .

'I will see that you get back to Rome safely,' Cornelius told her, 'if that is where you want to go.'

'I am not going to Rome,' she answered.

And saying it Procula let go forever the world of the Caesars, fixing her gaze instead on distant Jerusalem, with her prophets, her apostles . . . and her risen Messiah.

Historical Notes

The historical scenes and those details of history discussed within the novel are all based on actual or reported events. Josephus and Philo give somewhat different accounts of Pilate's handling of the Jewish protestors in Caesarea. Josephus describes the encounter in Jerusalem that ended in a massacre, and there is quite possibly a reference to this in the New Testament with the mention of blood on the Temple steps. Simon Magus was a Samarian magician who sold his image in various guises to the credulous with the promise that if they prayed to it they would live forever and never grow old. Nicodemus was the richest man in Judea during the reign of Tiberius. There was also a wealthy Nicodemus who was a friend of Jesus.

Tacitus gives a full account of Tiberius and Sejanus – that partnership which went awry as Sejanus became increasingly ambitious. Tiberius gets bad press from Tacitus and Suetonius as a profligate and paedophile (he apparently took up his wicked ways sometime in his old age, having been sexually virtuous to that point). Tiberius was a world class alcoholic and a very competent scholar (especially of Homer). He was also the most politically astute individual of his age – after his mother, Livia, the wife of Augustus, had passed away.

While Sejanus and Tiberius agreed on most issues, we do know that with respect to Jerusalem Tiberius wanted to maintain the policies of Augustus, while Sejanus preferred to raze the city and sow the earth with salt. This latter policy was essentially carried out within forty years of the Crucifixion of Jesus and changed the course of history.

Senator Publius Vitellius, who makes only a brief appearance in this story, is a curious figure in the story of Tiberius and Sejanus. Having served as the second in command under Prince Germanicus, Vitellius was politically aligned against Tiberius up until the unexpected death of Germanicus (most believe Tiberius had the prince poisoned); however, Vitellius saved the emperor in the aftermath of that event and became one of Tiberius's most trusted friends. After the fall of Sejanus in AD 31, Vitellius took his own life, presumably because he had shifted his alliance away from the emperor and was working with Sejanus.

It is generally assumed that Pilate was fluent in Greek, since every educated Roman would study Ancient and classical Greek. I have suggested the contrary from my own experience with the language. It is one thing to read classical Greek, quite another to speak it or for that matter the *Koine* of the New Testament. Moreover, I doubt some administrators could even read Latin, there being no such thing as a pair of glasses – or even glass, as we know it. I have therefore given Pilate difficulties with Greek and have him insist on good old Latin. Pilate, being only human, would naturally have had the occasional run-in with interpreters.

Pilate's venality is a matter of less contention. While he is not specifically mentioned as being especially corrupt, the custom of the day was to return to Rome quite rich after an assignment in the provinces. It was said Tiberius kept his administrators in place for long periods of time so they would not feel obliged to build their fortunes too quickly.

It is almost a cliché to call Judaea a backwater but I find no evidence of it. The East, as it seems to me, fed Rome financially, culturally and, yes, even literally. Caesarea, as we now know, was an extraordinary city – a model of Roman engineering, second only to Antioch of Syria in its ostentatious display of wealth. The Temple compound in Jerusalem was one of the great creations of the ancient world – and Rome did not pay for it. The Jews did.

While it is generally assumed that Caiaphas was the power in Jerusalem, he in fact owed allegiance to his father-in-law, the former High Priest Annas (aka Annanus). Caiaphas was probably appointed not by Pilate but by his predecessor, Gratus, after the prefect quarrelled with Annas. Caiaphas's marriage to the daughter of Annas came immediately after his appointment (obliging him to answer to his father-in-law). It is a virtual certainty that the spur to the Jerusalem aqueduct was paid for with Temple funds.

There are a number of ancient accounts about Pilate's wife – all the stuff of legend. Other than her dream in the Gospel of Matthew, we know nothing about her – including her name. Legend calls her Claudia Procula, making her a Claudii. In the Orthodox tradition she is a saint. We know wives did travel with Roman administrators. Many set up shadow courts and became as powerful as their husbands. Tradition gives Procula two children, but many Roman patricians at this time were childless – often by choice.

Cornelius, the centurion, is mentioned in Acts, and is said to be the first gentile to convert to The Way (the terms *Christianity* and *Christians* had not yet been coined, this being before the conversion of Paul). Cornelius had a vision of Christ (perhaps on the Cross) and may even have been the same centurion who participated in the Crucifixion. Peter brought him to the faith in Caesarea.

The existence of Pilate's Portrait of Christ is mentioned in the second century by Irenaeus – after which I can find no further historic reference to the painting. Irenaeus says the Gnostic sect in possession of this panel believed that whoever prayed to it (the mood of the verb suggests continuously or regularly) would live forever and never age.

The history of the Holy Face of Edessa is far more complex, a mix of verifiable fact and undeniable legend. In one tradition Jesus sent a cloth he had touched to his face to Edessa to heal the king of leprosy; when Abgar (aka Agbar) saw the cloth, he also saw the face of Jesus and was healed. In another account, Paul sent a panel (?) painting 'made by no human hand' to the King of Edessa. Both of these stories (along with a Syrian text telling the tale somewhat differently) pre-date the discovery of the actual image or painting buried inside Edessa's city wall in AD 525.

Some believe the image of Christ that was found in Edessa was the Shroud of Turin (taken to France by the

Templars and kept now in the Italian city of Turin); others speculate that a cloth with Christ's image was sent to Constantinople and then on to Rome, where it became known as the Veil of Veronica. A third theory is that this image inspired one of the famous icons of the Russian Orthodox Church, and still another theory associates the Holy Face with the oldest known icon of Jesus, the 6th century painting now in the monastery of St. Catherine on Mt. Sinai. The idea that it was Baphomet, the image the Templars worshipped, is so far as I know wholly original.

To my knowledge no one has connected Baldwin I, the first king of Latin Jerusalem from 1100 to 1118, to the Holy Face, the Grail, or the legend of the Fisher King – though he does fit the bill perfectly.

During the nineteenth century, the Arsenal Library in Paris contained the Vatican Archives (courtesy of Napoleon), including every known work on magic and all of the Templar records and artefacts. This made the Arsenal ground zero for the occult revival – which saw public and private acts of necromancy (raising spirits) and the birth of modern magic and occult belief. Both Oscar Wilde and his wife maintained strong ties with occult groups throughout their lives, though in his last hours Wilde converted to Catholicism – in my opinion a genuine conversion that was years in the making.

Wilde did meet a young painter named Armstrong in Paris shortly before his death and the painter was subsequently instructed by his parents to sail home on the next ship (to save him from Wilde's sin). On the last night that Wilde was out of his bed, we know he sat without his usual friends in an out-of-the-way tavern (quite naturally unable to pay his bill) and may have talked to another young painter named Bill Landi, but then that is only the speculation of a storyteller.

At the end of the twentieth century Switzerland came under legal attack for not returning bank funds to the survivors and heirs of victims of the holocaust. The banks insisted they had lost the records of these accounts. Then one night a security guard discovered a cart-full of these records set out with instructions to have the material incinerated the following morning. The guard stole several pages to prove his story, and found someone who helped him take the news to the world. The Swiss bankers, impeccable for three centuries, were caught in their collective lie and agreed to settle. In the aftermath of their disgrace, a number of new treaties have been put in place obliging the banks to cooperate with international inquiries about suspicious accounts. Banking secrecy in Switzerland is now, presumably, a thing of the past.

In Switzerland, there are billionaire fugitives, intelligence operatives, disenfranchised aristocracy, wealthy art dealers, master thieves, mountain climbers, and of course independent bookstore owners, but those in *The Painted Messiah* are all the work of my imagination.

For more on *The Painted Messiah* visit my website: *www.craigsmithnovels.ch*

CS

Acknowledgements

I am grateful to the following individuals who read an earlier draft of this novel and gave such cogent remarks: Harriet McNeal, James McNeal, Marilyn Bisch, Mike Jefferson, Martha Ineichen, Shirley Underwood, and Burdette Palmberg.

For their continuing support and encouragement, thanks also to Herbert Ineichen, Doug and Maria Smith, Don Jennermann, and Rick Williams.

And a special thanks to Jeffrey Simmons and Ed Handyside – the men who made this happen!